THE MASKS OF ROME

THE
MASKS
OF ROME

by Caroline Llewellyn

SIMON & SCHUSTER

LONDON • SYDNEY • NEW YORK • TOKYO • TORONTO

First published in Great Britain by
Simon & Schuster Ltd in 1989

Simon & Schuster Ltd
West Garden Place
Kendal Street
London W2 2AQ

Simon & Schuster of Australia Pty Ltd
Sydney

British Library Cataloguing-in-Publication Data available
ISBN 0-671-69679-3

Printed and bound in Great Britain by
Richard Clay Ltd, Bungay, Suffolk

For Ted

THE MASKS OF ROME

CHAPTER

1

The drone of the Vespa ought to have warned me. Six months in Rome had taught me to walk with my purse to the wall, glancing over my shoulder at the sound of a motor scooter's approach from behind. A rider alone was rarely a threat, but two together were dangerous until they had passed. Only a tourist walked with her purse dangling from her hand, trailing like bait. The way I was walking.

And so it began with a cliché, with the crime that is the predictable fate of so many foreigners who come to Rome, the report of which provokes only a bored official shrug.

I came out of the Palazzo Torreleone into one of those quiet Roman squares made empty by mid-day and the closed grilles of small shops, giving it the shuttered look of sleep. The sun was the color of pale honey, and it poured a soft golden warmth down on terra-cotta roofs and yellow walls, sweetening the last days of the month. February in Rome was almost bearable.

It was Carnevale, carnival time, and confetti seamed the cobblestones where passing children had scattered it in dirty pastel drifts. Rows of empty-eyed masks stared out at me from the window of a stationer's. But my mind was on the work I had left behind in the palazzo; I barely saw the masks, or heard the scooter. When I did, it was already too late. In the instant that I recognized the danger and thought of my purse, something snatched at the bait. An arm shot out and jerked down on the purse strap, wrenching it free from my hand. A masked face leered into mine, a monkey's plastic grin on a man's body, before it was borne away on the back of a little red Vespa. And my purse with it, brandished aloft like a trophy.

That contemptuous gesture with its one-in-the-eye for female impotence enraged me more than the theft itself. Furious, I looked around for a rock or a stick, some sort of weapon, saw an empty bottle and scooped it up, hurling it at the scooter just as it started to turn the corner out of the square.

The bottle bounced off the rear wheel, and the scooter fishtailed in a wild, skidding arc, throwing the man on the back into the street before the driver could right his machine. When he had it under control again, he gunned the motor and shot off down the alleyway, leaving his hapless partner prone in the blast of exhaust, still masked and clutching my purse.

I stood there gaping, stunned by my luck and more than a little unnerved at the prospect of an opponent who, now that he had struggled to his feet, looked half a foot taller and considerably stronger than I. My courage and the desire to reclaim my purse were rapidly ebbing.

But I never found out what he meant to do next or whether discretion might have triumphed over valor on my part, because before either of us could move a man hurtled out of nowhere onto Monkey Face, spun him around and down to his knees, and forced the purse out of his grasp onto the cobblestones.

I ran forward, but as I reached them Monkey Face jabbed viciously at the other man's groin with his elbow. The man jackknifed back to avoid the blow and his grip must have loosened, for Monkey Face twisted up out of his hands and was free. In an instant he, too, vanished down the alley, his escape accompanied by the roar of the waiting Vespa.

I muttered an unimaginative but highly descriptive English obscenity as I picked up my purse, then turned, with proper, polite Italian ready on my tongue, to thank my rescuer.

But he was there before me. "Nicely put. And you might add that they're cowards too. Luckily for us."

The American-accented English came as a shock. I had taken him for Italian, Sicilian perhaps—the smooth veneer of the beautifully tailored businessman over a darker, rougher grain. He was middle-aged, a dozen or so years older than I, with an unremarkable face and a big, powerful body that seemed at odds with the elegant suit. Then he smiled. His face lightened, shifting the heavy features into a distinct and unsettling sensuality, a sensuality leavened only by the humor in his eyes.

"And they say that women can't pitch worth a damn. Do you hit as well as that?"

I shook my head. "I've noticed that people have a tendency to hit back. It inhibits me. So thank you for taking my lumps for me just now." I rubbed my arm, which had begun to ache a little, and inwardly cursed myself for the foolhardy pride that had risked my work to retrieve the few thousand lire and replaceable papers in my purse. Their loss would be nothing compared to a sprain in the arm that earned me my living.

Then I saw that he hadn't escaped unscathed from the encounter himself. There was a long tear in a seam of his jacket. "I really am grateful to you. And I hope you aren't hurt. Your jacket—"

"Nothing to worry about." He glanced down as he spoke to where I was pointing and gave a rueful smile when he saw the tear. "I'm likely to suffer more at the hands of my tailor. He was very proud of this suit."

"Let me pay to have it mended then. I'd hate to think I was responsible for a breach between you and your tailor."

"I suspect I'll only rise in his estimation when I tell him how it happened."

I laughed. "Well, if you're sure . . . But how on earth were you able to come to my rescue so quickly?"

At this he looked oddly uncomfortable. He half turned away from me, and as his gaze left my face I felt such a queer sort of relief that it disconcerted me. For the first time I really looked at him, and realized with a small shock that he was vaguely, unplaceably familiar.

"I was in the bar over there, looking out the door." He pointed to the Bar Tiberina, across the square from the Palazzo Torreleone, where I occasionally stopped for a morning cappuccino. Perhaps I had seen him there. "I noticed the scooter following you. They looked like typical *scippatori*." He grinned. "Don't misunderstand me, please, but you were an easy target."

"I'll bet. And I've been in Rome long enough to know better. I once watched a pair of those thugs lift a fur coat off the shoulders of a woman who was silly enough to wear one in September. They twirled it in front of her like a matador's cape. I feel about as foolish as she looked."

Again that unsettling smile. "I've found that a glass of Frascati can do wonders for wounded pride. Have one with me." Abruptly, as though he had suddenly remembered his manners, he added, "My name's Nick Taliaferro."

"So you're Italian, after all."

"Actually it's pronounced 'Tolliver' in Virginia, where I grew up. But try explaining that over here."

I hesitated, then thought, Why not? "I haven't eaten at all today, so I need more than a drink. There's a restaurant not far from here with some of the best pasta that I've had in Rome. And a garden, so we could eat outside. If you won't let me pay for your jacket, at least let me treat you to lunch."

"How can I refuse? You're persuasive, and I'm easily led. So please lead on."

He struck me as anything but easily led. Quite the reverse. Tough, very sure of himself, the only bit of softness that hint of a southern accent that slid now and then over the educated

4

transatlantic speech. He walked with a reined-in impatience, clear from the way he would edge imperceptibly ahead of me and then, catching himself, slacken his pace, as though he were used to getting where he was going in a hurry and had to remember to slow his steps to mine. I had the distinct impression of a man accustomed to having his way more often than not, though why I felt this so strongly I couldn't have said.

"You're Canadian, aren't you?" he asked after a few moments of awkward silence in which I'd had time to wonder if I was going to regret my impulsive invitation.

"How did you know?"

"Your 'out' and 'about' give you away." He pronounced them 'oot' and 'aboot,' and I protested the exaggeration but had to laugh. "What part?"

"Montreal. I'm half-English, half-French. A half-breed."

"Divided loyalties?" There was a trace of sympathy in his voice.

"You might say that." Or none at all. I'd come to the end of them—the struggle that had never really been mine and a marriage that was no longer. Sometimes the only choice left is retreat, and if you go far enough, it can seem like progress. Rome was far enough.

"You still haven't told me your name."

"Sorry. It's Kate Roy."

"Roy is a fairly well known name in Quebec, isn't it? Gabrielle Roy, the writer. And there's a separatist politician— I've forgotten his first name. . . ."

"Michel," I said. "He was my husband."

He looked at me with curiosity. "Past tense?"

"We divorced last year."

Something in my tone must have told him that I wanted a change of subject, for after a moment's pause he said only, "Why are you in Rome?"

"I'm working here. I'm a conservator, someone who fixes up works of art, antiques, things like that. Oil paintings are my specialty. I work for Faltecchi and Stillitano. I'm Giorgio Faltecchi's assistant."

5

"I'm sorry, but I have to plead ignorance. You say the name as though I ought to know it."

"Only if you were in the same field. He has a great reputation among restorers."

"I thought you said you were a conservator. Or is it the same thing."

"Pretty much. But Faltecchi has the expertise and the experience to paint in the missing bits of a painting. I stick to cleaning them—until my apprenticeship is over."

We were walking along a narrow alley where the buildings on either side tilted in toward the street, all but blocking out the sky above, when a man came suddenly out of a doorway, colliding with us in his haste. The brown paper parcel he was carrying fell to the ground. Hurriedly, he snatched it up again, murmured an apology, and rushed on up the street ahead of us, clutching the parcel to his chest.

"A man with a mission," I said.

"Or an assignation."

Both, as it turned out. When we came out into the Piazza Navona, we saw him surrounded by pigeons, feeding them spaghetti from the brown paper parcel. Two pigeons were tugging on a strand that looked like a long white worm. Overhead bells were ringing the hour, drowning the gentler music of the fountains.

"They would never have forgiven him if he'd been late," Nick Taliaferro said dryly. Then he asked me how long it would be until I was a restorer myself.

"Probably a few years yet. Restoration is so complex these days that you have to be an art historian, a bit of a scientist, and a decent painter yourself in order to be a really good restorer. A detective, too, for that matter," I added as an afterthought. "I mean, you have to like solving problems."

"It sounds daunting."

"Does it? I suppose in a way it is. But there are rewards." The revelation of beauty hidden or marred, the restoration of truth, or simply the shedding of light—rewards that were, to me, so great as to be worth the years of training and preparation. "At the moment," I went on, "I'm cleaning some paintings for the Torreleones." I looked up at him as I said this and caught surprise, just a flash of it, on his face. "Do you know them?"

His face was smooth again. "By reputation. I know that Massimo Torreleone was a communist resistance hero during the Second World War. And that he's a count."

"But you know that Massimo Torreleone refuses to use the title?" There was something about the old man, however, a quality that the Italians call *grandezza*, a grandeur without the pomp and circumstance, that made it impossible for me to think of him as anything but Count Massimo.

"Really? Why not?"

When Giorgio Faltecchi, who knew the family, had told me the story of this refusal, he made it a domestic tragedy of irreconcilable ideals, of a father—Massimo Torreleone's father— set against his son, a father so unbending and unforgiving that Count Massimo had apparently vowed to forgive his own son everything, whatever the provocation. And the provocation, I understood, had once been great. The son, Alessandro, was notorious.

But all I said now was "The war had something to do with it. Count Massimo fell out with his father over the fascists, and his father was furious because Massimo had become a communist. And too many aristocrats collaborated or found the Nazis socially acceptable. It must have been terrible for those who didn't."

He shrugged. "And yet Rome got off comparatively lightly."

"If you can call starvation and torture getting off lightly." I had done a little reading on that period of Rome's history since Faltecchi had told me Count Massimo's story.

"I only meant that Rome wasn't bombed, not that there wasn't suffering." He said it quietly, but there was an underlying emotion in his voice, strong enough to make me uncomfortable.

I accepted the implied rebuke and changed the subject. "Are you working here too, or just visiting?"

"A bit of both." He did not elaborate. His silence made me feel as though I'd been prying, illogically, I knew, for I'd done no more than return his own question to me. But I had the impression of a barrier going up, and I was not going to push for details—or volunteer any more of my own. We walked on in silence until we reached the restaurant.

Moments later we were sitting at a round table covered with a red-striped cloth debating the virtues of spaghetti alla carbonara and paglia e fieno. The spaghetti won, and while we waited for it, we drank the recommended Frascati and chewed on the rough, crusty Roman bread. It was glorious to be able to sit outside again—I could feel my spirit expanding in the warmth of the sun. Five of the other half-dozen tables were occupied by Italians who were hunched over their plates, eating with the concentration that they give to good food, or lounging back in their chairs, satisfied, while they argued and laughed, hands sketching arabesques in the air or stabbing the tabletop to make some point.

I was quite content to sit there with the sun warm on my face, enjoying the prospect of a delicious meal, leaving it up to Nick Taliaferro to tell me about himself or not, as he chose. I was curious, however, to know what kind of mind lay behind that oddly provocative, attractive face. And I was still puzzled by its familiarity.

I looked up to find his eyes on me. Instinctively, we smiled at each other, the uneasy social smile that covers an awkward moment, and turned with relief to the waiter, who had arrived with our food.

As we ate, we talked about Rome. It was clear that he loved the city and knew it well. I found myself relaxing, liking him, because I could see some of my own feelings about Rome reflected in his. There was a comfortable ease to our conversation.

We decided on fruit and espresso to follow the pasta. He motioned the waiter over and in fluent, idiomatic Italian gave him the order, then told him that it had been the best carbonara he'd had in some time—almost as good as his mother's, he said, and she had been a Roman born and bred. The waiter, who looked no more than sixteen, blushed and said that he would pass on the signore's compliments to *his* mother, who was the cook.

"Now I really am confused," I said when the waiter had gone. "Are you or are you not Italian?"

"I'm a half-breed like you. My father was American, a Virginian. He was here during the war, in Mark Clark's army when they liberated Rome in '44. He met my mother over a Hershey bar."

I smiled. "So she was a war bride?"

"No."

The smile died from my face.

He picked up his wine, swirling the golden liquid around the bowl of the glass. "Later he made a lot of money and sent some each month to my mother. It happened that he and his wife couldn't have children, so when I was four years old he came back to get me. The spoils of war." In one gulp he finished the wine, then shifted in his seat and fished a crumpled pack of cigarettes out of his jacket pocket. He offered me a cigarette, but I shook my head. "Do you mind if I do? I've just about given them up, but it's hard to resist after a good meal."

"Your mother let you go?" I asked him.

He blew a thin line of smoke upward. "People were very poor here after the war."

So he knew something about Rome's suffering after all. I flushed, remembering my words to him.

"My mother had no money apart from what my father sent her. She knew what kind of life I would have growing up in a Roman slum." His voice was matter-of-fact, almost expressionless, and he watched the glowing tip of the cigarette with a look of distaste before stubbing it out. "Maybe I'm closer to quitting these than I'd realized."

"The separation must have been terrible for you both." The only consolation I'd salvaged from the wreck of my marriage was that Michel and I had not had children. A cold comfort.

"Yes, I think it was. But it's more than thirty years ago now." He drank some coffee and leaned back in his chair, stretching his long legs out to one side. "Later on my mother did marry, a good man with a good job, but I don't think she ever got over my father." He gave a crooked smile, apologetic, as though his tale might have bored me. "Sorry. Ancient history."

9

I smiled back at him. "One of my favorite subjects. Did you see your mother again?"

"She and my father came to some sort of agreement when I was ten. I came over to spend that summer in Rome, and I've been coming back almost every year since."

"Is your mother still here in Rome?"

"She died just before Christmas." His face was blank, like a slate wiped clean, his downcast eyes invisible. Before I could say anything, he went on. "But look, enough about me. Tell me how you find working in Rome. And," he added, too casually, "what it's like working for the Torreleones."

I wondered why I should feel so certain that he was really interested only in the second. Something in his voice, perhaps, its studied casualness. "Rome is not Montreal, for which I'm daily and profoundly grateful. Everything else—the people, the buildings, the beauty—is icing on the cake. But the best part is my work. As for the Torreleones . . ." I paused, watching him. Did he lean forward slightly, or was it my imagination? "I've only met Massimo Torreleone. He's very old, very frail, and utterly charming. A remarkable man. His wife is dead, but he has a son, Alessandro, and a niece, both living in the palazzo. I haven't met them. The son's been away, and the niece hasn't appeared while I've been there. I think her father's a diplomat in Washington and she lives with Count Massimo while she's studying at the university." Deliberately, I added, "Mind you, I've heard enough about Alessandro Torreleone to make me curious." I was amused to see interest in his eyes.

"Oh yes?" he said very blandly, almost indifferently.

"Well, he does have a certain reputation."

"Does he?"

"As the stereotype of the Italian playboy, I mean. Though I gather it's pretty much a thing of the past."

"If you ever meet him you'll have to tell me if the gossip is true."

I gave him a sharp look, but his face was unreadable, and I couldn't hear any malice in his voice. Keep it light, I told myself. "Oh I shouldn't think he'd notice anyone with less than a

10

billion lire to her name. I gather that the Torreleone fortune isn't what it used to be, and apparently Alessandro contributed his share to its decline. But then I'm told he may surprise people someday." I threw this in as a wild card, merely quoting Giorgio Faltecchi, who had known Alessandro since he was a boy and whose opinion of him was higher than most people's.

But my wild card made Nick Taliaferro show his hand for the first time. "What exactly do you mean by that?" There was an edge to his voice now. I'd provoked a reaction of sorts.

"Why exactly are you so interested?" I countered, echoing his tone.

He gave his seductive smile. "Sorry, I didn't mean to be nosy. You make him sound interesting, that's all."

That was far from all, I said to myself, and far from convincing, too. But aloud I said only, "Well, I may never get to meet him. Why should he bother with an unimportant conservator who has no reputation of her own yet?"

"But who will have someday." He said it lightly, and I knew I was being teased for the 'yet' but stood by it. I had no false modesty about my work; perhaps it was arrogant, at twenty-six, to be so certain of my power, but that certainty was my life raft. Unlike love, unlike my failed marriage, my work always made me happy. It carried me away from the scenes of my defeat.

"Your 'out,'" Michel had called it. "Your escape from us." He meant our marriage, and in the end he was right—it was. But he should have been the last person to accuse me of that particular sin. What cut more deeply was his accusation that I had no commitment to anything but my work, not to ideals, not to people, not to him.

I moved uneasily away from the memory.

Nick Taliaferro poured some more wine for both of us, then raised his glass. "To your reputation."

"Thank you." I picked up my own glass. "May we both get whatever it is we're after."

He stared at me and laughed. "Am I that transparent?"

"Let's just say that I think you're interested in more than my opinion of the Torreleones." He could interpret that any way he liked.

He chose an interpretation I hadn't intended. "I *would* like to see you again."

I looked away, surprised by my response to his words. A part of me wanted to take them at their simple face value, to believe him. A cool wind was blowing now, and the sun had shifted. The insinuating chill of the winter that still lingered in the shadows crept into my bones; the courtyard no longer seemed so pleasant. With a glance at my wristwatch, I mimicked surprise. "It's time I was starting back to work."

"May I call you?"

Again I hesitated. He was attractive, even appealing, but there was an intensity that reminded me all too sharply of Michel, although admittedly of a very different kind. After the divorce I had promised myself that I would avoid serious men for a long time to come.

But in the end I gave him my phone number. It was obvious that he was interested in the Torreleones and was after information; I supposed that he was hoping I could supply it. It might be amusing, I told myself, to discover precisely what Nick Taliaferro wanted. And that was my first illusion.

Rome is, of course, the great city of illusion, of tricks played on the senses and the mind. Like the trick of the light as it skims the weight from St. Peter's dome if, at a certain hour, you stand in a certain place up on the Gianicolo. Or the trick of a fountain or church so large for the space that contains it that even as it delights it threatens, a reminder of power, of a city built, destroyed, and built up again by power brutally or subtly wielded. And the greatest trick of them all, the baroque, played on a willing city and people all those centuries ago and still at work in the piazzas, where life is lived as theater and spectacle.

I dealt in illusion myself, the illusion of paint on canvas; it was my job to sustain the illusion that the artist created. But in my own life, I thought, I would see things straight, as they were.

I hadn't reckoned on a modern Cagliostro with tricks of the senses to baffle the mind. It was Carnevale, after all.

CHAPTER

2

There were bombs in Rome the night after I met Nick Taliaferro. Terrorism was on the wane that year, but it was still capable of spasmodic, vicious bursts of energy, and bombs were the preferred outlet. They went off late at night, bursting into my dreams like thunder.

In the morning, very early, I took my watercolors and went out onto the balcony of my hillside apartment to look down over the city that sprawled before me, rose roofed and hazily golden in the growing light.

I worked quickly, but the sun was swifter, sharpening the city and the sky until the dreaminess had vanished, all the edges hardened into clarity against the bright blue above. The air, at first pierced only by the songs of birds, gradually filled with the

13

muted roar of the traffic that raced along the Tiber. Rome was awake.

But I had caught a moment well enough to satisfy me. Later perhaps, with luck, I could work the sketch up into some semblance of the Rome whose beauty on paper still eluded me. Inside, I washed and dressed, then went downstairs, out into the sloping street.

I had to run for the bus that took me from my apartment on the Gianicolo down to the workrooms of Faltecchi and Stillitano in the city center. There was a seat free near the rear, and I sank gratefully down onto it. When I'd caught my breath, I glanced around, prepared to enjoy one of the few pleasures of traveling by bus in Rome—studying faces. But this morning the faces around me were uniformly serious, even angry, and I heard the words "terrorists" and "Red Brigades." I asked the man sitting beside me what had happened.

"Bombs, signora," he replied gravely. "All over the city. Some say it was the Red Brigades, some say the fascists." He shrugged.

"They're all criminals." An elegantly dressed woman across the aisle leaned forward, hissing the words out.

A sharp-faced girl in a green loden coat turned on the woman. "Not all. Some of them have ideals you know. Maybe there's a reason for the bombs."

"There's a reason all right," someone shouted at her. "Ask the communists. They'll tell you."

With that the people around me erupted in argument. My Italian was serviceable—with a drink or two even good—but it was not up to the speed and intensity of the seemingly inexhaustible debate that now raged. I sat silently, with a sense of déjà vu. For a moment I was back in Montreal, in our apartment on Sherbrooke Street, while Michel and his friends harangued each other with their beliefs.

It took the bus a long time to cross the Tiber. In the Via Arenula two cars lay belly-up on the sidewalk, gutted by fire, their insides torn out and trailing on the pavement. Police in riot gear, shields held in front of them, stood outside the Ministry of Justice. I watched one of them move forward threateningly when a passerby stopped to stare.

And then it struck me. I had forgotten my papers on a day when Rome would be thick with police. If they stopped me for questioning—and they routinely did spot checks on the street after an incident like the car bombings—it would be awkward for me. But it was too late to go back. I would have to take my chances.

The bus was barely moving now. At the next stop I got off. I was tempted to go straight to the Palazzo Torreleone, near the river and far from the noise and confusion around me, but I was running low on certain supplies that I knew I would need for the morning's work. There was nothing to do but to head first for Faltecchi and Stillitano, collect my supplies, and then go to the palazzo. Resigned, I set off down the Via dei Cestari. The long way around seemed safest—there were no police or bombed-out cars in the quiet back streets.

Normally thronged with schoolchildren, shoppers, and civil servants on their way to work in nearby government buildings, the streets seemed curiously deserted today, empty except for a few dark-suited men who brushed past me with heads bent, like beetles escaping from a storm. One of them muttered something unintelligible as he passed by, but when I realized that he had been speaking to me and turned around to him, he had disappeared.

I turned into a warren of narrow, winding side streets and was halfway down one of them, a twisty little street lined with small shops, when I heard shouting. The noise, a babble of angry, frightened voices, was moving my way, and swiftly.

"What's happening?" I turned to ask a shopkeeper who, a moment before, was lounging in the doorway of his fruit store. But he was gone, and the corrugated metal sheet that covered his shop at closing time was almost down. Then it clanged shut.

Suddenly, running figures waving placards above their heads appeared at the end of the street. The slam of closing shutters echoed in my ears. There was no refuge, nowhere to go but back.

As the runners in the lead came closer, followed soon by others, then a throng that filled the street, my eyes began to sting, and tears blurred my vision. All at once the air was needle sharp, pricking at my nose and throat. Tear gas, carried on the wind. I had walked right into a demonstration, or a riot.

Struggling with panic, I wheeled about, raced back up the street, and turned the first corner. And stopped dead. A solid line of shields blocked the way ahead. Riot police, their faces all but invisible behind visors, stood like a gray wall, a human barricade. But they seemed hardly human.

Any rational person would prefer the police to a mob; they were sanctuary, after all, from that madness at my back. But I remembered my missing papers, could only see that faceless, impersonal wall. Instinctively, I turned and ran, away from that terrifying blank barrier toward the river of bodies. As it streamed closer, I made out faces that looked younger than myself. A white placard danced above the sea of heads, Studenti per l'Operaio—Students for the Working Man—splashed across it in bold red letters. It was a student riot, that much was obvious.

I began shouting to warn them off. "Go back! They're waiting for you! The police are just around the corner!" In my own ears my voice sounded hoarse, strangled by tear gas and fear. I prayed that my Italian was clear, but I soon saw that it hardly mattered—they certainly couldn't hear me over their own roaring. Then they surged over me.

I saw the big white placard bobbing past on a wave of bodies. Desperately, I grabbed at the girl who was carrying it. Clutching at her arm, as much for balance as in an effort to halt her headlong course, I screamed into her face, "Police! Around the corner. Go back!"

For a long moment, wavering in the torrent that streamed past us, we stood there staring at each other. I was stunned by the look on the girl's face. She was like a maenad in a Bacchic frenzy, wild and beautiful, worked up to some sort of outrageous ecstasy so that she hardly took me in. Then her face cleared, the eyes grew hard, and it was as if a shutter had come down.

"Police?" she asked in a dazed voice, and without waiting for an answer shook herself free of my grasp and plunged back into the mob, battling her way upstream against the crowd as it thickened in the bottleneck of the street, her placard dropped and abandoned by my feet.

"Daniella, wait!" The harsh shout came from a dark cavelike doorway close by. A young man with the fierce face of some bird of prey, narrowly handsome, lunged out to fasten on the girl as she struggled in the sea of bodies. They argued furiously for an instant before he began pulling her back to the doorway where he'd been standing. When he reached it, he gave a quick look around, then pushed her roughly through it, following closely behind until both were swallowed up by the shadows.

At once I gave up my hopeless attempt to warn anyone of what lay before them. I only knew that if there was a refuge from the insanity around me, I was going after it. With my eyes fixed on the doorway through which the two had vanished, I concentrated on keeping my balance and fought my way over to it.

In the dark recess of the arched and narrow entryway there was a door. I was sure it would be locked, but I was determined to pound on it until they let me in. But the knob turned easily in my hand.

I found myself in a dim and tiny space. The air was cool, much colder than it was outside, and very damp. When my eyes adjusted to the darkness, I saw that I was at the bottom of a steep stairwell ending abruptly in a door. I heard angry voices. The name Daniella, shouted in that same harsh way, confirmed that it was the man and girl from the mob. I hesitated, uncertain whether I should let them know I was there, risking that anger turned on me, or whether I should simply sit there quietly until the demonstration ended and then slip away before they came out. I decided that I'd had enough of violent emotions for one day, so I sat on the bottom step in the chilly half-light, waiting. I kept my eyes on the door, expecting someone else to come through it in search of a bolt hole as I had. But no one did.

After what seemed an age but was probably no more than

fifteen minutes, the noise outside began to die away. As it faded I could make out something of what the two upstairs were arguing about. At first I was embarrassed at my predicament, at the thought that at any moment they might come out and find me there, to all appearances a deliberate eavesdropper. But gradually, as I began to understand precisely what the subject of their argument was, the embarrassment changed into a horrified fascination.

He was trying to persuade her to steal something.

I crept upstairs as quietly as I could, wondering if she might be in some sort of danger from him, thinking that perhaps I ought to be near so that I could at least bang on the door if she called out for help or began to scream. The wall felt clammy under my touch as I felt my way gingerly up to the door. Bits of plaster flaked off at my touch, drifting down over my feet.

There was a protest from the girl over something I couldn't make out. Then I heard the man say, in a voice ugly with sarcasm, "You play at revolution, don't you, Daniella? Like all rich people, you know so well how to let others take the shit for you. The way you were about to just now, before I stopped you."

"That's not true!" the girl cried. "You know I'm loyal. But why should I run into a trap? Getting arrested would prove nothing."

"And it was too much trouble to warn our comrades, wasn't it? That would have slowed you down."

"I don't see you at the barricades," she retorted angrily. "And you made sure you had this place to run to."

There was the sound of a slap and a muffled cry before the man's voice continued. "The group has ordered you to set up the robbery. If you won't, you're finished."

"But it's impossible! He's been good to me, Marco. And he isn't rich, whatever you and the others think."

"*Merda!* He and his kind are parasites. Whatever they've got is too much." His voice was hard. "Make up your mind. You have a week, no more. Not that there's any choice . . ." He didn't finish his threat. Abruptly, and quite revoltingly, his voice changed, grew caressing, voluptuous.

There was a long silence.

By now the noise outside had completely died away, and when the voices beyond the door resumed they had dropped to an indistinct murmuring. Terrified of being found, I made my way cautiously downstairs again and opened the door a crack to look out into the street. It was quiet once more. I went out into the entranceway. Only the tear gas lingered, an invisible, unpleasant reminder of all that had gone before. With a scarf from my shoulder bag pressed to my nose and mouth, I left my shelter and walked quickly away until I reached the next corner.

I waited there, around the corner. When I heard footsteps approaching a few moments later, I flattened myself against the wall, in the shadows. The man and the girl went past, talking in low voices, his arm around her shoulders, her head bent and her long tawny hair curtaining her face. They looked like a couple in love, oblivious to anything but each other.

When they were safely past, I retraced my steps to the small door and looked around, hoping to find something that might tell me who lived in the apartment upstairs. But there was nothing, no nameplate, no letter box. While I stood there wondering what to do next, an old man came slowly up the street carrying string bags filled with groceries in both hands. I went up to him and asked him if he knew the people who lived in the upstairs apartment opposite.

"No one lives there, signora. It has been empty for three months now." He wished me a good morning, coughing a little with the fumes of the gas as he shuffled inside.

I was dumbfounded. What could I tell the police now? That two people whose last names I didn't know were planning to rob someone I didn't know and that they had planned this robbery in an apartment where no one lived. It was too fantastic to sound believable. The police would listen politely and call me a crazy foreigner behind my back. There was nothing I could do. Besides, I told myself, if the girl had her way, the robbery might never take place.

I walked slowly along, turning the problem over in my mind, but by the time I reached the Corso I was no closer to a solution. Traffic there was moving sluggishly. Policemen with blank faces and watchful eyes stood in groups of two and three. Tempted, I took a hesitant step toward the closest, but when they turned to look at me my nerve broke and I pretended to be watching for a lull in traffic. I darted between two stopped cars, paused to gauge the speed of an oncoming bus, then gained the other side with the sensation of having crossed a border. Down a side street, a right turn onto the Via Livia, and I was there at last. Tears were streaming down my face, a reaction to the tear gas, as I walked into the lobby of the old building where Faltecchi and Stillitano had their workrooms. While I waited for the ancient elevator to make its noisy, laborious descent, I wiped them away and watched the porter clatter among the mops and buckets in the little broom closet behind his lodge. He smiled cheerfully at me, the first happy face I had seen that morning.

Upstairs, on the third floor, in the honeycomb of small rooms and studios that served as the offices of Faltecchi and Stillitano, Restorers and Conservators of Fine Paintings, I said good morning to Ilaria, the secretary, and went in search of Giorgio Faltecchi. I found him bent over his desk, studying a small oval portrait.

"Ah, Kate. Come and look at this." He hunched forward as he concentrated, shoulders stooped from years of bending in just that way. He had a short, compact body, solid all the way down, a peasant's body—he came from a poor family in the mountains of Friuli—but the broad hands splayed out on either side of the painting were the hands of a craftsman, supple and delicate despite their size. It was a comforting sight to see him like that, perhaps because he was so far removed from riots and robberies and the violent, inexplicable world of which I'd just had a glimpse.

"I'm sorry I'm late," I said. "I ran into a demonstration. Literally."

He looked up at me with a vague but benign concern. He had one of those mild, round faces, pouched and wrinkled now as he approached old age, that have a calmness that seems to come from inner peace. I had never seen him angry.

"Are you all right?"

I nodded. It never occurred to me to tell him what had happened. Men and women might riot, plan robberies, topple the state—it would all be as remote from him as a dream. He would murmur his distress and turn his interest back to what really mattered.

"Good. Then tell me what you think of this."

I picked up the portrait. Late-sixteenth-century oil on canvas, I thought, and with that elegantly long neck and body, in the mannerist style. I did not recognize the artist. The woman looking out at me was handsome, richly dressed, and serenely indifferent to the world's opinion. It was a wonderful face, although badly discolored by darkened varnish and dirt.

"And now this," Faltecchi continued, drawing a large color photograph from a manilla envelope and handing it to me. Again a woman's face, plain this time and stupidly arrogant, without the portrait's calm certainty and with a prominent, and none too attractive, nose and chin. I looked questioningly at Faltecchi.

"The photograph," he said, "is of the customer. She wishes us to clean the portrait and at the same time 'correct'—her word for it—the nose and chin to resemble her own more closely. A family portrait. Or so she claims." He allowed himself a faint gesture of disbelief. "Her husband is a rich industrialist, and I believe she would like to put her past more securely behind her."

"Does she think we're in the business of manufacturing ancestors?" I asked. Faltecchi shrugged. "But how would she get that impression?"

"I wondered that myself." He replaced the photograph in

the manilla envelope. "I shall tell her that we are not, of course. But I do not doubt that she will find others willing to do as she asks. She offers a very generous commission." Carefully, he wrapped the portrait up in brown paper and placed it, along with the envelope, on one of the shelves by his desk.

At the thought of that loveliness perverted for the sake of vanity, a sudden rage swept over me, rage at my own powerlessness to protect the painting. All I can do is repair the damage done by time or accident, I thought. Against a man or woman like that I'm helpless.

"It's maddening," I said, "to think there's no protection from vandals rich enough to do as they please with what they own."

Faltecchi looked at me with amusement. "Why, Kate, I believe you have the makings of a radical. Were you in that demonstration this morning?"

"In a manner of speaking. Though not of my own free will." I didn't mind Faltecchi's teasing; I knew he cared about the painting as much as I did.

"Well, I will tell this woman that if she does have the portrait altered she will drastically reduce its value. Perhaps the appeal to her purse will have some effect." With a sweep of his arm he knocked some tubes of paint littering the seat of the chair by his desk into a small box and gestured to me to sit down. "Now, we must talk about your work for the Torreleones. Sit, sit."

The Torreleone paintings were my first major commission. There were three of them, each an oil on canvas: a Vanvitelli and two views of Venice by Guardi. Although they needed no restoration, the job of cleaning them was complicated by the fact that the paintings could not be removed from the palazzo because the Torreleones were unwilling to pay the considerable insurance premium required. The work was going well, there were no problems, and my description was straightforward and brief.

When I finished, Faltecchi smiled. "I spoke with Massimo Torreleone yesterday. He is pleased."

"Thank heaven."

Faltecchi's smile widened. "Oh, I think you may take a little credit as well. Although a sense of piety is not a bad thing in our work."

"Some of the credit belongs to you, too," I told him. "After all, it was thanks to you that I got the commission. I never asked you what persuasion you used."

"The truth persuaded him. I showed him examples of your work, and I told him that you are the best assistant I have yet employed. I said that you could be trusted with his paintings."

I had always known that Faltecchi approved of my work—obviously he wouldn't have given me the Torreleone commission if he hadn't—but this was the first time he'd been so lavish with his compliments. I flushed, caught between delight and shame at my greediness for praise. I recognized my own vanity about my work, and I suspected Faltecchi was well aware of it, too.

But before I could thank him, he went on. "I also took the liberty of saying to Massimo Torreleone that because you are young and eager to establish yourself here in Rome, you would not be costly to employ. Whereas I—" Here he opened his hands wide in a gesture that acknowledged his own worth. Faltecchi was one of the best restorers of paintings in Italy and was, consequently, expensive. "The Torreleones were once a rich and powerful family, but no longer. So the matter of your fee was a persuasive argument."

"I would have done the work for nothing, I wanted it so badly."

Faltecchi pretended to be shocked. "Do not let Franco hear you say that. A craftsman must have pride, he would tell you. Most people do not respect work that costs them nothing."

Franco Stillitano was Faltecchi's partner, and opposite. He and I had disliked each other from the moment we met, an instinctive dislike that I tried and failed to suppress and that seemed to deepen into something more on Stillitano's part as my relationship with Faltecchi grew. I preferred to have as little to do with Stillitano as I could. I was always relieved when, as now, commissions took him out of Rome.

Stillitano had his own assistant, and there was little reason for me to go to him about the technical aspects of my work, but he was responsible for the finances of the business, and I found that he could be meticulous to an almost grasping degree where money was concerned. To his credit, he kept Faltecchi and Stillitano well in the black, something I suspected Faltecchi himself would never have managed on his own. Faltecchi was casual about bills.

Faltecchi's previous assistant, Paolo Flacco, had been a student with me in Florence years before and had recommended me to Faltecchi as his replacement when he resigned six months previously to return to Florence and a job at the Uffizi. "Faltecchi," Paolo had told me, "is a genius at what he does. You'll learn more from him than you'll ever suspect." Paolo was right about this. "The only problem with the job," he added, "is Stillitano. He's a frustrated artist with the soul of a bookkeeper. And poisonous. You won't like him." He was right about that, too. "But he *is* a brilliant restorer—in his own peculiar way." Paolo had refused to explain what he meant by that curious remark.

"While we are speaking of Signor Stillitano," Faltecchi said to me now, his face serious, "I must ask you not to mention the Torreleone paintings to him when he returns from Sicily today." He paused briefly, as if searching for the right words. "It is a question of the fee. I am sure Franco would consider it too low. Let me think a little about the best way to tell him."

Another reason for Stillitano to dislike me, I thought grimly. But I agreed, grateful that Faltecchi would handle it. When I tried to thank him for all he had done for me, he just laughed and held up one hand. "My motives are not wholly unselfish, Kate. I want to keep you here in Rome. You have learned much in the past six months, but perhaps you were growing a little bored with the simple tasks that came your way. It was time you were challenged, is this not so?"

I nodded, chagrined that he read me so easily. In the last month or two I had chafed against the restraints I felt he placed on my abilities, his insistence on the repetition of tiny details of techniques and skills I thought I'd mastered months before. I checked my impatience, however; I knew Faltecchi did nothing without a good reason. And I was consoled by the growing affection I felt for him, and his own quiet approval of me. We worked together easily, with a mutual, wordless understanding that had come to mean more to me than any amount of praise. Still, it quietly infuriated me to see Stillitano's assistant given commissions I was certain I could carry out with ease while I labored over unimportant and uninspiring pieces. Until the Torreleone paintings.

Faltecchi rested one of his hands on mine. "I know I have held you back a little, Kate. But you are impetuous, and while your instinct is often right and your skill impeccable, you do not always pause to consider every aspect of a problem down to the ultimate detail and then beyond. And that is crucial in our work. But you have been patient."

"And I have my reward," I said, without irony.

"Just so." He leaned back in his chair, turning a paintbrush over in his hands. "Tell me, what do you make of the Torreleones?"

"I've only met Massimo Torreleone so far. I'm under his spell already. If the rest of the family is half as irresistible— But, to be honest, I haven't heard much about the son that makes him sound as appealing as his father."

"No? Well, perhaps you have heard only gossip. I promise you that he can be very appealing. But he is a mystery. I doubt if anyone really knows him. For every rumor that one hears, there is another to contradict it. As a young man, he was undoubtedly wild and extravagant—in the most charming way, of course." Faltecchi gave a tolerant smile; it was clear that Alessandro Torreleone's charm must be considerable. "Some say that he cost the family dearly, that the Torreleones will never recover from Alessandro's youth. Now, on the other hand, he appears to have reformed and is a responsible, if not very illustrious, government official, his wild past behind him. His mother's death several years ago may have been the shock he needed. Who knows? I must confess to a certain liking for

Alessandro, even when he was behaving so badly. Women, of course, have always like him." Faltecchi scratched some paint off the sleeve of his jacket. "He is certainly nothing like his father in one respect. I am sure he has not the slightest sympathy for leftist causes, and I think that he will resurrect the family title when Massimo dies."

He rose to his feet. "Now I am gossiping myself. Perhaps Alessandro has that effect on people." As we walked out of his office together, he said, "You will do a fine job, I am certain of it. But remember, *pazienza*."

Patience. I liked the word better in Italian. There was a flourish to *pazienza* that expressed the slightly crazy quality it had in this city where so often the word was spoken with a wink and a certain irony. In English it just sounded dreary and long-suffering. And that, I suddenly thought as I said good-bye to Faltecchi and went into the storeroom for supplies, was probably precisely how Michel had thought of me near the end of our marriage—dreary and long-suffering. It would amuse him to know how I'd come to loathe the word.

I was following this unprofitable line of thought as I came out of the storeroom—and walked straight into Franco Stillitano.

CHAPTER
3

The impact was slight, hardly more than the touch of his arm against mine, but, instinctively, I recoiled so violently away from him that I banged my left elbow hard against the doorway and let out such a cry of pain that Stillitano looked shocked.

Embarrassed, I tried to explain the reason for my shriek while I fought down the wave of nausea that had come with the pain. "I'm sorry, but that elbow happens to be a sore point. I injured it long ago, and some nerve or other never recovered."

Stillitano gave me an unsympathetic look. "Then for your own sake, Signora Roy, and for the sake of the nerves of other people, you must not be in such a hurry. *Pazienza.*" The word flicked against me like a tiny hailstone, cold and sharp. It echoed Faltecchi's, without his kindness to soften the sting.

27

Stillitano was dressed in his "uniform," a black suit, white shirt, and dark tie held by a plain gold pin, all immaculate and just the least bit funereal. His body was very thin and tall, with unusually long arms and fingers, and he moved in a strange gliding fashion, as if he were flexible to the point of bonelessness. With all this, and his long pointed nose and chin, he reminded me of a toy I'd had as a child, a black india-rubber man who could be twisted into any shape one chose.

Out of courtesy rather than any desire to prolong our conversation, I asked him if the commission in Sicily had gone well. He answered me politely enough but so coldly that I escaped as soon as I could, grateful for the work at the palazzo that would keep me away for the rest of the day.

I walked back to the Corso. Almost all the signs of the demonstration were gone, apart from the inevitable leaflets fluttering on the sidewalk and in the gutter. Traffic had resumed its murderous way. Faltecchi once told me that in the old days during Carnevale riderless horses were turned loose to race along the Corso, wild with fear and rage provoked by the lead-spiked harnesses they wore and by the shouts and blows of the crowd, many of whom went down beneath the horses' hooves. The faintest trace of that terrified anarchy still hung about the street, now grown gray and bourgeois.

Fixing my eyes firmly on those of the driver of an approaching car, I stepped deliberately out into his path and held my breath, not quite trusting him to stop. But of course he did; they always did. That was the miracle of the Roman driver.

I threaded my way through the streets to the little piazza that fronted the Palazzo Torreleone. The palazzo was one of Maderno's less successful efforts, almost too severe in its plain four-square facade, as though the architect had grown tired of baroque extravagance and, aiming at a simpler effect, had gone too far in the other direction. Its charm lay in its size, which, for a palace, was small, and a certain well-proportioned grace about the windows, the bottom row of which was caged in iron grilles. Like many Roman palaces, the ground floor was given over to one-room shops—a baker, a shoe repair, some sort of workshop where a great deal of banging and hammering went on but nothing much seemed to be produced. The middle floor, the *piano nobile*, held the great staterooms and family apartments, while the upper floor was occupied by servants' quarters, down-at-heel dependents, distant relatives, and rented rooms.

The *portiera* greeted me as I passed through the gate. She leaned on the windowsill of the lodge, her plump bosom resting on equally plump arms, a wide smile running like a banner across perfect white teeth. It was impossible to tell her age. She was one of those large olive-skinned Roman matrons who might be forty or sixty—once they lost that ephemeral beauty of their early twenties, they would look the same, comfortable, motherly, until old age shriveled away their plumpness.

A lovely day, we both agreed, but such a terrible night. "What must you think of us, Signora Roy?" Signora Gambino said, her smile vanished. "We are a crazy people."

"Was anyone hurt in the bombings?" I asked her.

"*Sì.* The radio said one man killed and a *carabiniere* with one arm and half his face gone. The bombs were left in cars outside government buildings. *È terribile!*" She sighed. "You know, I was in Rome during the last war, and we did these things to each other, but I thought then, Never again. There must be some devil at work in our country. Tell me, do they do such things in Canada?"

I thought of the separatist bombings, long ago as they seemed now, and was forced to say yes, sometimes they did. "But not often. Canadians are so different from Italians. Some of us think we have too much respect for authority." I remembered Michel's unprintable comments on the subject of our national passivity.

"Ah well, then we are different indeed." She sighed again, then opened her eyes wide. "But I am forgetting! The signore wishes to see you as soon as you arrive. He is in his study. Have you been there?" I shook my head. "You must cross the courtyard and take the stairs in the far left corner up to the first floor. It is the door nearest the stairs. *Buon giorno.*"

I went along the vaulted stone corridor, through the arcade that ringed the four sides of the courtyard, and out into a pretty square of parterred flower beds set among low boxwood hedges and pebbled paths. The silence here after the noise of the piazza was startling, a rich, tranquil silence centuries old. Reigning over this peace, pipes in one hand, the other raised in a pagan blessing, was a small marble faun set on a pedestal above the water of the fountain. He was laughing, and when you saw his face you couldn't help but smile back at him, as though you shared some secret. I greeted him and continued across the courtyard to the staircase that led to Count Massimo's study.

There was a muffled reply to my knock on the door, and I went in. Count Massimo was at the other end of the room, seated at a desk. For a moment I thought he was talking to himself, then realized he was speaking into a tape recorder. He switched it off and rose to his feet.

The room was large, wood-paneled, and much too hot. A fire burned furiously in the big stone fireplace. Shabby chintz-covered furniture, hunting prints, and books, hundreds of books—spilling out of bookcases, scattered over chairs and tables, and stacked in piles on the floor—made the room seem more like the library of some seedy English country house than a palace in the center of Rome. But the old man who came toward me was pure Italian.

He was beautiful in the way that old porcelain is beautiful, finely made and elegant but worn to a fragile translucence with use and age. Nature had refined away all the grosser aspects of the flesh until his skin lay close to his bones and one could see the delicate modeling of his head. He had a narrow, high-browed face, a long, aquiline nose, and brown eyes that were intelligent and kind but filmed by cataracts. He was struggling now with a pair of wire-rimmed glasses, hooking them down over his ears, frowning a little as he did.

"*Ecco!*" he said, and his face smoothed out into a sweet smile. "Signora Roy! Forgive me, I did not know you at first. Without my glasses I am an imbecile."

"I hope I haven't disturbed you."

"Not in the least. I wanted to invite you to join me for coffee. I have already rung for it, and flattering myself that you would not refuse, I asked that an extra cup and some cakes be sent up."

"It would be a pleasure to have coffee with you," I said, meaning it.

We sat down. I was careful to choose the armchair farthest from the fireplace. It seemed remarkably uncomfortable until I realized that a book was wedged under the seat cushion and fished it out. Count Massimo reached out to relieve me of the book. "I must apologize to you for the confusion, but I—" He got no further because one elbow knocked against a precarious pile of books on the arm of his chair, which promptly fell to the floor.

"Please, let me." I knelt and gathered up the books.

"Thank you, my dear. On there I think." He pointed to an already overburdened table. "I was about to explain that the chaos in this room is the result of a book I am writing about my family—or rather dictating, as writing wearies my eyes. I have only a few more chapters before it will be completed but I am finding them the most difficult, for they are about the times and people I remember. That sounds peculiar, I know, but it seems to be harder for me to write well and with detachment about those I knew." He rubbed his face wearily.

I think he had forgotten I was there—he seemed really to be talking to himself—but a knock on the door brought him back from his reverie. "Good, that will be Mario with our coffee. Now let me see, where shall he put it?" In a haphazard way he began piling books on top of each other in order to clear a space on the low table in front of the fire as a man even older than he came into the room carrying a tray with a silver coffee-pot, cups and saucers, and a plate of little cakes. He set the tray down on the table beside a leaning tower of books, then stooped over and began picking up the litter.

"Never mind, Mario," Count Massimo said. "It does not matter."

But it obviously did matter to Mario, because he ignored his master and continued his tidying until he was satisfied that he had restored some order. Finally, he straightened, poured our

31

coffee, and handed each of us our cup, accompanied by a small bow, then left the room as silently as he had entered it.

After the door had closed behind him, Count Massimo smiled at me as if to say, What can I do? "Mario's brother is the majordomo for an English duke who lives in great style. I believe Mario thinks I shame him by my behavior. He scolds me for it frequently and plainly would prefer that I continue the traditions of my father's day."

"I suspect a lot of people would agree with Mario in finding the ideal of aristocratic behavior irresistible. Mind you," I added, laughing, "as long as they were the aristocrats and not the servants."

"I am sure you are right. It seems that even the most democratic of countries have secret yearnings for the trappings of the aristocracy."

"In Montreal I knew liberals who imported their servants from the Caribbean so that they wouldn't have to pay them decently and Marxist millionaires living in mansions who somehow reconciled the contradiction." I was warming to my theme when I remembered his communist past. Feeling tactless, afraid I'd offended him, I came to an abrupt halt.

But he seemed, or pretended, not to notice my gaffe and merely said, "Contradictions make us human, and interesting."

As he spoke, his narrow hands moved in a graceful accompaniment to his words—watching him was, for me, almost as great a pleasure as listening to him. Because of the impression he gave of tranquil and gentle reason, there was never anything forced or frenetic about this play of hands; on the contrary, I found it soothing. Count Massimo raised the Italian language of gesture to an art form.

While we drank our coffee, he asked me about my work. He seemed genuinely interested in the methods I used to clean oil paintings, and as I described the approach I was taking to his own paintings, I was struck again by how easy he was to talk to.

"You speak of your work with passion, Signora Roy," he said when I'd finished. "You are blessed to have such a feeling."

"Yes, I think I am. I can't imagine working at anything else, or at something I hated."

"And are you happy in Rome? Forgive me if the question seems impertinent, but it is not your city, and perhaps you find that difficult at times."

"I don't mind the question," I told him. "I love Rome. Perhaps all the more because I was unhappy before I came here. My marriage had ended and I was feeling like a stranger in the place I was born. Rome seems such a generous city, so tolerant. But," I added, "I'm a foreigner, and I suspect that no matter how long I live here, I'll always be one."

"My wife also felt that way. She was Anglo-Irish. She suffered from the feeling that she was an outsider in Ireland because her family was originally English, although her sympathies were with the Irish people. Then she felt an outsider here in Rome. But we are all outsiders in some sense if we choose a path other than that prescribed for us by custom. My wife should have married one of her own people, although I am happy for my own sake that she did not. And I should have . . ." But he left whatever it was he was going to say unspoken. "However, there is not much use in 'should haves,' is there? I hope you haven't many of them at your age, Signora Roy."

"A few," I said ruefully. "Enough, anyway, to agree with you." There was a silence while we finished our coffee. In the fireplace a log burned through and collapsed in a flare of sparks, blue and yellow against the blackened stone. We set our cups down simultaneously. "Now I should go and do some work—I've been spoiled long enough."

Count Massimo rose to his feet with me. "How are you progressing?"

"It's going well. Would you like to come and see?"

"Thank you, I would." Once Count Massimo had made the decision to trust me with his paintings, he left them in my hands absolutely and would come to see them only on my invitation. Several days had passed since his last visit.

As we turned to leave the study, I noticed for the first time a small painting in the left-hand corner of the room by the door, half-hidden by an oriental lacquer screen. It hung on the oak paneling above a wooden prie-dieu, a Madonna and child in an oval gilt frame, at first glance made insignificant by the dim light of the corner in which it hung. But I recognized the famous Torreleone *Madonna and Child* by Guido Reni.

Count Massimo heard my faint intake of breath and noticed the direction of my gaze. "How stupid I am," he said quietly. "I had forgotten to show you the jewel of our collection. Come, let me take you closer to it." He led me around the screen to stand before the painting. "The Reni is my favorite because my wife loved it. It used to hang in her bedroom. This was her prie-dieu. She was a better Catholic than I—I had almost forgotten how to pray when I met her—but she reminded me by example only. She was never the fanatic so many of her countrymen are."

I stood there staring up at the painting, feeling sick.

The baby lay on a tangle of violet cloth, abandoned to sleep, his head resting on one plump arm. He was any holy child of early baroque paintings, an angelic rosy baby, half putto, half human. But the Madonna bending over him was unmistakably a Reni. A smoothly oval, upturned face, lips slightly parted, eyes raised to heaven in a gaze both sorrowful and tranquil, her arms outstretched to frame the sleeping child. The gesture combined protective mother love with sacrificial resignation. She was offering up her child to God's will, and the look in the large blue eyes made it clear that she knew what He would ask.

It was a painting from Reni's controversial last years, the period when his celebrated golden palette turned to silver, the paint tones softened into lavender, blue-grays, and pale whites, and over them that luminous pearly light. The period some called a decline, when his style had loosened, the brushstrokes broadened, grown impressionistic—unfinished, said some critics. The period when, pressed by popular demand and gambling debts, the "divine Guido" had gone into mass production. Or so critical opinion contended. Like much else in art criticism, that opinion changed, and the late work came into its own. The

Torreleone *Madonna and Child* was at last recognized for the masterpiece it was.

But this was not the Torreleone *Madonna and Child*.

It tried hard to be. The breathtakingly accurate colors, the typical "unfinished" style, even the famous expression on the Madonna's face, all came close. Close, but a million empty miles from the real thing.

I desperately wanted to hold the painting in my hands. I asked Count Massimo if I might take it down from the wall, to see it more clearly.

"But of course you must take it down. My own sight is so poor that I see only a glimmer of what I saw in the past. In my mind I remember this painting so well that I forget others might find it difficult in this light. And, to be truthful, few others come here. As a rule, we meet our guests in the *salone*. There is an alarm, however, and I must first switch it off." He went across the room to his desk, reached down behind it, then came slowly back to me. "There, now it is safe. You may lift it down. Or I could ring for a servant if you would like help. I am sorry that I am so useless, but I dare not offer to help you myself. My doctor is very strict with me."

"Thank you, but I can easily manage it myself. It's small enough for that." I moved the prie-dieu forward and reached up for the painting. Holding it out before me—as though arm's length would somehow protect me from the unpleasant feeling the painting aroused in me—I took it over to the window.

The light fell ruthlessly on *Madonna and Child*. No, there was no doubt. From a distance the deception succeeded, but seen in a good light by a trained eye, it fell apart.

Reni's characteristic brushstrokes were too tight here, overly controlled—the unmistakable stamp of a copy. Or a forgery. The "autograph" of his work, that firm, accomplished drawing of facial features, was missing; the modeling here was too careful, copycat careful, lacking the spontaneity, the direct quality, of an original. There was a clumsiness of line that could never have been Reni's no matter how "unfinished" his work.

I turned the painting over to look at the back. The work was on canvas, and that in itself was odd. In his last years Reni usually painted on silk, convinced that it held up in a way that canvas and linen did not. The story went that Reni was present during some excavations in a church in Bologna when workmen opened a tomb. As soon as the air touched the contents of the tomb, everything crumbled to dust—apart from the silk robe covering the body. From that moment, he worked on silk.

The canvas itself and the wooden supports were both convincingly old, but there were no certificates of guarantee, no collectors' marks, none of the inscriptions—those fading scraps of paper that testify to a painting's provenance—that one normally finds on old paintings. Not that their absence necessarily meant the work was a forgery, but it was peculiar not to see them.

"Has this painting always been in your family?" I asked Count Massimo. If it had, that might explain the missing marks.

"No. In fact, it is a comparatively recent part of the collection. My grandfather was an ardent collector of paintings. He bought the Reni in the late 1890s. I believe it had been through many hands before it came to us."

That made it very peculiar indeed that there were no marks.

Count Massimo went on. "That one painting would, I am told, bring us enough money to save the others. If I would consent to sell it." He spoke dispassionately enough, but the words shocked me. I looked at him in surprise, although I ought to have guessed.

He caught the look and said quietly, "Giorgio Faltecchi did not tell you why I am having the paintings cleaned?"

"No, he didn't."

"Well, perhaps he does not know. I must sell them. They must be sold."

The "must" was repeated with a burst of conviction, as though to persuade himself. It was obvious that he hated the fact. I didn't need to ask why the Torreleones were selling their paintings. I knew from the little Faltecchi had told me that they needed the money.

"Now," Count Massimo said gently, "shall we go and see what you have been doing."

I could only nod. What in heaven's name could I say to him? That the painting he loved best of all was a fake? Plainly, he had no suspicions. I hung the painting back on its hook, pushed the prie-dieu into place below it, and turned my back on the troubling *Madonna and Child*. They would have to wait. And I would have to speak to Giorgio Faltecchi; he would know what to do.

Out in the chilly passageway I shivered a little after the warmth of the study while Count Massimo searched his pockets, producing a key that he fitted into the lock of a door across the way. We went through several small and very beautiful eighteenth-century rooms, sparsely furnished but so wonderfully decorated with frescoed scenes of the Roman *campagna* populated by peasants and shepherds that what little furniture there was seemed almost superfluous. Still, once there must have been tables and chairs and sofas, and I wondered if these had gone the way the paintings were destined to go.

The last door let out onto the landing of the great central staircase. We crossed this, unlocked a handsome set of double doors, and found ourselves in a room of surpassing loveliness, an incandescence of light shimmering on gold and white, shattered by marble, crystal, and glass, pooling in blue shadows and finally, triumphantly, warmed by yellow, scarlet, and rose. Gradually the riot of shape stilled, the swirling colors separated, sharpening into specific detail, and the room came into focus, a long room running half the length of the palazzo, where a baroque imagination had staged an elaborate fantasy of paradise.

To my left, light poured in through tall windows along the western side of the room. Paintings, tapestries, and extravagant mirrors thickly crusted with gilt hung between the windows and along the unbroken eastern wall, while ornate gilt chairs, gilt tables frosted in black-and-white marble, busts and statues, and graceful sofas rich with rose brocade filled every bit of space apart from the path down the center of the room. The ultimate effect was to carry the eye along and up, up to the vaulted ceiling, where laughing cupids held garlands of flowers up to the gods who reclined lazily above them in a sky of pure, transparent blue.

Each time that I saw the Salone d'Oro, the Golden Room, I forgot that the flower-filled vases in the corners were painted, not real, that half of the tapestries were murals on the wall, not cloth, and that the ceiling that arched above me was no higher than the other rooms on this floor. It was trompe l'oeil, a trick, and a trick that worked, unlike the Reni, a trick that brought pleasure instead of the anger of betrayed belief.

Count Massimo came quietly up to where I stood looking at a tapestry of commedia dell'arte characters who were strolling, flirting, deceiving each other in an Arcadian landscape. "It is ridiculous in this day to own such things, is it not? Yet I struggle to save this remnant of a past age as if it could make a difference to the future." His tone was dry, without self-pity.

"Perhaps the future will need beauty like this," I said. "We seem to make so little of it ourselves. If we can't create, we should at least preserve what there is." How pompous that sounds, I thought. Aloud, I added, "I'm sorry. I didn't mean to give you the conservator's apology for her work."

"You need not apologize, Signora Roy," he said mildly, "for speaking the truth. You are right, of course. The difficulty, however, is that there is always a cost to be paid for the past. The price of a Reni, perhaps. But that I cannot bear to pay. My son Alessandro will have to be the ruthless one."

"Will I, Father?"

I spun about, startled by the voice so close behind us. I hadn't heard him come into the room.

At first I saw only his eyes, which were on me, eyes as blue as the ceiling above. They were slightly slanted and fringed with thick black lashes, and the look in them was both direct and ambiguous. He had his father's carefully modeled features, the same good bones, but broadened across the breadth of the face, with a shorter, more sharply angled jawline, and the same curving, attractive mouth. He had nothing, however, of his father's ascetic quality. Not really conventionally handsome, not even conventionally masculine, he was a man, I was certain, who would always notice, and be noticed by, women.

Aware that I was staring at him, I shifted my gaze and noticed a commedia dell'arte figure in the tapestry hanging just behind him. It was Harlequin, smiling enigmatically out at me from over Alessandro Torreleone's shoulder. The two of them looked disconcertingly alike—the angle of Harlequin's head, the fluid, elegant body, the slanted eyes, all echoed Alessandro's. Amused by this, I imagined Alessandro in pursuit of the pretty tapestry Columbine and found myself smiling at him.

"Alessandro," Count Massimo was saying, "this is wonderful. I had not expected you back so soon."

"I returned last night, Father. Very late. Otherwise, I would have come to you." He looked at me again. "I don't believe—"

"Ah yes," his father broke in, "you must meet Signora Roy. Signora Roy, may I present my son, Alessandro." He spoke his son's name with obvious affection, and, remembering Faltecchi's words, I knew that whatever Alessandro had cost the Torreleones, it was not his father's love. "Alessandro, this is Signora Kate Roy."

"I'm delighted to meet you, Signora Roy." He made the trite expression sound genuine.

"Signora Roy is here cleaning some paintings for us," Count Massimo said. "The paintings we agreed should be sold."

"Here?" There was an instant when I could have sworn something very like anger flashed across Alessandro's face, but in his voice I heard nothing more than curiosity and surprise.

"In the end I decided that we could not afford the extra insurance needed if the paintings were to leave the palazzo." Count Massimo said this so firmly, or with what passed for firmness in one who normally spoke so gently, that I had the impression this was an issue on which father and son disagreed. "And Signora Roy comes to us very highly recommended by Giorgio Faltecchi."

"Then you must be skillful indeed, Signora Roy. Signor Faltecchi doesn't praise lightly." He let the half smile widen, and the blue eyes widened with it. "And so we'll have the double pleasure of your skill and your company."

I began to understand that Alessandro himself was very skillful, with a social ease that disarmed and invited intimacy. There were no flourishes in his compliments; he said them easily, simply, as though he meant them. And of course I wanted to believe that he did.

"I was about to show your father what I've done so far. Would you like to join us?"

"Yes, come with us," Count Massimo said eagerly. "She is a miracle worker, you will see."

"That is what we need, Father—a miracle." But Alessandro spoke so softly I doubt if his father heard him. Perhaps he wasn't meant to hear.

My studio was in the southern wing of the palazzo, a large unused room that had been cleared of debris, fitted out with tables, a comfortable chair, and a stool, and turned over to me with the understanding that I should ask for whatever I required for my work and it would be provided. I had chosen it because both ventilation and light were exactly what I needed—there were large windows overlooking the courtyard that let in plenty of air and a strong north light—and because it had, for some inexplicable reason, a small pantry off it with a sink where I could clean up.

The Vanvitelli was on the easel, one of his many views of the Castel Sant'Angelo, the round colossus by the Tiber that was successively an emperor's tomb, a prison, and a papal palace, a frank reminder of death and power and the one threatening note in a scene of sparkling gaiety, of boats on the river and people gathered on the green riverbank, under racing white clouds in a sky of radiant blue. I showed the Torreleones the way in which I was reducing the old, darkened varnish to let the colors through in the bright, clear tones they had once had.

Alessandro pleased me with his comments on my work; they were knowledgeable enough, however, to make me wonder idly whether he had his own suspicions about the Reni. I was debating with myself how best to ask him about it in a way that would seem innocently curious rather than probing when he anticipated me.

"You and my father were discussing the *Madonna and Child* in my father's study when I came up. Do you like Reni's work?" In his voice I heard only the polite interest of someone inquiring about the tastes of another.

I hesitated a moment before replying; any answer I could give seemed dangerous in one way or another. In the end I decided to hedge a little. Feeling like a hypocrite, I said, "Yes, I do—purely as an onlooker. Of course I've never worked on any of his paintings." This much was the literal truth; I did not add that I'd spent a semester in graduate school studying his work. Why I felt that urge to cover my suspicions I had no idea; it disturbed me, made me uncomfortable. "And you?" I asked him.

Alessandro said, "I prefer this." He pointed to the Vanvitelli. "Or a Watteau. But I know very little about painting."

"You do yourself an injustice, Alessandro," his father said. He turned to me. "Despite his modesty, my son has an excellent eye for such things."

"Nonsense, Father. You have always been charitably blind to my failings. I'm a hopeless amateur in this as in so much else." He smiled. "Now, if you ask me about the art of a Lamborghini—well, that's another matter. There I was an expert long before my tenth birthday."

To my relief, the conversation shifted to the other paintings in the room, a pair of Venetian scenes by Guardi, and then Count Massimo thanked me in his courteous way. ". . . but now I must return to my book. We will have dinner together, Alessandro? I would like to hear about your trip."

"Of course, Father. Nothing would please me more. I must go to the Treasury in the afternoon, but I will see you this evening."

Alessandro showed no inclination to leave when his father had gone. While I set out my tools, I asked him where his trip had taken him.

"To Switzerland, on business. I'm a civil servant in the Treasury Department. A dull trip. The Swiss are very correct, and my business was financial. There wasn't much opportunity

41

for pleasure. However, one always eats magnificently in Switzerland, and that is a great consolation." He laughed, and Harlequin was there again in the tilted eyes and the curve of the mouth. "Money and chocolate, a powerful combination for happiness, you'd think, but the Swiss treat them so seriously. As they do everything."

"Unlike the Italians?"

"Well of course foreigners always think we're too much the reverse. A frivolous people, some say. And perhaps we are."

"Not your father. He's a remarkable man."

"Yes, he is a remarkable man. I'm glad you see that. Do you know his story?"

"A little of it. That he was a resistance hero."

"A great one, with great ideals and hopes for Italy. As had my grandfather—but they were very different men. Tragically different." He began to speak very rapidly. "My grandfather was an honorable man, a *galant'uomo* who was prudent, cautious, not as intelligent, perhaps, as my father, but still perceptive. When the fascists came to power, he did not like them, but he endured them. It was the communists he hated.

"My grandfather believed that the nobility's role in Italian life was to steer a careful course using the maps of tradition. My father, who was a young man of impatient and deeply held beliefs, disagreed. He was a typical idealist of the thirties. It's enough to say that in the end he became a communist himself, and my grandfather banished him from this house.

"When my grandfather died, my father refused to use the title. But after the war he became disillusioned with his friends in the Communist party, perhaps recognizing that the past cannot be disposed of as easily as the communists would have us believe. He found himself in a no-man's-land, between allegiances and, I think, turned in a little on himself, and toward my mother also. From a man of action he became one of contemplation. Did you know that he has written many books, histories of our country?"

I nodded. "And that he's writing one now of your family."

"A book that will be as unhappy as the others."

"What do you mean?"

"The history of Italy is notoriously unhappy, Signora Roy. Individual families are no different. Our own especially."

"And yet the Italians are spoken of as a happy people."

"By those who do not know them. It's called '*bella figura*,' putting on a good front, you would say. To fool yourself as well as others." Alessandro's voice was dry, sharp with irony. "One puts on a good show to make life bearable."

"That sounds so cynical."

"Many Italians would consider it simply a pragmatic way to live."

I wondered if he did. I also wondered what had become of Harlequin; this was a different person, someone darker.

Suddenly he gave a mischievous smile. "Don't take what I say too seriously. I do enjoy life occasionally you know, despite myself."

"So I've been told." I could be mischievous, too.

He obviously knew what I was referring to, because he said, "And don't take that gossip too seriously, either." Then he added, "In Italy you have always to look beneath the surface. Nothing here is what it seems."

I found myself liking Alessandro very much. Perhaps that sudden liking showed too clearly on my face, because his expression changed, the mischief gone, and his eyes held mine an instant too long. I turned and went across to the metal cabinet where I stored my solvents. Idly, to fill a silence now grown uncomfortably long, I asked him if he had heard the bombs the night before.

"Only the deaf or the dead could have been here in the center of Rome and failed to hear them. However, we're accustomed to such sounds—most Romans simply cross themselves and go back to sleep."

"And in the morning . . . ?"

"We mourn. But not for long. If we went into mourning each time this city suffered, we'd never escape sackcloth and ashes. We're easily consoled—a dish of pasta, a beautiful woman . . ." He sketched out the parody of a courtly bow. "And now,

43

unfortunately, I must go. Even a bureaucrat must pretend to work."

Before he went through the door, he said, "I seem to have talked only about myself. A typical Italian male, you see. But the next time we meet it will be your turn, Signora Roy."

I smiled at him. "I enjoyed our conversation, Signor Torreleone."

"Alessandro, please."

"Alessandro."

I was about to transfer the solvents I'd brought with me from their metal containers into the small glass vials I used when I remembered to open the windows to get a draft. Some of the fumes were dangerous. As I unlatched a window, I saw Alessandro below in the courtyard, strolling past the fountain. Then he paused, opening his arms wide, and a woman ran out from under the arcade opposite, straight into his embrace. He whirled her around, both of them laughing, and when they stopped her head was thrown back, eyes closed as though in ecstasy, so that for a moment, before she turned, I could stare down into her face. A face I recognized. The face of a maenad, wild and beautiful—the girl from the riot.

The two of them, arms linked, disappeared into the shadows of the arcade.

CHAPTER
4

I worked into the early evening to make up the time I had missed that morning. Every so often, when I paused to rest, the image of those two linked figures, Harlequin and the maenad, came into my mind, and I felt an inexplicable sense of exclusion. Later, looking back, I could see that I was already under Alessandro's spell.

When I left the palazzo, a thin rain was falling, chilling the warmth of the day, a reminder that it was winter still despite orange and lemon trees heavy with fruit. The only brightness against the gray was the shiny yellow of the taxis that splashed their way through puddles and pedestrians.

Before going home, I wanted to talk to Faltecchi, to discuss the Reni with him. I caught him as he was leaving the workrooms. That habitual abstracted look was on his face but he seemed pleased to see me, and we walked together under his umbrella, talking of the day's work. By the time we reached his car, I'd worked up the courage to ask him if he knew the Torreleone Reni.

He nodded. "I remember it well—a wonderful painting. We cleaned it for the Torreleones, you know, some months ago. Before you came to work for us. Perhaps ten months ago. Yes, it was at the time of Massimo Torreleone's illness. He might have died had his will to live not been so strong."

I was stunned. "Do you mean you actually had it in the workrooms? That you worked on it yourself?"

"Not personally. Franco did all the work." Faltecchi laughed. "I remember he was very jealous of it. He is possessive about some commissions and refuses to let anyone in to see them while he works. A bad habit of his." His smile faded, and he ran a heavy hand over his hair, smoothing it back. "He can be very secretive you know."

"Yes." The briefest of looks passed between us, and I suddenly knew that Faltecchi understood perfectly well how I felt about his partner, and sympathized. But it was small comfort at that moment. My mind was grappling with the knowledge that both Faltecchi and Stillitano had seen the Reni, Stillitano himself actually working on it, and presumably neither had thought it a forgery. I was confused, doubting my own judgment. Until I remembered those tight brushstrokes. No, there was no doubt, no possibility that I was wrong.

Faltecchi took his car keys out of his trouser pocket. "Why do you ask me about the Reni, Kate?"

"Because I think it's a forgery." I said it baldly, flat out. I couldn't think of any other way.

The car keys jingled. Faltecchi turned away from me and unlocked the passenger's side. "You had better get in. You're shivering."

It was no warmer in the car, but at least we were out of the rain. When Faltecchi looked at me, the abstracted air was quite gone from his face. "So. Why do you think this?"

46

"Because there are too many good reasons not to." He listened without questions as I listed the clues, until I came to the last. "Whoever did it was meticulous in so many details that it makes me think it was meant to be more than a copy. I'd swear it's out to fool you into thinking it's an original. Even the canvas is old enough—"

Faltecchi interrupted for the first time. "It is on canvas, not silk? You are sure?"

"Yes. I checked, because I remembered that Reni generally painted his last works on silk."

"But the Torreleone *Madonna and Child* was on silk. *That* I am certain of." There was no doubt in his voice.

Neither of us said a word. I felt a curious mixture of exhaustion and guilty relief, as though I'd passed a nasty burden on to someone better able to carry it than I. The windows of the car were fogged up, and I rubbed a circular patch in mine. The rain was still coming straight down, swirling the litter along in the gutters.

Faltecchi stirred in his seat. "And you think Massimo himself has no suspicions?"

"I'm certain he doesn't. For one thing, his eyesight is so poor—he says he sees it much better in memory than in fact. And it obviously means so much to him. He told me that he realized he could sell it for a price that would save the three paintings I'm cleaning but that he couldn't bear to part with it." I remembered the alarm and told Faltecchi how, unlike the other paintings in the collection, the Reni was protected. "So you see, they must believe it's genuine. Otherwise, why bother?"

"You said nothing of your doubts to the Torreleones?"

I shook my head. "Not to Count Massimo. I couldn't. And not to Alessandro, either. I met him for the first time today, and we talked a little about the Reni. I was curious, too, to know what he thought about it. He said he doesn't know that much about painting."

Faltecchi gave an ambiguous grunt, falling silent for some moments. His face was grave, the dark pouches under his eyes seemed more pronounced, and when he spoke again his voice sounded hoarse. "If the Reni is indeed a forgery—and I am inclined to agree with you that it must be—it will be disastrous news for the Torreleones. They had it as an insurance if the worst came and there was no more money. And, as you say, it has great emotional value for Massimo." He rubbed the back of his neck wearily. "But I am certain that the painting was not a forgery when I saw it ten months ago. I would stake my reputation on that. So the question is, when was it made?"

"From the quick look I had, I couldn't tell whether it was an old copy or a modern forgery. I suspect we'd need to get it into the lab for that." It was hard to ask the next question, but I had to know. "Did you see the painting when Signor Stillitano finished working on it, before it went back again to the Torreleones?"

"No. Apparently Massimo asked to see the painting, to have it in his bedroom while he was ill, and it was rushed back to the palazzo. Alessandro told me later that he sent it to us for cleaning during his father's illness because normally his father refused to let it out of his sight."

Faltecchi was slumped in his seat, his head bowed forward into his hands. I could hear his heavy breathing, and above it, the steady drumming of the rain on the car roof. Then he straightened and said, "Well, I will have to see the painting myself, and to do that I will have to tell the Torreleones of your suspicions. But I think we would be wise to go slowly in this. How much more time do you need to complete your work in the palazzo?"

"If all goes well, and there's no reason to think it won't, I should be done by the end of next week."

"In the meantime, then, please do not tell anyone of your suspicions, Kate. When it is time, we will go together to the Torreleones."

I agreed. I knew that I had just given Faltecchi more to worry about than how to break the bad news to the Torreleones. If the Reni was last in Franco Stillitano's hands . . . The fleeting comfort I had taken from Faltecchi's involvement in the dilemma vanished.

Faltecchi asked if he could drive me home. No, I thanked him, his journey was long enough as it was—he lived on the opposite side of the city—but his courtesy was a sweet echo of Count Massimo's, reminding me of how I hated to hurt a man who had been kind to me, willing to trust me.

"I'd better let you go," I told him. "Elsa won't thank me if dinner is overcooked because I held you up." Elsa, Faltecchi's unmarried daughter, acted as his housekeeper, a fiercely protective, loving one who scolded her father constantly for his shortcomings but had made sure he was well fed and cared for since her mother's death.

Faltecchi insisted that I take his umbrella, then leaned across the seat to take my hand and give it a gentle squeeze of reassurance. "*Pazienza*, Kate. There may be an explanation." He wished me good night and drove away, adding his diesel fumes to the smog that was building with the onset of the evening rush hour. I found a bus and joined the passengers who stood wearily leaning against each other in a damp warmth thick with wet wool and stale tobacco. I was feeling distinctly weary myself by the time I opened the front door of the house where I lived and came face-to-face with Clara Palmieri, my friend and landlady.

"Kate! You look so tired. Come in, *cara*, come in." She took me by the waist and steered me gently into her apartment.

Clara and her husband, Gianni, were two halves of a wonderful whole, both vital, attractive, and very different from each other; they completed each other and knew it. I had never seen a happier marriage. Though they occasionally had terrific rows, with much shouting and hurling of breakables, their love seemed solid.

Clara's father had bought the big nineteenth-century hillside house for her when she married Gianni, with the warning that she'd better have something of her own to fall back on if she really was set on leaving home and marrying a good-for-nothing Milanese journalist. Clara came from Naples, where her father was a successful and very rich land speculator. Although she loved him, she had no illusions as to his connections. He had little reason to like journalists, for he had been the subject of numerous investigative articles, none to his credit. But Clara was his only child, his darling, and if her heart's desire was one of the accursed breed, well, how could he refuse her?

The Palmieris had divided the house up into apartments, two on each of the upper two floors, keeping the entire ground floor for themselves and their children. Paolo Flacco, Faltecchi's previous assistant, was their friend and the former occupant of my apartment. He had passed it on to me along with the job; the friendship with Clara and Gianni followed naturally.

Gianni refused to use any of the money that the house brought in for himself, so Clara kept most of it for Giannino and Cecilia, their children. Gianni's principles were high, often unyielding, and a source of both pride and baffled amusement to Clara, whose own approach to the complexities of life was more typically southern, flexible and easygoing.

The Palmieris' apartment was very modern, all curves and bright primary colors, the soft, cushiony furniture heaped in great splashes of red and yellow against white walls. I sank back into one of the oversized sofas, kicking off my shoes with relief, while the children, scrubbed and shining from their bath, came running in to hug me and to search for the candy I sometimes had in my pockets specially for them. They were in luck tonight and, after some chocolate and several stories, went contentedly off to bed, leaving Clara and me alone to talk.

"You'll stay for supper, Kate?" Clara said as she poured me a glass of wine. "You don't look as though you could cook for yourself tonight."

"Bless you, I'd love to." I held the glass of straw-colored wine, enjoying its delicate scent, the opulent comfort around me, and, most of all, the sight of Clara curled up in the chair opposite. She was lovely, all soft, curved edges and bright colors herself; she suited the room perfectly. Her face was typically Neapolitan, round and sensual, with great brown eyes fringed by thick black hair. Around her mouth, like whimsical parentheses, were two deep lines that gave her smile an odd, deprecating downturn.

I sipped the wine and felt the weariness and tension inside me slowly ease as the wine, the comfort of the room, and Clara's presence worked on me.

"Better?" she asked.

I nodded. "Much."

"Good. I was beginning to think that you needed to practice a little of the restorer's art on yourself. Though you rarely look anything less than beautiful, *cara*—no, truly—tonight you worried me."

I smiled at the compliment—it seemed so ridiculous in the light of her own real beauty—but let it pass because it pleased me. "I'm bone weary tonight, Clara. A lot has happened."

"Ah," Clara said with pleasure. "Tell me. Has Alessandro Torreleone returned, and have you seduced him already?" She knew about my work for the Torreleones, and we had speculated a little together about the son and heir, wondering if he would live up to his reputation.

"Yes, he is back, and no, I haven't had my way with him. But it's easy to see why women want to."

"Tell me all," she repeated eagerly, plumping the cushions around her and settling herself comfortably into them. She loved a good gossip and was a remarkable source of information for the goings-on of Roman Society. Despite that, she could be absolutely discreet if asked.

So I told her about Alessandro, leaving out only the strange encounter with the maenad Daniella that I'd seen from my workroom window. I did not, or course, mention the Reni. "He's as charming as his father, though in a very different way. The two of them together are very sweet. If he is to blame for the Torreleones' money troubles, you'd never know it from the way his father looks at him and speaks to him. Do you think it *is* just gossip, Clara?"

The parentheses around Clara's mouth deepened. She shook her head. "I'm afraid not. A friend of mine had an affair with him—it was a long time ago, and she's happily married now—

but she told me that he thought nothing of flying the two of them off to Paris for the weekend. They always stayed at the George V and ate at La Tour d'Argent. And he always bought her something glittery and expensive from Cartier. No, it's not just gossip, Kate."

"Well, I suppose a colorful past never made any man less attractive. I admit I can see the appeal of a weekend in Paris with Alessandro. And I'm not sure he'd have to buy me something glittery to persuade me."

Clara raised her eyebrows. "So soon? His technique must be formidable."

"I'm teasing. He's obviously well aware of the effect he has on women. And it doesn't detract one bit from his charm." I grinned at Clara over the rim of my wineglass. "Anyway, I sense there is something more to Alessandro Torreleone than that playboy image."

"I'd be delighted to pack your suitcase for Paris, Kate." Clara gave a wicked laugh. From time to time she and Gianni tried to link me up with some of their unmarried friends, but although I enjoyed myself when we were together as a four-some, the attempts to duet were dismal and usually, I suspected, my fault. I simply wasn't ready for anything more than a friendly dinner with a man, and although I was flattered by the intensity of the attention as long as it stayed verbal, I retreated, with as much grace as I could manage, once it became physical.

"Paris might be fun," I said, "with the right man." For some reason I thought of Nick Taliaferro and added, "Yesterday I met a man who reminded me of just how much I don't want to get involved again with anyone as serious as Michel." I told Clara about the attempted purse snatch and my rescuer. "He was almost too competent, if you know what I mean. One of those Americans who is so clearly able to deal with anything he comes up against. Nothing fazes him—or at least he'd never let you know it if it did. He'd never let you see any strong emotion, or anything of himself, for that matter."

"You didn't like him?"

I felt guilty, as though I had done Nick Taliaferro an injustice and been untruthful, too. Why did I find it so hard to admit that he attracted me? "It's not that I disliked him exactly. He did rescue me, after all. But there was something secretive about him, too. He asked me to have dinner with him, and I think he's after something. I'd swear, though, that it's more than the pleasure of my company."

"He sounds fascinating," Clara said. "Tell me more."

But before I could go on, we heard loud, tuneless singing outside the door. "That's Gianni," Clara said happily, jumping up.

The door opened, and Gianni Palmieri came into the room, smiling broadly, his arms filled with groceries. At that moment— dressed in a chocolate-brown corduroy suit and darkly furred with thick brown hair, bushy eyebrows over black eyes, and a heavy beard that left much of his face to the imagination—he looked like nothing so much as a friendly bear. He disappeared briefly into the kitchen before returning with an embrace and a rose for each of us.

"Have you started dinner, Clara? Good, because tonight I am the cook. I've bought everything for a meal that will be exceptional, I promise you. You must stay and eat with us, Kate." He was exuberant, full of a good humor that made us smile for the sheer pleasure of his obvious happiness.

"I've already invited Kate, and she said yes," Clara told him.

"*Bene*. Then if you will begin chopping onions for the sauce, I will go and kiss the children."

"I thought you said you would do the cooking," Clara protested, laughing. "I should have known it was too good to be true."

"But I will. You will simply be my assistants. I will do the real work." With a wink for me, he started down the hall to the children's room, a stocky, energetic figure bristling with life.

Clara turned to me, her eyebrows raised. "I wonder what that was all about?" Dutifully, we went into the kitchen to chop onions.

The tears running down my face from the onions reminded me of the tear gas and the demonstration. I described the mob to Clara, who nodded sympathetically when I told her how I'd taken cover and felt cowardly in consequence.

"But it wasn't your fight, Kate. You did the right thing. Those students are crazy. Half of them are manipulated by the far right and the other half by the left. And they are being used." She sighed and chopped the onion more fiercely. "Still, I know they're right to be angry. The situation is terrible—"

"Which situation is that?" Gianni asked as he came into the kitchen, wiping water from his hands and face with a towel; some if it still dripped from his beard. He threw the towel over one shoulder and began pulling pans out of a cupboard.

"Take your pick," Clara replied. "You have a lot to choose from."

"My God, yes," Gianni said explosively. "Everyone has a legitimate cause. You should have heard the story that came in from Naples today." He launched into a complex but remarkably clear account of some local government-housing scandal. Gianni was a good journalist, and I watched for his byline, for I had a hope of understanding what he wrote. That wasn't always the case with other reporters' stories, particularly political stories, which were Gianni's specialty.

By this time he was sitting perched on a tall kitchen stool, smoking his pipe as he talked, while Clara and I, with occasional meaningful glances at each other, progressed with the actual cooking. Every now and then he paused to direct operations, calling for more basil if he thought we'd skimped, or rising to tip wine into a pot.

"Ah well, Naples—what do you expect?" he said when he finished the story, with a sly grin for Clara. "They're all corrupt there." She faced him, wielding her knife, and he flinched back in mock terror. "*Basta, basta*, I'm only an ignorant northerner who doesn't understand."

Clara turned back to me and to the subject of the demonstration. "But how lucky you were to find shelter, Kate. A mob can be unpredictable, and dangerous."

"I think I was more frightened in my shelter. And as it turned out, I was probably in greater danger there, too."

"What's this all about?" Gianni asked.

When I paused dramatically, Clara said impatiently, "Don't be a tease, *cara*. What happened?"

So I filled Gianni in on what he'd missed and then told them both what I'd overheard in that dank stairwell, adding the subsequent sight of the pair, apparently harmonious once more, and the old man's account of the empty apartment. But I could not bring myself to mention the next appearance of the maenad—in Alessandro's arms. I told myself that I was being ridiculous—after all, why should it matter if the two knew each other—but because I felt such confusion, I wanted to know more before I confided that part of the story to anyone.

I finished with an appeal. "What could I have done? What would you have done?"

But Gianni, of course, was a journalist and had a ready answer. "Followed them. What else?" I must have looked crestfallen, because he added hastily, "I don't mean that you should have, Kate. After all, you aren't a journalist or a detective."

"You did the right thing," Clara said. "How were you to know that the apartment wasn't theirs? And you were right about the police, too. What use could they be?"

Gianni laughed. "Spoken like a true southerner." He looked at me thoughtfully. "But now we must think what would be the best thing for you to do."

"At the moment, I'd like to do nothing. I do have one clue. But," I added as Gianni and Clara began to speak at the same time, "I want to wait a bit to see what comes of it." I didn't look at them, concentrating my attention instead on layering slices of mozzarella and tomato.

"And if the robbery goes forward as planned?" Gianni asked after a moment's quiet in which I sensed rather than saw his questioning glance at Clara.

"The man named Marco said she had a week to decide. If I don't learn anything more in the next few days, I'll do something, I promise."

Clara gave me a serious look. "Be careful, *cara*. Someone may not like your curiosity."

I promised to be careful and deflected further questions with the observation that Gianni's pasta water was about to boil over and the olive oil was smoking in the pan. With a curse, Gianni grabbed a pot holder in each hand and leaped for the stove. We spent the next few minutes furiously grating and stirring and generally getting in one another's way until Gianni pronounced the pasta ready to eat.

The kitchen smelled deliciously of basil, onion, and wine, and I found that I was ravenously hungry. But as we went into the dining room, Gianni took the edge off my appetite with a murmured "Clara is right, you know. Curiosity can be dangerous. We are your friends, Kate, so . . ." He didn't finish the sentence, but I was grateful for the implied offer of help and told him so.

As we began to eat, Gianni suddenly slapped himself on the forehead. "*Stupido!* I had almost forgotten—this is a celebration."

Clara and I looked suitably impressed.

"My name is about to be made. I will be the Italian Woodward and Bernstein, destroyer of governments, revealer of corruption—"

"Gianni," Clara said as he waved his glass enthusiastically around, slopping wine onto the tablecloth, "just tell us. Enough of the rhetoric. You sound like a politician."

Gianni composed himself and announced, very seriously, "The biggest story of my life. That's what it will be."

"And just what is this story about?" Clara asked him.

He did not answer her directly; instead, he turned to me. "You have Freemasons in Canada, don't you, Kate?"

I heard Clara give a faint sigh and say, "Oh, *that*."

Startled, I said, "Yes. But I don't know much about them apart from the fact that they're some sort of secret organization and do good works. Do they exist in Italy, too?"

"Yes. They have a long, and mostly honorable, history here. There are several big lodges in Italy today—one very powerful lodge in particular. It's called Mestola Rossa, after the red mason's trowel, one of their symbols. But its members don't do good works—except for each other."

"You're still on that story?" Clara said. She sounded disappointed.

Gianni said to me, "Clara thinks I make too much of what I've learned about this lodge. The Italian love of mystery at work, our desire to believe that complicated plots lie under every aspect of our life. But sometimes we have been proved right."

"I don't deny that an organization like Mestola Rossa exists, Gianni," Clara told him calmly. "But to see it as some insidious destroyer of the state when it's probably merely a matter of patronage—no, that's too much. I've seen such groups all my life. It's the way to get ahead in this country, to be a success."

"That may be," Gianni replied. "But these Masons are after success in its largest sense, an absolute control of the state. They're determined to subvert democracy in order to replace it with fascism." He was speaking slowly and seriously now. "The members of this lodge belong to all parts of government and society, including the Church. And they're all to the far right."

"But I thought that Freemasons were anti-Catholic," I said. "Doesn't the Church forbid Catholics to be Masons?"

"Yes, it does. But it appears that this particular lodge doesn't direct its activities against the Church and may even work with its blessing." Gianni said this on his way into the kitchen for the *secondo*, rolls of veal scaloppine in a tomato sauce, which he set in front of Clara and me with a flourish. "Taste that now and tell me you've had better!"

"Never," I reassured him after I'd eaten a forkful. It really was delicious—Clara and I had worked hard on it, after all. "But how did you find all this out about these Masons?"

"Now you've done it," Clara groaned with mock despair. "Eat, Kate. If anyone's food has to get cold, it should be Gianni's."

He ignored this. "The leader, a man named Bassi, has been under suspicion for some time now. He's made some mistakes, but he's come a long way for a former mattress manufacturer from Rimini. He was a fascist during the war, one of Mussolini's faithful in Salò, the *Duce*'s last stronghold. But somehow he convinced people after the war that he'd fought in the resistance, so he escaped trial and prospered. He built up an astounding network of powerful connections and created his private kingdom with Mestola Rossa. But his kingdom is about to collapse, and a lot of people will go down into the mud with it." He attacked his food with relish. Between bites, he went on, "When it all comes out, the government stands a good chance of collapsing as well. Too much collaboration and cover-up have gone on for it to survive. Though you can bet they won't give up without a fight." He looked up from his plate with a grin. "I'm looking forward to that fight."

"Gianni, the crusading journalist," Clara teased him; but it was said affectionately.

"When will you publish all this?"

"Soon, I hope. There are details to tidy up and connections we need to make. An American friend has been working on part of it with me. Much less suspicious, in some ways, to have an American nosing around. And he has a personal interest in it, anyway. His sister was involved with a member of Mestola Rossa, may have been used by him somehow. And then she died in a way that my friend thinks might not have been an accident. He won't tell me the details, he says, until he's sure of them himself." Gianni pushed his plate away. "That was magnificent, if I say so myself. There's a dessert, too, in the refrigerator. I picked up a *torta* on my way home."

"Oh, Gianni," Clara wailed, "you know I'm on a diet."

"Then Kate and I will eat your share for you." He winked at me.

"Not a chance." She and I gathered up the dirty dishes while Gianni leaned back in his chair, filling his pipe.

As we ate the chocolate cake, our conversation moved on to other paths, the children, a film we'd seen together, a painting Clara wanted to buy.

We did the dishes, Clara and Gianni arguing good-naturedly over whose technique left them cleaner, rewarding ourselves afterward with a brandy, which left me sleepy and thinking of bed. After I said good night to the Palmieris and the door closed on their warmth and company, the problems of the day came back to haunt me. Suddenly I felt isolated, and a little frightened.

I trudged upstairs to my apartment. As I put my key to the lock, my telephone began to ring.

"*Pronto.*"

Perhaps something of what I was feeling came through in my voice, because Nick Taliaferro began with an apology. "Sorry if I've disturbed you. I tried to call earlier, but you were out. I was wondering if you'd have dinner with me tomorrow night."

"Tomorrow? Why, yes—yes, that would be fine." My curiosity, which really did seem to be getting out of hand, was stronger than any reluctance. More than ever I wanted to know why he was interested in the Torreleones, and Alessandro Torreleone in particular.

"Good. If you'll give me directions to your apartment, I'll pick you up at seven-thirty. We'll have a drink somewhere first, then go on to dinner."

"I'd rather meet you, if that's all right. I may work late, so it would be easier. There's a bar I like in Trastevere, the Bar Apollonia, near Santa Maria in Trastevere. We could meet there."

"I know the place. Till tomorrow, then. Good night." And he was gone.

Vaguely, irrationally, annoyed by his haste, I stripped off my clothes, washed, and fell asleep the instant I pulled the blankets over me.

CHAPTER
5

Although it was Saturday, I went early the next morning to the palazzo to work. As I entered the gate, I saw Signora Gambino drawing water from the fountain in the center of the courtyard. She lifted the overflowing bucket with two hands and made her way toward me with a slow hip-swinging grace. That brilliant white smile was, if possible, even broader as she called out her good morning to me.

"We're early birds, you and I, Signora Gambino." I reached for her bucket. "Let me help."

"No, no, Signora Roy. It is not heavy. And you would only get water on that pretty skirt of yours." She set the bucket down by the door to the porter's lodge, panting a little despite her disclaimer, and smoothed one hand across the dark blue apron she was wearing over her dress. "We will all be getting up earlier in these next days. There is so much to be done." I must have looked puzzled, because she added in explanation. "For the Carnival Ball."

"Which Carnival Ball?"

"Why, the one the family is giving here in the palazzo. Did you not know?" She looked at me with mild surprise.

I shook my head. But then I remembered gardeners suddenly busy raking the gravel paths and weeding flower beds in the courtyard, women sweeping and polishing in obscure corners, and the delicious smell of baking mingled with the scent of beeswax. I had thought it merely a grand spring cleaning.

"Ah, it will be wonderful," Signora Gambino went on, clasping her hands in front of her. "For one night, the palazzo in its glory again."

Before I could help her, she had swung the bucket of water up onto the window ledge. There was another bucket still sitting by the fountain, and I went to fetch it for her.

The fountain was ringed round with miniature lemon trees in terra-cotta pots, pale yellow and green against ocher, made vivid by the sun. Sunlight danced off the water, off the laughing faun on his rock in the middle of the fountain, and off the back of a bright green lizard that lay like an emerald bracelet around the faun's wrist, a slash of color on white marble.

As I stood there, a movement above caught my eye. I looked up and saw Alessandro framed in one window of the long gallery that ran the length of the eastern wing, at the southern end near the door to my workroom. I waved at him, and he smiled, one hand raised in greeting, before fading back out of sight.

I took the bucket of water over to Signora Gambino and left her washing the windows of the porter's lodge, perched precariously on a rickety ladder as she sloshed water onto glass with enthusiastic abandon. At the angle where the arched entryway opened under the courtyard's arcade there was a narrow staircase that led up to the main floor and my workroom. I went upstairs to find Alessandro leaning casually against the locked door, arms folded across his chest, waiting for me.

"Good morning." He looked so cheerful that I felt my spirits rising at the sight of him. "Such eagerness to work, especially on a morning as beautiful as this, is inspiring. A pity I've never found it easy to follow good examples." He considered me, his eyes slanted with amusement. "Perhaps you could teach me."

I smiled at him. "I'm not sure I'm fit to be anyone's good example." Or that I'd want to be yours, I added to myself. Much too dangerous. I suspected that Alessandro would take a certain pleasure in undoing good examples, although, to be fair, the pleasure would probably be mutual.

He stepped aside to let me unlock the door, following me into the room. "Well, perhaps for now you could simply show me something of your work." He watched as I laid out my tools, asking me why I used this or that solvent, surprised to see lancets, scalpels, and tweezers beside the brushes. "It looks as though you're about to perform major surgery."

"Of a very satisfying sort. The patient is almost always restored to a better life."

He was sitting on the edge of my worktable, one foot in its boot of glossy chestnut leather swinging slowly back and forth while he picked up the various tools that interested him. "My father tells me that you come from Montreal and that Signor Roy has stayed behind there."

"Yes, my husband did stay behind. Permanently." I said this as repressively as I could without being rude.

But Alessandro was not easily deflected. "You are divorced, then?"

"Yes." I moistened the cotton-wool swab on the end of my tweezers with white spirits and dipped it into the solvent. Then I bent forward to the painting. Carefully, with light, quick strokes, I dabbed at the varnish blurring one corner of Vanvitelli's sky.

While I worked, Alessandro was silent; when I paused and straightened, he asked, "May I stay and watch? Would I disturb you?"

Yes, you do disturb me, I was tempted to tell him. But I only shook my head. "This part is straightforward. When it gets complicated and I need to concentrate, I'll probably ask you to leave."

But it was no good. He *was* distracting, and although I could generally work through any amount of noise, I found it increasingly difficult to focus on the painting in front of me. I was about to tell him so, no matter that it might flatter his ego to hear it, when the click of footsteps on the stairs made us both look around to the doorway.

"Daniella," Alessandro said as a girl appeared there, a lovely girl, golden skinned, with gold tints in the amber hair that streamed down her back, and in the eyes, lustrous and shaped like large, perfect almonds. It was, of course, the maenad.

She barely noticed me, greeting Alessandro with a smile dazzling in its seductiveness, followed by an extravagant embrace, like a declaration of ownership. Alessandro gently detached her arms from around his neck. "Have you met Signora Roy?" he asked her.

I waited while her eyes flicked over me and dismissed me in a glance. She made it very plain that I was of no interest to her whatsoever. And clearly she didn't remember me.

"No? Then let me introduce you," Alessandro continued. "Kate Roy, my cousin Daniella Nerone."

I felt an odd mixture of dismay and relief at these words "my cousin." The dismay was understandable; that Daniella was Count Massimo's niece meant I now knew two very unpleasant secrets, secrets that I had no right to keep from him, or from Alessandro for that matter, but that could only cause the count pain: He not only possessed a forgery but a potentially larcenous niece. It suddenly occurred to me that the victim of the robbery plan might well be Count Massimo himself. But no, I told myself, that was too improbable; after all, Daniella must have many rich friends.

As for the relief—I didn't care to examine that emotion too closely. But the cousinship conveniently explained the obvious warmth between the two of them.

Daniella crossed the room to the Vanvitelli on its easel. She stared at it for a moment before turning to me, and said, so aggressively that I was startled, "Aren't you afraid that you'll strip away the painting itself? What makes you so sure it's meant to look like this?" She pointed to a cleaned patch.

"That's a problem with all cleaning and restoration work," I answered quietly. "When to stop. What the artist intended. You just do everything in your power to put the odds in your favor. I've looked at Vanvitelli's paintings, I work slowly, and I don't take risks."

Daniella looked bored, and I was left with the uncomfortable impression that I'd been lecturing her. Immediately I felt at least twenty years older than she, though the real difference couldn't have been more than seven or eight. I also felt dowdy, in my plain sweater and skirt, set against this epitome of student chic in jeans so tight I wondered how she could sit down, stiletto-heeled boots, and a thin blouse of pale olive silk that was close to the tone of her skin, giving the disconcerting impression of a nudity only barely covered. She was magnificent, I was forced to grant her that much.

She turned away, back to Alessandro. "You must come with me now, Sandro. It's important."

Alessandro ruffled her hair. "I'll come in a little while, Dani." He looked at his watch. "In half an hour, in the *salone*."

Her eyes were mutinous, but he had spoken so firmly that she did not protest and left the room with a muttered "*Ciao*" that only tangentially included me.

Alessandro gave a wry smile. "You must excuse Daniella. She finds it impossible to be polite to any woman more beautiful than she. In fact, she has little time for women in general. So you mustn't mind her lack of courtesy. It's not meant personally."

Despite the consolation of Alessandro's compliment, I did mind it, I minded it very much indeed, and I said to myself that it was going to be easy to find reasons to dislike Alessandro's beautiful cousin. But of course I said none of this aloud. Instead, I smiled with hypocritical tolerance and murmured some rubbish about the single-mindedness of the young. Even to my ears it sounded pompous.

Alessandro looked amused. "I wouldn't have said you were so very old yourself. And as for single-mindedness . . ."

I could feel myself flushing under his shrewd gaze. Awkwardly, I said, "Yes? My husband called me obsessive; unfair, I thought, but now I wonder if he wasn't right."

"And was that why your marriage ended?"

"Partly. Obsession on both sides. But there is never just one reason, is there?"

"I wouldn't know. I've never been married."

"Why not?" I could be direct in my turn; Alessandro invited it.

He laughed. "That's what I like about North Americans. They don't waste time in the elaborate formalities of the Europeans. And it makes life so much simpler."

But something about Alessandro failed to convince me that simplicity was really his goal.

"So then," he went on, stretching a little as he got up and walked over to a window, "why haven't I married?" He leaned back against the windowsill. "The answer is really very easy. I've never met a woman I thought I could spend an entire life with. The women I've loved have spread their egos like cloaks at my feet. And I have no wish to trample on another's soul." The words were melodramatic, but he said them quietly.

"What is it you do want?" The words were out before I realized how they sounded; I didn't stop then to reflect that Alessandro himself had provoked them.

But he didn't seem to mind. He was a man, I discovered, who preferred the personal note; it was part of his appeal. "Someone who doesn't need me," he said. "Someone with a life of her own."

"But if you love someone, can you be independent of them?" I had my own ideas about that question, but I was curious to know what he would say.

"Why not? Freedom, giving someone their freedom, is the highest form of love. Don't you agree?" His voice was light.

"Perhaps. I haven't had that kind of love—or given it, for that matter. But you're right. The other kind, the possessive kind, can destroy."

"Your husband was possessive?"

"Not in any obvious way. He preached freedom, wanted it for Quebec and fought for it. But on his terms. And he could never see the parallel with our marriage."

"Ah, but the state is different. The freedom you grant one individual should not, perhaps, be given to all. You must discriminate."

This chilled me; it seemed so at odds with what he'd said before. It was a perverse, inverted echo of Michel's beliefs. Freedom for everyone, Michel had argued, but within marriage the chosen yoke. Although he had dignified it with another word, bond.

"Freedom for the elect few," I said dryly. "And who elects them?"

"It worked in Athens," Alessandro replied.

"For a while. But do you have a Pericles here in Italy?"

"You're a democrat, Kate? I'd have thought your work would teach you the illusion of that particular creed. What is more undemocratic than artistic genius and the power to buy its products? And haven't the great ages of art come during enlightened tyrannies?"

" 'Oppression is good for creation'? I think you'd have a hard time selling that one to the masses. And I haven't noticed much great art coming out of Russia."

"I did use the term *enlightened*."

There were a thousand good arguments against Alessandro's sophistry, but at that moment I could not produce one of them. I did not want to argue with him, and instinctively I did not want to know more. I wanted him to be Harlequin—light, teasing, and infinitely seductive. I was sick of politics. I'd finished with all that when I left Michel. So I gave him the last word, smiled, and turned back to the Vanvitelli.

Abruptly, he changed tack. "Will you join us for lunch? We dine at one."

Thinking of the uninspired cheese roll in my bag, I said I would be delighted to.

"We use the Sala della Marina, next to my father's study, as our dining room. Until one, then." He went out, closing the door gently behind him.

I worked steadily on through the morning without interruption, carried along on a rush of energy and excitement that I didn't stop to analyze. A few minutes before one o'clock I put down the scalpel I was using to scrape off a stubborn patch of varnish and tidied up. Then I went along the gallery to the Room of the Seascape.

As I approached the open doorway, I could hear father and son talking together and, as punctuation, a woman's husky laugh. The two men rose to their feet as I entered the room, and Alessandro came forward to lead me to my place at the table, opposite Daniella. She was lounging back in her chair, unsmiling, tapping the bowl of a spoon against the edge of her plate; she acknowledged me with the barest of nods. Her gaze lingered pointedly on my sweater, and I looked down to see flakes of dried varnish scattered like fish scales on the black wool. With an immense effort of will I restrained myself from brushing them away, greeting Daniella with my friendliest, and most hypocritical, smile. "You have met each other then?" Count Massimo asked as he beckoned Mario, who was standing by the sideboard.

"Several times." I couldn't resist the impulse to disturb Daniella's equanimity. If she questioned the "several," I was quite prepared to mention our encounter at the demonstration, although not what followed. But it seemed that Daniella had lost what little interest she had in me. She ignored my reply, helping herself to the soup that Mario was serving as she began to talk to her uncle and cousin.

The Sala della Marina was almost as lovely, in its less flamboyant way, as the Salone d'Oro, a cooler baroque vision— this time of an undersea world. The walls were paneled in a pale green watered silk between flat pilasters of veined green marble. Family portraits hung on the silk, although in places, where the silk was ovaled or rectangled in a darker shade, it was plain that some had gone, sold perhaps.

The ceiling was the palest aquamarine, with enormous gilt

scallop shells in each of the four corners; above them was a bestiary of mythical sea creatures at play in a storm-tossed ocean, presided over by a benign Neptune blessing them, and those of us below, with his upraised trident. There were worn but still-beautiful carpets in tones of blue and yellow on the floor to complete the effect of immersion in some luxurious marine paradise.

Count Massimo leaned forward to pour wine into my glass. The hand that held the bottle trembled a little; he looked paler today, his skin like thin parchment, and I wondered if he was ill. "We are giving a *ballo in maschera* on Tuesday night, for Carnevale," he said. "It would please us if you would come to it, Signora Roy."

Surprised, I told him truthfully that I could imagine nothing I'd like more.

At that, Alessandro broke off his conversation with Daniella to turn to me with a smile. "Wonderful. I would have asked you myself when we met earlier, but my father wanted the pleasure of inviting you himself."

From her lack of response, it was plain that Daniella wasn't quite so enthusiastic about my invitation, but the warmth of the two men made up for her silence. Count Massimo reached out to take her hand. "This ball is really for Daniella. It is her birthday present. Not very grand, I'm afraid—nothing like the balls at Carnevale I remember from my youth—but we hope it will be an evening she will long remember with pleasure."

"Dear Uncle." Daniella kissed the frail hand that held hers. For the first time, she let the young girl she still was show through the facade of bored sophisticate, and I wondered how she had got mixed up with someone like Marco.

"It will be a costume ball," Alessandro told me. "The theme is the commedia dell'arte—inspired by the tapestries in the Salone d'Oro. Do you remember them?"

"Harlequin and Columbine and the 'lean and slippered Pantaloon,'" I said in English. "Yes, I remember them. So we should come as players?"

"Exactly. I hope we've given you enough time to choose a costume."

"If you have any difficulties," his father said, "you must tell us. There are chests full of costumes that my mother and grandmother used to wear. They are beautiful dresses and deserve to be worn again by a beautiful woman. If you wish, I will ask Mario to have some of the chests brought down from the storerooms."

I was touched by his generosity and tempted by the offer, for I knew that it wasn't going to be a simple matter to come up with a costume, given the likelihood that Rome's costume suppliers had been booked up for months. But there was something in the set of Daniella's mouth that suggested I had better not accept her uncle's offer, and much as I might have liked to annoy her, I didn't want to provoke controversy. It was, after all, her party. I thanked Count Massimo and promised to ask if I had any trouble finding a costume. Privately I was hoping that Clara would come to my rescue.

As we ate our lunch, we talked about the preparations for the ball. "We are going a little mad, as you see," Count Massimo said. "But occasionally madness is good for the soul. Or so my son persuades me."

Alessandro took an apple from a silver bowl heaped high with fruit in the center of the table and peeled it with one smooth curve of his knife. "In the past, all Rome would go mad at Carnevale. Now there's more madness at a soccer game." The spiral of apple peel dropped onto his plate. "These days we take our pleasures vicariously."

"Through our children, perhaps," I said, thinking of those I'd seen promenading under the proud gaze of their parents in the park on the Gianicolo. "I'd love to paint some of the children I've seen this week. A few of the costumes are so elaborate they must take weeks, not to mention a fortune, to make."

"The poorest often spend the most," Alessandro said dryly. "*La bella figura* again."

Count Massimo objected, "But that has always been a part of Carnevale, Alessandro. In a way, that is precisely the point."

"Yes, of course you're right, Father. It's the chance to be somebody else, to mask reality. And it is amusing to see which masks our friends choose, to see their fantasies and illusions." He smiled at Daniella. "Perhaps you'll come as La Pasionaria, Dani?"

There was no mistaking that pointed reference to Spain's revolutionary heroine; Alessandro knew something of his cousin's inclinations. But how much?

She gave him a sharp look. "That would be as suitable as your coming as the pope."

He laughed.

Curious, I picked up the subject. "I saw a number of would-be Pasionarias myself yesterday." Briefly, and vaguely, I described my part in the demonstration. Daniella's head came up, and she stared at me; there was genuine interest in her eyes.

"You were fortunate to escape injury," Count Massimo said when I'd finished. "A mob can be a violent creature—headless, but so many arms, all striking out blindly."

"And was your morning as exciting as Kate's, Dani?" Alessandro asked.

But she refused to be drawn. "Hardly. I spent it in the university library." The image of Daniella reading a book wasn't easy to conjure up.

"Such a good student," Alessandro said blandly. "A pity there aren't more like you. Rome might be more peaceful if there were."

"And if all civil servants had your concern for the public good, it would also be better governed," she retorted.

"Now, now. What will Signora Roy think?" Count Massimo chided gently.

"That Dani and I are a quarrelsome pair, Father. But isn't that the image we export in our films for consumption abroad—decaying aristocrats wandering about their crumbling palaces arguing with one another? Or worse."

Count Massimo turned to me, his upturned hands spread wide in a gesture of resignation. "Alessandro pretends that he takes our past lightly. But in reality his faith is much the strongest of us all."

Alessandro got up from his chair. For a moment he stood with his back to us; then he turned around to his father, his face serious, almost fierce. "There *is* something of value in the past. But I think we—I mean the aristocracy—have cut ourselves off from it. It surrounds us in paint and plaster"—he pointed to the portraits that were hanging on the walls around the room— "but there is nothing deeper. We have lost our place in the flow of life that carries the past into the present. Most of us have chosen to be obsolete or *déraciné*." In a voice so low I could barely hear it, he added, "But we aren't alone. All of Italy seems to be rushing ahead to escape as much of the past as it can."

"That's just as well!" Daniella shoved her chair back noisily and jumped to her feet. "So much talk of loss and escape. *Merda!* I'm sorry, Uncle, but Sandro makes me so angry sometimes. Life is change, and if we don't adapt, we deserve to go to the wall."

I was willing to bet that was a direct quote from her friend Marco.

"The voice of the future, God help us." Alessandro came over and put his arms around Daniella's waist, smiling down at her. "You're right, Dani. You've known me all your life, and so you should also know better than to take me so seriously." I watched Daniella's anger melt away under his caress.

Count Massimo spoke, and his voice was both wistful and resigned, and very weary. "Daniella is partly right, Alessandro. As you are." He sipped a little of his wine, and when he spoke again, the words came slowly. "When I was a child, I would visit my grandparents each spring in Sicily. Their palazzo was sold before Alessandro could know it, but when I lived there as a child I saw the harmony and respect between the people and the nobility that he regrets as lost.

"In my grandfather's house the gate stood always open. Anyone who wished to enter and speak to my grandfather could do so. But the *portiere* would ring a bell as they came through the gate. No one entered without being seen. Sometimes we were at dinner when the bell sounded, but I never saw my grandfather show by the smallest sign that he resented the intrusion. He knew his responsibilities. He gave his time and his wisdom to his people, and they, in turn, gave him respect and deference. But"—and here Count Massimo's voice became an echo of his son's, the bitterness more pronounced in one who so rarely showed it—"of course in Sicily the people needed more than wisdom. Beyond my grandfather's gate was a misery his wisdom never seemed to cure." He touched his upper lip with his napkin and then rose to his feet, holding on to the armrests of the chair. "Forgive me, I find I am very tired. I think I will go and lie down now." Alessandro got up with him, but Count Massimo shook his head. "Stay with the ladies, Sandro. Mario will help me to my room." He took his servant's arm, and they made their way slowly to the door, two old men together.

As we sat down again, I told Alessandro how sorry I was that Count Massimo was unwell.

"My father had a bad night," he replied, "but he refuses to see his doctor. He says there's little the doctor can do for him except to tell him to take the pills he's already taking. But I do know that he wouldn't want you to worry over him. You must eat your dessert and have some more wine."

Before I could stop him, he filled my glass again. The wine was delicious, deceptively light and as easy to drink as water, but I had already drunk more than was good for me if I wanted to work that afternoon. I decided then that I didn't and picked up my glass.

Daniella clattered her fork against her plate. She seemed on edge; there was tension visible in her restless movements, and I wondered if it stemmed from a pressure I had no difficulty imagining. Abruptly she rose, saying she had to get ready to meet a friend. Something in her voice, a hesitation, suggested that she would prefer not to leave me alone with her cousin.

But then we were alone. A trace of tension lingered in Daniella's wake, like the musky perfume she wore, and I hunted, without success, for something inconsequential to say. Alessandro, on the other hand, seemed content to sit drinking his wine in silence.

Mario returned with coffee on a tray for us. As he poured it out, he told Alessandro that Count Massimo had suggested I might like to see more of the palazzo, the secret passageway, for example.

"We won't disturb him?" Alessandro asked.

Mario shook his head. "No, signore, he says not. He has closed the door to his bedroom, and he has taken his medicine. I think he is already asleep."

"Very well. Then I will show the signora myself." He looked across at me. "Well, Kate, does that appeal to you?"

"A guided tour? Very much. You'll have to give me five minutes to try to find the passage myself."

"Take all the time you like. But I doubt that you'll have any luck. When he built the palazzo, Baldassare Torreleone had the passageway made to ensure an escape route—and he was a very clever man."

"Escape route?"

"He was never on good terms with the Inquisition. He knew there might well come a day when he would need to leave his home quickly and quietly."

"Did he ever have to use it?"

"No. In the end he found it wiser to accommodate than to flee. We Torreleones have always been pragmatists. Apart from my father."

"And you?"

"I'm a traditionalist. But I don't believe in lost causes. I suppose that makes me a pragmatist. . . ." He drank off the last of his coffee and set the cup down. "I must get the master keys from Mario. I won't be long."

While I waited, I daydreamed a little, seduced by the wine and the beauty of the room into a romantic, foolish vision of what it would be like to live in the Palazzo Torreleone, with all that loveliness around me, a part of a life so very different from any I had known. Then I remembered how fleeting that life might be for the Torreleones themselves and was suddenly sad. Alessandro belongs here, I thought as I gazed at the portraits on the wall, looking for a likeness in the faces that stared back at me. But none of them had his eyes.

I heard footsteps coming back along the gallery and got up—too quickly. The wine was stronger than I'd realized. Suddenly dizzy, I had to grip the table edge for support and stand like that while my head cleared. I gulped down the remains of my espresso, then poured myself another cup and drank that, too. It helped—not much, but enough to keep me steady on my feet.

Alessandro came into the room. "If you're ready, Kate, we'll go to my father's apartments first. The secret passage is in his study. You've been there, haven't you, so perhaps you already know where to find the passage?"

"I haven't a clue. There were so many books I doubt if I noticed anything else." Except the Reni. My heart sank. The last place I wanted to be with Alessandro was in the same room as that painting. But it was too late; I could only hope that the *Madonna and Child* would stay safely hidden by the screen.

Alessandro tapped quietly at the study door before opening it. "My father's bedroom is through there," he said as we went into the room, pointing to a closed door near the desk on the opposite side of the room. "It would be better if we spoke as quietly as possible. Now, you may have your five minutes."

It was no use. For one thing, there was such a muddle of books and such a number of bookshelves that any search would take hours; for another, I could not bring myself to give a thorough look for fear of being too obvious in my avoidance of the corner with the Reni. "It's hopeless," I conceded. "You'll have to show me."

He laughed. "So soon? I thought simple feminine curiosity would keep you at it longer. All right, then. It's over here. . . ."

To my horror, he turned and walked straight to the Reni.

Ignoring the painting, he set the lacquer screen aside and ran his hand over the wood molding that edged a section of the paneling nearby. "Here," he said, "come and look at this."

Doing my best to seem indifferent to the Reni, I went over to his side. He took my left hand in his and raised it to the molding, which was slightly above my eye level. "Press there," he told me. I did as he said and felt a section of the molding sink a fraction below the level of the rest. "Harder." The strip of wood gave under the pressure until it met some sort of resistance and would go no farther. There was a loud click that seemed to come from somewhere behind the paneling.

"Now push there with your other hand," Alessandro instructed, pointing to a place on the paneling below. As I pushed, a part of the paneling began to turn on its axis until there was an opening something over five feet high and roughly three feet wide on either side of the panel. A current of cold air rushed out at us. Beyond was darkness.

"Quite a trick."

"Isn't it? That spring has worked for almost four hundred years. The passage leads down to the cellars. There were stables in one part of the cellars—horses were kept there even within my memory. My grandfather rode until he was a very old man. One of my earliest memories is of his taking me down to the stables through this passage so that I could feed sugar to the horses. That's all gone now, of course." As he spoke, he bent his head and stepped into the opening, disappearing into the darkness.

"Why don't you come, too, Kate," I heard him say.

In spite of Alessandro's invitation, I had a good mind to stay where I was—dark and drafty passages reminded me too forcibly of spiders and bats and Edgar Allan Poe—but I hated to be thought a coward, and besides, I told myself encouragingly, Alessandro was there to step on the spiders and fight off the bats.

Resolutely, I followed him into the secret passage, blinking until my eyes adjusted to the darkness. Alessandro was a formless shape nearby, moving about as he groped for the light switch. In the moment of silence, I heard a rustle, like the wind in dry leaves, and then the quick patter of claws across the floor. Rats. Worse than spiders or bats. Right, I thought, this is where I show my true colors. Turning, I stretched my hand out blindly for the wall. But before I could do more than take one retreating step, Alessandro said, "At last," and the light came on.

At first I thought we were in a cavern carved out of the rock itself, but that absurd idea gave way to the reality of a dimly lit stairwell, low ceilinged, shadowy, built of ancient-looking stones that might have come straight from the Colosseum; I wondered which Roman ruin Baldassare Torreleone had plundered for his palace. Ahead, shallow stone steps curved down into the gloom.

"Once we would have had to make our way with a candle or lantern. Electric light is less romantic, I'm afraid, but far more practical."

Alessandro's voice made me jump. I turned and found him so close beside me that we brushed against each other. The electricity was as sudden as the light. At once I found myself in his arms, his face angled above mine, dark and beautiful in the shadows, but I've no idea which of us took the first step toward the other. I saw the faintest of smiles on his mouth before it came down on mine in a kiss as light as a breath, infinitely gentle as it moved across my face and back to my mouth again, to rest there, growing hard and sweet, opening as I felt my own opening under it.

I don't know how long we stood like that while the chilly dampness gathered around us, filtering through my clothes until it lay like a cold finger against my skin and I broke away, shivering.

Alessandro touched my cheek. "You're cold. We'd better go back."

Like a sleepwalker, I turned and went ahead of him through the opening in the wall, grateful for the warmth of the study. I rubbed my arms to stop my shivering while Alessandro closed the panel. Out of the corner of my eye I saw the *Madonna and Child;* involuntarily, I gave them a skeptical glance, then turned away and found Alessandro looking at me. Wordlessly, he put the screen back into place, and we left the study.

Out in the corridor he said, "I didn't mean to hurry you away. Perhaps you would have liked a longer look at the Reni?"

"No—that is, I had a good look at it yesterday, with your father."

"My father did tell me that you seemed very interested in it. But then it is such a very interesting painting, don't you think?"

"Oh, yes, it certainly is," I said, wishing desperately that I could find a way to turn the conversation into safer channels.

"What exactly do you think of it, Kate? I'd be glad to have an expert's opinion."

Somewhere in my mind the penny dropped. He knew my doubts. Reluctantly, I accepted the inevitable and turned to face him. "I think you know." I felt quite calm now, regretting only that I would have to disobey Faltecchi, though I was sure he would understand. And the charade could not go on.

"Yes, I think I do," Alessandro said. His voice was still relaxed, unsurprised, but his face was serious. "And you're right."

"I am?" Confirmation came like a shock; anticipation did not weaken its impact. "You're sure?"

"Yes, it is a copy." He said it flatly, with certainty.

"It is?" I echoed like a simpleton. Relief was immediate and overwhelming, followed almost at once by an equally overwhelming curiosity. There were a dozen questions waiting to be asked, but I spoke the one that mattered most. "Does your father know?"

Alessandro looked grave. "No, he has no idea. And I mean it to stay that way. He must not be told." Both eyes and voice held a cold determination so unlike their usual warmth that I might have been frightened if I hadn't understood and sympathized with the feeling that prompted it.

"Of course not," I said quickly, to reassure him, resting my hand on his arm. "I do see that, Alessandro. He loves the painting, and—well, naturally there are other reasons, too . . ." I trailed off weakly, uncertain how to say that I recognized what the painting meant financially to the Torreleones.

He smiled at me then, and the warmth came back into his eyes. "You do understand, Kate. Thank God. I was afraid . . . But that doesn't matter now." Slowly, we began to walk down the corridor together. "I can't tell you much about it, but as you could probably guess, it was a question of money. We needed it badly, and selling the Reni was the quickest way to get it. It was a difficult decision, of course. As you say, my father loves the painting. And so I had the copy made, a deception to spare him pain. I don't mean to excuse what I did, but I warned you that I was a pragmatist, and it seemed the best way. We needed the money to pay our bills. It was a very simple issue. Unfortunately, my father has little understanding of money."

I said nothing; I hardly knew what I could say that would sound neither puritanical nor too much like Dr. Pangloss. Besides, I hadn't yet sorted out my emotions well enough to know what I felt. So far they seemed to be a confused mixture of sympathy with his dilemma, a tentative understanding of his reasons, and a vague, murky unease when I thought of all that forgery implied. That the Reni was a forgery, not a copy, as Alessandro called it, was the one thing I was clear on; the genuine Reni had belonged to Count Massimo. Only he had the right to commission a copy to replace it.

If Alessandro was worried by my silence, he didn't show it. With a certain wryness he said, "It's not the most successful of copies, is it? I take it you knew almost at once?"

"Almost. But that's because I was trained to. It's good enough to fool a lot of people." What a queer conversation, I thought unhappily; it's almost as though I'm reassuring him on the quality of his forgery. Aloud, I asked him, "But weren't you worried that someone would come along, as I did, and spot it for what it was?"

"Of course. I've been trying to persuade my father to lock it away, for safekeeping. Luckily, very few people are allowed into my father's study." He gave me a sideways look. "You seem to have made an impression on him."

I said simply, "I like your father very much."

"Then you won't mention this to him? Or to anyone else?"

We had stopped walking and were standing in front of a closed door in the northern wing of the palazzo, a wing with which I was unfamiliar. I looked up at Alessandro. "I'm afraid I've already told Giorgio Faltecchi that I thought it might be a forgery. I needed his advice. He agreed to talk to you and your father, though he wanted a little time to consider how to go about it."

Alessandro's face remained impassive as I spoke. There was a silence when I finished; I could hear a door slamming shut a long way off and, somewhere in the courtyard below, the sound of voices and laughter. Finally, he said, "I see. Well, that can't be helped. I'll have to explain to Faltecchi."

"He is a very discreet man," I said. I meant to be comforting, but after I'd spoken I realized how conspiratorial the words sounded—the effect of the empty, silent corridor streaked with dusty rays of sunlight, our low voices, or perhaps simply my own imagination.

Alessandro was turning the bunch of keys he held over in his hand, sorting through them one by one, as though they could somehow unlock the problem he faced, when Mario came silently up behind us.

"Signore?"

Startled, I overreacted with a gasp of surprise, but Alessandro calmly turned and said, "Yes, Mario?"

"A word with you, signore."

"Excuse me, Kate. Would you like to see this room while you wait for me?" He began to fit the key to the lock.

I stopped him. "That's all right. I'll wait over by that open window." It would give me time to think. I wandered over to the window and looked out at the courtyard; gardeners below were clipping the low boxwood hedges. I could see their secateurs clicking along the top of the green like the beaks of busy birds.

But though I tried to fix my mind on all that Alessandro had told me, it refused to stick. The kiss completed what the wine had begun; I found it impossible to think clearly.

When Alessandro came over to say that there was a problem with a new servant that might take some time to clear up, I told him the rest of the tour could wait for another day, grateful for the chance to escape. We parted without mentioning the Reni again, but Alessandro touched my hand once as we said good-bye.

I went back to my workroom. Trying to work, however, was more than useless; it was dangerous. I needed all my wits about me when I worked, and at the moment they were hopelessly scattered. But I was filled with a restless energy crying out for exorcism, or exercise, so I decided to walk over to Faltecchi and Stillitano for a solvent I needed.

As I came out of the palazzo into the square, I saw Daniella disappearing up a side street, a long red scarf wound around her neck, mingling with the tawny hair. Suddenly, a brilliant idea— or so it seemed at the time—seized me. I hurried after her.

CHAPTER

6

I'd told Nick Taliaferro that a good conservator had to be, among other things, something of a detective. You had to like a mystery and long to solve it. A painting sat before you on an easel, unsigned, its provenance unknown, a mystery. The clues were there—the style, the subject, the paint and canvas, a hundred smaller but still significant details—and you pieced these together until you saw a glimmer of the truth, and finally, if you were lucky, the bright flash of inspiration.

But Daniella was not a painting confined within a frame, with a set of clues that, once mastered, yielded a certain answer. She was the unknown, another human being, and Italian. She belonged to a country where mysteries flourished like a parasite vine on a crumbling wall, each mystery more convoluted than the last, mingling, tearing at the fabric of life. No mystery is

81

ever truly solved; no story ever really ends. Each solution, each ending, only reveals a further mystery or the beginning of a new story. Or so the Italians believe.

I was at a disadvantage. I came from a country where there are few conspiracies, few secrets of any magnitude, where privacy is cherished—but not because anyone has much to hide—and where order is based on the assumption that most people lead blameless lives. Canadians tend to believe that people are, for the most part, what they appear to be. The Italians know better.

Some of this went through my mind as I crossed the piazza in pursuit of Daniella. Blame the melodramatic thoughts on the wine and on the interlude with Alessandro, both of which had left me quite bereft of plain common sense. I was filled with a mysterious and totally unjustified feeling of power, which in turn gave me a dangerous self-confidence.

And so, as I followed Daniella, the beginnings of a plan were forming in my mind.

She was walking quickly, her head bent, hands thrust into the pockets of her leather jacket, the long silk scarf around her neck fluttering back across her shoulder like a scarlet pennant. I caught up to her, calling out her name until she turned around, irritation on her face.

As I greeted her, I made some casual remarks about our lunch together and then, before she could shake me off, added, "Did you know we've met before?"

She made an impatient gesture with her head, which I interpreted as a mixture of denial and indifference. But I continued, oblivious to her rudeness, "It's true, we have. At that demonstration near the Largo Argentina yesterday. I was the one who warned you about the police. Remember?"

I watched her as she took in the significance of what I'd said. We had stopped walking now and were facing each other. Those almond eyes narrowed, and I saw recognition there. But I didn't give her a chance to say anything; I wanted to start the process of seduction at once, before she could remember too much about the incident.

"You were great," I told her. "Really impressive." She was watching for signs of irony; it had been pretty clear that she was abandoning the field, leaving others to fight, but I pretended to think otherwise. "I saw you go off to warn people just before I found a place to hide. I didn't have any identity papers with me, so I found an alleyway and disappeared down that." I thought of her claim to Alessandro that she'd been in the library studying, and I added, "I didn't say anything at lunch just now because you obviously didn't want your uncle and Alessandro to know about it. They don't approve, eh?"

She ignored that. "What were you doing there anyway?" She began to walk again, with sharp, scissorlike strides of her long legs. I could barely keep up.

"I used to work for the separatists in Quebec. I missed the excitement, so I thought I'd see how things were done here." I said this with a naive eagerness I hoped would convince her. I was already breathless from hurrying beside her.

Even if her suspicions were far from conquered, her curiosity must have been aroused, because she slowed down and said, her head half turned toward me, "What sort of work did you do for the separatists?"

"Oh, a bit of this and that. Organizing meetings, demonstrations . . . You know the kind of thing."

"So why did you leave?" Her voice was neutral, almost bored, her face hidden by the amber hair hanging down beside her cheeks. But as long as she was asking questions, I knew I had her interest.

"My husband and I divorced. He got in with the establishment, and I could see that nothing much was going to happen in Quebec. The power structure is too solid there. And you know how Canadians are . . . I got fed up. Besides, ever since I read Gramsci I wanted to come back to Italy."

I was afraid that this might be laying it on a bit thickly, or that Daniella might not know who in the world I was talking about, but I had misjudged her. She let a little warmth creep into her voice. "You're a Marxist?"

And I was off, on a rush of adrenaline and wine. I could

quote chapter and verse if necessary. It was all there, stored away in my mind, the result of interminable evenings with Michel and his friends, all of them up on the latest Marxist thinking and all eager to educate Michel's unregenerate bourgeois wife. I trotted out Marcuse, Mao, and threw in Tonio Negri for good measure. I touched all the stops. I was Jane Fonda and Vanessa Redgrave rolled up in one, and I was heartily ashamed of myself. Until this moment I hadn't realized my own acting ability, as I warmed to my theme, growing passionate, even profound, while I paraded with conviction and fervor beliefs that weren't my own.

I wasn't sure that I liked the ease with which I produced these lies—no one likes to discover that they have the makings of a successful hypocrite—but it did the trick. I could see some of the mistrust leave Daniella's face. She believes me, I told myself, she thinks I'm ripe for the picking.

However, she wasn't naive; she knew enough to go slowly. All she said to this travesty of the committed Marxist disciple was that she agreed with me.

I went a little farther along the way. "I know there must be opportunities for me to help—so much seems to be happening here. Those bombings the other night, for instance, do you know anything about them?"

But she shied away from this. "No!" Then, more calmly, she added, "Not that I would tell you if I did. But I do know that it was a complete waste of time. If you're going to all the trouble of killing people, you should at least make sure you kill people whose deaths make a difference."

Another pragmatic Torreleone. "You study Machiavelli, too?" I asked her.

She jerked her head around to look at me, but I'd kept sarcasm out of my voice and my features bland. "Why bother with that old stuff?" she said. "There are others who matter more now."

"True. I'd rather read Debray any day." I'll be writing jingles for the Red Brigades next, I thought disgustedly.

With a show of indifference that I suspected was a mask for an important step, she asked me if I had considered continuing the struggle for the cause in Rome.

I wondered which cause she meant but said only, "Perhaps. If I met the right people."

"Maybe that can be arranged." She gave me a direct, challenging look.

I pushed things along a little. "By you?"

"If you like. I know some people you might find interesting."

At that moment I glanced ahead to see a man I recognized immediately, a tall, hawk-faced young man in blue jeans and a black pullover lounging against a motorcycle with a badly dented rear fender. He was smoking a cigarette, looking every bit as sullen as his voice had sounded when I'd overheard him threatening Daniella. My heart sank. I'd thought that I might learn something useful by playing this silly charade with Daniella, something that would help me decide how to tell her uncle. Fencing with Daniella was one thing, however; dueling with Marco, quite another.

"*Ciao*, Marco," Daniella called out to him.

He did not reply. With a flick of two fingers he threw his cigarette into the gutter, then turned his fierce stare on me, running his eyes over me with an insolent appraisal that made me long to tip his motorcycle over and send him into the gutter after the cigarette.

"Who's she?" he asked Daniella.

"Her name's Kate Roy. She's a Canadian, but she speaks Italian," she added, possibly as warning. "Right now she's cleaning some paintings for my uncle." To me, Daniella said curtly, "This is Marco." No last name.

There was a pause while Marco digested the information and watched me with greater interest.

"She was in the demonstration yesterday." Daniella went on, like a faithful lieutenant, to give my bona fides while I stood there making every attempt to keep my face friendly and eager under Marco's unpleasant scrutiny. When she finished, Marco grunted and asked us, with more politeness than he'd shown before, if we'd like some coffee. The three of us went into a nearby bar.

I suppose if I'd had any sense or been more my usual self, I would have made some excuse, however feeble, and beaten a hasty retreat. But my curiosity was insatiable. So I ordered a *caffè doppio,* double-strength black coffee, and stood with them in a quiet corner of the bar, listening.

Daniella was, to my surprise, very skillful. She had something of her cousin in her when she cared to use it, and she used it now to charm Marco out of his rudeness and to play up to my supposed enthusiasm for their cause. I wondered if she got points for recruiting new members to their group; it seemed the only reason why, given her apparent dislike of me, she was going to so much effort on my behalf. She succeeded so well with Marco, stroking his arm while she soothed his ego, that he began to boast of what he proposed to do, come the revolution. In the meantime, he added with a knowing wink, he would lay the groundwork. Then he abandoned the braggadocio and got down to business, and I began to understand his appeal for Daniella.

He was very good-looking in a dark, brooding fashion, quite the romantic, humorless revolutionary whose fanatical absolutes would have great attraction for any woman who liked to be dominated, whose sensuality thrived best when her will was submerged by some man's. But there was more than a hint of posturing in Marco's attitude, and I had the impression of a hypocrisy that might even match my own—and under it a wide streak of ruthlessness.

But he wasn't stupid, or at least he had a sort of cunning that passed for intelligence; it took all my skill to fit the right responses to his questions, an inquisition, really, disguised superficially with friendly overtures and interruptions by Daniella.

While Marco grilled me, I gave a silent prayer of thanks for the reading I'd done when I was trying to be a good wife to Michel. But as Marco's interest in me grew—like all such men he enjoyed the role of high priest initiating the acolyte into arcane mysteries—I could feel the tide of wine and self-confidence receding, replaced by a bleak stretch of fear.

What in God's name was I doing? I asked myself. I had no business to be mixed up in this affair of Daniella's. I wanted desperately to leave, but it was difficult to find an opening in Marco's performance that would let me do so casually and easily.

He seemed especially interested in the fact that I was working for the Torreleones. He knew nothing about restoration, but he clearly liked it that I worked with valuable paintings, the Torreleone paintings in particular. "And do you take these paintings home with you?" he asked me at one point.

"No, no, of course she doesn't," Daniella answered for me. "Don't be ridiculous. They're much too valuable to leave the palazzo; it would be too great a risk." She crushed out a half-smoked cigarette in her saucer and lit another, pulling at the smoke with short, nervous movements of her mouth. I sensed a growing nervousness on Daniella's part with the line that Marco was taking, and I thought I knew why. Even if the Torreleone collection wasn't originally the object of Marco's criminal attentions, it might well become so.

Daniella was eager to change the subject, finally accomplishing it so abruptly, with a glance at her watch and a reminder to Marco that their friends were waiting for them, that she gave me the excuse I'd been waiting for to make my escape.

I told them halfheartedly how much it meant to me to talk to people who cared about the important issues of life and, after giving them both my widest and most naive smile, started for the door. I was almost there when I heard Marco's voice behind me.

"We'll be in touch."

I turned, nodded silently—by that time I couldn't have managed a word—and left the bar. I felt almost sick with relief as I went out.

There was a palpable air of violence about Marco that terrified me; I wished that I'd kept myself out of things that didn't really concern me. But then I thought of Count Massimo and admitted to myself that I was involved because I cared for him. And Alessandro? That was more complicated. But, I told myself firmly, when you go back to the palazzo on Monday, the first thing you'll do is go to Alessandro and tell him that his cousin is mixed up with a probable terrorist and potential criminal. Immediately, the resolution made, I felt better.

The walk to Faltecchi and Stillitano did me good. By the time I reached the workrooms, my head was clear and I had resolved to keep my detective instincts where they belonged—on my work. I would let Alessandro deal with Daniella and the forged Reni.

The main door of the office was locked, but I had a key. I let myself into the apparently deserted workrooms and went down the hallway to the storeroom. The solvent I needed was kept in an alcove off the storeroom, carved out of space taken from Faltecchi's office, which lay next to it. I went into the tiny space and was pouring solvent from its large tin can into a glass container when I realized that there were people in Faltecchi's office. Raised voices were coming through the thin wall. I recognized Stillitano's voice, loud and angry, and under its flow Faltecchi's gentler tones.

"She should never have been given that commission," Stillitano was saying. "She's much too inexperienced. Moreover, in the past I have been responsible for the Torreleone paintings. The commission rightly belonged to me."

There was a long, incomprehensible murmur from Faltecchi. Stillitano broke into it with horrible clarity, each word icily, devastatingly, distinct.

"My God, Giorgio! She has certainly pulled the wool over your eyes. So you think she has the makings of a first-rate conservator, do you? Are you certain that those are the only skills of hers that you admire?" His voice grew insinuating. "I can appreciate that at a certain age a man might find her act of wide-eyed admiration irresistible. Although personally I think she's somewhat too obvious. That touch-me-not look, together with a body that—"

"*Basta*, Franco!" Faltecchi forced him into silence.

Stillitano's words crawled over my skin. I knew whom he was talking about. I felt sickened by them and frightened by the intensity of his dislike of me. All I wanted to do was get out of there before I heard any more. In my haste, clumsy with outrage and humiliation, I spilled some of the solvent onto the countertop. It ate into the Formica as I grabbed a cloth to mop it up. While I scrubbed at it, I heard Faltecchi say something that stopped my hand.

His voice was low, but hard and clear, obviously responding to another accusation Stillitano was making about me. "I disagree. I trust Kate. I wish that I could say as much for everyone I work with. If I could, I would have spared us the search of the files, which you seem to find so disagreeable." His voice dropped away again, and I strained to hear, a deliberate eavesdropper now. ". . . the portrait. You still have not explained that to me satisfactorily. And it is not the only one. A number of people seem to believe that we will do questionable work for them."

Stillitano's voice grew soft in its turn, a low mutter of Italian that sounded thick, like an oversweet syrup. Whatever he said must not have persuaded Faltecchi. "It began with the Brandini painting, Franco. At the time I thought it merely bad luck. It could happen to any conservator, and nothing, after all, came of it. But since then I have wondered about one or two others. And now the Torreleone Reni. No, it is too much."

Stillitano turned defensive. "Alessandro Torreleone needed a copy of the painting. I merely supplied one. Unethical, perhaps, but hardly forgery."

"Alessandro does not own the Reni," Faltecchi said firmly. "Not yet, anyway. Count Massimo is the owner, and he believes that the painting is geniune. That makes it forgery, Franco. And what became of the original, can you tell me that?"

"I do not know," Stillitano said shortly. "You must ask Alessandro."

"I intend to. But in the meantime I have other questions that only you can answer. Although I must tell you frankly that what I have learned today from these files has made me doubt that we can go on as partners."

I was shocked by what I was hearing, but suddenly, with a jolt of fear, I remembered the open storeroom door. If Stillitano should come out of the office and find me here . . . It didn't bear thinking about. Quietly I crept out of the alcove and went across the storeroom to close the door. Just as quietly I went back again. I was determined to understand what was happening between the two men, and why.

But their conversation was over. I'd thought of the storeroom door just in time. I heard Faltecchi's door open and the sound of a double set of footsteps in the corridor, then the click and slam of the main door. They had gone.

I was shaken and confused by all that I'd heard. Why did Stillitano dislike me so much, hate me, really? We didn't get along, it was true, and inadvertently I'd trespassed on territory he considered his own, but that could hardly account for the way he'd talked about me. I felt my stomach tighten at the memory of it and wondered how I would be able to face the man when next I saw him without betraying something of what I felt. But perhaps I would not have to face him much longer if Faltecchi really intended to end their partnership.

I was fishing around in my purse for the key to the main door of the workroom when I heard swift footsteps on the stairs outside and, before I could do more than step back a few paces, the rattle of a key in the lock.

When the door opened, Stillitano stood before me. He looked shocked. I'd had a few seconds to arrange my face into what I hoped was nothing more than surprise.

"Oh, it's you, Signor Stillitano. I thought I heard voices. Were you here? Have you forgotten something?" I prayed I sounded convincingly innocent and must have succeeded, because some of the black anger died out of his eyes. But not all.

He ignored my questions. "What are you doing here?"

"I needed some things for my work in the palazzo and came in to get them. If you'll excuse me," I said quickly, to forestall any other questions, "I should be getting back there now." I made a forward movement, but Stillitano stood his ground.

He said quietly, "I should like to talk to you, Signora Roy. In my office, if you please. It will not take long."

"Of course." I followed him obediently back down the hall. Unsuccessfully, I tried to swallow the fear that was rising like bile in my throat. I consoled myself with the thought that, although he might suspect, he couldn't be sure that I'd overheard him with Faltecchi; he was hardly about to attack me, whatever his suspicions. So why was I so frightened? Anger would better see me through whatever he had in mind, anger that would give me courage, like a concealed weapon.

Stillitano's office was very much like its occupier, correctly and discreetly elegant in tones of gray and beige, neat, and decidedly chilly in overall effect. The business files were stored here in tall wooden cabinets; several were standing open, with a drawer pulled out and gaping. Stillitano closed these and then, with extreme courtesy, moved a chair forward for me, offering me some of the brandy that he kept with several glasses on a tray on the wide top of his desk. When I refused, he poured a glass for himself and sat down behind the desk. For what seemed a very long moment he stared at me, his long fingers steepled, elbows resting on the desktop.

Unnerved but trying very hard not to show it, I stared back at him.

"Signora Roy," he began slowly, "I will pay you the compliment of honesty. You are, I believe, an intelligent woman. I do not think that you are unaware of my feelings about you." He gave a cold smile. "However, although I have not found it easy to work with you, I have the highest respect for your abilities." He paused to sip a little of the brandy.

I said nothing. My face felt frozen with the effort of concealment. I wondered where this remarkable beginning would take him.

"But still," he continued, "it would be useful, I think, if we were to work apart for a while. I have work I must complete here in Rome. Therefore, I will be in the offices more than I have in past months. We would necessarily see a certain amount of each other. That would be difficult for both of us, would it not?"

I made an ambiguous sound, neither polite denial nor agreement—let him interpret it any way he wants, I thought. I was not about to match his so-called honesty. And I kept my face a blank and my eyes on his.

When I did not speak, he went on. "Good. I see you feel as I do. So then, what is the answer to our dilemma? Perhaps the following: It happens that a friend of mine has an important collection of paintings and is looking for someone to clean a number of them at his villa near Palermo. His name is Pietro Bassi. Do you know it?"

"No, I've never heard of him. Should I have?"

"Not at all. He does not like publicity, and his collection is so remarkable that it would be a target for thieves if he were better known."

"And you want me to work for him?"

"Precisely. It would be a long project, several months or more. I would arrange a leave of absence for you here."

"Let's be perfectly frank with each other, Signor Stillitano—as you suggested. If I refuse this commission . . . ?"

His face gave up its attempt at a simulation of friendly concern. "That would be unwise. You were lucky to get a permit to work in Italy. That sort of luck is easily reversed."

I was so angry that I could feel my hands shaking; I clasped them tightly together in my lap. I was also frightened. Faltecchi's threat to end the partnership should have meant that I had nothing to fear from Stillitano, but oddly enough it did not. The man was incalculable and, under that chilly reserve, menacing.

"Your way with words is persuasive, Signor Stillitano, if not original." I was consoled by the sound of my voice as the words came out, cool and seemingly unafraid. "But then originality isn't your strong point, is it?" Right away I wished I could bite the words back.

But he seemed to take them at their surface value. "Results are more important to me than originality, Signora Roy. I would like your decision by Monday."

I struggled to stay in control. "That's too soon. I'll tell you in the middle of the week."

"Very well." He stood up, his manner brusque, all traces of the formal courtesy gone and his dislike of me plain in his eyes. "Don't mention this conversation to Signor Faltecchi. I will be able to persuade him when you accept."

"*If* I accept." I looked up at him, then got to my feet.

"As you say, if you decide to accept. And now, Signora Roy, I will let you go. . . ." There was the slightest emphasis on that simple word "let," just enough to make the implication clear. I turned and left the workrooms without another word.

I needed to think, and at the same time I wanted to get away from the whole business, to immerse myself in something completely separate, more remote. I walked aimlessly up the Corso until I found myself facing the Victor Emmanuel monument, bombast and power writ large. Without hesitating, I crossed the Piazza Venezia, daring the traffic to do its worst, turned my back on that enormous white wedding cake, and made my way along the streets that led around it, back to an older Rome.

Behind iron railings, on sunken ground littered with broken marble, lay the wrecked power of an earlier age. I bought a ticket from a surly guard and went into the Forum, picking my way around the heaps of stone, the lone shattered columns that pointed to the sky, pathetic in their solitariness, yet a more evocative reminder of glory than the great white monument on the Piazza Venezia, and went up onto the Palatine, home of the emperors, now all pretty gardens, grassy meadows spotted white and yellow with tiny wildflowers, and the subterranean house of Augustus's wife Livia.

With my back against a warm stone wall, I settled down in a patch of sun and pulled out my sketch pad and pencils. High above me the branches of the stone pines opened like green parasols against the bright blue sky. Clumps of shiny acanthus, the crown of so many Roman columns, spread their jagged leaves against a wall whose brick was exactly the same shade of brown as the earth below it. A bee shot past, dove into the mouth of a wild purple crocus, and disappeared. The silence was broken only by birds and bells and the occasional sound of tourists, more adventurous than most, who wandered up from the Forum.

Like the scent of summer, wild thyme mingled with the clean smell of freshly cut grass, thickening in the heat of the sun until I closed my eyes, the pencil dropping forgotten from my fingers, and gave myself up to a blessed, drowsy forgetfulness. I think I slept.

But only briefly. A host of questions clamored on the edges of my consciousness, like persistent petitioners demanding to be heard. Sleep vanished, and I sat up, trying to marshal my thoughts into some sort of order. I picked up the pencil again, but this time I used it to list the questions as they came to me.

First: Where was the original Reni now? Who would buy it without being able to show it, if in fact that was part of Alessandro's condition for the sale? But, of course, the answer to that was easy. Hundreds of stolen works of art were sold under precisely such conditions every year; an unscrupulous dealer would know whom to approach.

Next: How would Alessandro account to his father for the sudden appearance of the money he received for the painting? Again, that would probably not be so very difficult, given his knowledge of financial transactions and his father's unworldliness about money. Perhaps he would simply put it down to clever investments.

But what had happened to that money? Why were the Torreleones still selling off paintings? I had no answer to that.

Why had Stillitano made the forgery in the first place? Why risk his considerable reputation in such a dubious undertaking? And not for the first time, either, if I'd understood Faltecchi's accusation rightly; he'd said something about the "Brandini painting," whatever that was. Moreover, how had Alessandro known that Stillitano would be open to such a proposition? These, too, were unanswerables.

Finally, the hardest question of all: What should I do about all of this? That I would have to do something was quite clear, if only in response to Stillitano's stated and implicit threats. I would refuse Stillitano's so-called commission, of course—of that much at least I was sure—but I needed some way to check him from further threats when the time came to turn it down. I had to protect myself. But how? I could tell Faltecchi that I had overheard his argument with Stillitano, tell him about Stillitano's threat, and ask his help. I had no doubt he would give it, but I was unsure how much protection he could be from someone like Stillitano.

I looked down at the questions on the piece of paper in my lap. Impatiently, I stuffed them in my purse, out of sight, and stood up. I felt bad-tempered and confused; I wanted to do something, not just be a listener and onlooker. I was sick of my own passivity.

As I walked out of the Forum, I suddenly thought of Paolo Flacco, Faltecchi's previous assistant; I remembered how much he'd disliked Stillitano and the hints he'd dropped about his darker side. Perhaps he knew more than he'd told me; perhaps he would know what to do. I would call him in Florence and find out.

When I got back to my apartment, I did precisely that. With luck, I found him in. Unsure of how to broach the whole matter over the telephone, I hedged a little and simply said that I had a problem. Could I come to Florence the next day, Sunday, to see him?

But of course, he replied cheerfully. It was time we saw each other again.

With a lighter heart, I dismissed all my worries from my mind and hurried to prepare for my dinner with Nick Taliaferro. I took a very deep and very long bath until I felt each knotted muscle loosen and relax, then polished my nails and chose my clothes with a care I hadn't given to such things in months. I began to enjoy myself and by seven o'clock was almost inclined to feel sorry for Nick. He would have to bear the brunt of all my pent-up energy and curiosity. I might not have the answers to those questions on the Palatine, but I was going to make sure I got some from him. And if I couldn't persuade him to be more forthcoming . . . Well, he was one potential complication at least that I could eliminate from my life.

CHAPTER

7

The early-evening air was mild, deceptively gentle with the lingering warmth of the day. As I walked toward the bus stop, swifts darted and wheeled in the dusk that was gathering among the trees, so like bats that only their plaintive cries of "Gesù, Gesù" reassured me. I came around a corner to the sight of my departing bus, early for once and indifferent to my pursuit. As I knew that I would have to wait a quarter of an hour for the next, I decided to walk down into Trastevere to the bar where I had arranged to meet Nick. It wasn't far, a twenty-minute walk at most through a quiet, aloofly opulent neighborhood of foreign embassies, academies, and mansions, one that I enjoyed for the delights it offered along the way—a richly baroque splash of a fountain set like a marble waterfall into the back of a triumphal arch and a small church with a sublime view over the city.

I was in good time, thinking that I would arrive early and treat myself to a drink with friends who were generally there at this time of day, and it was one of those lovely evenings that defy you to stay indoors.

But it was already growing dark. Many Romans, and more foreigners, would not venture out by themselves after the sun went down. Rome had changed, I was often told. It was no longer the city where a woman could walk alone after dark with the certainty that she would attract only those attentions she had grown used to in daylight. However, that was mostly in the center of the city; I always felt safe in my own neighborhood.

Occasionally I met someone I knew, a neighbor or friend of the Palmieris, who would smile and nod as they hurried homeward, but there were few people about on the streets. Through open windows I could hear the clattering of pans and smell frying garlic and oil. The shouts of children playing street soccer punctuated the gradually fading clamor of traffic on the busy Via Carini. A motorcyclist gunned his engine and shot past me down the street, a shadowy figure in black merged with his machine.

I passed the extravagant, noisy fountain and walked along to the small terrace beside the church. For a moment I stopped there to gaze out on the city; it was losing its definition as the sky darkened, turning into a haze of light points.

Night doesn't fall in Rome; it rises from the city's heart, from the gloomy little alleys and courtyards where the sun never gets much more than a brief look-in, and then, like the mist from the Tiber, it creeps over the rooftops and spreads up into the hills. Those hills still showed the last traces of day, a glaze of gold above the deepening blue.

Directly below me the ground sloped steeply away in a jungle of bushes to meet the road that wound its way down into Trastevere. To my right, just beyond the end of the low wall against which I was leaning, was a gate that opened on to a narrow passageway, a twisting cobblestone path between walls painted with the Stations of the Cross, inspiration for the priests and pilgrims who used the passage as a shortcut from the street below up to the church. Now the gate was locked, and when I peered through the grille set into it, I could see that the path beyond was sad with neglect, thick with weeds and garbage, even a little frightening at this time of the evening.

I turned away and crossed the street to the sidewalk that bordered the patch of park opposite the church, a plot of stubbled grass dignified with a few forlorn oaks and pock-marked statues where people came to exercise their dogs. At the far side of the park, straddling his machine, I saw the motor-cyclist silently watching the view.

The street skirted the park before descending in a series of *S* curves through a stretch of large houses cut off from the street by high vine-covered walls with shut gates. During the day I rarely saw anyone entering or leaving these houses, and tonight they seemed especially lonely. They were lifeless terra-cotta monuments to the taste and discretion of the rich.

I thought of Nick Taliaferro and of the No Trespassing sign he wore as plainly as these houses did. The same well-tended and seemingly invulnerable facade, the same watchfulness. I wondered if I would get more than a glimpse tonight of the emotions behind the carefully placed mask.

As for his interest in me—well, I didn't flatter myself that the invitation to dinner was a compliment to my own irresist-ibility. Seduction? Perhaps—though not, I was willing to bet, of the usual kind.

It was quiet now. There was no one in the street, only the occasional car flashing past. In each returning silence I noticed the motorcycle. It hung back in the darkness, somewhere behind me, neither close nor remote, simply there, like the buzzing of some hovering insect poised to sting, distracting if inconsequen-tial. But all at once I wanted to be down in the light and life of Trastevere.

I was halfway along the longest and darkest stretch of road, in a canyon where it snaked downward between walls like sheer cliffs, when suddenly the motorcycle's engine crashed against the silence of the night and then, as suddenly, died away into that monotonous, by now maddening, hum.

I felt my nerves tingle along my spine at the sound, slipped the long strap of my purse over my head, and quickened my steps. I did not want a replay of Monkey Face and his friend. I looked behind me, but the motorcycle was back around the last curve of the road, out of sight. All I could see was a beam of light sliding along the wall and over the torrent of greenery that brushed against my shoulder as I hurried past.

Absurdly, I felt hunted. Although I told myself sternly that I was being foolish, that it was probably only some teenager out for a joyride, I began to run, my purse bumping against my side, my feet—mercifully in flat-heeled shoes—slapping the pavement.

There were only two more blocks until I reached the steep cascade of steps that led down to one of the main streets of Trastevere, steps that seemed defeatingly mountainous when I was standing at the bottom, bags of shopping in my arms, but that now offered the refuge of a sanctuary where no motorcycle could follow.

But then, as though someone else remembered those steps and realized that they would have to strike soon, the motorcycle exploded into sound again, like a buzz saw gone wild.

I couldn't bear the thought of that thing at my back, and I knew I could never outrun it. Like a creature at bay, I whirled around to face a stabbing yellow light hurtling at me on a blast of noise. Terrified, I threw myself back against the wall, wishing I could bury myself in the rough mass of ivy that cushioned me, as the motorcycle screamed past—a black blur of speed with a shadowy figure leaning forward into the wind—and off around the next corner. There was a cough and a splutter as the motor died. And silence. The only noise I could hear was the roaring of my own blood in my ears, the heavy thud of my heart against my ribs.

He was waiting for me, I was sure of it. And if I didn't appear soon, he would come back for me. Frantically, I looked around for some way of escape, but the long, smooth walls curved past me, too high to scale even had I been much of a climber and spiked with broken glass at the top, protecting houses whose darkness suggested that ringing bells would produce either no response or only a servant trained to screen out unknown callers. Kidnapping was too real a threat for the people who lived in such houses to retain much of their natural Italian instinct to help someone in distress. That trick had worked too often in the past.

Where could I go, what could I do? Scream my head off, hoping someone would open a gate to me? That wasn't even a choice. I was too much a product of callous times to have faith in the usefulness of screams. Fling myself in front of the next car to come along? Or go back the way I'd come, back to the dubious haven of the park and the church where there might be people to help?

I heard a car coming fast up the hill. In a moment it swept into sight around the corner, and instinctively I stepped out into its path, waving my arms. Without slackening pace, the car swerved to miss me, the driver swore at me from his window, and the car shot past and on up the hill.

That decided me. I couldn't go forward, so I would have to go back, back up the road and out of this walled canyon that trapped me like a blind alley. I started running again, arms pumping, grateful for the full skirt and comfortable shoes I was wearing. Over my own panting I heard the inevitable roar of the motorcycle as its throttle opened.

Like a hound on the scent, the motorcycle came baying after me, as though it sensed my desperation and my flight. I was only halfway back to the park when its headlight pierced the darkness ahead of me. The light lit up a mass of plastic garbage bags put out for the next day's pickup, just in time to stop me stumbling into it. Without stopping to think, I dropped to the ground behind it and huddled there, curling up into myself as tightly as I could; I gave thanks to the gods or whomever it was watching over me that the pile lay on the gloomiest patch of sidewalk. Dressed as I was in dark clothes, perhaps I would pass as part of the black heap when the motorcycle went by.

There was a crescendo of noise echoing in the gully of the road with a diabolical pitch that reduced all thought to a desperate impulse to bolt from my refuge. I stamped down on my fear and stayed rooted to my reeking hiding place as the motorcycle screeched past—and, to my relief, on up the street.

As soon as it retreated, I leaped to my feet and headed uphill toward the church. Never mind that the motorcycle had gone that way, too; there were lights and space and possibly people in that direction and no hope at all the other way.

When I reached the corner by the park, I stopped, peering through the shadows that darkened the bit of ground between me and the church. But the street was empty apart from a lone parked car. There was nothing—no help, but also no motorcycle. The only sounds were the faint splash of the fountain and the distant hum of traffic.

Now that I was calmer and felt safer, I began to think that perhaps I had overreacted to an incident that could have any number of explanations. Even if the motorcyclist had wanted to do more than frighten me, he had gone off in search of easier prey, and I could relax. I abandoned the idea of a walk, however; I decided that I'd had enough of fresh air and exercise and would sensibly go home and order a taxi.

I was crossing the street to the church when a blinding glare of light caught and pinned me like a searchlight. He was sitting there, behind the parked car, waiting.

But I didn't stop. In three running steps I crossed the road. Five more brought me to the gate of the passageway by the church, and then I was clutching at the wire mesh of the grille set into the gate, one foot on the doorknob, the other leg swinging up for a foothold while I hauled myself hand over hand up onto the top of the wall. There was only one thought in my mind, one impulse governing my body—to scramble over that wall, run down the passageway, and escape over the wall at the other end. It never occurred to me that he might follow me; by now I think I saw him as so much a part of his machine, almost welded to it like some modern centaur, that I couldn't imagine he would get off.

With a sob of relief I gained the top and was about to drop down onto the other side when I stopped short. And felt sick.

A wire netting covered the top of the passage to prevent

precisely what I was trying to do, or perhaps simply as a support for the vines that trailed over it. No matter; I was trapped.

Crouched there like a treed cat with nowhere to go, I turned my head slowly around. He stood there, just below me, his hands on his hips, in black leather from boots to jacket, with a visored helmet hiding his face.

He stook a step forward. I opened my mouth to scream, futile or not. But when he pushed up the helmet's visor, the scream died in my throat. It was Marco.

For a brief moment I was speechless. I could only gape at him while a grin of self-satisfaction spread over his face. Terrifying women was doubtless an art to Marco; he probably prided himself on his technique.

Well, I was damned if I was going to let him go on feeling so pleased with himself. Oddly enough, I wasn't afraid anymore. I was simply relieved to find that my tormentor was someone I knew.

Filled with the glorious energy of righteous rage, I scrambled down from my perch, indifferent now to safety or dignity, shouting at Marco with every bit of pent-up fear turned to fury. I have no idea what I actually said to him, only that it was whatever insulting Italian I could dredge up from my inadequate store of obscenities. When I began to repeat myself, I switched over to English and French—he might not understand, but I found it wonderfully satisfying.

It was some comfort to see the complacent smile disappear from Marco's face during this tirade. He looked taken aback by my anger, as though he hadn't expected me to do anything but quail before him.

Without pausing to consider whether it was wise or not, I pressed my advantage. "Who do you think you are? Some sort of tenth-rate Marlon Brando?"

But that went right past him. He smiled down at me again, a different smile this time but no improvement over the last. "You're angry." He sounded pleased.

"You have a way with the obvious."

"I like a woman with balls." He tapped my cheek lightly with the tip of one finger. The nail rasped my skin; it needed trimming.

I moved back several steps. "Why? To compensate for your own deficiencies?"

There was an evil spark in his eyes at that, and I wished fervently that I'd kept my analysis to myself. What little I had seen of Marco's psyche should have warned me away from certain subjects.

He reached out and grabbed my arm, my left arm, near the elbow.

I stood my ground, determined that I wouldn't be cowed by him again but equally convinced that I'd better abandon my pride and play up to his ego. "Don't do that," I said as calmly as I could when his grip tightened. It was very painful. "You don't have to prove that you're stronger than I am. It's quite obvious enough."

He relaxed the pressure but kept his hold. "You know," he said smoothly, "we should be friends. If we're going to work together."

We weren't, but I couldn't tell him that now. "You have a strange way of making friends. Don't you find that your methods put most people off? Or does Daniella like to play rough?"

His grin widened, and he dropped his hand from my arm. I rubbed it with exaggerated care, although it really did hurt. Let him think I was weak and in pain and therefore less likely to cause him trouble.

"Ah, Daniella," he said, laughing. It was a remarkably unpleasant laugh. "You don't need to worry about her." He put a hand heavily on my shoulder.

The conceit of the man, I thought, torn between outrage and amusement; he actually thinks I'm jealous of Daniella.

"And why do you think I was trying to frighten you?" he went on. "I only wanted to invite you to a meeting we're having tonight."

"Next time try the telephone. It's simpler."

"But I wanted to see what you're made of," he replied,

contradicting himself. "If you're going to be one of us, you need to be strong." He was giving me that insolent stare of his again.

The Marco stamp of approval, I thought wryly; what more could I ask for? Aloud, I said merely, "Tonight's impossible. I'm meeting a friend for dinner."

"*Me ne frego!* Forget your dinner. This is more important. If"—and his face lost its smile and went frighteningly dead looking—"you meant what you said. And I hope you did. For your own sake."

The superficial attempt at charm dropped away from him. Suddenly he was every bit as menacing as he no doubt wanted to be. He rested both of his hands on my shoulders and looked straight down at me. Then, slowly, he moved his left hand up and around to the back of my neck, lifting my hair away until I felt his long, bony fingers—like the talons of some cruel bird fastened lightly onto its prey—against the bare flesh of my neck. His mouth parted slightly, and I could see the crooked edge of his teeth. His eyes were quite dead under their heavy lids.

The other hand dropped down to my left elbow again and began to squeeze it, harder than before, until tears came into my eyes. "Where does it hurt?" he asked. "There?" He looked pleased at my gasp of pain. "A pity to have to break it again."

At the time I hardly took in his words; I was only aware of the pain, and his eyes. He enjoys all the preliminaries, I thought through the pain, as much as any hawk with a mouse. Quite content to watch the victim struggle until it's exhausted and then take pleasure in its last despairing passivity.

Well, I wasn't cut out to be a victim, and I wasn't going to give Marco the pleasure of my fear again. I let my eyes glaze over and stood there, as passively as he liked, while my mind raced.

I wasn't sure what he meant to do with me, or why; I only knew that he terrified me and I wanted to get away from him. I had just decided to knee him as hard as I could in the groin when I heard the sound of a car coming down the street. Over

Marco's shoulder I saw the yellow gleam of headlights, then the car itself. Miraculously, it slowed and stopped by the park.

Marco turned to look at it, and in that instant I went limp, sagging like a dead weight in his hands. Perhaps he expected a struggle rather than this sudden yielding. Whatever the reason, I must have taken him by surprise, because I slipped down through his hands. It was all I needed. With a wrench and a twist, I broke loose and went racing across the street, over to the car.

A man was getting out of the driver's side. He looked up in astonishment as I practically threw myself into his arms. A dog barked fiercely from the back of the car.

"Please, signore," I said frantically, "there's a man over there—by the church—who's been following me. Please, may I stay with you until he's gone?"

He looked to where I was pointing. Marco was still standing by the gate of the passageway, but as we watched he pulled the visor of his helmet back down over his face and walked quickly to his motorcycle. He jumped on the seat, gunned the motor with a threatening flourish, and shot off down the street.

The dog was still barking. The man leaned back into the car, gave a quiet command, and it fell silent. He turned to me again, "Now, signora, you are all right? Did he harm you?"

I shook my head, giving him what I hoped was a reassuring smile; I didn't want too many questions. "No, he didn't. I'm fine. Really. I don't know what he intended," I said half truthfully, "but you came along just in time."

He looked pleased at this. He was a small man, neatly made, balding, with a rim of dark hair around the crown of his head and a sharp, intelligent face. I liked his smile, which was mild and friendly. He asked me where I was going, if he could give me a lift. It really didn't seem a good idea, he said, to walk alone while that man was in the neighborhood.

I agreed. "I'm going to the Bar Apollonia, near Santa Maria in Trastevere. Do you know it?"

He said that he could drop me off close by and opened the passenger door of the car for me. The dog in the back seat turned out to be a large German shepherd with a manner considerably less friendly than its master's, though firmly under control, and I could see why the man hadn't seemed much alarmed by my approach or by any threat from Marco. I suspected that a command from its master would have brought the shepherd snarling from the car.

When we reached the Apollonia, I thanked him profusely for his help, so warmly, in fact, that he seemed on the verge of proposing that we dine together some evening. He was charming, and I was grateful, but he was also married. I already had too many problems to wish for another, and I managed to parry his discreet suggestions. Unperturbed, he gave me his telephone number—his office number, he told me—should I change my mind, paid me a few compliments that raised my spirits considerably, and said good night. The shepherd gave a final growl before they drove off.

I paused to run a comb through my hair before I went into the bar, wondering if any of the elaborate preparations I'd made for this evening had survived Marco's attentions. Feeling very much in need of a drink, I opened the door and stepped inside.

CHAPTER

8

The Bar Apollonia was loud, smoky, and hot. The walls were papered with drawings and paintings, the drinks were generous. It was popular with the artists, both genuine and would-be, who made Trastevere chic, with cultured foreigners who lived in Trastevere because they liked to be in the thick of things but couldn't quite afford the climate of central Rome, and with the wealthy hangers-on who were steadily sending rents up in their wake. Out of my range, anyway.

Whenever I felt cold and lonely, I would wander into the Apollonia. I enjoyed the passionate conversations of the bar's clique, a nucleus of artists and their constantly shifting satellites whose only demand was that one be either *"simpatico"* or talented. I was never quite sure which they considered me to be.

Tonight it didn't matter. After Stillitano's words and Marco's treatment I was grateful for the uncritical warmth of the welcome, and as I made my way slowly over to the corner where Nick was waiting for me, stopping for greetings and a few words of gossip en route, I could feel some of my confidence returning.

I had an ulterior and not very creditable motive in suggesting to Nick that we meet in this particular bar. It was, in a sense, my territory—as much as any in Rome could be—and I thought it might give me some advantage over his cool self-possession to be in a setting where I suspected he might feel out of place.

But he surprised me. When he stood up to greet me, I saw, instead of the proper businessman in well-cut flannel and rather formal manner, a relaxed, younger-looking man wearing a black velvet jacket over white open-necked shirt and jeans, as much a part of the place as anyone in it. He was grinning slightly as he came forward to help me off with my jacket.

"You missed that fellow over there" were his first words to me. "The one with the Andy Warhol hair."

Surprised, I glanced around to see a pallid young man with remarkable straw-white hair sitting at a nearby table. He looked up, disconcerted to find us staring at him, then down again with sudden interest in his drink. "What do you mean?" I asked Nick.

"Only that he seemed pretty disappointed when you passed him by without so much as a smile. I sympathized. Seems like just about everybody in here got a kiss but Andy and me."

He exaggerated his southern drawl for effect, and the words and the tone were teasing, though not in the least malicious. I had to laugh, but I was uncomfortably certain that he'd seen through my poor plan and couldn't help replying, somewhat defensively, "It *is* a bit clubby in here, I admit. But I like it."

The grin widened. "I can see that." Then, as I was about to protest the teasing, he added, with mock contrition, "Sorry, Kate. I'm just jealous. And I like the Bacchic touch."

"What?"

In response, he leaned forward and plucked something from my hair, then gave me a trailing piece of ivy. "You can tell me the story when I get back with our drinks. What would you like?"

"Ordinarily, I'd say white wine. But tonight I'll have a whiskey. It is quite a story."

As I sat absentmindedly shredding the ivy, I watched him maneuver his way through the crowd in front of the long nickel bar. Stefano, the barman, was generally overworked and slow to respond to strangers on a busy night, but I was amused, and not the least bit surprised, to see how quickly Nick managed to get his attention and our drinks. I told him so when he returned.

"I have a way with barmen. Long years of practice, I'm afraid." He gave me an appraising look as he handed me my glass. "You look pale. Is it anything to do with the ivy?"

Instinctively, my hand went to my face. "Is it that noticeable?"

"Don't worry, you're fine. Better than. Just paler than I'd remembered."

"Well, it's been a wretched day. Topped off by a repeat performance from Thursday. Or almost. That's where the ivy comes in." Without mentioning Marco by name, leaving Nick with the impression that he'd been a stranger, I described my adventure—most of it, anyway.

"It confirmed everything I've ever felt about men in black leather and motorcycles," I finished bitterly. "Wasn't it Byron who said that Italy was a paradise for horses but hell for women? The horses are all inside engines now, but otherwise it's still true."

"It was Robert Burton," Nick said. "And you don't really believe it."

"No," I admitted, "I don't. Who?"

"Robert Burton. He wrote *The Anatomy of Melancholy*."

"Oh. Well, that explains it. However did you know such a thing?"

"I was an English major years ago. Some things stuck—God knows why. But look, do you want me to do something about this character? Call the police? Report it?"

I shook my head emphatically. "I just want to forget it. Besides, nothing much happened." I sipped some of the whiskey and felt a little warmth seep through to my skin.

Nick touched my hand briefly. In a voice I hadn't heard him use before, he said, "I'm sorry, Kate. What a rotten start to the evening. I'll try to make it up to you."

I smiled at him and got his wonderful, sensual smile in return. There was a silence then, friendly enough to feel comfortable with—both of us, I sensed, ready to find the other attractive, disposed to be satisfied with each other if only we could sort out that slight wariness that edged all our conversation.

Impulsively, without stopping to measure my words, I said, "I expect great things tonight, you know."

"Oh yes?" He sounded taken aback. "Then I hope I don't disappoint you."

"Oh, you won't," I said recklessly. "All you have to do is satisfy my curiosity and my appetite." Abruptly, I stopped. I could feel myself flushing scarlet as I realized how my words might sound. "I mean I'm—"

But before I could flounder on, Nick gave me a wolfish grin and said, very smoothly, "I'll do my best. As long as your tastes aren't too exotic. It'll certainly be a pleasure to try."

With as much dignity as I could muster, I said, "I simply meant that I'm very hungry, and I'm sure you know good restaurants in Rome. As for the curiosity, there's a lot about you I don't know. . . ."

"I could say the same about you. That's one of the reasons I asked you to have dinner with me. I thought we might like to know each other better. Or rather, I *know* I'd like to get to know you, and I'm hoping you feel the same. I'm delighted to see, by the way, that you don't look so pale anymore. The whiskey must be doing you good."

I refused to rise to this, turning instead to watch Stefano, during a lull in business, polishing the already gleaming espresso machine that had pride of place among the ranks of obscure liqueurs behind the bar. Nick turned, too, to watch Stefano, who was at that moment smiling and nodding, with a look of almost clinical interest, at something a regular was telling him. "He must know a lot of secrets."

"Useful for journalists," I said idly, thinking of Gianni, who'd once told me that a certain bar near the Chamber of Deputies, popular with politicians, was occasionally his best source.

Nick gave me a startled look. "Why do you say that?" He picked up the cardboard coaster from under his glass and began turning it around between his fingers.

"I have a journalist friend who says that an indiscreet bartender can ruin a man faster than an angry mistress."

He laughed. "Your friend is probably right."

There was a hint of relief in his voice, but I had only a moment to register it before he moved the conversation smoothly along into a mildly flirtatious fencing, brief verbal skirmishes that revealed a wicked sense of humor and at the same time concealed any deeper feeling. I wondered if this was another mask, amusing, sophisticated, and equally effective as a disguise for the real man.

He glanced at his watch. "If you're ready, we should be going."

Outside, the night had grown dank, blurred by a thin mist off the river. The cobblestones were greasy underfoot, slick with oil that rainbowed under the streetlights, and I slipped and might have fallen if Nick hadn't put out his hand to catch me. I kept my arm in his as we walked down the street to the small piazza where he'd left his car. The solid feel of this arm under the velvet sleeve disturbed me; I wasn't sure if I liked the sensation or not.

The square was filled with cars and empty of people except for a group of boys on and around a red Maserati. Two of them were draped on the hood, smoking, and one, a gangling fellow with an incongruous cowboy hat on his head, sat cross-legged on the roof, tapping out a rhythm as if he were playing drums. It was, Nick muttered, his car. Whatever it was that he did for a living, I reflected, it paid well.

The boys fell silent at our approach. I could feel my stomach tighten as we got closer. They reminded me of the *scippatori* who'd tried for my purse, thugs in training. Nervously, I looked around for a black motorcycle with a dented back fender, but that, at least, was missing. And none of these boys had Marco's predatory menace.

Nick walked coolly up to them while I trailed behind. The boys watched him, their faces expressionless, and then, at the last possible moment, slid gracefully off the car and moved away, enough to let us through. They bowed with elaborate, mocking courtesy as we got into the car, and I heard one of them, the skinny drummer, say something to Nick in a rough dialect I couldn't understand. Nick laughed shortly and answered back in the same dialect. There was a shout of laughter from the boys. They broke up and walked away across the square, nothing more now than bored kids looking for a way to relieve some restless itch. Once they were safely behind us, I asked Nick what he and the drummer had said to each other.

"It was pretty crude. Basically, he was complimenting me on my taste in cars and companions."

"The car naturally coming first," I said without rancor.

"Naturally." Nick glanced at me and grinned. "And I agreed and thanked him for polishing my car with his behind."

"Not a bunch I'd care to meet alone."

"They're harmless enough, despite appearances. They just like you to think the worst." We were driving now across the Tiber, along with half of Rome; the little Tiber island glimmered in the water beyond the bridge. "They're a type I know fairly well," Nick added. "My sister had friends like that."

"An Italian or American sister?"

"Italian. She was my half sister and much younger than I. She came along late in my mother's marriage. My mother and stepfather spoiled her outrageously, especially my mother. They wouldn't let her grow up. But despite that she was very lovable."

"Was?"

He took a moment to answer. "She died a few months before my mother. My mother had been sick for some time, but Susanna's death finished off her will to live." Once again his voice was absolutely flat. He was reporting a fact; that it was a tragic fact was apparent only from the words themselves.

"How terrible. I'm so sorry, Nick." I meant it, but my words sounded weak, echoing hollowly against the hard shell of his self-sufficiency. It was impossible to say more to him, to ask him how she died, and I found myself wishing again that he were more approachable. He gave a muttered thanks, more a grunt than a word, and lapsed into silence.

I watched the city, hazy in the mist, flow past as Nick unhesitatingly took the car through a maze of one-way streets and tiny piazzas. He drove well, with that mixture of controlled aggression and assurance so essential in Roman traffic.

The restaurant he took us to had no sign in front, nothing to tell the passerby that it was anything more than a dilapidated house, scabbed with peeling plaster and torn posters, just like its neighbors. It was in a part of the city that had little charm and none of the indefinable atmosphere that can make even the most run-down areas in old Rome so appealing to tourists. This was a plain down-at-heel working-class neighborhood; no tourist would ever come here.

Inside, in the plain square room lit with a cruel neon brightness, every table but one was filled. The walls were covered with enormous photographs of Che and Mao, and other icons of the left whose faces were familiar but unnameable, and scored with slogans and calls to arms in every language imaginable. By the door a large slate announced that meals were free to workers on strike, brothers and sisters of the revolution, and anyone in want. All others should pay what they could. There was a short list of suggested prices.

I found Nick watching me. "Another surprise," I told him. "What's the name of this place?"

"Il Ristorante Rivoluzionario." The Revolutionary Restaurant. He grinned. "What else?"

"What else," I agreed.

If the ambience was unusual, the delicious smell of roasting meat, herbs, and wine that hovered in the room was reassuringly typical of all good restaurants. Before I could ask Nick any questions, a thin, intense-looking man came through the swinging kitchen door and over to welcome us, greeting Nick by name. He looked more like an intellectual than a restaurateur, with round, tortoiseshell glasses on a beaky nose and a way of leaning forward as he spoke, hands moving all the time, that I found intimidating until I got used to it.

After Nick introduced the two of us, Giangiacomo Maurelli led us over to the empty table, spreading a clean white paper across the tabletop, fetching glasses and knives and forks, pouring wine from a liter bottle, and talking all the while.

"You've been away, Nick. Antonia and I, we've missed you." He clattered plates down in front of us, and brought bread and two huge bowls of minestrone.

"I've been in the States. How's business?"

Maurelli spread his arms wide and shrugged. "You know, people don't pay, we don't open. And we've been open more than shut. Sometimes only pasta, though. But tonight you're in luck. Antonia's father took pity on us and gave us a lamb. He's got a farm in the Marche. Eat now. We'll talk more later. *Buon appetito.*"

"A singular way to run a restaurant," I said to Nick when he had gone.

"Isn't it? The restaurant is really Antonia's. She'd feed all of Rome if she could. Giangi publishes an underground newspaper. One supports the other, though it's never clear which does which."

"How did you meet them?"

"Through my sister. She used to bring me here. The Maurellis tolerate my bourgeois leanings for her sake. Whenever I'm in Rome, I try to come here."

His sister sounded interesting, and I wanted to ask him about her, but the opening his last sentence gave me was too tempting. "Why are you in Rome this time?"

Slowly, almost grudgingly, he replied, "A mixture of things. Winding up some business from my mother's death. Family stuff, mostly."

We were eating the soup; it was thick with vegetables and very good. I scooped up another spoonful before asking my next question. "And you can get away from your job for long enough?" Clumsy, I told myself angrily, not subtle at all. Why don't you just ask him straight out what he does for a living? Just get all the basic facts out early on in the evening so you can relax and enjoy this marvelous food.

But Nick made it virtually impossible to be that direct. He was so very different from Alessandro Torreleone; I suspected that an invitation to simplicity such as the one Alessandro had given me would only provoke an amused smile.

"I'm pretty well a free agent." He paused a moment, as though considering how much to tell me, before he went on. "I write about international finance. On a free-lance basis. There are some things I'm looking into while I'm in Rome, for a possible book."

I wondered how this fitted in with his interest in the Torreleones, but it was too soon to ask that particular question.

He talked about his work in vague generalities, something about banking, international money markets, making it all sound so dull that I wondered why a man who seemed so far from dull himself should choose to do it. All he said left me no wiser. But before I could see this, he turned the talk about his work into talk about mine so skillfully that only later did it occur to me how well he'd deflected my questions. He learned much more about the restoration of paintings than I did about whatever it was he really did.

But I had to grant him a genuine interest, or else the perfect portrayal of it, in what I was saying, and naturally that made me like him better.

Once or twice I looked up from my plate or back from scrutinizing the other diners—family groups complete with ancient *nonna*, students in regulation denim, workers in overalls—to find Nick's eyes on me as though he'd been considering me, wondering about me as I wondered about him, still unable to make up his mind just what he thought.

When we finished the costolettine, baby lamp chops fried in an egg and parmesan-cheese batter, Giangiacomo came over to ask us if we wanted fruit or the *dolce*, which in honor of the occasion—the lamb, he explained—was Monte Bianco.

"You choose," I told Nick. "I'm in your hands."

"The Monte Bianco, then, Giangi. Antonia's is wonderful I remember, and we can have fruit anytime."

As we ate the creamy chestnut dessert, Nick said, "You know, Kate, I can't imagine you allowing yourself to be in anyone's hands but your own."

I looked across at him, surprised. "My husband once said something similar. He meant that I was too stubborn to be much good at partnership. I'm afraid that I took it as a compliment."

"Which is how I intended it." His voice was serious. "You don't like partnerships?"

"I haven't much experience of them. And the marital kind was a failure."

He gave me a shrewd look. "Idealists can't be easy to live with."

"They're not." I spooned up the last of the Monte Bianco. "But then, who is? It's ironic—lies wreck so many marriages, but we lied to protect each other. Not to cover up infidelity, at least not the sexual kind; we lied to hide the differences between us. But in the end even lies weren't enough. We each felt betrayed by the other's work. Michel thought mine was pointless, and I felt his made him fanatical. We gave up trying to understand." I drank a little wine to quench a bitterness I could almost taste, although the potency was dying. "But I've learned one thing— that it's no use trying to protect someone from the truth."

Immediately after I'd said all this, I felt foolish. What on earth had possessed me to tell him my tale of woe? I also felt a hypocrite. Concealment was a form of lying, and I knew it.

"I wish I had your certainty."

"I don't mean to sound holier-than-thou. It's simply something I've thought a lot about since my marriage ended." I shrugged. "Maybe I spend too much time looking back."

Nick took out his cigarettes, laid them on the table, and searched his pockets unsuccessfully for matches. I found some in my purse and held the packet out to him. When our hands touched briefly, I registered the contact; it meant something. Curious to know what, I watched the top of his head while it was bent over the flame. His hair was thick and shiny, clean looking; I wanted to reach out and touch it. Maybe that's all it was, just a sudden urge to make physical contact, to break through the barrier.

"My own marriage ended years ago," Nick said abruptly as he leaned back in his chair, "but I don't suppose I've ever stopped looking back at it." My face must have shown my surprise, more at the admission than the fact of the marriage itself, because he went on. "We were very young. Each of us after something the other couldn't give."

"What was it you were after?"

He tapped the ash on the end of his cigarette into a saucer. "It's hard to put a name to it. Equilibrium is as good as any I suppose. A balance or harmony. Something I didn't see in the marriages around me, either."

At that moment, Giangiacomo brought his wife over to say hello. Nick stood up, and he and Antonia kissed each other on both cheeks. She flushed with pleasure when we praised the meal. Nick grinned down at me and said, "Antonia and Giangi are an example of what I was after." To the Maurellis, in explanation, he added, "We've been discussing partnerships. It's nice to see one that works."

Giangiacomo laughed. "That's because I always do exactly as Antonia says. Now, we have something for you. Something special." He produced a bottle filled with a clear liqueur. Sambuca, he told us, from Viterbo. The best in Italy. "You must taste it."

Then they must join us, we told them. While Nick pulled up two more chairs, Giangiacomo filled glasses with the anise liqueur and dropped three coffee beans in each. "Some say it's very bad luck, or an insult, to put in an even number of beans," he told me. "Personally, I don't think it matters a damn. But in some things I preserve the old mythologies."

Nick raised his glass. "To old myths."

Giangiacomo smiled back at him. "To hell with them all."

And we drank to that.

The restaurant was almost empty now; it was growing late. We spent the rest of the evening there talking, not politics but a safer subject—the perils and pleasures of the restaurant business. Not surprisingly, the Maurellis came in for more than their fair share of freeloaders; Giangiacomo was very funny on his method of detecting them.

"You can almost always tell by their shoes," he said. "They may wear an old coat and suit, but they rarely bother to disguise their shoes. I always check those first."

Then we were the last ones in the Revolutionary Restaurant. Although Giangiacomo was just gathering steam and gave the impression he could go on all night, Antonia began to look weary, and I signaled to Nick that we should go. As we said good night, with invitations and promises to come again soon, Giangiacomo drew Nick aside, and their faces grew serious.

We went outside into a brisk and biting wind that had blown away the mist. While we walked to Nick's car, it occurred to me that he had not once mentioned the Torreleones. So perhaps, I told myself, my suspicions were groundless. I had been making mysteries where there were none. It was as simple as it seemed on the surface. Nick liked me for myself, not for what he might learn from me. And I . . . well, I found him much more sympathetic than I'd expected to.

We took a roundabout route to my apartment, weaving our way up onto the Gianicolo through the narrow park dedicated to Garibaldi's memory, that plateau where he and his soldiers fought the French and where some of them remain in stone to gaze over the city they had freed. Nick stopped the car and we strolled together to the hillside balustrade to look down on the city lights. The cold wind had driven all but the most determined of lovers away; the hardy few who remained seemed to be clinging together as much for warmth as out of passion. Nick took my hand; we stood like that, without speaking, until the wind chilled us, then walked slowly back to the car.

In front of us, on a rearing horse, one hand clutching a pistol, the other a baby, was a statue of Anita Garibaldi. She seemed far more the burning revolutionary than her husband, sitting so sedately on his horse nearby. We stopped and looked up at her.

"A formidable lady," Nick said.

"And as decisive as her husband. Do you know how they met?"

"How?"

"Garibaldi was in Brazil. He saw her from the deck of a ship—she was washing socks or doing something equally domestic by the river—and he decided to marry her. Even more amazing, she said yes."

Nick glanced once more at the statue before he got into the car. "Poor Garibaldi."

"Why do you say that?"

"I'll bet it was the last pair of socks she washed. He probably thought he had himself a useful camp follower, and look what she turned out to be."

"A lesson to us all," I said, smiling at him, "not to judge by first impressions."

Nick paused with his hand on the ignition and gave me a speculative look. "Do you often revise yours?"

"Sometimes."

When we reached my apartment, I asked him if he would like to come in for a drink, a quick one only, I was careful to add, because I was going to Florence in the morning to visit a friend and would have to be up early.

While Nick looked at the sketches and paintings on my walls, I poured a brandy for each of us, then walked over to his side and handed him his glass.

"Are all these your own work?" he asked me as he took the brandy.

"Most. Some are by friends—that one over there and the

one above the sofa. One or two are things I've bought in Rome. The only real regret I had when I left Montreal was having to leave most of my paintings behind. I miss them."

As we talked about the paintings, Nick spoke so knowledgeably about technique that I asked him if he'd ever painted himself. Yes, he said, long ago; he'd given it up for lack of time. "But I go to galleries when I have the chance."

"Well," I said helplessly, "you *are* a surprise to me."

"How do you mean?"

"It's hard to say. Only that you leave me feeling continually uncertain of what you're really like."

He smiled. "Do you mind that?"

"I'm not sure." I set my empty glass down on a table. "But I look forward to finding out."

"Let me help you with your research," he said quietly, and took me by my shoulders, turning me gently around to him. He cupped my face in his hands and looked down at me, the shadow of a question in his eyes before they closed. His lips were hard against mine; they tasted of brandy. When, after what seemed a very long time, he stopped kissing me, when I had caught my breath and looked back at him, the question in his eyes was gone.

"Will you come with me to a Carnival party on Tuesday night?" he asked when he finally released me.

I hesitated, caught off balance. "I'd like to, Nick, but I've already been invited to one. I'm sorry." Then, because I couldn't see why I should hide it, I added, "The Torreleones have asked me to their Carnival Ball." I felt inexplicably embarrassed, and angry with myself for showing it.

Nick seemed disconcerted at first but recovered smoothly. "So you've met the famous Alessandro. And do you like him?"

"Yes, I do. He's really so much nicer than rumor has it. Very funny and quick. You'd like him, too," I finished lamely, and untruthfully. Intuition told me that the two men would be anything but friendly.

We were sitting on the sofa, at either end. I had my shoes off and my feet tucked up under me; Nick was leaning back, long legs stretched out in front of him, his hands clasped behind his head.

"Tell me more." He said it quietly, but I sensed an intensity in the words that put me on my guard.

"There isn't much more to tell. I've just met him. But he and his father have both been very kind about the work I've been doing for them, and I think the invitation is probably some sort of expression of that approval." Why was I finding excuses? But it seemed important, for whatever reason, to establish the innocence of my relationship with Alessandro in Nick's eyes. I added that I'd also met the niece, Daniella.

Nick looked so interested at this, and I was so relieved to have attention deflected from Alessandro that I described her in some detail, editing out only Marco. As Nick asked his questions, I felt my doubts coming back. Why was he so interested in the Torreleones? I was working up the courage to ask him when abruptly he got up and said he had to be going.

He put his glass down beside mine. "But I'll call you on Monday, Kate, if that's okay."

"Of course. I'd like that."

At my door we kissed again. This time it somehow seemed inevitable that I would move into his arms, raise my face to his. And under the passion I sensed something else, a friendliness, almost a comradeship.

With clasped hands we walked downstairs together to the front door. But before we reached it, the door opened and Gianni Palmieri came in. "*Ciao*, Kate," he said cheerfully. Then he saw Nick, who was standing just behind me. "Nick! But this is wonderful—"

"What are you doing here, Gianni?" Nick asked him, sounding surprised.

Gianni stared at him, then laughed. "Why, I live here. I had no idea that you and Kate—"

Impatiently, I interrupted him. "Do you mean to say that you two know each other?"

"Of course," Gianni replied. "Nick is the American I told you about last night. The one working with me on the Mestola

Rossa story. This man is one of the best journalists around; he could get secrets out of a stone. But surely you knew that?"

I turned around to Nick in time to catch the quick shake of the head that he aimed at Gianni. He had the grace to look abashed when he saw I'd noticed. "No," I said, "I had no idea."

By now Gianni realized that something was wrong but clearly didn't know what or how to fix it. "Listen," he said awkwardly, "why don't you both come in for a drink? Clara's probably still awake, and I think, well . . ." His voice trailed off.

Nick said, "Fine," and looked questioningly at me, but I didn't answer right away. It had just occurred to me why Nick had seemed so familiar when we first met. I'd seen him on television, on some news program or other. "So you're a journalist?" I said to him.

"Yes." The way he said it, grudgingly, made it more of a confession than an acknowledgment.

I didn't know what to think. Why had Nick avoided telling me that straight out? Did it have anything to do with his interest in the Torreleones, and, if so, was I right in suspecting that his interest in me was the direct result? My head was swimming. I was confused and tired and wanted nothing more at that moment than to be alone to sort out my thoughts. I felt betrayed, and I wasn't quite sure why. What exactly, I asked myself, did Nick mean to me?

"Thanks, Gianni," I said, "but I think I'll just go to bed. I'm tired. Good night." This last was for Nick as I went past him up the stairs.

"I'll call you tomorrow, Gianni," I heard him say behind me.

"*Va bene.*" Tactfully, Gianni disappeared into his apartment.

"Kate!" Nick's footsteps sounded on the stairs.

But I didn't stop. I was about to go through my own door when he leaned forward and put one hand on the frame, blocking my way.

"You're angry," he said. "And I'm sorry—"

I didn't look at him. "I'm not angry. Just confused." Then, in a burst I couldn't help, I said, "You seem so secretive. I'd like to know why you find the Torreleones so fascinating—you don't strike me as a simple *paparazzo*—but I realize that I probably wouldn't get a straight answer to that. Not that it matters. Given time, I might be able to figure it out for myself. And now I'd like to go in please."

He dropped his arm from the doorframe, and I went inside and shut the door.

CHAPTER

9

I went to Florence on an early-morning train. Despite the hour and the overcast sky, the vast square in front of Rome's Stazione Termini was dotted with families that had come into the city to show off the children's Carnival finery. Tiny masked Harlequins and Columbines chased each other through pools of dirty water, ignoring their parents' threats and outstretched arms. Cries of outrage mingled with their laughter as mothers cuffed the children they could catch, then grabbed them once again to administer ferocious hugs of forgiveness.

The Florence train was virtually deserted. A few gray-faced workers, slumped in their seats, stared at me incuriously as I walked along the corridor, looking for an empty compartment. As the train rumbled out of the city, I felt an immense relief. Rome and its complications were, for the moment, behind me.

But it wasn't to be so easy. The city itself might retreat into the distance, but its complications kept pace with the train, creeping back into my mind, repeating themselves with the monotonous insistence of the clack of the tracks beneath me. I picked up a magazine and riffled through it halfheartedly and in vain. It was no use, I could not be distracted.

All right, then, I thought resignedly, perhaps this was the time I needed to think. First about Stillitano: I had no intention of accepting his "offer," but on the other hand I believed him when he said that he could get my work permit withdrawn if I refused. I did not want to leave Italy, and I particularly did not want to be exiled by Franco Stillitano's machinations, but I needed some persuasion of my own to oppose his, something that would force him to leave me alone. Perhaps Paolo would have an idea where such persuasion might be found. A long shot, but all I had.

The Reni was, if anything, more complicated. Complicated by Stillitano's involvement and by my feelings for both Alessandro and his father. I wanted to believe Alessandro's explanations, but there were too many unanswered questions. And a small voice far back in my mind was whispering, asking if I didn't find Alessandro's duplicity just a bit distasteful.

Finally, there was Nick and his investigation. If he and Gianni were interested in the Freemasons' cabal and if Nick was also interested in the Torreleones, it seemed to follow naturally that one of the Torreleones must somehow be involved. The obvious candidate was Alessandro. But I wasn't going to suspect him of anything until I knew more. Stillitano might be a villain; I couldn't quite, however, believe it of Alessandro. The memory of that moment in the secret passage was still too clear.

I was almost grateful for the simplicity of Daniella's problem. There at least I knew what to do. Marco was troubling, but I expected that once I made it clear I wanted nothing more to do with his and Daniella's affairs, he would leave me alone. Wishful thinking, I realize now, but at that point I considered Marco the least of my worries.

The soft green countryside slipped past, luminous in a mist-ing of fine rain, the hillsides topped with villages picked out by flashes of light as the sun burned its way through the clouds. The train passed through small towns, each with its new religion, the Sunday morning soccer game. Small figures in brightly colored shirts ran across grass green as emerald.

For some inexplicable reason best known to the unions, there was a go-slow when the train reached Florence and we crept at a snail's pace through the suburbs to the station in the center, only to come to a grinding halt tantalizingly close to the platform. And there we sat. No one seemed to mind, no one complained, everyone simply hung out of the windows and called good-naturedly to the passengers on more fortunate trains that went slowly by us. It was all very pleasant.

When the train was finally allowed to move into the station, Paolo was waiting for me. He called my name as I stepped down onto the platform, and I turned to find his round face in its frame of thin brown hair close to mine. We hugged each other enthusiastically.

"Oh Paolo," I told him, "you don't know how I've missed you." He looked so solid and straightforward, full of good humor and sense, and I realized that even if he couldn't help me with my dilemma it would do me good just to be with him. We were never more than colleagues and close friends, although I found him so appealing that I might have tried my luck if he hadn't already been in love with the well-brought-up daughter of a good Tuscan family whom he'd known all his life. Clara and I called Paolo "the monk" because he looked so much like one, a modern monk in blue jeans, and because one night he vowed to us extravagantly to live like a monk until his Beatrice could marry him.

Beatrice's father insisted that Paolo establish himself before marrying his daughter; I had often listened to Paolo's lament that the two of them were going to be middle-aged before he measured up to her father's standards. I tried to console him with the poetic notion of himself as the constant lover à la Dante but wasn't really surprised when this failed to comfort him. He wasn't cut out to be Dante, he told me. He was too fat for the part, and besides, he wanted more than glimpses of his Beatrice from afar.

For the first hour after my arrival we walked through the city, talking about our work, while I reacquainted myself with old loves—the sturdy defiance of the Bargello guarding its treasures, in particular Donatello's charmingly effete *David* and a Della Robbia *Madonna* that was more convincingly holy than the thousands on display in the city; Gozzoli's fresco of the Medici as Magi; Giotto's beautiful bell tower, a shaft of pale-pink-and-green marble, like ivory tracery against the bulk of the Duomo; and the yellow line of houses against the yellow Arno.

Paolo showed me the restoration work he was completing on a Ghirlandaio fresco in the private chapel of an old Florentine family. The smell of incense from the morning mass still hung in the air. It was peaceful, calm with the certainty of faith and continuity, as though the present never came within its walls, never disturbed the serene faces of the men and women painted there. I found it difficult not to envy a tradition where, for the lucky ones, the path of life was so clear. And I thought of Alessandro and understood a little of what he believed he had lost.

Afterward we drove out into the hills for lunch. Behind the wheel of his miniature Fiat, Paolo abandoned the careful precision and patience that made him such a wonderful craftsman, giving himself up to the intoxicating rapture of speed. If he had been a better driver and his car something other than an egg-shell on wheels, I might have enjoyed that swift, winding ascent through terraces of olive groves with their delicate silver-gray foliage like motionless clouds of smoke, past black spears of cypress, and sleepy villages.

As it was, I offered up a small prayer of thanks when we arrived safely in a skidding shower of stones at a restaurant set among umbrella pines high above a valley.

The sun was shining on the little terrace fringed with ilex that overlooked the valley. We asked the waiter for a table outdoors, and there, in the warm air scented with pine and mimosa, we traded gossip and laughed over the inflated egos and rivalries of rich patrons we had known. Paolo told me that it was no different in Florence, if anything more incestuous, since so many of the families were related.

"But," he said, "I have no complaints. I am doing well here. Well enough, anyway, to suit Beatrice's father. She and I will marry in the summer, and you must come to our wedding, Kate."

"That's wonderful, Paolo! Of course I'll come." I leaned over and kissed him. "Beatrice is a very lucky girl." I couldn't resist adding, "And I'm delighted that she'll come to you unwrinkled and under thirty."

"If not quite the blushing bride her father would like," Paolo said with a grin.

The smile faded from his face, and he took my hand. "But you, Kate—are you in some sort of trouble? You sounded very strange on the telephone yesterday, and I worried."

Before I could answer him, the waiter arrived with our lunch. I let a moment go by while he set the food down, opened another bottle of wine, and wished us a good appetite. After he'd gone, I said, "I *am* in trouble. In a way." I told him about the Reni, about the other painting, the one left with Faltecchi by the social-climbing industrialist's wife, and finally about the overheard conversation between Faltecchi and Stillitano. Once again, I found myself editing my story. I did not mention Daniella, Marco, or Nick.

When I finished, Paolo said flatly, "None of this surprises me. I always thought Stillitano would go too far."

"Why?"

He looked as grave as anyone can who has been blessed, or cursed, with the plump, good-natured features of a benevolent friar. "Because of that trouble over the Brandini painting. Do you know anything about it?"

"That was the name Faltecchi used when he was arguing with Stillitano. But I didn't have any idea what it meant."

I waited while he chewed his steak. After a great gulp of wine, he went on. "The painting was a Canaletto that belonged to a minor branch of the Brandini family. It was Stillitano's

128

commission, and he did all the work. After it was sold, the buyer claimed that it was a forgery—there was very nearly a scandal, accusations were made against the Brandinis and against Faltecchi and Stillitano. But it was effectively hushed up. I don't know the details, only that there threatened to be a stink, then there was no stink, after all. Stillitano took a long vacation, and it seemed some time before relations between Faltecchi and him were friendly again.

"But naturally it made me wonder, and it made me watchful. When Stillitano was as secretive with the Reni as he had been with the Brandini painting, I thought he might be up to something. However, the Torreleones seemed content with his work, and there were no more scandals, so I decided that it was just my dislike of Stillitano that made me so suspicious. But what you've just told me means my instincts were right. Still, if Faltecchi is breaking with Stillitano, do you really need to get mixed up with any of this? After all, the Reni is Alessandro Torreleone's problem, not yours."

"It's too late. Stillitano hates me for some reason. I think he's afraid of what has already happened, that I'll get a good look at the Reni and tell someone. He's been trying to get rid of me."

"What do you mean?"

"He wants me to take a commission with a friend of his in Palermo. A long-term commission, he says. He encouraged me strongly to accept—no threats in so many words but the implication that he'd get my work permit revoked if I refused."

Paolo stopped with his glass halfway to his mouth and gaped at me. "My God, Kate! Have you told Faltecchi this?"

"Not yet. Stillitano told me not to. But I will, first chance I get. What I'd like to do is go to him with some proof that Stillitano is everything we all think he is. Faltecchi suspects him, you and I suspect him, maybe others do, too. But we need proof." I put my fork down and drank some wine. "I thought you might know what to do."

"I wish I did. But I can't see how I can help. . . ." He paused, looking down on the valley that fell away from us in

129

folds of hills where vineyards and olive groves fought for space. A flock of sheep grazed near an old farmhouse; in the silence I could hear the faint jingling of their bells. I wondered what I was going to do now.

But then Paolo said slowly, "There was something—"

"What?" I asked eagerly.

"He used to have a notebook, a black leather-bound one. I always thought it might give me an idea of what he was up to."

"He still has it. I've seen him writing in it."

"He was always very secretive with it—"

"Yes, that's right," I broke in excitedly. "I remember once when I'd just begun at Faltecchi and Stillitano . . . I was working late and was very keen to tell someone about a bit of canvas I'd managed to save, which everyone else was convinced had rotted through. Stillitano was the only one around. I didn't know him well enough then to be wary of him, and I sort of barged into his office—the door wasn't shut all the way—and he jumped up and turned on me as though I'd caught him doing something criminal. At the time he only seemed to be writing, and the lecture he gave me was so furious, in his icy way, that it seemed out of all proportion."

Paolo gave a short, contemptuous laugh. "The *stronzo* probably thinks he's Machiavelli. Writing down his great thoughts. Ugh!" With a gesture of disgust he tore a roll in two. "Does he still keep it locked away in his desk, that big old brown one?"

"Well, he still has the desk. But I've never actually seen him put the notebook away in it. Do you remember which drawer he kept it in?"

"As a matter of fact, I do." Paolo grinned at me. "At one point I considered a little burglary; I was so desperate I would have done anything to pin something on the man. Working with him had become intolerable. Then the job here came along, so it wasn't necessary after all."

"And you've made me a present of it instead," I teased him.

He looked sheepish. "Yes, I'm sorry, Kate. But you must admit that I did warn you that he was a *cazzo*."

"Granted. Anyway, I'll forgive you if you'll tell me which drawer holds the notebook."

"It used to be in the right-hand side, second one down. God knows if it's still there or if it will be any use to you." To my surprise, he said, "But I wouldn't mind helping you find out. To even the score, so to speak. Do you want a companion in crime?" As he said this, he looked exactly like my childhood picture of Friar Tuck, the modern version of a well-fed monk not above a little lawbreaking in a good cause.

"I'd love it. Come back to Rome with me. We'll do it tonight." I was delighted with the prospect of Paolo's company and moral, or immoral, support. The idea of breaking into Stillitano's desk when I had no real proof that he had actually done anything wrong filled me with a confusion of sensations, fear not the least of them.

But Paolo was looking crestfallen. "That's impossible, Kate. I can't get away until next weekend at the earliest. Can you wait till then?"

Disappointed, I shook my head. "Things have been happening too quickly. And Stillitano wants my decision before then."

"Then you must find someone to help you, Kate. Stillitano is too much to take on alone."

"Yes, I know. I've had a taste of his methods. But one way or another I intend to find out what's in that notebook. It's the only real lead I have." I said this with more conviction than I felt.

But Paolo, at least, seemed convinced. "It won't be easy, you know, breaking into that desk. But there may be a way I can help you after all. Wait here a minute. I'm going to make a phone call." He pushed back his chair and went inside the restaurant.

I drank my coffee, imagining myself as, successively, a would-be burglar, a criminal on the run from the police, and a prisoner languishing in Rome's bizarrely named Queen of Heaven Prison—I had passed it often enough on my walks along the Tiber to appreciate how unpleasant it would be to live there.

The more I considered the possible consequences of my actions, the less inclined I became to any course other than the strictly law-abiding. I was trying to come up with legal alternatives to our mad scheme, without much success, when Paolo came back, beaming as though he were about to produce the notebook itself.

"We're in luck. Come, I've already paid the bill." He hustled me away from the restaurant, into his car, and back down to Florence. As he drove, with no concession to any other vehicle on the road, passing everything and provoking even the hardened Italian drivers' outrage, he described his plan.

"Naturally you will not want to let Stillitano know that someone has broken into his desk. You must be discreet. No crowbars, for example, because they leave marks. Therefore, you need certain skills, and certain keys. I don't suppose you could get a key to that desk somehow?"

I shook my head glumly. "Maybe we ought to forget this burglary idea, Paolo. It really is crazy to imagine that I'm going to be able to get that notebook."

"Nonsense," he said with an enthusiasm that more than made up for my own waning spirits. "By the end of today you'll be able to begin a career as a jewel thief if life as a conservator grows too dull." He swerved violently back into his own lane in time to avoid an oncoming bus.

"I'm rather partial to my life as a conservator. And to life itself, for that matter. Do we have to go so fast?"

At once Paolo looked repentant. "Does it frighten you, Kate? Then I'm sorry. Beatrice often tells me that I drive badly. I was thinking of the adventure ahead of you and wishing I could take part in it." He sounded like a small boy who has been told he's too young to join in the big boys' game. But he did slow down a little, enough so that I no longer felt the need to clutch the dashboard.

"Just where are we going? If it doesn't spoil your fun to tell me."

"To visit a friend, a woman I used to work for when I was a student. She has an antique shop specializing in old furniture, with a collection of bureaus, cabinets, and desks. And they have many different kinds of locks. Signora Renzini is going to teach you how to pick a lock."

I must have looked shocked, because he laughed. "It's a skill she must have in her business. She often buys pieces of furniture for which the keys have long been lost. In some cases, it isn't possible to remove the locks without damaging the piece itself. So she has become an expert at picking locks, of necessity. She has also acquired a set of what in English you call skeleton keys. This afternoon she will teach you something of what she knows. She has also agreed to lend you her set of keys. But only because she and I are old friends has she agreed to do this without asking any questions. She has that rare and blessed quality in a woman—discretion."

I was too familiar with Paolo's occasional attempts at blatant male chauvinism to rise to the bait that was dangled to distract me from my worries. I confined myself to saying, with a nastiness I immediately regretted, "I suppose your Signora Renzini is a very proper lady as well as a safecracker?"

"She picks locks, she does not rob," Paolo said.

"I'll never understand this country of yours, Paolo. Everyone seems so willing to blur distinctions here. There's never any clearly defined right or wrong, good or bad. I wish you'd teach me the language instead of the fine art of breaking and entering." As I spoke, I knew I was being unfair and unreasonable, that I was taking my frustrations out on poor Paolo.

He gave me a sidelong look. "You speak it well enough, Kate."

"You know I don't mean Italian."

"Neither do I." His voice held a note of impatience. "If you were really a good Canadian girl, you'd go straight to the police. I notice you haven't mentioned them once in our discussion. And you wouldn't hide so much. Do you think I don't realize that there are many things you haven't told me?"

I felt ashamed. "You're right, of course," I said slowly. "But it's as though I only have enough of the code to decipher half the message, to know what I can't do, not what I can. There's so much I don't understand."

"Well, perhaps you must go on trying." The car slowed and pulled up to the curb. We parked in front of a discreetly grilled and shuttered building of soft golden stone that had, despite its severe facade, a distinct look of opulence. Paolo pushed a button set into a highly polished brass plate marked Renzini Antichita. In a moment there was an answering buzz, and Paolo turned the handle of the heavy front door. We walked into a marble foyer and over to another door with an opaque glass window protected by elaborate black metal scrollwork. Before he could knock, the door opened and a woman beckoned us inside.

There were extravagant embraces and a flurry of rapid Italian between Paolo and Signora Renzini before he stepped back to introduce us to each other. She was as bronzed and gleaming as the brass plate that announced her business, formidably coiffed and dressed but with a warmth that softened the professionally hard edges and an energetic, enthusiastic manner that I liked.

She led us through a large room that seemed more like the *salone* of someone with impeccable taste and unlimited funds than the traditionally overcrowded antique shops I was used to, a room rich with walnut, mahogany, and fruitwood, lightened by pale oriental rugs in tones of apricot and rose and smelling pleasantly of lemon oil, wax, and camphor. Behind it, through another door, was a storage room crammed with tables, chairs, cabinets, and desks in varying states of repair. Signora Renzini went over to a heavy, battered-looking walnut cabinet, unlocked it, and opened a small safe inside.

"First, I will show you how to use these." She dangled a large bunch of keys from the crook of one finger. The fingernail was lacquered bright red. "Then we will look at some locks."

We were able to tell her roughly the period of Stillitano's desk, and I remembered that the lock of his office door was the same type as mine, although no key but his own would fit it. Then we set to work.

By the end of the afternoon I learned to distinguish among a confusing array of modern locks and was able to judge with a reasonable degree of accuracy the skeleton key to use on each. The office door, Signora Renzini told me, would probably be a fairly simple matter. But because the desk was older, it would likely prove far more difficult, and if the skeleton keys did not work on it I would have to use one or a number of the picklocks she had in her collection. We spent a long time practicing with these instruments until, to my surprise, I became quite deft in manipulating the locks on which I was working, probably because in my own work I was used to managing tools that resembled them. And, again because of my work, I had the requisite steady hand and sure touch.

Somehow it seemed appropriate, despite a strangely unreal quality, to spend a Sunday afternoon in the city of Machiavelli and the Medici pursuing one of the fundamental Italian pastimes—intrigue.

"You learn quickly," Signora Renzini told me when we'd done all we could and I said it was time to catch my train. "If luck is with you, I think you have a fair chance of success." She smiled at me, and her eyes were ironic.

"I'm very grateful for all you have done," I told her. "I'll have the keys and picklocks back to you by next weekend."

"Agreed. Then good-bye, and good luck." She opened the door into the foyer, we slipped out, and it closed behind us with a brisk click.

Paolo drove me to the station. We said very little to each other on the way except to skirt around the question of my great adventure with some talk of when would be the best time to try my luck. Paolo thought that very night, because it was Sunday and my skills were fresh, but I was more inclined to Tuesday night, Carnevale; there would be noise and confusion from the celebrations, and it was unlikely anyone would work late.

"You'll call me when you've done it?" he asked as we walked along the platform to the train.

"If I can. Otherwise, I'll have my lawyer call you."

We said good-bye and embraced, Paolo looking very grim by this time. I was even more reluctant to leave the comfort of his company to embark on a course I felt had chosen me rather than the other way around. But I pretended to a bravery I was far from feeling and made a *V* for victory as I waved to Paolo from the window of my compartment. He turned the sign into its less polite, and more common, version, shouting, "And that's for Stillitano!" I sank down onto the seat, trying not to think, as the train took me back to Rome.

CHAPTER
10

When I got back from Florence late that night, Clara Palmieri was waiting for me. As soon as my footsteps echoed on the stairs she came out of her apartment. "At last," she said. "I was beginning to grow anxious about you, *cara*. Gianni told me what happened last night."

I smiled at her. "Did you think I'd vanished just because of Nick Taliaferro?"

The parentheses around her mouth deepened as she laughed. "But of course not. No woman runs away from a man as attractive as that one. But I wondered . . ."

"I went to Florence for the day, to see Paolo Flacco."

"Yes? And how is our good monk?"

"In fine form. And shortly to be relieved of his vows. Beatrice's father has consented to the wedding."

"My faith in miracles is restored!" Then her smile died away, and she said, "May we talk a little, *cara?*"

Although the sight of Clara was, as always, a pleasure and a stimulus, almost a promise that she would help me forget my problems, I wanted the solitude of my own apartment, where I could sit down and try to figure out a way to put my questionable new talents to work with the least possible risk to myself. But I came downstairs to her and said yes, of course we could talk.

She touched my arm. "You look worried, Kate. What I have to tell you may add to that, and if so, I am sorry."

I thought bleakly of straws and camels' backs but told myself philosophically that any worry compared to those I already had would seem insignificant.

She drew me down to sit beside her on the stairs, tucking her skirt up under her, then smoothing it out again around her legs. Irrelevantly, and with a trace of envy, I noticed that, as with everything Clara wore, the skirt managed to be both chic and sensuous, made of a thin, diaphanous material—lozenges of red, purple, and blue—that flickered under the yellow light of the hallway as it rippled around her. The shifting colors mesmerized me.

Clara seemed nervous; her fingers plucked at the cloth of the skirt, and she watched me anxiously as she spoke. "Nick is inside with Gianni. They want to talk to you."

I made no reply apart from a noncommittal murmur that I hoped sounded more indifferent than I felt.

"They would like to explain to you what they're doing. And why Nick felt he couldn't tell you at once."

"Gianni doesn't have to justify his stories to me, Clara."

"He knows that. He wants you to understand, that's all. Now that Nick has told him why he has been investigating Alessandro Torreleone, Gianni's worried. He knows you're working for the Torreleones. And that you like them."

"So it *is* Alessandro." I felt no surprise, merely a dull acceptance of the fact, the confirmation of my guess. "Why?"

"Let Nick tell you. I think you should listen to him, Kate.

138

Although it might not be pleasant to hear." Her voice was as anxious now as her face.

I put my arm around her shoulders; she was soft, and I could smell the light perfume she always wore, the jasmine that reminded me of summer. There was comfort in the simple contact with her, and I sat like that for a while before saying, "I'm tougher than I look, Clara."

She smiled, but her voice remained serious. "You're fond of Alessandro?" she asked me gently.

"Yes."

She sighed. "Well, they may be wrong, Nick and Gianni. Nothing is proved yet." But her voice told me differently. They had persuaded Clara, and, inexplicably, I felt betrayed.

I got wearily to my feet. "All right, I'll listen to them. But they'll have to be very persuasive to make me believe that Alessandro's done anything wrong." This, I knew, was as much for my benefit as for hers; I could feel my doubts beneath the bravado of the words.

We stood facing each other, Clara's hand resting on the handle of the door. She said, "Gianni trusts Nick. And I like him, too. He told me the story of how you met. So he's the mysterious American you described yesterday."

"And do you remember what I said about him? About all those barriers he puts up?"

"Yes, and I do see what you mean. But I think you may have made a dent in them, *cara*." With that enigmatic pronouncement, she turned and opened the door.

Inside, we found Gianni sprawled across the shaggy white rug, his head propped on a pile of cushions, filling his pipe from a tobacco jar on the floor beside him. He was talking to Nick, who stood by the window looking out into the darkness. When Gianni saw me, he got clumsily to his feet, still talking, the words directed now at me. Nick turned around with the briefest of nods to me, saying nothing. His face was a blank.

At once Clara became the good hostess, urging us all to sit down, pouring a glass of wine for me, easing the tension with her usual grace. Finally, when we were more or less comfortably settled—with the exception of Nick, who remained standing by the window—I said, "Just tell me what you believe, Gianni, please. About Alessandro Torreleone."

Gianni looked at Nick again. "I think you should tell her. You've done the work on it after all."

Nick didn't answer right away. He lit a cigarette; the match flared, and for a moment I could smell the sharpness of sulphur in the air. A thin plume of smoke rose lazily to the ceiling. I watched Nick's reflection in the window behind him, blocks of light and dark, and wondered how he managed to look at once so solid and so shadowy. Slowly, almost reluctantly, he said, "All right. Since Gianni feels you ought to know, Kate . . ." Making it abundantly clear that he did not.

"I told you that my sister died. But I didn't tell you how." He was looking at me now, and I took a sip of wine, distraction from his cold stare. "One night last November she fell—or was pushed—onto the tracks of the Metropolitana." The Roman subway. I opened my mouth to speak, but he went on, "It was rush hour, the platform was crowded, but no one clearly saw it happen. Suddenly she screamed, and then she was on the tracks. Then the train hit her."

He turned back to the window, the unsmoked cigarette dangling from his hand. I looked over at Clara, who was biting on her lip, but neither she nor Gianni said anything. And I could not.

"A woman who'd been standing beside my sister told the police that she thought Susanna might have been with a man— that there was, at any rate, a man right behind her, and this woman had the impression his arm was around Susanna's waist. But it was so crowded she couldn't be sure. And she didn't remember anything of the way he looked. Anyway, no one came forward to say they'd been with Susanna. For a while the police thought it might be suicide, but there was no evidence to support that. In the end, they had to call it an accident.

"When I came to Rome for Susanna's funeral, my mother told me that my sister had been mixed up with a radical group. My mother knew very little about them. Susanna wouldn't talk

140

about them much except to say that they were struggling for workers' rights. Just like dozens of others. My mother did know the name of the group, however. They call themselves Studenti per l'Operaio, Students for the Working Man. The usual presumptuous misnomer," he added sardonically.

As he said the name, I remembered that big white placard dancing above the mob before it was dropped, abandoned by Daniella, onto the cobblestones. Studenti per l'Operaio. That was the slogan scrawled across it in crimson letters three feet high.

Nick went on. "My mother told me that Susanna had an affair with a man she worked for which ended badly. She fell out with this man and with Studenti per l'Operaio at about the same time." He paused, smoking his cigarette. He was still looking straight at me. "Susanna was a clerk at the Treasury. The man was Alessandro Torreleone."

I didn't look away; as calmly as I could, I asked him how he could be sure of that.

"In the beginning Susanna talked about it quite freely with my mother; they were always very close. But later, in the weeks before she died, Susanna changed. My mother said she seemed a different person, secretive, almost frightened, but she refused to tell my mother what the trouble was. Eventually though, one night, she admitted that she'd decided to leave Studenti per l'Operaio. She wouldn't say why. And she told my mother that she and Torreleone had broken up over a dispute at work. She'd done some routine checking on the figures for a currency trans- action between an Italian company and its foreign subsidiary—a transaction Torreleone had approved—and found that the fig- ures didn't add up. She didn't go into details because my mother wouldn't have understood them, but she did say that when she went to Torreleone about it he said he would look into it, and he took the file away with him for several days. When he returned it, he told Susanna that he couldn't find any inconsist- encies. Susanna checked again and saw he was right, but she was sure that the figures had been changed. She confronted Torreleone, but he told her to forget it. She said he was very pleasant about it—no threats, nothing crude—but it was clear she was to keep quiet about it. And that was the end of their affair. A few days later she died." He walked over to the coffee table and stubbed out his cigarette in an ashtray.

"When my mother first told me, I didn't know anything about Alessandro Torreleone, not even the gossip. And I'd never heard of Studenti per l'Operaio. So I did a little research. It was all very interesting, but the most interesting fact of all was the name of another member of the unpleasant little group my sister had belonged to—"

"Daniella Nerone," I said quietly, before Nick could go on. "Alessandro's cousin."

I'm ashamed to confess that I was pleased with the look on their faces, the same look of astonishment. Both Gianni and Clara spoke at the same time, but Nick interrupted them. "How the hell did you know that?"

I didn't answer him. Part of me longed to comfort him for the sadness that lay behind his story, but another part, the worse half, wanted to be as hard as he was, as cold and unapproachable, and to hold a few cards of my own. Why, I thought nastily, should he have all the surprises?

The worse half won. "Why don't you tell me the rest of your story first."

He shrugged. "All right. I'll give you the simple facts. You can put them together any way you like." As he sat down on the long red sofa, he looked, if anything, even more remote, and although I felt sorry for him I put my sympathy away. It was plain he didn't need it.

"I'd worked with Gianni a couple of times in the past," he began. "After my sister died, he came to me with this Free-mason story. He needed help with some of the international and financial ramifications. As it sounded interesting and as I wanted to stay in Rome until I'd learned more about my sister's involvement with Studenti per l'Operaio, I agreed to do what I could. After a little digging, whose name should turn up but Torreleone's, in connection with the leader of Mestola Rossa. So I dug some more.

"For a start, I looked at his job at the Treasury. I discovered that, among other things, he okays the loans Italian companies make to their foreign subsidiaries. He checks the paperwork, and makes sure everything conforms to government regulations before the request goes on for its final Treasury approval, a rubber stamp once Torreleone has passed it along. In other words, he's in the perfect position to control one way of getting money out of the country legally. And that's something almost every rich Italian longs to do.

"According to our sources, Torreleone rose remarkably swiftly through the ranks of civil servants to his present position—a position that makes him very useful to powerful people. Gianni and I think we know how he did it. The name of one man turns up at every important point in his career, a man who appears to be his patron. That man is the head of Mestola Rossa. Torreleone's probably a member of the order himself, though we don't have proof for that yet, just hearsay."

Nick leaned forward to pick up his glass, and the room was silent for a moment. After a sip of wine, he went on. "Another fact. He has known two women in the same radical group. Why would he entangle himself with leftists when he's so right wing himself? Curious, don't you think?"

Suddenly I didn't want to hear any more; and the sympathy on Clara's face was almost more than I could bear. I said, much too sarcastically, "Well, he can hardly help the fact that he's Daniella's cousin. And maybe he has a thing for revolutionaries. Maybe all that finance gets so dull that he longs for a little vicarious adventure. Just like reporters who go off to cover foreign wars or create great mysteries where none exist to fill some gap in their own lives." Immediately, I felt ashamed. "I'm sorry, Gianni. I didn't mean you." But I found it impossible to apologize to Nick.

It didn't seem to touch him, though. "Maybe you're right" was all he said. His face was heavy, and the eyes gave nothing away.

Gianni stepped in. "Kate, you must understand. We are certain that Torreleone has been helping certain companies vio-

143

late currency regulations. We are close to proving it. And we know that he is mixed up somehow with this bunch of crazy leftists. This is not fantasy or coincidence." His voice lowered, grew somber. "Beyond that, Nick's sister found him out, and now she's dead."

"So you've decided he's guilty of murder, too?" I could have bitten my tongue, but Nick was sitting with his head back against the sofa cushions, his eyes closed, and he did not visibly react; perhaps he hadn't heard. "I'm sorry. But you seem to have constituted yourselves judge, jury, and hangman, all in one."

Gianni made a spluttering sound and sank back onto the pile of cushions on the floor. The room seemed much too hot and filled with smoke, and my head was aching. I rubbed at my forehead and wondered why it was so hard for me to accept what I was hearing.

Slowly, as though he were talking to a recalcitrant child, Nick began again, looking up at the ceiling as he spoke. "We know this: Torreleone was once famous for his debts—they don't seem to be a problem for him any longer. He has a job that puts him in a position to help the rich get their money out of the country. He has links with an extreme right-wing organization. He also has links with a Marxist revolutionary group. Make of it what you will."

"Let me put it another way," I replied evenly. "He has reformed and is now a conscientious government official cursed with a taste for revolutionary types. Like a lot of other Italians at his level in society, he has friends with questionable political leanings." But this was hardly a convincing portrait, given all that they, and I, knew about Alessandro. Doggedly, I went on. "I'm so sorry about your sister's death, Nick. It's horrible. And I can understand why you'd want to believe the worst of Alessandro if you think he made her unhappy and if she seemed a threat to him. But . . ." I stopped, uncertain what to say in the face of his silence. There seemed nothing left to say.

We had failed to convince each other, though they had left me with enough doubts to taint whatever it was that I felt for

Alessandro. Oddly, however, it wasn't Alessandro I worried about; he was so obviously someone who could look after himself. It was Count Massimo. If Nick and Gianni's accusations were even partly true and Alessandro was exposed, it would undoubtedly hurt him badly, a man who once had suffered from his father and now faced the disgrace of his son. These thoughts followed of their own accord, and it was only after I was well on the way to blaming Alessandro for his father's unhappiness that I saw I was implicitly accepting Nick and Gianni's version of the facts. I dug in my heels then, partly out of sheer contrariness.

"What do you want me to do? Spy on the Torreleone family for you?"

"Not at all," Gianni replied, scratching his beard as though it irritated him. All at once he looked exhausted. Clara came to sit on the floor beside him, linking her arm through his. "Simply be careful, Kate. That's all we ask. But if you notice anything out of the ordinary, we'd like to know."

Out of the ordinary! I wanted to laugh, but the expression on Gianni's face kept me serious. Everything about the Torreleones was out of the ordinary. How in heaven's name would I know what to look for? I sat back and thought of all the mysterious, and downright frightening, things that I'd encountered since I began to work for them just over a week ago: the forged Reni, Daniella's connection with the ominous Marco, Alessandro's with Stillitano.

I was dizzy with fatigue—it was an awful hour for this discussion, anyway—and confused by all that I did and did not know. Suddenly it was too much for me. I longed to tell Clara and Gianni—even Nick, for all his provoking aloofness—everything, to lay the whole burden down at their feet, just as I'd done for part of it with Faltecchi and Paolo. And why not? After all, I trusted Clara and Gianni, and they trusted Nick. I remembered Paolo's words to me that afternoon, his advice to find someone to help me. Stillitano, he had said, was too much to take on alone.

I looked up to find three pairs of eyes on me, all weary, two imploring, and the third, Nick's, with a puzzled cast to them I didn't understand. Playing for time, I asked them to tell me more about Mestola Rossa. "I know that men like Thomas Jefferson and Tolstoy were Masons, so the Masons can't always have been sinister. They've had a reasonably honorable past, haven't they?"

"Certainly," Gianni replied. "Like the Mafia. No, I mean it. Once upon a time—it seems like a fairy tale, I admit—the Mafia began as the Robin Hoods of Sicily, to help the poor against local tyrants. That didn't last long."

Nick said, "Be fair, Gianni. Most Masonic lodges are harmless enough. Some do good—"

"Admitted," Gianni said. "In fact, in the nineteenth century here in Italy, Kate, the Masons represented freedom and enlightenment. Garibaldi was a Mason, too. No wonder the Church feared and hated them."

"And they hated the Church," Clara told me. "Did you know that you can see St. Peter's from almost everywhere in Rome, if only the dome, but not from the Prati quarter? Because Prati was designed by Masons. They turned their back on St. Peter's."

"But the Italian Masons changed at the beginning of this century," Gianni went on. "They lost some of their idealism and became more interested in promoting the political and financial fortunes of their members. When Mussolini came to power, he banned the Masons—a real compliment—because he felt that they'd become a state within a state. In fact, he made it illegal to belong to any secret society. That law is still on the books. It isn't illegal any longer to be a Mason, only to have a secret Masonic lodge."

"Which is precisely what Mestola Rossa is," Nick said. He stretched and got to his feet again, rubbing the back of his neck with one hand as he spoke. "Its leader insists on secrecy. He even keeps the members from knowing each other unless it serves his purposes. It isn't that all the members are up to no good; many have probably joined because it's the way to get ahead," he added, echoing Clara's words when Gianni had first told me about Mestola Rossa. "Patronage has a long history in Italy, right back to the Romans. But it's pretty clear that others are using it for different ends. There are men who fear socialism like the plague, who'll do anything to keep it from spreading here in Italy. And democracy has no great charm for them, either."

"And you think Alessandro Torreleone is one of them?" I asked him. He only shrugged. But I didn't really need his answer. Alessandro's words echoed in my ears: The freedom you grant one individual should not necessarily be given to all, and something more about enlightened tyrannies. It was all too plausible. I went a step further and forced myself to acknowledge that Alessandro had kissed me because I knew about the Reni. He was afraid of what I might do with that knowledge; he needed me on his side. Bitterly, I remembered his saying that he wanted someone who could not be used by him.

I had the catalyst I needed for my story.

"You're looking at a potential burglar and thief," I began, "so I'm hardly in a position to judge Alessandro for what he may or may not have done." I stopped, brought up short by the delight on Clara's face.

"Go on, Scheherazade," she urged. "The night is still young."

I laughed for the first time. "You haven't looked at your watch lately. And even if the night is young, *I* feel at least a hundred." Turning to Gianni, whose face was as startled as Nick's, I said, "Scheherazade told her stories to save herself. Maybe that's why I'm going to tell you mine. You asked for my help, but I need you more than you need me."

"Anything you want, Kate. You know that." Gianni reached up and gave my knee an affectionate squeeze. All was forgiven; I was back in his good graces again.

"Wait till you hear what it is. You're allowed to change your mind." But I was grateful for his immediate response; Nick hadn't said a word. "There's such a lot to tell you, I hardly know where to start. But"—and here I looked at Nick—"I think you were my first hint that all was not well with the Torreleones. You seemed to want something from me that could only have to do with them."

"Not only," I thought I heard him say under his breath, but it was followed so quickly by what he said next that I couldn't be sure. "I was afraid I'd been less than subtle," he said ruefully, and added, almost as an afterthought, "But you know, Kate, I never lied to you. It's true that I didn't tell you what I was up to. But we barely knew each other after all, and—"

"It wasn't that so much," I said, "as the feeling that you were using me to get information. And would have gone on if Gianni hadn't come along and spoiled things for you."

"It wasn't just my story to tell," he said. "I had no idea you were a friend of Gianni's and knew some of it anyway. And I wasn't sure how you'd react to the knowledge that I was investigating the Torreleones. After all, you made it plain that you liked Massimo, and just look how you've risen to his son's defense."

Something in the way he said this, the hint of something other than simple annoyance at my disbelief of his and Gianni's allegations against Alessandro, made me wonder—and then feel absurdly pleased. "So you didn't intend to pry information out of me about Alessandro?"

"Okay, Kate, I'll be completely honest with you. Meeting you like that was a godsend. I'd wondered what your connection with the Torreleones was. I'd seen you coming and going at the palazzo." So he had been using the Bar Tiberina as a vantage point. "And I knew about Alessandro's weakness for beautiful women."

He grinned at me, and I felt myself flushing. Damn him, I thought resentfully, why does he inevitably make me feel this way?

"But," he continued, "once I realized you didn't know him, I let that idea go." What "that idea" was he didn't say, but I could guess. "You know, I enjoyed last night." His voice was very low. He was standing close to my chair now, looking down at me as he took a packet of cigarettes from his pocket and lit one. "And it had nothing to do with the Torreleones."

Uncomfortably aware of Clara and Gianni's amused interest—they were silent during this exchange—I said awkwardly, "Where was I? Oh yes—has Clara told you about the demonstration I got caught in? And what happened afterward?" When he shook his head, I went on to describe what I'd seen and heard, finishing with a deliberately dramatic pause. "There's one thing I didn't tell Clara and Gianni. The name of that girl."

But Nick was there before I could say it. "Daniella Nerone."

"*Madonna!*" Gianni sat bolt upright.

"There's nothing the least bit saintly about her," I said. "Or virginal, either. The only thing I've been able to find in her favor is her affection for her uncle. Anyway, she's up to her ears in something dubious, though to do her justice I'm not sure how willing she is. I've met the awful Marco . . ." I told them first about my encounter with Daniella and the subsequent conversation in the bar with Marco, following it with a description of the motorcycle chase.

"It's my turn to say I'm sorry," I conceded to Nick. "I suppose that I was guilty of hiding things, too."

"You're forgiven," Nick said quietly. "Am I?"

I looked up at him, feeling suddenly happier, and nodded.

"Good. Next time," he added, "I'll pick you up. No more walking alone in Rome after dark." To my surprise, I did not resent the proprietary tone.

"How terrifying it must have been for you, *cara*. Why didn't you tell us?" Clara asked me.

"I haven't had the chance. I still can't believe all this has happened so quickly."

Gianni was cleaning and refilling his pipe, carefully packing the tobacco into the bowl. He looked across at Nick. "So this Marco is another member of Susanna's group?"

"Yes. His last name's Gatti. The name was on the list that Cucchi gave us. I've been trying to find out exactly what his relationship with Susanna was. A friend of mine has been checking into it for me."

I broke in, confused. "What list, and who's Cucchi?"

"A man I know in the state security division of the *carabinieri*," Gianni told me. "He investigates radical groups like Studenti per l'Operaio. Cucchi has been a good source in the past, so I asked him if he had anything on them, and he produced a folderful. Nothing in it for which they could be prosecuted but enough to make them interesting to the police."

"Gatti had his own folder," Nick added. "He's not what he seems. At least not what Daniella and her buddies probably think he is. He's been in prison a couple of times—for criminal, not revolutionary, activities. Car theft, petty larceny. Once he was arrested for assault, but the charges didn't stick. The police thought the witness had been intimidated. In short, not a nice boy."

"That's putting it mildly," I said. "He's like a time bomb waiting to go off and quite happy to take everyone along with him."

Gianni puffed on his pipe, then said reflectively, "I wonder if Torreleone knows him?"

"He can't possibly," I said. "He'd never let Daniella get mixed up with someone like Marco. He really seems fond of her."

Nick ignored this. "But now Gatti thinks you're interested in joining Studenti per l'Operaio, Kate?"

"I'm afraid so. I was trying to play detective with Daniella, but it backfired. I certainly didn't want to get involved with Marco, too. That was pure bad luck." And sheer silliness on my part, I added to myself. "But there's more besides Marco and Daniella. They are really the least of my worries. There's the Reni, you see, and all those other forgeries. And now Stillitano's trying to get rid of me—"

"Whoa," Nick said. "Back up a little. You're throwing too much at us too fast. What forgeries do you mean? And who the hell is Stillitano?"

So I began again, more slowly, going over the ground for the third time, but this time leaving nothing out. I started with the Reni *Madonna and Child*, avoiding Nick's eyes as I told them that Alessandro had admitted it was not the original and his reasons why. I'd just reached the overheard conversation between Faltecchi and Stillitano and Faltecchi's threat to end his partnership with Stillitano because of his suspicions when I began to cough. My throat was very dry, and I felt intolerably thirsty. I asked Clara for some water.

She made us promise not to go on until she returned. While she was gone, there was a companionable silence; Gianni smoked his pipe, Nick paced the room, thinking. He paused once to smile at me, the seductive smile that took my breath away.

As Clara came back into the room with my glass of water, I heard a faint ringing. It took me a moment to recognize what it was. When I did, I jumped up. "That's my phone. I'd better go answer it. I'll be right back."

Why would anyone be calling at this hour? I wondered as I took the hall stairs two at a time. I unlocked the door and raced across to the telephone. *"Pronto?"*

"Signora Roy?" A woman's voice, thin, somewhat shrill, came down the wire. "I am sorry to disturb you at such a time of the night, but it is urgent. You must come at once—"

"Who is this, please?" There was a barely controlled hysteria in the woman's voice that frightened me; I tried to make my own as calm as I could in response.

Perhaps it helped; when we spoke again, she sounded slightly more in control. "This is Elsa Faltecchi, Giorgio Faltecchi's daughter. My father . . . Oh Signora Roy, it is terrible, what has happened to him. He is very badly hurt. The doctors say . . ." But she got no further, for she began to weep.

I was too stunned to speak. I stood there with the receiver pressed hard against my ear, listening to Elsa Faltecchi cry, unable to take in what she had told me. Finally, I forced some words out. "Please, Signora Faltecchi . . . I'm so sorry . . . Please tell me what's happened. Will he be all right?"

Between shuddering sobs she told me that her father had been attacked, presumably by a mugger, earlier in the evening. "He was unconscious, and at first we thought—but now, it is better, he can speak a little. He is not really awake, and what he says makes no sense. . . . Only your name—he says that over and over. You must come, Signora Roy. As quickly as you can."

"Of course I'll come. Right away. Tell him I'm coming."

She was so distraught by this time that it was only with

difficulty that I managed to get the name and address of the hospital out of her before she began sobbing again. I mumbled some inadequate words of comfort and hung up.

I ran back downstairs to the Palmieri apartment. Nick was talking to Gianni and Clara, who had their backs to me as I rushed into the room. When he saw my face, he stopped abruptly. "What's wrong?"

"It's Giorgio Faltecchi. Someone attacked him. He's in the hospital. That was his daughter on the phone. She says he's been asking for me. I've got to go right away."

"I'll take you," Nick said immediately. "My car's just outside."

At that moment, awakened by the noise, the Palmieris' daughter, Cecilia, came into the room, sleepily rubbing her eyes and demanding to know what all the fuss was about. Clara gave me a swift hug and then went over to soothe Cecilia. Gianni came with us to the front door.

"Would you like me to come too, Kate?" he asked with concern.

"Thanks, Gianni, but there's no point. You might as well get some sleep. I'll see you and Clara in the morning."

He put his arm around me. *"Coraggio."*

I nodded—I couldn't speak—and went with Nick down the walk to his car.

CHAPTER
11

There were few other cars on the road—it was almost three in the morning—and Nick drove so expertly, with the concentration and skill Paolo had so notably lacked, that I would have enjoyed the ride at any other time but this. I was desperately frightened by Elsa's obvious fear that her father would die, equally frightened by suspicions growing in the fertile soil of my fear.

But I blessed the Maserati's power and speed. We shot across the river over the Ponte Savoia and headed northeast on the Lungotevere, the main road that runs along the Tiber. When Nick shifted into high gear, the car surged up the straightaway. Lights on the opposite bank of the river streamed past in a ribboned blur.

Up in the winding curves of the Gianicolo Nick had been

silent, although once he'd reached across and briefly touched my hand, but when we gained the bridge he asked me if I would mind finishing the story I'd begun in the Palmieris' apartment. "If you can stand to talk about it right now?"

"I'd be glad of the distraction." So I went on with the story. I described how Stillitano had found me in the workrooms after his confrontation with Faltecchi and taken me back to his office for his own particular brand of advice. "He said he has a friend with a villa near Palermo who needs a conservator for a long-term project, one that would take me out of Rome for several months." I managed a wry smile. "In those immortal words, he made me an offer I can't refuse."

"Which was?"

"To take the commission and make myself scarce. Or lose my working papers. He claims he has powerful friends who could arrange it for him."

"Charming. Did he say who his friend in Palermo was?"

"A man with a major collection of art, though I'd never heard of him. I think the name was Bassi, Pietro Bassi—"

Nick gave a low whistle. I turned to him in surprise. "Do you know him, Nick?"

"Yes. Or rather, I know who he is. He collects more than paintings."

In the silence that followed this cryptic statement I could hear the swish of the car's tires on the road beneath us, then the sudden shift of gears as Nick slowed to go around a ramshackle old pickup truck rocking along under its load of even more disreputable looking furniture. Once we were safely ahead of the truck, I turned expectantly to Nick.

In an unemotional, deliberate voice he said, "Pietro Bassi is the head of Mestola Rossa." He let that sink in before adding, "He's guilty of God knows how many crimes, but always indirectly of course—he's a clever son of a bitch. So far, no one's been able to touch him. Bassi's known to have Mafia links, too. If Stillitano is passing you along to him, he wants you out of the way all right. Maybe permanently. Bassi would have no problem disposing of one troublesome conservator."

"My God, Nick! How melodramatic." But his tone had been as cool as the night wind coming in at my window.

"Not at all. A number of people who crossed Bassi in one way or another have come to an unhappy end. One unfortunate man was appointed by the Bank of Italy to look into some of Bassi's more questionable financial dealings and saw too much. He was shot to death in front of his house one morning on his way to work. And there have been others. . . . There's no proof to link Bassi directly, needless to say, but— The question is, why should you be such a threat?"

"I wish I knew." I was shivering again, with more than the cool air rushing past. But as much as I disliked Stillitano and as frightening as he'd seemed during those final moments in his office, I couldn't believe that he would go so far as to have me "disposed of." Then I thought of Faltecchi, and no longer felt so sure.

Those insidious suspicions were spreading. If Nick was right, Stillitano must be worried about more than my knowledge of the forged Reni. After all, Alessandro himself had commissioned it, and of the two of them, that made Alessandro technically the guiltier if Stillitano could prove he believed he was simply making a copy. How could I be any threat? It was more Alessandro's problem than Stillitano's. No, there had to be some other danger in my knowing that Stillitano had forged the Reni.

And then I remembered Nick's allegation that the leader of Mestola Rossa was Alessandro's patron. I'd wondered about the link between Alessandro and Stillitano, how Alessandro knew Stillitano would make a forgery, what precisely their connection was, and here was my answer. The connection, the sinister link, was Bassi. I watched the houses flick past as I tried to sort out the implications of this unpleasant fact.

By now we were threading through streets that led over to the chic Parioli quarter of the city, the quarter where Faltecchi lived. The hospital to which he'd been taken wasn't far off.

Uneasily, I said to Nick, "I've just realized something."

"Oh yes?"

"It's still jumbled in my mind, and I'm not sure what to make of it yet, but if Stillitano, Bassi, and Alessandro all know each other and if Stillitano really does want to get rid of me as permanently as you say, then Alessandro . . ." But I could not finish the thought aloud.

At first Nick said nothing, apparently concentrating on the road ahead. Then, in a bitten-off voice emptied of emotion, he said, "I'm sorry. I know how you feel about Torreleone."

"Do you? Then you know more than I do." I couldn't keep the anger out of my voice. Nick's face shut down again, all the life and warmth in it since that moment in the Palmieris' apartment when I'd decided to throw my lot in with theirs quite gone. I found, with a sudden shock of knowledge, that I couldn't bear it.

Tentatively, I went on. "It isn't Alessandro so much, Nick. I hardly know him. Oh, I admit he *is* attractive, and I'm hoping he isn't what we think he is. But for his father's sake, not mine. I'm fond of Count Massimo, and I know he'll be badly hurt if he finds out his son has done what you say. But I'm not on Alessandro's side, whatever you may think."

"It's really not my business, Kate."

"Isn't it?" I asked him bravely. "Then I'm sorry you care so little."

"Christ! If you knew—" Nick began, but suddenly we were at the hospital gates and he had to stop to speak to the *portiere* on duty in the little lodge by the entrance.

There was a parking lot close by the main door. We got out of the car without another word to each other and spent the next few minutes untangling a confusion of directions as we were told first to go to Emergency, only to be informed there by a tired nurse whose shift was ending that she knew of no Giorgio Faltecchi admitted that evening. Then, as we were turning away in search of someone more helpful, she called out that, yes, on second thought she remembered that he'd been transferred to Intensive Care.

156

"Third floor. The elevator is straight ahead." Wearily, she turned to deal with a well-dressed drunk whose demands that he be treated at once were growing simultaneously louder and less comprehensible.

When we came out of the elevator, I saw Elsa Faltecchi at the far end of the corridor talking to a white-jacketed man, presumably the doctor. She slumped against the wall, shaking her head a little at whatever he was telling her. When he finished, he patted her arm briskly and left her, passing us with a nod. Elsa's pale face was haggard with worry. Then she saw me and started forward to meet us.

In Elsa, Giorgio Faltecchi's calm, assured certainty and focused energy were unhappily translated into a stolid literalness coupled with a fussy preoccupation with the minor details of life, especially the domestic, that I usually found impossibly irritating. But tonight I felt a wave of sympathy at the sight of her suffering and a pang because she looked so much like her father. Her beautiful long-lashed green eyes were the only concession nature made to her femininity, but they were swollen now with weeping.

I introduced Nick as a friend who'd driven me to the hospital. With a genuine sympathetic warmth that surprised me until I remembered what he'd been through with his mother and sister, he told Elsa how sorry he was about her father, then excused himself, saying he would go in search of coffee for us. Before I could ask Elsa any questions, she began, apologetically, "I am sorry you have had to come all this way, Signora Roy. My father is no longer conscious. I tried to call you to tell you that you need not come, but I was too late. Papa was conscious for only a little after I spoke with you, and he said nothing more. I am sorry."

I touched her arm gently. "I would have wanted to come, anyway. I'm glad you called me, Signora Faltecchi." I used the respectful "signora" rather than the more youthful "signorina," despite her single state, because we were always very formal with each other and because, although she wasn't much older than I, she already seemed resolutely middle-aged.

"Is there somewhere we can sit down?" I asked her. "I know you must be exhausted, but I'd be grateful if you would tell me what happened to your father."

"Of course." She led me to a small alcove with several shabby and uncomfortable-looking chairs and a low table littered with newspapers and magazines. The corridor stretched away, empty and silent. As we sat down, I asked her if she'd had to deal with everything herself.

No, she replied, her sister and brother-in-law had only just gone home, and a friend of her father, a man who lived in the apartment next to theirs, had come to the hospital with them. He was the one who'd frightened off the man attacking her father. The police, too, had been and gone.

"My father went out," she told me, "as he does every evening, for a walk before bed. He likes to take scraps from the dinner to the cats that live in the park near us. Papa—" Her voice broke, and she wiped the corners of her eyes with the back of one hand, like a child. "Papa loves cats, but they are such a nuisance in the house, so dirty . . . Well, as I was saying, my father's friend Professor Carbone happened to be out walking his dog. Usually he does not take the dog into the park at night out of respect for my father's time with the cats, but he thought he heard a man cry out for help. When he went into the park, he saw someone lying on the ground—at that time he did not know it was Papa—and a man bending over him. He thought the man was about to hit my father with something, so he shouted and let the dog loose. When the man saw Professor Carbone, he ran off, out of the park. Perhaps he had a motorcycle; Professor Carbone heard one start up almost at once.

"He could see that my father was badly hurt. He was bleeding from the head"—she touched her temple to show me the place—"so he put his coat around him and went for help. My father was very lucky, the doctors told us. If the blow to his head had been even this much deeper, he would have died right away. But as it is . . . Well, we have hope." She fumbled in her purse and took out a crumpled handkerchief.

"Did Professor Carbone see the man's face?"

She shook her head, raising her eyes helplessly to mine. "Of course the police asked him that, too. But it was dark. All that Professor Carbone could see was that the man was tall and wearing black, or some dark color, and he picked up something from the ground before he ran. He said it looked to him like a motorcycle helmet. Professor Carbone had the impression it was a young man, but he could not be certain. We do not even know why the man attacked Papa. Perhaps he tried to rob him and grew angry when he found my father had no money. He never has his wallet when he takes his evening walk."

It was absurd, I know, to feel that cold touch along my spine at the mere mention of a motorcycle. I told myself that in a city overrun by the wretched machines it was more than probable a mugger would use one as his means of escape. Still . . .

Aloud, I said, "And when your father asked for me, did he give you any hint as to why he wanted to see me?"

"He said only your name, several times, with such concern that we felt we must call you. I knew that he tried to reach you during the day yesterday, but again I do not know why." She spread her hands wide. "I am sorry; I wish I could tell you more. But I do not know why he wanted to speak to you."

In an effort to ease her mind about this much at least, I said, "You mustn't trouble yourself about it, Signora Faltecchi. It's probably simply something to do with our work, and I came to his mind the way these things do."

"Perhaps you are right. Once or twice he spoke of Guido Reni also, and I wondered why. There are painters he prefers to Reni. It seemed strange that he would think of that one at such a time."

I said nothing, but it occurred to me that this might well be why Faltecchi was so eager to talk to me. Perhaps, since he had no idea I already knew, he wanted to tell me that Stillitano had made the forgery, or perhaps, in a last attempt to keep his partner out of trouble, he'd decided to tell me to leave the whole matter alone.

"Your father will soon be able to tell us why he asked for me. He's strong and healthy, and I know he'll recover. I'm sure of it." I tried to sound encouraging, but inside I felt bleak and miserable. "Does Franco Stillitano know about what's happened to your father?"

"My sister telephoned earlier to his house. Apparently he is in Sicily, but he is expected to return tomorrow. Naturally Signor Stillitano will be concerned—my father's condition will make a difference to the business." Her voice was stiff with hostility.

I saw Nick coming along the corridor; he was carrying a tray with three steaming cups and a pile of rolls. "How did you manage this miracle?" I asked him, taking one of the cups of coffee and handing it to Elsa.

"I found a sympathetic nurse who'd just made a pot of coffee. She took pity on me and threw in the rolls for good measure."

I smiled up at him. "A way with barmen and now nurses," I said in English. "What next?"

"Conservators, I hope."

After we finished, Nick and I tried to persuade Elsa to let us take her home. But she was adamant; she wanted to stay at the hospital until her sister came back in the morning or until her father was out of danger. There must be, she told us firmly, some member of the family nearby should he awaken and need them. I said that I would telephone the hospital in the morning; if her father was conscious before then, she should call me, whatever the hour, and I would come right away.

Before we left, Nick found the same friendly nurse and got a pillow and blanket for Elsa. We left her curled up in the hard chair, already half-asleep.

Outside, the air was chilly, with traces of mist lying low over bushes and grass. There was that first faint lightening of the sky that signals night is ending. As he got into the car, Nick reached into the backseat and pulled out an overcoat, which he tossed into my lap. "Here, put this around you. You're shivering." I did as I was told. Once we were clear of the hospital gates, he asked me to tell him what I'd learned from Elsa about Faltecchi's attack. "For a start, how did it happen?"

I told him what Elsa had said, ending with the motorcycle. "Nick, I can't help thinking of Marco, who seems to wear nothing *but* black *and* has a motorcycle."

"But what would Marco have to do with Giorgio Faltecchi?"

"That's what I keep asking myself. And I haven't any answers. No, it must be coincidence—a grim coincidence."

"Did Signora Faltecchi tell you why her father was asking for you?"

I shook my head. "She has no idea. He lost consciousness again shortly after she called me. But there is one clue: apparently he mentioned the Reni, too, or rather said the name Reni, so I'm assuming he meant the Torreleone painting. It was obviously on his mind." I pulled Nick's coat more tightly around me. "I'm so tired, and it's all so confusing. But oh God, if anything happens to Faltecchi, if he dies ..." Before I could prevent them, I felt tears on my cheeks. I was rooting in my purse for something to dry them with when Nick held out his own handkerchief. "Thanks," I said in a muffled voice as I blew into it. "I'm sorry, but tonight's been such hell."

"I know. But the nurse I talked to said Faltecchi has a good chance of surviving. They got to him in time, and he's in good shape for a man his age. So keep your courage up." His tone was matter-of-fact, and it cured my tears, though the glance that accompanied the words made up for the lack of sympathy in the voice.

I leaned back against the seat and closed my eyes. I was slipping into a drugged half-sleep when Nick spoke again. "You know, there's another nasty aspect to this business you haven't considered. Or perhaps you have ... ?"

I opened my eyes. "What's that?"

"Franco Stillitano. Doesn't it strike you as odd that immediately after he and Faltecchi have their argument and Faltecchi accuses him of making forgeries, Stillitano offers you that commission with Bassi, *and* Faltecchi is attacked?"

"Yes, I've been thinking about that," I said slowly, "but they've been partners for years, and Stillitano always seemed fond of Faltecchi."

161

"Do you think he's a dangerous man? One who could conceivably hate you so much he'd want to get you completely out of the way? And might feel that way about others, too?"

Reluctantly, I said, "Yes, yes, and yes. But murder? I just don't know. It seems fantastic."

"Then let's just say it's a distinct possibility. And since Faltecchi was eager to talk to you, presumably about the Reni, it makes sense to guess he'd discovered something, something that might have meant disaster for Stillitano. Or danger for you."

I admitted that the same thought had occurred to me, and then, because of the cold and an intense weariness, I yawned and snuggled farther down into Nick's overcoat. My hands were chilled, so I found the pockets of the coat and thrust them well down for warmth. But at the bottom of the right hand pocket I touched metal. My hand closed over a distinctive shape. Startled, I sat up, pulling the gun out of the pocket.

"What in heaven's name is this?" As though it might go off at any moment, I held the gun gingerly away from me.

He glanced over and said, too casually, "Sorry, I forgot it was there." Opening the glove compartment, he took the gun from my hand and slipped it inside on a pile of maps. "Gianni gave it to me today."

"Why?"

"One of his contacts told him Bassi found out about our interest in his affairs and isn't pleased. Gianni thought we ought to be prepared for the worst." When he saw my face, he added, "Don't look so worried. I have no intention of using it. And no expectation of needing to. Gianni gets too worked up at times."

But I was not persuaded. "Does Clara know that Gianni's story has become so dangerous?

"She suspects. Her father's been at her to get Gianni to turn his attention somewhere else. But Clara has always kept out of Gianni's work, and she refuses to interfere despite her father—"

"But the children . . ." I protested.

"They'll be all right. After all, they have a very special

grandfather. I'm more worried about you, Kate. If we could only figure out where Stillitano comes into this—"

"I might be able to find out," I broke in. "I was going to tell you when Elsa called. Stillitano has a notebook . . ." I told him what Paolo and I suspected. "I thought if I could get my hands on it I might learn something about the forgeries. Who knows, it might even tell us what Stillitano's connection to Bassi is."

"And how do you plan to get hold of it?"

"Theft. I got some lessons in burglary yesterday." I laughed at the startled look on Nick's face. "Yes, it's true. You and Gianni aren't the only ones playing cloak and dagger." I described my day with Paolo and Signora Renzini. Slightly shame-faced, I added, "Paolo pointed out to me that I never even mentioned the police when we discussed how to deal with Stillitano. And he was right. But in my own defense I have to say that there isn't any proof to go to the police with. That's what I was hoping the notebook would give me."

I sighed, and stretched to get some of the achy tightness out of my muscles. "Everything's so murky, Nick, so . . . so confusing and impossible to be certain of. I can't prove that Marco's up to no good or that he and Daniella are actually going to commit this robbery they talked about. And I can't prove that Stillitano's involvement with Alessandro goes beyond the forgery of the Reni or that Alessandro meant any harm by it."

"On the other hand, too," Nick said quietly, "it leaves him open to blackmail from Stillitano, among other things. And vice versa, for that matter."

We were driving slowly back up onto the Gianicolo by the route I'd taken on Saturday night when I'd gone to meet Nick at the Apollonia. As we passed the park and the church, I thought of what had happened. "You know, Marco's the one who really bothers me in all of this. I remember something he said to me on Saturday night, just before I got away from him. Something that implies he knows more about me than I told him or Daniella. Or any of the Torreleones."

We pulled up in front of the Palmieris' house. When I got

163

out of the car, I could see the first streaks of dawn in the east; some of the chill was gone from the air, and there was already the promise of a beautiful day.

"What was it that Marco said?" Nick asked as we walked up the path to the front door.

"He was threatening me. He grabbed my elbow, the left one, and began to squeeze it. It was horribly painful. And then he said that it would be a pity to break it again. He did say 'again'—that was the odd part." We were climbing the stairs to my apartment, and I was whispering in order not to disturb the Palmieris or the other tenants. "When I was in college, I slipped on a patch of ice and went down on that elbow, smashing the bone. It healed pretty well—I haven't had any problem with it since except that it's always been sensitive to any sort of direct pressure. But you know, Nick, I don't think I've ever mentioned it to anyone here in Rome. . . ."

And then, as I was about to open my door, I remembered. I could only stand there, resting my forehead against the smooth paint of the door, letting the sudden memory return, the memory of that moment in the corridor when I'd bumped into Stillitano and knocked my elbow against the angle of the storeroom doorway. Stupid, stupid, I thought—how could I have forgotten?

I raised my head and said to Nick, "You'd better come in. I've just remembered who knows."

I told Nick what had happened. ". . . and I caught it right smack on the most painful part. I really let out a yell. Stillitano was shocked; it was almost comical, his reaction. Anyway, I told him why I'd overreacted. But, I'm certain I've never mentioned it to anyone else here."

Nick gave a long, low whistle. We were standing just inside the door, facing each other. "If that's the case, it means—"

"It means Stillitano knows Marco and probably sent him after me on Saturday night, and after Faltecchi, too, I'll bet. I knew I was right to be suspicious of that man in black with his damned motorcycle. It was Marco; it had to be." Abruptly, I stopped. My nerves were jumping with tiny shocks of electricity each time my mind touched some new possibility. But there were connections I couldn't make, and this was one of them. "How can Marco be mixed up both with Daniella *and* with Stillitano?"

Nick started to say something, thought better of it, and merely said quietly, "Perhaps the answer will be in Stillitano's notebook." Then, with sudden intensity, he added, "Look, Kate, if Stillitano did send Marco after Faltecchi in such a murderous fashion, he'll have no qualms about trying to get rid of you, too. And I'm not about to let that happen. The thought of what that bastard tried to do to you . . ."

There was a flash of that darker, rougher grain I'd sensed on our first meeting, the hint of something very like brutality under the smooth veneer. He looked so formidable that I was almost inclined to feel sorry for Marco if he should come up against Nick in such a mood. Almost, but not quite. I was, I'm ashamed to say, quite delighted I'd inspired such atavistic feelings in Nick.

Maybe something of my own feelings showed in my face— I was too tired to have much control over anything by now— because Nick took a step toward me. And I was in his arms.

CHAPTER

12

Nick wasn't gentle. But then neither was I. I found a blessed release from doubt, however momentary, in the certainty of his mouth hard against mine, the certainty of desire—as though I knew him now as vulnerable, if only through the senses, and could let my own defenses down.

He said my name once, tenderly, almost with surprise. I felt his grip soften, become more kind; it was as if whatever had broken free from his will was once more under its control. He traced the outlines of my face, moving his fingers lightly across my flesh in the first tentative motions of discovery.

I closed my eyes and stood before him with my head tilted back, angled to trap his hand between my cheek and shoulder. I could hear the faint ticking of his wristwatch and somewhere, like an echo, bells tolling the hour. Then I looked up at him.

The smile was in his eyes, shadowy, remote, before it reached his mouth—a half-tender, half-mocking smile. He said, "I should go."

"No, stay."

"Sure?"

"Yes."

He kissed me with more tenderness than he'd shown before, holding my face cupped in his hand, gazing down at me. I felt the catechism of his look, my own questions turned back on me, but I said nothing, wondering if he would find the answers in my face. Perhaps he did, for he said, "There are some lines of Eliot's I've always liked: '. . . the end of all our exploring, will be to arrive where we started, and know the place for the first time.' "

"And are you back where you started?"

"With a difference. This time I know where I am." He picked up a tendril of my hair and wound it around one finger, letting it spiral loose again. "You once told me you weren't sure who I really was. Remember?"

I nodded.

"And now? Do you know me better now?"

"I'm starting to." I heard the hoarseness in my voice. Impatiently, I moved my hands over the rough tweed of his jacket, up to his shoulders, and put my mouth to the hollow of his neck where his shirt lay open. On his skin I could taste the cool night air that blew against us while we were in the car.

We found the bed and lost our clothes somewhere along our stumbling way. There was a shiver of recognition as our bare flesh touched all along our bodies, the briefest moment of surprise at mingled hard and soft, heat and coolness, everything familiar yet a difference beyond the simple catalog of lips and hands and thighs. The driving insistence I sensed in him from our first meeting was undisguised now, but always with it was a tender care that my pleasure equal his, the overwhelming need to satisfy desire fused with the generosity of love.

Afterward there came a gentler repetition, the softer variation on the theme, and the long, sighing notes of pleasure sustained beyond imagined limit. So dreamlike in the wordless harmony of feeling, of movement, that I have no memory of the moment when sleep took me as easily and tenderly as Nick's body in the last embrace.

I woke to bright sunlight on my face. A bird's raucous cry as it flew by my window pierced my sleepiness, mockingly. The empty place beside me, the empty apartment, might have mocked me, too, had my contentment been more fragile. But I only stretched, yawning, and looked at the alarm clock by my bed— eight o'clock—then headed for the shower. I let the water sluice down over me, lathered my hair into suds, rinsed, and lathered again. Only when the water was running cold did I step out of the shower and dry myself off, toweling my hair until my scalp tingled.

When I'd dressed, I telephoned the hospital to ask after Faltecchi. No, I was told, he had not regained consciousness. Yes, they had my telephone number and would telephone me if there was any change. Signora Faltecchi was still with her father.

I stood there listening to the dead end of the wire with misery tightening in me.

As I put the receiver down in its cradle, I heard footsteps on the stairs coming up quickly. Nick appeared, his arms filled with packages and flowers, looking so much like the answer to any woman's prayer that I simply stared at him, smiling idiotically. He smiled back, an unvarnished smile of happiness at first, then tinged, infuriatingly, with mischief at my answering blush.

"Sleep well?" he asked with an innocent air.

"Quite well, thank you. What little I had. And you?"

"The finest sleep I can remember. And thank *you*." He dumped the parcels down on the dining table and, with the sudden pleased look of a little boy, a look that disarmed me completely, held out the enormous bunch of flowers.

"Oh Nick, they're lovely." I took them, overwhelmed. They were as lovely as flowers from an old fairy tale illustrated by Edmund Dulac. Plump pink roses, their petals wide to the sun, enormous purple anemones, carnations frilled with red and smelling deliciously of cinnamon, yellow-throated iris on spiky green stalks, and daisies like great white stars splashed with gold at their hearts—all tied together with ivy and still glistening with the dew of the morning.

I rummaged in my cupboard for something large enough to hold them, but all I could come up with was an ugly chipped pitcher that I'd shoved to the back of a shelf. It didn't matter; the flowers cascaded over it, obscuring its failings. "Where did you find such a gorgeous bouquet?"

"An old woman was just setting up her stand on the Via Carini. I told her I wanted flowers beautiful enough to wake up Sleeping Beauty."

I set the pitcher carefully down in the middle of the table. "Oh, I think you'd already done just that. Only the most determined Sleeping Beauty could fail to wake up after last night."

"Thank you. That's the first time anyone's implied I'm a Prince Charming."

"That's not exactly—"

He held up one hand. "Please don't spoil it. Let me have my illusions. Now, shall we eat at once . . . Or later?" He looked up from opening parcels to smile at me.

"Breakfast first. Other things will keep for a few minutes, anyway. I'm ravenous." I took the espresso pot from the cupboard. "Shall I make coffee?"

"Do you make good espresso?"

"Not very," I admitted. "Why bother in a country where you can never match what's sold in the bars? I gave up trying to compete long ago."

"Defeatist. I'll do it, then. Where do you keep your coffee?"

I found it for him and set about loading a tray with cups and plates and the rolls and melon from the paper bags. When everything was ready, we went out onto my balcony, already warm from the sun, and had our breakfast as we sat on pillows, our backs to the bumpy stucco wall and our faces turned up to the sun. We ate in a contented silence. Sparrows hopped optimistically on the balustrade, just out of reach, swooping down for the crumbs we tossed to them and away again. I could smell the little boxwood bushes set out in wooden tubs in each corner of the balcony as the heat of the sun released their fragrance. Above us swifts slipped sideways in the air, wheeling around for a closer look at the sparrows' banquet. Their shrill cries were like the calling of little children at some game.

"Any news yet from the hospital?"

I shook my head. "But I called them. Still no change." I thought of Faltecchi, unconscious, cut off from this beautiful day, and found I wasn't hungry anymore. I crumbled the rest of my roll for the sparrows.

Nick shifted his back against the wall, half turning toward me. "I saw Clara and Gianni this morning. I told them what happened to Faltecchi. Plus the rest of your story. Gianni and I want to help you get that notebook, Kate."

"You're sure you want to be mixed up with a lady of dubious character?" I tried to make a joke of it, but I had a few doubts about this joint enterprise. I could see that once Nick and Gianni were involved, things might move too fast for me.

Nick took my hand. "I have a weakness for dubious characters. Didn't I tell you once that I was easily led? We'll have to be careful, that's all."

Despite the doubts, I felt something inside me relax, as though a tightly wound spring had eased just a little.

"What will you do about your work today?" Nick asked as I poured him another cup of coffee.

"First I'll call the workrooms and find out if they need me there. If not, I suppose I'll go to work as usual at the palazzo— until last night catches up with me." I turned Nick's hand over in mine and traced his lifeline with the forefinger of my other hand; his palm was broad, strong looking, the lifeline reassuringly long.

"You know," I said, "I was going to tell Alessandro about Marco and Daniella and let him deal with it. But now I'm not sure if that's a good idea. If Marco is working for Stillitano and if Stillitano does have some connection to Alessandro beyond the Reni, it might be wiser to wait until after we try for the notebook. What do you think?"

"I agree. The less that other people know about what you know, the safer you are." He spoke slowly, and I sensed that he was choosing his words with care. "Maybe we ought to try for the notebook tonight?"

"I'm not sure . . . No, it really does seem better to wait until tomorrow night, for Carnevale. People probably won't work late, and our chances of finding the workrooms empty will be greater." How much of this was good sense and how much simple procrastination was beyond me. I only knew that as far as I was concerned, the later it happened the better. Once this burglary was under way, and real, it was going to be terrifying.

Nick was too good a journalist to miss the truth behind the matter-of-fact tone. "Look, Kate, why don't you let me do this? Traditionally it's man's work anyway."

"I wish you could. But I suppose it would be a real waste of my new talents if I didn't at least have a try at it." Then, more seriously, I added, "Besides, I have a valid reason to be in the workrooms, whatever the hour, and you don't." I drank the last of my coffee with little pleasure; it was cold and I'd put too much sugar in it. "And you," I asked him, wanting a change of subject, "what will you do today?"

"I have a contact at the Bank of Italy—remember I told you that the Bank is carrying out its own investigation into some of Bassi's affairs? My contact is willing to talk to me about the links between some of the banks that Bassi's connected with and the Treasury—and the way that Torreleone's job at the Treasury fits into it all. We're going to try to figure out precisely how Torreleone is useful to Bassi."

"I see. Poor Count Massimo." I set my coffee cup down. "Well, whatever I end up doing today, I'm liable to see either Stillitano or Alessandro—or, at the worst, both. I really dread it. I don't know how I'll face them without showing something of what I suspect."

Nick gave me an odd look and said levelly, "I'd say you

have a remarkably good face for poker. You managed to keep a good deal of what you were thinking from me."

"Really?"

"Most." He smiled. Our heads were close together; his breath was warm against my skin. Just before we kissed, he whispered, "But not all."

Nothing more was said for some time to come.

In fact, I saw neither Stillitano nor Alessandro that day. When I called the workrooms, Ilaria, the secretary, told me that Stillitano had not yet returned from Sicily but was expected sometime in the afternoon. Yes, she said in reply to my question, he knew about Signor Faltecchi's condition and was very concerned but had said that work should continue, as Signor Faltecchi himself undoubtedly would wish.

When I arrived at the palazzo, I found Signora Gambino at work, cheerfully singing as she swept the flagstones under the arcade. I explained that a friend of mine was in the hospital and that I'd given the palazzo's number to the hospital so that they could reach me if I was needed. The palazzo had several different lines, but those for the family members were private and unlisted; I knew only the general number that rang the porter's lodge.

"But of course, Signora Roy," she replied. "I will come to you at once if the hospital should call. And I will say a prayer for your friend."

I thanked her and asked after Count Massimo.

"Ah, the count is much better, praise God. But Dr. Guareschi has ordered him to rest, and so he keeps to his rooms. The doctor thinks he should not go to the ball, but the count insists he must be there. Signor Alessandro says his father must do as he wishes."

"Where is Signor Alessandro this morning?" I asked rather nervously.

"I was told that he left suddenly for Palermo last night. Naturally he will come back in time for the ball. A dirty place, Sicily," she said, with the Roman's contempt for the south, "and one hears such terrible stories. Still, Signor Alessandro must like it there."

"What makes you say that, Signora Gambino?"

"Why, because he goes so often." She gave a broad grin. "The servants all believe that he has a lady love there. But no one really knows. Some say—but there, I mustn't gossip." Infuriatingly, she set to sweeping again.

If it were only as innocent as that, I thought, as I went slowly up the stairs, torn between relief that Alessandro at least was out of the way and dismay at his whereabouts. Sicily again. And Stillitano there, as well. *And* that villa near Palermo of Pietro Bassi.

I spent a quiet morning working, with one interruption to call the hospital, only to be told yet again that Faltecchi's condition was unchanged. As I worked, I tried to keep my mind clear of everything but the painting before me, but whenever I paused—to mix solvents, to clean brushes—the insidious thoughts wormed their way back into my brain.

If only Count Massimo were stronger, I could go to him and tell him everything with the hope that he might be able to persuade Alessandro and Daniella to give up their dangerous games. Once Alessandro learned about Marco, he might realize that there was more to his game than power and money. I still couldn't believe he was so ruthless that he would condone the uses to which Marco was put. I couldn't believe he knew what had happened to Faltecchi.

But I could not go to Count Massimo. I simply couldn't risk the shock to his frail health even had I the courage to shatter his illusions about his family. I remembered, too, what Nick had said on my balcony that morning: The fewer people who knew what I knew, the better. For safety's sake.

I thought of Faltecchi then and of his safety. As he grew stronger, recovered consciousness, and was able, perhaps, to identify his attacker, to reveal whatever it was he had so urgently wanted to tell me, even to expose Stillitano, the danger to him would increase. A danger that came, I was certain, from Stillitano rather than Marco. Marco was a tool, a tool that had proved inefficient and might be replaced with one more reliable. While Stillitano was in Sicily, Faltecchi might be safe, but when he returned . . . I put down my brush. Suddenly I was terribly frightened for Faltecchi, unconscious and vulnerable as he was in his hospital bed.

Unable to work any longer, I had an overwhelming urge to go to the hospital, to see for myself that he was safe. Swiftly, I put away my supplies, cleaned up, and hurried down the stone stairs. As I went past the porter's lodge, I waved good-bye to Signora Gambino, but she called out after me.

"Signora Roy, one moment, please." She leaned out of the window of the lodge. "Count Massimo asked me to give you a message. You are to have tomorrow off, to rest for the ball. And he has sent you a surprise. Come." Like a Judy in a puppet show, she jerked back inside, one beckoning hand outstretched for a moment before that, too, disappeared.

I was desperate to get to the hospital, to reassure myself that Faltecchi was all right, but I obeyed her and for the first time went into the porter's lodge, or rather, tried to. But I could only stand in the doorway, amazed. Outside of an antique shop I hadn't ever seen so much bric-a-brac in one small place. It was as if furniture from the palazzo's various staterooms had all been crammed together, claustrophobically and without a thought for any kind of harmony, let alone taste. The little room fairly burst apart at the seams.

In spite of the surfeit of furniture and a general air of luxury gone rampantly to seed, however, the room was perfectly neat and clean.

Fortunately, Signora Gambino took my stunned silence for awestruck admiration. "Beautiful, is it not?" she asked me, looking proudly around her. "Countess Anna, Count Massimo's wife, gave all these things to my father, who was the *portiere* before me, when she changed some of the rooms in the palazzo. It is a pleasure to spend my days here."

"I can see that it would be. You keep it beautifully, too."

"But of course. It deserves no less." Then, with an air of mystery, clearly enjoying herself, she told me to close my eyes

174

and hold out my hands. I did as I was told, and what felt like a large box was placed in my outstretched arms.

"Now you may look."

Opening my eyes, I saw a long oblong dress box wrapped around with string. It was bulky but not heavy.

"Count Massimo said you were to open this in your own house," she told me, "and that you were free to wear it tomorrow night or not, as you choose. He said to be certain to tell you that he will not be offended if you wear another instead."

I tucked the box under one arm. "Please tell Count Massimo how touched I am by his generosity, Signora Gambino. He's very kind to trouble himself about me when he must have so much else on his mind right now. I'm tremendously grateful." It was the simple truth. Why, then, did I feel so sad, and obscurely guilty, at the thought of that kindness?

I knew very well why. But there was not, I told myself, one blessed thing I could do about it.

However, I thought, with a grain of relief, at least one minor complication was solved by that kindness. So far I hadn't given a moment's reflection to what I would wear to the *ballo in maschera*. Now it seemed I wouldn't have to.

I took a taxi to the hospital; when it slowed to follow a bus or stopped for a light I was jumpy with impatience. Always with me, like a nagging pain, was that undercurrent of fear. But the taxi driver was one of those irrepressible types who talk to you over their shoulder without expecting more than "Yes" or "Really?" in return, and I found his observations on everything from the pope to the Lazio soccer team irreverent enough to amuse and distract me. A lurid pink-and-blue plastic madonna simpered at me from the dashboard, *la Madonna della Confusione*, he told me, the madonna of traffic jams. Perhaps she was watching over us, for we made it to the hospital in nerve-shattering time. I overtipped the driver, but it was a pleasure to pay for the distraction.

When I reached Intensive Care, I asked the nurse on duty at the main desk if Signor Faltecchi had had any visitors that morning. To my relief, she said no, visitors were forbidden;

only the immediate family were allowed into his room. His daughter was with him at the moment. At my request, the nurse went to fetch her.

Elsa looked very bleak. Faltecchi's condition had worsened, she told me. The doctors thought they would have to operate if he did not show signs of improvement within the next few hours; they were afraid that blood might leak into the brain. Wordlessly, I took her hand and held it. We went to the unfriendly alcove and sat down amid the crumpled newspapers.

"I was suddenly frightened for your father," I told her hesitantly. "It occurred to me that his attacker might try to hurt him again—out of fear that he could identify him. I thought . . . well, that perhaps it would be better if he weren't left alone. I'm sorry if this adds to all your other worries, but it did seem a possibility to me that—" I stopped, uncertain of how to continue. I hadn't quite worked out what I was going to say if Elsa asked me why the attacker would risk coming to the hospital. Or how he would find out where Faltecchi was or who he was. In other words, why he should be more than a casual mugger.

But I needn't have worried. Elsa had been there before me.

More calmly than I expected, she said, "This occurred also to me. And I am even more determined that some member of our family be with my father at all times. My sister agrees with me. We have certain suspicions, you see . . . But they are only suspicions. You will understand that I can say no more than that. But I am very grateful for your concern, Kate. Until my father is safely home, you can be sure he will never be alone."

I registered the "Kate," and it pleased me. "Then, unless I can do anything for you . . . ?" But she shook her head. "If you can't reach me at my apartment, try this number." I scribbled the Palmieris' number on a scrap of paper. "But I'll call every few hours to find out how things are going."

"Do not forget your package." Elsa held out the box, which I'd left propped against the chair. "A new dress?"

"A costume for Carnevale. The Torreleones are giving a ball tomorrow night. I don't have the heart for it now, but the family has been so kind to me."

"My father would be the first to say, 'Go, enjoy yourself.' " Elsa looked down at her hands, which were clasped tightly in her lap, so that all I could see was the straight parting that ran across the top of her black hair. "I have disappointed him, I know. He thinks I do not take all the pleasure from life that I should." Her voice was muffled. She looked up at me again, an opaque look. "He has always liked your enthusiasm."

I touched her shoulder hesitantly and said, "I only know that whenever he says your name he always says, 'My Elsa,' as though no one else could mean as much to him." I tried to make her smile. "Do you know that he refuses to order pasta in restaurants whenever we go out to lunch because he says only you achieve perfection?"

"Yes?" She gave the ghost of a smile, and her heavy body straightened. We said good-bye, and I left the hospital. As I walked away, one question kept coming back: Were Elsa's suspicions about her father's attacker in any way connected to her hostility to Stillitano? I thought I knew the answer.

CHAPTER

13

I did not go back to the palazzo. Instead, I decided to take the afternoon off in lieu of the following day offered me by Count Massimo and went home to sleep, awaking only to the simultaneous sounds of my telephone ringing and a knocking at the door. I felt dazed but came sharp awake at the thought that it might be news of Faltecchi.

"Door's open," I called out as I went to answer the phone. Nick came into the apartment, smiled at me, and raised one hand in greeting, then made as if to leave again to give me privacy for the call. I shook my head and pointed to a chair.

Elsa Faltecchi was on the line. She said her father had just come out of the operation; the doctors thought it had gone well and were hopeful that he would recover. However, it was plain to me from the tone of her voice that she didn't have much faith in their assurances. She was going home, she told me, but her sister was there and would stay overnight with their father. We spoke for a few moments more, then said good-bye. I hung up, discouraged by her dejection.

Nick put his arms around me. "Bad news?"

I told him what Elsa had said and about my own fears for Faltecchi. "He's so vulnerable, Nick. That's what I can't stand to think about. I'm terrified for him."

"I know. But if Stillitano thinks Faltecchi is dying, he may seem less of a threat. Stillitano might even think he can afford to leave him alone."

As I stood there in his arms, I could feel myself absorbing some of his calm and managed a smile. "Would you like a drink before you tell me what you learned at the Bank of Italy?"

"Something cold. The weather's turned muggy."

While Nick carried two chairs out onto the balcony, I poured white wine into glasses, adding chilled soda water and the few cubes of ice my tiny refrigerator could produce. With our legs propped up on the balustrade, we sipped our drinks in a companionable silence. I thought, for the first time in what seemed a very long while, how pleasant it was to be on the edge of love; I liked the pleasurable uncertainties of a new beginning, the promise of a fresh, unexplored territory entered without maps but with the conviction that the discoveries waiting there would be exciting. All at once, despite everything, I felt remarkably happy.

Nick reached over and stroked the back of my neck. "Penny for them?"

"Only ... oh, that at this moment I'm content. Maybe something more." I smiled at him.

He didn't reply, but I felt his hand tighten against my skin. After an interval in which I had another opportunity to recognize how much I enjoyed kissing him, he murmured, "I'd better tell you what happened today, or I may never get started."

"Is there any hurry?"

"Come to think of it, no."

But eventually we had to pause for breath. We leaned back

in our chairs, holding hands. Somewhere in the garden below us we could hear the Palmieri children playing happily together, and beyond, the noise of the city muffled by the distance. The late-afternoon sun gilded the rooftops through a haze of rose and umber, the deceptively beautiful mist that pollution lays over the city at the end of the day. The air was heavy, but I liked its drowsy quality; it made me feel languorous and infinitely lazy. That and the wine combined for one instant to make the mysteries and sorrows of the last few days as remote from me as the hills still capped with winter snow far away across the Roman *campagna*.

When Nick began to speak, however, his words were a brutal reminder of all I'd so fleetingly wished away.

"Torreleone's a clever bastard. The links to Bassi are there, all right; we can see them pretty plainly. What's missing is clear proof he's done anything illegal. He's left that to Bassi. At the most, he can be accused of favoring Bassi's interests, of smoothing the way for government loans to Bassi's companies."

The chair creaked as Nick shifted to take out a pack of cigarettes. He lit a cigarette and blew a plume of smoke upward. I watched it hang suspended in the still air, then vanish.

"It's complicated, Kate, so stop me if you don't follow what I'm saying, okay?" I nodded. "Basically, then, the government and a number of major banks lent huge amounts of money to companies controlled by Bassi, persuaded that they were investing in developing Italian industry. Instead, the money was siphoned through these companies into shell companies that Bassi set up in Liechtenstein and the Bahamas, and in Argentina, where Bassi has powerful connections."

"Stop!" I was already confused. "What are shell companies?"

"Just that—hollow shells. Companies that exist only on paper. Oh, there might be a room somewhere with a telex and a secretary, maybe even an opulent front office designed to impress. But that's it. Primarily they're conduits for certain transactions. Bassi uses these companies to channel money out of the country, a good part of which eventually finds its way into secret Swiss bank accounts. For example, he sells stock in the

Italian parent company to the shell subsidiary, then buys it back at vastly inflated prices, with the perk of outrageously generous commissions to those involved as a reward. None of this is legal, you understand, but the maneuverings have been so complex that only now has the Bank of Italy been able to piece together Bassi's methods."

"How long has this been going on?"

Nick shrugged. "Who knows? A decade, maybe."

I was astonished. "He's got away with it for that long?"

"Yes. That's where he's so remarkable. Bassi's like a juggler, adding more and more balls to the show. Up to now he's been able to keep them all in the air, but he added one too many, and . . . What's really amazing is that it's clear those balls started falling some time back, yet he created the illusion of still being in control. He's manipulated money and people so well that he's been able to go on getting the money he needs to maintain the illusion."

"Just like a modern Cagliostro." The eighteenth-century charlatan whose magic potions promising riches and eternal youth seduced the powerful and the innocent all across Europe.

"That's the perfect analogy," Nick said. "Did you know that Cagliostro had his own Masonic lodge, too? He called it the Egyptian Order; he claimed that membership would grant the initiate all sorts of magical secrets and powers. Like Bassi, he had a long run for his money. But he finished up in prison."

"And Bassi?"

"I'm not sure. He pulls too many strings—maybe too many ever to come to trial." He paused to light a cigarette from the remains of the first, realized what he was doing, and with a shamefaced grin at me, stubbed them both out.

As tranquilly as I could, I asked, "Where exactly does Alessandro fit into Bassi's operations?"

"Very neatly," Nick replied. "On the surface, his role looks innocuous enough, but he's been instrumental in getting Bassi's applications for the Treasury approval of these loans past the red tape. He doesn't have the power to give the final okay, but he can make Bassi's requests look good on paper from the

Treasury's point of view." Staring out at the expanse of sky and roofs and treetops, he said bluntly, "In his own way, Alessandro Torreleone's as skillful a manipulator as Bassi. He must have learned a lot from his master." The bitterness was back in his voice.

"Do you think the Bank of Italy will be able to prove all this?"

"Perhaps. Though of the two of them I'd say that Torreleone has been more successful in covering his tracks."

I swirled the melting cubes of ice around in my glass. "Did you know that Alessandro has been in Sicily, in Palermo, these last few days?"

He looked surprised and shook his head.

"Stillitano, too. I don't think I told you that. Elsa mentioned it last night at the hospital. I gather she likes him as little as I do, by the way. Today she implied that she has her own suspicions about her father's attacker. She wouldn't say what they were, but I'd be willing to bet they involve Stillitano. Do you happen to know if Bassi's in Palermo, too?"

"No, but I may be able to find out."

"The *portiera* at the palazzo did say that Alessandro may be visiting a girlfriend when he makes these trips to Sicily. Apparently he goes quite often. But . . ." I let my voice trail off.

"But," Nick finished dryly, "you're about as convinced of that as I am."

"There are just too many coincidences—and too many questions—to be convinced of anything." I drank the last of my wine and got up, stretching out my hand for Nick's empty glass. "More?"

"Please. And you can skip the soda water and ice this time. With that wine they're a sacrilege."

"If you were brought up on wines like London Dock, you wouldn't have much of a palate, either," I said defensively.

Nick laughed. "Another good reason to stay in Rome."

"I'm beginning to discover there are more reasons than I'd realized."

I went inside and was just opening the refrigerator when there was a light tap on the door and the sound of Clara's voice softly calling my name. When I let her in, she apologized for disturbing us. "Gianni and I saw Nick's car outside. I said to Gianni, 'Perhaps they want to be alone. We should wait.' I thought perhaps . . ." She glanced around the apartment, then back at me, her eyebrows raised.

"It's all right, Clara," I reassured her, laughing, "Nick's on the balcony, and quite respectable."

"But of course. What else would he be? It is nothing to me that he comes with flowers in his arms at such an early hour this morning. . . ." She smiled and gave me an affectionate pinch on one cheek. "I'm happy for you, Kate. Nick is a dear."

"I know. And so are you. Come and have some wine with us."

As I reached into the cupboard for another glass, I felt her hand on my arm. "Not now, *cara*. Gianni is like Vesuvio, ready to explode if he can't tell Nick this news of his. It *is* important; I wouldn't have bothered you otherwise. Something to do with Bassi."

"Come on, then, let's get Nick. I hate to think of Gianni suffering."

The three of us found Gianni prowling up and down, pipe in one hand, glass in the other, muttering to himself. He pounced on Nick the moment we came through the door. "At last!" Thrusting the pipe into his mouth, he grabbed Nick and excitedly began telling him something I found incomprehensible because of the speed of the delivery and the impediment of the pipe. Finally, Nick persuaded him to stop and begin again, this time without the pipe. Good-naturedly, Gianni agreed, and we all sat down, Gianni perched on the arm of a chair as though poised for lift-off, Clara by his side to prevent it.

He told us that he'd just spoken with Cucchi, his friend at the *carabinieri*. "It's fantastic, Nick! Yesterday a magistrate gave the *carabinieri* a warrant to search Bassi's apartment in Rome. Bassi wasn't there; apparently he's been at that villa of his near Palermo." Nick and I glanced at each other. "Cucchi says they've made an incredible find. Many, many files and a long list of names, much of it to do with Mestola Rossa. He wouldn't give us details—he said his boss would kill him if he told me more—but he did say that we were right, you and I. In fact, maybe we didn't go far enough with our suspicions." He looked at Nick with a mixture of glee and triumph. "There were politicians, businessmen, even a general in the army on those lists of Bassi's."

"Christ, Gianni!" Nick said. "Do you know what this means?"

"Sure. Among other things that some *pezzi grossi* won't be sleeping too well for a while. They're going to sweat—"

"Yes," Nick broke in impatiently, "but we're going to have to move a lot faster. The first real shot has been fired, and all your *pezzi grossi* are going to dive for cover. Including Torreleone." He got to his feet abruptly and began pacing the floor, his hands shoved deep in the pockets of his trousers. "Cucchi wouldn't give you any names?"

Gianni shook his head. "But he as much as promised to leak what he could to us. I think he's worried that some of it may never get out if he doesn't. Too much pressure from above. He says he can feel it starting already." His face grew dark. "Some *cazzo* may have warned Bassi."

Nick looked over at me. "I wonder if your friend Stillitano is on any of Bassi's lists. You know," he said to Gianni, "there's a slant to this story that the *carabinieri* may not be aware of, and somehow Stillitano fits into it. It's pretty clear that he links up with Bassi and Torreleone. But we need to figure out how, and why."

"And that brings us to burglary," Gianni said with relish.

"I wish you wouldn't sound so cheerful about it," I told him. "If you knew Stillitano—"

"Oh, Gianni and Nick think it's all such a grand adventure," Clara said blithely. "The more horrible this man is, the more exciting it will be for them. You and I, Kate, will stay safely at home and pray for them."

I stared at her in surprise. "Why Clara, don't you know that I'm the one who'll have to do it?"

She looked back at me, appalled, and said flatly that I couldn't, it was far too dangerous.

"Yesterday afternoon I would have agreed with you," I told her. "But now that Faltecchi's been hurt, I'm going to go through with it. We've got to find some way to stop Stillitano, something to go to the police with."

Clara started to protest, but I cut her off, explaining once again why I had to be the burglar. Finally, she accepted it, still looking very dubious and adding firmly that she and Gianni would go with Nick and me.

I hugged her. "Thanks. The more of us there are, the safer I'll feel."

"So then, we must have a proper plan." Gianni was pulling paper and pencils out of a drawer when Clara stopped him.

"First we must have a proper dinner. I don't plot well on an empty stomach. If you'll give me half an hour . . ."

But Nick had a better idea. "You don't need to cook, Clara. We know just the place for plotting, don't we, Kate? Good food, too. You remember I told you about Giangiacomo Maurelli, Gianni— Well, it's his place, the Revolutionary Restaurant. He was checking on something for me, and I'd be glad of the chance to talk to him again."

Clara said she would ask the neighbors' daughter to look after the children. She returned a few minutes later with the girl and called the children in from the garden. We kissed Cecilia and Giannino good night, promising to bring them back a treat, and set off for the restaurant.

We were the first customers; it was early, and the Romans, as a rule, dine late. Giangiacomo put his head through the open kitchen door, saw us, and came out to greet us, calling for Antonia. The Maurellis and Palmieris took to each other at once, as I'd suspected they might. Clara and Gianni were fascinated by the restaurant, and their curiosity delighted the Maurellis, who proudly showed us around the kitchen and gave us each a taste of the veal stew that was to be the evening's dinner.

As Giangi led us over to a large table in one corner of the dining room, he said to Nick, "I'm glad you've come tonight. All day I've been trying to reach you. About that man . . ." He left the rest of the sentence unfinished.

"It's all right," Nick said in answer to Giangiacomo's hesitation. "They know all about it. Gianni's working with me on it."

"In that case, you remember that fellow you asked me about after Susanna died, Marco Gatti?"

Nick nodded.

"I knew then no more about him than you did. Until now I have learned little, except that he is not much liked or trusted. But this I have told you. Well, yesterday an old friend of your sister came in here; at one time she was a member of Studenti per l'Operaio. I had not seen her since Susanna's death, and we talked for a little. Then I thought to ask her about Gatti. She, too, remembered him very well."

Giangiacomo paused to scoop olives and salami onto our plates and, after a hearty "Eat, eat. It is possible both to eat and to listen," went on with his story. "She is terrified of this Gatti. I had to give her my word I wouldn't tell you her name, Nick. But she was willing to talk about him after I swore I would tell no one that she had given me the information. She said that when she heard Susanna had been killed—it was she who used the word 'killed,' not I, you understand—she wasn't surprised. It seems that Susanna was for a time under Gatti's spell and then became frightened of him. Her friend tried to persuade her to leave Rome when she decided to get out of Studenti per l'Operaio, but she wouldn't. Perhaps, so this girl thought, because of another man. But she wasn't sure.

"She said that Gatti is well-known for his violence and for the pleasure he takes in using the women who are unlucky enough to become involved with him. He enjoys their fear of him." As much as any cat with a mouse, I thought. Giangiacomo looked at Nick. "I am sorry, Nick . . ."

But Nick's face and voice held only that familiar expressionless calm. "Don't be. Go on, please, Giangi."

"There is not much more. Except that this girl is convinced Gatti killed Susanna. Susanna knew too much about Gatti's affairs, and when she decided to break with him, her friend warned her to be careful. That was the last time they spoke together."

Nick poured each of us more wine and drank his own slowly. I put my hand on his, wishing I could comfort him. After a pause, he said, "Thanks, Giangi. I'm grateful to you."

"One thing more, Nick. From what I hear, this man is no revolutionary. He is only scum, a man with no beliefs who plays both sides." Giangiacomo turned to me. "What is it you say in English? A hired gun?" I nodded. "Well, that is what he is." He got heavily to his feet and stood for a moment at Nick's side, then touched his shoulder. "If there is something I can do about Gatti, my friend . . . Perhaps through my paper?"

Nick smiled grimly. "Don't bother, Giangi. Gatti's career is about to come to an abrupt end. What you've just told me makes me sure of it."

After Giangiacomo had gone, I asked Nick if he'd suspected Marco before in his sister's death.

"It was always a toss-up between Gatti and Torreleone. I was convinced one or the other of them had something to do with it. But I thought Torreleone was the one with the most to lose if Susanna decided to tell what she knew, and the most to gain by her death. Perhaps I was wrong."

I suspected that was as close as Nick would come to an acknowledgment that Alessandro might not be quite the villain he'd believed him. "But I don't understand why his affair with Susanna should be such a threat to him?"

Through a forkful of food, Gianni explained for Nick, "Don't you see, Kate—if Torreleone's right-wing pals knew he was friendly with leftists like Susanna, they would drop him like a snake. Then good-bye career."

"And," Nick added, "on the other hand, if he was using my

sister to get information for his friends about the revolutionaries and she found out and threatened to tell, it might have meant retribution from Studenti per l'Operaio. Remember, too, she'd confronted him with her suspicions about that file. Any way you look at it, she was dangerous to him. But according to Giangi, she was more dangerous to Gatti."

Another idea occurred to me, though it seemed so farfetched I hesitated as I broached it. "If Marco attacked Faltecchi on Stillitano's orders, do you think your sister's death might also be connected in some way to Stillitano?"

"I don't think Stillitano is giving the orders," Nick said. "But again, that notebook of his might tell us."

"So," Gianni said impatiently, "now we'll discuss tomorrow night."

We spent the rest of the evening in the restaurant talking over the best way to tackle our project, Nick and Gianni with an enthusiasm straight out of the Boy Scouts. But their confidence and breezy assurance helped ease my doubts. If nothing else, I was grateful for the camaraderie, their automatic assumption that we were all in this together. Or at least as far as the door of Stillitano's office.

We decided we would go in separate cars, Nick and I together, Gianni and Clara in theirs, after I'd made my appearance at the Torreleones' ball. The ball would be an alibi of sorts, if I needed one. The later I attempted the burglary, the less likely it was I would run into one of my colleagues working late, though I couldn't imagine anyone working late on Carnevale, anyway.

If, by a stroke of bad luck, I did come across someone in the workrooms, I would say that I'd decided to stop by for supplies on my way home from the ball so that I could sleep in the next morning. As excuses go, it was pretty thin, but not, I hoped, entirely unbelievable. My colleagues knew I liked to work odd hours; perhaps that would stand me in good stead now.

So much could go wrong with this plan that I preferred not to discuss alternatives yet. One thing at a time, I told the others.

Privately, I doubted I would have the courage for more than one attempt.

Afterward, just before we said good night to the Maurellis, I called the hospital. I got the by-now-familiar litany: Faltecchi was sleeping, recovery might be slow, I would be informed if he asked for me.

As we got into the Maserati, Gianni announced that he and Clara were taking us to their favorite jazz club. "I like your friends, Nick. They're *simpatici*. But that sort of life isn't for me—much too serious. We need some amusement to prepare ourselves for tomorrow."

"The eat, drink, and be merry school of life, eh, Gianni?" I couldn't help a certain grim note to my voice.

"But of course, Kate. Is there any other that makes sense to you?"

I had to admit that at that moment there wasn't.

CHAPTER

14

When I walked into the Palazzo Torreleone the next morning, one of those undecided, blustery spring mornings that tremble on the verge of rain while the sun shines, Signora Gambino was busy with a brigade of delivery men bringing tubs of blossoming trees and bushes to swell the small forest already grown up, as if overnight, under the arched entrance and out into the courtyard. The air smelled sweetly of gardenia and mimosa, luring a cloud of curious bees to investigate this sudden flowering of *primavera* on their doorstep. Signora Gambino brushed them away with distracted sweeps of one hand while she directed operations, as serious as any general on the morning of a major battle and quite as impressive.

"The forsythia and mimosa are to go here, in the courtyard, a pot of each under every arch—no, no, not like that! Those are flowers not bricks you are moving. *Madonna!* Now see what you have done, *cretino!*"

The *cretino*, a young man who seemed not in the least offended by the abuse heaped upon his curly-haired and handsome head, retrieved the broken branch that was the cause of Signora Gambino's fury, plucked off a bright yellow blossom, and presented it to her with the added flourish of a low, extravagant bow and a charming smile. Mollified, she laughed with something of her usual good humor and tapped his cheek.

"*Grazie.* But I am not as easily taken in as I once was, *piccolino.* Come—the azaleas, camellias, all these over here, must go up to the Salone d'Oro. I will show you the way."

The men groaned good-naturedly and set to work, and slowly the forest began to move, the swaying greenery processing through the courtyard under the leadership of Signora Gambino like Macbeth's ill-omened Birnam wood on its way to Dunsinane.

Screened by a palisade of potted palms and hedged around with azaleas, the staircase to my studio was virtually invisible, but I pushed my way through the undergrowth and slipped upstairs, hoping to work unnoticed, undisturbed, and alone.

I prayed I would not see a single Torreleone until the ball. How could I talk easily with any of them, knowing and suspecting all that I did, feeling more and more like a viper in the collective bosom of the family? Tonight I would have to face them, but then at least they would be occupied with their guests and would hardly have time for more than a few words of welcome. I could put in an appearance and then, duty done, make my escape.

Alessandro was, of course, the Torreleone I least wanted to see. But when I reached the top of the stairs I heard voices and saw the door to my studio standing open, and when I stepped inside, there he was. He was talking to old Mario and to Claudio, another servant; he wheeled about, surprised, as I came into the room.

"Kate! But you were to have a holiday today."

"I know. I'm sorry," I said, wondering why I was apologiz-

191

ing. "Signora Gambino did tell me, and it was very kind of your father. But I took it yesterday instead. I . . . I needed it then." I could hear the nervousness in my voice and tried to relax, hoping that Alessandro would put my awkwardness down to the memory of that kiss. "If there's any difficulty about my being here today, if I'm in the way—"

"No, no, of course not." Alessandro himself seemed off balance, less smoothly in control, and the emphasis of the words did not quite disguise the hesitation in his own voice. But he recovered quickly, more quickly than I, and said, "My father and I thought it would be wise to put the paintings into safe-keeping for tonight. Mario and Claudio were about to move them to my rooms. But that can be done later, when you are finished."

"Thank you, but I'll need only the Vanvitelli. You can take the other two now if you like."

"Very well." He turned to the two servants who were standing silently beside one of Guardi's paintings, a small scene of the Grand Canal, Claudio a much younger shadow of Mario, with the same white jacket, hands clasped in front of it in precisely the same way, and the same unnerving ability to melt into the surroundings. I remembered Count Massimo's rueful admission that he failed to measure up to Mario's exacting standards of aristocratic behavior and wondered if Mario consoled himself by training his underlings to be servants in the grand manner. Alessandro pointed to the two paintings by Guardi and said, "Take those along to my *salotto* and lay them on the big table there. You have the necessary keys, Mario? Good. Signora Roy will let you know when she has finished with the other."

Under Mario's vigilant eye, Claudio lifted the larger of the two paintings from the easel and carried it off. As they went down the hall, Mario was solemnly lecturing the younger man on the value of what he held in his hands—if there was the slightest damage, etc.—and I hoped he wouldn't make Claudio so nervous that he dropped the painting out of sheer anxiety. The ball was not, it seemed to me, having the best of influences on the palazzo's servants.

It was also, to judge by the dark smudges under his eyes and the harsh downward strokes on either side of his mouth, taking its toll of Alessandro. Or were there other explanations for his visible weariness? His trip to Sicily, for instance. Had he found out that the police were tightening their net around Bassi—and so, perhaps, around himself? Or was he simply and understandably worried about Count Massimo, a worry compounded by the fear his father would learn that his beloved Reni was a fake?

I began to take out my tools from the storage cupboard. As Alessandro stood there, preoccupied, twisting the gold signet ring he wore on one finger, he struck me as suddenly older, and unhappy, like a man reflecting on his own fallibility. I felt an odd mixture of sympathy and dismay—the sympathy because he seemed so alone and so threatened, a man like any other and not the teasing, carefree creature he often appeared to be, the dismay because sympathy was a feeling I knew I couldn't afford.

Away from him, talking to Nick and Gianni, I could judge him coolly; I could accept that he had brought whatever lay in store for him upon himself. Here in the same room with him it was impossible. Whatever the magic was that he worked on women, it seemed I wasn't immune.

Alessandro yawned and stretched, then grinned at me, a mischievous grin that erased the tiredness from his face as thoroughly as if it had never existed. "Excuse me, Kate. Last night was one of those nights you bitterly regret the next morning."

That grin of his and the vivid, teasing blue eyes above it transformed the weariness into nothing more sinister than the aftereffects of a good time and the worry into a simple hangover. I felt foolish, a prey to romantic imaginings, and obscurely resentful, as though he had no business arousing those feelings in the first place.

I knew I was being perverse, but I also felt a twinge of pique at his easy reassumption of the role of the frivolous Harlequin in the face of my own, admittedly concealed, concern for him. With a certain sharpness, I said, "So you've been burning your candle at both ends, have you? And before the ball, too—"

He must have picked up something of what I was feeling—I'd swear he had a sixth sense as far as women were concerned—because the grin grew wider. "But of course. We're meant to burn our candles brightly during Carnevale so that the gloom of Lent will seem all the more unrelieved. Good Catholics do penance for their sins, and in order to be truly penitent, one must have truly sinned. I would hate to disappoint my confessor; he has learned to expect so much of me."

I had to laugh. "I see. You've simply been doing your duty as any good Catholic should. I had no idea you were so devout. Are you truly penitent now?"

"It's too soon to say. You must ask me tomorrow. After all, I still have a little time left. But it will be difficult to repent of a few of my actions. Saturday's, for example." He caught my eye and held it in a look that was both playful and directly sensual.

To my credit, I returned the look for long enough to seem untouched by it and then, composure presumably intact, turned to the Vanvitelli; it was easier to face. "Of course I can't answer for all your activities on Saturday, but I don't remember anything you should feel sorry for while we were together. Besides, I would hate to think I'd made you feel guilty."

"You make me feel a number of things, Kate, but never that." I couldn't see his face now that my back was to him, but his voice made his amusement infuriatingly plain.

"I'm delighted to hear it." My pretense of cool detachment was spoiled by my dropping the cap to a bottle of solvent I was holding. The solvent was toluene, one of the most dangerous; it was highly flammable, and the fumes were poisonous. I bent to retrieve the cap from under the table, but it was nowhere to be seen, and I stood up again, breathless and flushed. Alessandro came across to help me search, but the little cap had disappeared.

"Never mind," I told him after we'd looked fruitlessly for a few minutes. "I'll stick a piece of cotton wool in the neck. That'll have to do until I get a replacement. And now, I'm the one who's going to feel guilty if I don't get some work done today. After my holiday yesterday."

As hints go, it was hardly subtle, but it made no visible

impression on Alessandro, who blithely ignored it, sitting down instead in the studio's one comfortable chair as if settling in for a visit.

"I hope you don't mind," he said, stretching his legs out in front of him and looking very much at his ease, "if I rest for a moment before I go off to argue with the decorators over whether they should hang pink balloons or green ones from the statues. Today is going to be a day of important decisions, and I'll need to have all my wits about me."

With as much good grace as I could muster, I smiled at him, somewhat weakly, and said, "Make yourself at home." I re-signed myself to accomplishing nothing substantial with the Vanvitelli so long as Alessandro stayed, but perhaps, once I'd worked up my courage, I would learn something that would help me make up my mind about him one way or the other. I could feel his scrutiny as I set about my work, that slightly mocking, questioning glance that made me feel both flattered and uneasy, as though it were a dubious honor to have aroused such interest. His lingering there with me on a day when he would surely have so much to do made me suspicious despite the temptation to suppose that it was for the sake of my company alone.

He said, "You look tired too, Kate. You didn't use your holiday to rest?"

"Does anyone in this city use their holiday for that? I'm no exception. I do as the Romans do."

"Not in all things, I hope." He smiled at me.

"Such as?"

"Juvenal said that to live in Rome one must know how to lie. You strike me as too honest to live happily here."

"Really? You'd be surprised at how quickly I adapt to local customs."

He made no reply to that but waited until I'd turned around again from the Vanvitelli to say, "I'm afraid you work yourself too hard."

"Oh I burn my candle, too, in my own way."

He gave me a slow, speculative look. "Such a beautiful

way." But he said this so quietly and moved so quickly into his next question that I barely had time to register it and no time at all to wonder whether he was being serious or merely provocative. Provocation, however, was frank in what he said next. "So, you have done nothing to repent of, Kate?"

"Now you make me sound impossibly self-righteous and boring," I objected, laughing. "You of all people ought to know that no woman likes to be accused of goodness."

"*Mi dispiace*. I'll remember that. But you really don't seem so very wicked."

"Ah, but you see my sins are generally the duller ones of omission"—until tonight anyway, I added more honestly to myself—"while yours, I suspect, are far more interesting, and—"

"—and quite the reverse. Agreed. And what great sins do you suspect me of, Kate?"

He was still sitting down, one leg now hooked over the arm of the chair, the foot swinging idly back and forth, and his voice was still amused and lightly teasing, but suddenly I was afraid. It was as if, without any warning, we had skated out onto very thin ice—and I had no idea how we got there so quickly. I thought we were gliding along at random, flirting a little on the way, when all the while he had been guiding us gently to this point.

I tried to keep my tone as casual as his and replied, in mock seriousness, "Only a devastating charm you're very well aware of, and exploit mercilessly. And a healthy *amour-propre* that I'm feeding as I tell you this. Nothing beyond redemption."

"Is that the complete catalog of my sins? You've let me off very lightly. After all, charm and *amour-propre* are the Italian male's stock-in-trade. Where would we be without them? We might even be taken seriously, God forbid." He got up from the chair as he spoke and walked across to stand beside me in front of the Vanvitelli, looking down at it. The amusement was still in his voice, but I thought it had a bitter edge to it, and that surprised me. I hadn't meant to offend him and was about to say as much when he turned to me and quietly added, "I should have thought you would accuse me of something far more serious—"

"Which is?" I asked him, although I already knew the answer.

"The business of the Reni."

I paid him the compliment of honesty. What was the use of pretending? "All right, I admit I don't like it. But I understand why you thought you had to do it. Besides, it really isn't any of my business." But you've made it your business with a vengeance, I told myself fiercely. I might have said to Alessandro that I believed Stillitano the guiltier party in their conspiracy, but he couldn't know that I suspected Stillitano at all. And it would be safer to keep it that way.

However, he may have had his own suspicions, because his next question caught me off balance. "You've never asked me who painted the copy, Kate. Surely, given your work, you must be curious?"

As evenly as I could, I said, "Naturally I'm curious. But as I told you, it's not my business." In a feeble thrust at Stillitano, I couldn't resist adding, "Whoever it was, they helped you to break the law, so I assume they aren't reputable and their name would mean nothing to me." I hoped this would satisfy him, because I wasn't sure how well I would be able to parry his questions if they became more direct.

Perhaps it did, because mercifully he changed tack, although what came next was even more unsettling. "Did you know that my father wants to hang the Reni in the Salone d'Oro tonight, for the ball?"

"But that would be terrible!"

He gave a thin smile. "I'm glad you agree with me. I'm going to have to find some way to dissuade him."

"Wouldn't it be simpler to tell him the truth now?" Even as I spoke, I knew my words were a waste of time, but I was still eager to give Alessandro a chance to redeem himself.

Indulgently, as though to a naive child, he said, "The truth, in most cases, is rarely simpler, and in this it would be disastrous." He did not say disastrous for whom.

197

"What will you do, then?"

After a pause in which I had time to grow uneasy, he said, "I thought you might be able to help me."

I knew now why he'd lingered on in the studio. "What help could I possibly be?"

As smoothly as though rehearsed, his answer came pat. "You might tell my father that in your opinion the painting is in no condition to be displayed, that it has developed some problem or other. You're an expert, and I'm sure you could come up with a convincing reason. And my father's eyesight is so poor that he will believe you."

"But it was at Faltecchi and Stillitano only ten months ago for cleaning," I blurted out without thinking; the last thing I wanted to do was bring up the subject of Stillitano's connection with the Reni.

Quick as a cat, he caught me up. "So you know about that, do you? I thought you began work there later. Did my father tell you?"

I was tempted to lie, but what was the point? He could easily confirm the truth of what I said with Count Massimo, and that would create greater problems for me. "Giorgio Faltecchi told me when I mentioned my doubts about the painting to him." Before Alessandro could pursue this dangerous path, I hurried on, hardening my voice in an attempt to sound as discouraging as I could. "Anyway, that's beside the point. I already feel guilty enough for concealing what I know from your father; I'm not about to make it worse by lying. I don't want to discuss it anymore, and I do want to get on with my work. It's what you're paying me for, after all."

His hand caught mine, trapping it, although the pressure was light, his voice when he spoke equally light but underneath the playful tones a pressure of its own. "I've made you angry. I'm sorry, Kate. Lies are always sordid, aren't they? No matter how well-meaning. But it's too late now for the truth. If you can't help me, I will have to find another way."

He was standing very close to me, sideways to the window so that the sunlight fell slanting on him, gilding his skin, throwing the sharp planes of his face into relief, the high cheekbones, the clear angled line of the jaw; I noticed for the first time that there were tiny gold flecks in the blue of his eyes, surrounding the black pupils like a star. Those eyes gazed down at me with an appeal I understood too well. I was conscious of the warmth of his hand on my bare skin, the warmth of his voice, low and intimate as a confession, rich with the implicit promise that I would find more pleasure in surrender than in stubborn resistance.

It would be so easy—the thought was forming in my mind as his mouth brushed across my hair, moving slowly down to my face. He kissed me gently, the barest touch of his lips against mine, before he let me go. Then he turned and left the room without another word.

After he had gone, I spent a futile five minutes cursing him for his attractions, myself for my weakness, and the circumstances for their ambiguities. I had always disliked painters who tried to disguise their own deficiencies with the muddy colors and confusion of line that passed for chiaroscuro, shadows that masked a multitude of sins, and it seemed to me now that I practiced that shabby technique with my own life.

But my work on the Vanvitelli offered an escape from unpleasant reality as powerful as any drug. Within minutes I'd forgotten Alessandro and, what mattered more, myself. I was so wholly immersed in the painting that I failed to hear the knocking at the studio door until the sound of Signora Gambino's voice calling my name broke through my concentration.

"Come in." I looked at my watch and was startled to see that it was already past three in the afternoon. I had worked without a stop for almost six hours.

"You have a telephone call, Signora Roy," Signora Gambino said breathlessly. "Perhaps your friend in the hospital . . ."

I dropped my brush and hurried downstairs with her to the telephone in the lodge. It was Elsa Faltecchi, her voice made virtually unrecognizable with happiness. Her father was conscious, she told me; he seemed to be out of danger and was once again asking for me. Could I come at once?

Offering up a silent prayer of thanksgiving, I raced back to the studio and made a cursory attempt at tidying up. Normally I put everything away in the cupboard, but this time I merely threw dirty tools and brushes into a box and shoved it under the worktable, checked that all solvents were safely capped, and made a mental note to get a cap for the toluene. On my way out of the palazzo, I asked Signora Gambino to tell Mario that I was finished with the Vanvitelli for the day. Not long afterward I met Elsa in the corridor outside her father's hospital room.

CHAPTER

15

Elsa's sister and brother-in-law had not yet arrived at the hospital, and she was clearly desperate to pour out her relief and happiness to someone who cared about her father. Like many inhibited people, Elsa was torn by the need to confess to her anguish and the fear of revealing too much of herself. She spoke in short, intense bursts, as though gulping for air, with an honesty quickly smothered in conventional phrases when her reserve got the better of her. Listening to her was like going for a very jerky car ride. You were just gathering speed, feeling that you were finally getting somewhere, when she would stamp on the brakes. The delay, when I so badly wanted to see Faltecchi, was maddening.

Finally, she remembered. "But I am talking too much, and

my father is waiting. You must go in to him, Kate. But please do not stay long. He is very weak and needs to rest."

"I won't let him tire himself," I promised her. "Before I see him, though, I wanted to ask you if he said anything about the man who attacked him."

"To the police, yes. They were here before you came. They told me that he confirmed Professor Carbone's description—a young man wearing a motorcycle helmet. When they struggled, Papa managed to pull the helmet off. He says he will know the man again." An angry flush darkened her face; she looked very Sicilian and briefly quite unlike her father.

I asked her outright. "Do you have any idea who it might be, Elsa?"

"Ideas are not proof. That will come later, perhaps. It does not matter," she added enigmatically. "My mother's people have a saying: Revenge is a dish best eaten cold." She turned and opened her father's door.

I wouldn't care to have Elsa Faltecchi as an enemy, I thought, as I went past her into the room.

Faltecchi was lying with his eyes closed, his head swathed in bandages, propped against the inclined upper half of the bed and surrounded by the trappings of serious injury or illness, the monitors with their silent screens and the thin plastic tube that snaked through the air from the plasma bag suspended on its stand.

He must have heard us as we entered, because his eyes opened and he smiled. "Kate. Come, sit down here by me." There was a chair beside the bed. "Elsa, my dear, I would like a few minutes alone with Kate." She nodded and went out, closing the door behind her.

When I reached his side, Faltecchi took my hand and patted it softly, brushing aside my words of relief. Despite the heavy pouches under his eyes and the shocking grayness of his face, he looked so much more himself, now that his eyes were open, that it gave me hope.

"I am sure that the nurse will be here at any moment with something unpleasant for me to swallow, so let me tell you at once why I asked you to come. Apart, I mean, from the good it does me to see you." He smiled up at me. "I do not want Elsa to hear it, because she is already much too upset over this business." I took this as gentle hint that I should moderate my own reaction to whatever he was about to tell me.

"Before this happened"—he touched the bandage on his head— "I tried to reach you. I felt I must speak to you about an argument Franco and I had on Saturday afternoon. We are no longer partners, Franco and I—after twenty-five years." He was silent for a moment, his fingers moving restlessly on the sheets. "But then Franco is no longer the man he once was."

There was nothing I could say. I couldn't counterfeit surprise or regret. But I knew how painful the decision must have been for him, and I told him I was sorry. If Faltecchi noticed my lack of response, he didn't show it; perhaps he expected it—he knew how I felt about Stillitano.

Somberly, he continued. "Do you remember the Florentine portrait we were asked to 'correct' for its owner?" I nodded, and he gave a faint smile. "You were so angry, Kate, and I liked you all the better for your anger." His smile died away. "Well, when I looked at that painting, I saw many things I had been blind to in the past few years, willfully blind, perhaps. I always let Franco take care of the paperwork for us. He seemed content that it should be so, and he was undoubtedly better at such things than I. But it meant that I knew very little about the business side of our work. When I realized that there were problems at Faltecchi and Stillitano, I knew I would have to go back through our files to search for answers to the questions I had. There was so much I did not know—I have always been shamefully lazy about certain things, and now I must accept that it may have cost me my life's work."

I wanted to protest, to offer him some sort of hope, but I knew I had nothing more than a crazy scheme that would only worry him, and the words died in my throat.

"Franco found me with the files, and he was furious. I had trespassed, you see. But by this time I had begun to understand a little, and I had questions that he could not answer to my satisfaction. He grew even more angry—and, I think, frightened . . ." Faltecchi's voice faded, took on a puzzled note. "I had the feeling he was not so much frightened of what I might do as of something else."

Abruptly, he asked, "Did you mention your doubts about the Torreleone Reni to him, Kate?"

"No. Why?"

"Because he has somehow found out about them."

From Alessandro, I thought with a sinking heart. Who else? But did that mean Alessandro knew I suspected Stillitano of the forgery and had been playing cat and mouse with me in the studio that morning? Dazed, I tried to fix my attention on what Faltecchi was saying.

" . . . seems to blame you for my distrust of him, although I assured him you had nothing to do with it. There was too much else. He said terrible things, but they do not bear repeating." I knew what they were, however; I had heard them. "I spent the rest of Saturday and all of that night thinking about what I must do. At first it was very hard for me to accept this great change in my life, but on Sunday I began to see more clearly. I realized that I must warn you of Franco's anger against you." He was silent, then said, with terrible simplicity, "You see, I am no longer sure of his sanity."

That shocked me. "Why?"

"He is not the same man I once knew and trusted; he is changed. He behaves now so strangely . . . Perhaps insanity is not the right word. He seems, at times, unbalanced, as though he is under some great pressure. I asked him to tell me what was troubling him, something that might explain his behavior in these last few years, but he denied there was anything and grew even more angry."

"I'm sorry," I said helplessly. "To be honest, I've had my own suspicions—"

"I know." He looked at me, and when our eyes met, there was a world of understanding between us. Faltecchi had not said, and I had not asked, precisely what it was he believed Stillitano guilty of, as though it didn't need to be said.

For all our rapport, I knew Faltecchi must be very worried, or very frightened, to reveal so much. But I didn't want him to know how frightened I myself was—that much at least I could spare him—and so, with a confidence I was very far from feeling, I told him, "You mustn't worry about me. I'll stay well out of his way until things are settled between you." I wondered, then, how far Faltecchi's suspicions went; I had to know if, in fact, they went as far as mine did. "Do you think there's any connection between all of this and what happened to you?"

He gave me a brief, agonized look, then shifted slightly in the bed, as though with pain. At once I regretted the question, but it was too late to take it back. "There is no proof," he said, "and my heart refuses to accept that someone I worked with for so long would do such a thing. But I would be lying if I denied that I had thought of it."

"Will you tell the police?"

Again there was a short silence. "I need a little time, Kate. Perhaps in the end I will have to. But I would spare Franco . . ." With a certain wistfulness, he added, "I hoped I would be able to persuade him to give up this, this . . ." He struggled to find the right word and finally, out of charity, perhaps, said, "This folly. Forgive me, Kate. I cannot be more specific. I am unsure of so much, and until I know more, I cannot—"

"I understand. I really do," I tried to reassure him. That uncertainty was an emotion I knew too well. "I just wish there was something I could do to help you."

"There is one thing—"

"What is it?" I asked him eagerly.

"There was a file . . . I took it from Franco's office on Saturday. It seemed important, but he was so angry I thought it wiser not to mention it just then. I meant to come back later, to look at it more closely, but of course I could not. I thought it might help me to persuade Franco—"

"If you tell me where it is, I could get it for you."

Faltecchi looked relieved. "When Franco came into my office, I slipped the file under a pile of papers on my desk." It struck me that if he had felt such a need for concealment, the file must be very important indeed. "It should still be there. It is a manilla folder, the only one. You will see the name Brandini written in pencil on the cover. Elsa will call Ilaria and ask her to unlock my office for you."

Brandini. The near scandal over the Brandini painting had caused a temporary falling-out between Stillitano and Faltecchi. Had Faltecchi found something to confirm suspicions he'd had at the time?

A nurse came in, tray in hand, to announce that it was time for Faltecchi's injection and my departure. I stood up. "I'll go and get it now and bring it to you as soon as I can."

"No more visits today," the nurse said briskly. "Signor Faltecchi must rest and sleep. The doctor has ordered it."

"Tomorrow, then." I touched his hand. "You must get well. We need you."

As I was going out the door, he called my name. When I turned, he said, "Be careful, Kate."

I went straight to Faltecchi and Stillitano. The trip was slow and the taxi driver as obnoxious as the traffic fumes thickening in the heavy warmth of the day. But I minded none of it. I felt like a condemned prisoner given a reprieve. Faltecchi would be all right—the intensity of my relief told me just how much he mattered to me. And, like the condemned man, I suddenly had a future again; I could think beyond today, or rather, tonight. If the file was as important as Faltecchi thought it was, there was a good chance I wouldn't need to turn burglar after all. I could leave the pursuit of truth and justice to Nick and Gianni, who seemed to have a greater taste for it than I did anyway.

I had to admit I would just as happily continue ignorant of Alessandro's crimes, whatever they were, and let Daniella go her own way to perdition. All I really wanted was protection from Stillitano, some sort of magic charm to keep him, and Marco, well away from Faltecchi and me. I hoped whatever was in the file would be just that. I didn't stop to consider all the questions this was begging; I was too far gone in my relief.

When I walked into the workrooms, Ilaria jumped up from behind her desk and called out, "Kate's back!" Half a dozen heads popped out of doorways, and at once I was surrounded by colleagues eager for news of Faltecchi. Mercifully, Stillitano's long face was nowhere to be seen. He wasn't back yet from Sicily, Ilaria told me.

After I'd convinced everyone that Faltecchi really did seem to be out of danger, they began to pack up for the day, some to take children to Carnival parties and parades, others simply glad to leave early for once. When Ilaria and I were the only ones left in the workrooms, I asked her if Elsa had called with Faltecchi's request to let me into his office.

"I almost forgot," she told me. "I have the master key here."

We went down the hall together to the door of Faltecchi's office. Ilaria unlocked it. "If you don't need me, Kate, I'll go home, too. When you're finished here, you have only to shut the door and it will lock automatically. You have your key for the main door?"

I nodded. "Thanks, Ilaria. See you tomorrow."

I waited until I heard the main door slam behind her before I crossed the room to Faltecchi's desk. It was his usual seemingly chaotic jumble of crumpled paper, journals, skimmed-over half-drunk cups of coffee, and mangled tubes of paint. Faltecchi refused to allow anyone to touch it. But an untidy heap of papers was just visible amid the debris, and I scooped it up eagerly. Too eagerly. The papers slipped out of my hands and went sailing into the air and all over the floor. I stood looking at the mess with despair; it was obvious there was no manilla file.

Gathering up the papers, I turned to the desktop. I searched it thoroughly but without success. Desperately, I went through all the drawers—typical of Faltecchi, they weren't locked—but with no better result. The file was gone.

Stillitano had taken it, of course. There was no other answer. He must have found that it was missing, guessed who had it, and searched Faltecchi's office for it. Or perhaps he'd noticed Faltecchi's attempt to hide it. At any rate, it was gone, and with it, any hope Faltecchi and I had of stopping Stillitano so easily.

I was almost tempted to start to work on Stillitano's office right away, but I didn't dare to. The risk was too great. Anyone might come back to the workrooms; worse, Stillitano himself might appear. And, more practically, I didn't have Signora Renzini's keys and picklocks with me.

The only consolation I could find was that at least I wouldn't have to face Faltecchi with the news today; he would have some hope for a little longer. All I could do now was go home and wait for tonight.

Before I walked the block to my bus stop, I went into the bar across the street for an espresso. When I came out again, I saw a taxi pull up in front of Faltecchi and Stillitano. A man got out and went into the building. Luckily, he didn't see me. Stillitano was back.

The bus was crowded and hot, and I had to stand all the way home. It was unnaturally warm for the time of the year, with a sullenness to the air that promised a storm and made my head ache. I felt edgy with frustration and fear.

Nick arrived soon after I got back to the apartment. I was glad to see him, I wanted him there, and yet . . . To cover an awkwardness so slight I hoped he hadn't noticed, I plunged into an account of all that had happened, omitting only my conversation with Alessandro. I thought I would broach that later.

When I said that Faltecchi was better, Nick put his arms around me. "Happier?"

"Much. For a while I even thought everything was going to be all right. More fool I."

"What do you mean?"

I told him about the missing file. "It must be important, Nick. Otherwise, why would Stillitano bother to take it back?"

Nick hardly seemed to be listening; almost abstractedly, looking out the window as he spoke, he asked me, "You say that Faltecchi never actually mentioned forgery, but did he know if Stillitano was connected to Torreleone in any other way?"

"No, I didn't ask."

Nick looked at me then, a sharp look. "Why the defensiveness?"

"What on earth do you mean?" I moved away from him and picked up the pitcher of flowers to give them fresh water.

"You sounded as though I'd touched a nerve."

"You didn't."

Nick probed further. "Did you see Torreleone today?"

"Yes." I snapped a dead anemone off its stalk and dropped it into the sink.

"That explains it. The famous Torreleone charm at work again."

This was too near the truth for comfort, and I reacted predictably. "For heaven's sake! You talk as though I were some sort of impressionable schoolgirl."

He didn't reply.

Exasperated, I tried again. "Look, Nick. Frankly, I don't much care what Alessandro has or hasn't done. That's your and Gianni's affair. I'm really only interested in Stillitano and Marco, and I'm only doing what we've planned tonight in hopes of putting an end to the pair of them. If a by-product happens to be information on Alessandro, well, that's his lookout. But it isn't my aim."

He lifted his jacket from the back of the chair with the crook of one finger. "I understand." His voice was cool. "Shall I come by around nine-thirty tonight? Or would another time suit you better?"

"Nine-thirty's fine." I kept my own voice as cold as his.

"See you then." He left the apartment.

I looked down at the flowers in my hand; methodically, I began to weed out the dying blossoms.

CHAPTER
16

At eight-thirty I began to dress for the ball. Feeling distinctly like Cinderella to Count Massimo's fairy godmother, I untied the box he'd given me, took off the top, and parted the yellowing layers of tissue paper. The faintest scent of sandalwood drifted for a moment in the air as I lifted the costume, cocooned in a length of muslin, from its nest of tissue paper. Once unwrapped, the muslin revealed a dress as beautiful as any butterfly, a shimmer of silk, satin, and taffeta glowing under the light from my bedside lamp.

It was a dress for the most elegant and extravagant Columbine imaginable, fit for Marie Antoinette playing at dairy maid in the Petit Trianon or for a contessa at Carnevale. I spread it out across the bed and lightly ran my hand over the satin of the skirt. Once it must have been bright yellow, but it was faded now with age to a pale lemon. Cool and infinitely soft to the touch, the skirt looked deliciously like a creamy froth of *zabaglione.*

Arabesques of black lace edged in velvet circled the hem of the skirt and banded the cuffs of the long-sleeved, tightly fitting jacket top. The jacket was a stained-glass window in silk and taffeta, diamonds and triangles of purple, red, orange, and yellow—the traditional motley of Harlequin transformed for a Columbine with exquisite, and expensive, taste. The silk ribbons sewn to the bodice fluttered as I picked up the dress and slipped it over my head. Once again, more strongly this time, there was a fragrance of sandalwood clinging to the cloth, like an echo of the past.

The fit was almost perfect. Perhaps a little too tight and low over the bosom for modesty, but that was very much in the tradition of the coquettish Columbine. I took a deep breath and did up the little jeweled buttons—they seemed alarmingly fragile for their purpose—and wondered if I would dare to eat anything at the ball, let alone dance any but the most sedate waltzes. Then I turned to the mirror and saw with relief and pleasure that I did not disgrace the wonderful dress.

As I put the muslin back into the box, I noticed a snippet of black velvet caught between the layers of tissue paper. When I pulled it out, I found it was a *loup,* the tiny mask worn by the female players of the commedia dell'arte—the final touch to my costume.

There was a knock on the door, and Clara came in, carrying a garment bag in one hand and a small white box in the other. Her eyes widened satisfactorily when she saw me. "*Cara,* you're magnificent! Turn around, let me look at you."

I pirouetted for her, swirling until the satin skirt belled out around me and the ribbons on the bodice streamed like tiny banners. Laughing, I executed two perfect jetés before I remembered the buttons and came to earth abruptly; the buttons, however, were stronger than they looked, for they held beautifully.

"Will I do?" I asked Clara a little breathlessly.

"I don't know what you have in mind, but I think you will

do very well." She held out the box to me. "These flowers came for you earlier, when you were out. I put them in the refrigerator to keep fresh."

"Would you open it for me, Clara." I was struggling to untangle a ribbon from one of the little buttons where it had snagged on what I hoped were only paste diamonds.

Clara held up a cluster of camellias, waxy white blossoms against green leaves. "Very pretty. From Nick?"

"Isn't there a card?"

"I don't think so, but let me look again." She rustled through the cellophane in the box. "Ah yes, here's one." There was a pause. "Not from Nick," she said.

As she handed me the oblong of white cardboard I could see the large black *A* slashed across it; I turned it over, but the back was blank.

Clara was silent, with the proverbial silence that speaks volumes. Finally, very dryly, she said, "A pity Nick won't be at the ball, isn't it?"

Before I answered her, I pinned the flowers on at my waist, then looked up at her. "I know what you're asking me, Clara. But I don't have the answer yet. At least not all of it. Maybe I will by the end of the evening. But not all fairy tales have happy endings."

"That depends, doesn't it, on your definition of happiness?"

The sound of a car outside saved me from any more of Clara's questions. I opened my window and saw Nick shutting the door of the Maserati. As he looked up, I called out that I would meet him downstairs; he nodded and started toward the house.

I smoothed some perfume on my arms and on the back of my neck under my hair, but perhaps my hands weren't steady, because I tipped the little bottle too far and the perfume splashed down onto the jacket sleeve, soaking into the silk before I could wipe it off with my fingers. The scent was much stronger now than I usually wore it, but there was nothing I could do about that; at least the small stain was drying fast in the air and would soon be invisible.

"So, the adventure begins. Perhaps if I drink enough champagne at the ball I'll be in the proper spirit by the time I have to turn into Raffles."

"Who?"

"Just someone who took burglary more lightly than I seem to be able to. It's not important. Now, tell me, what's in that?" I pointed to the bag on her arm.

"Oh! I almost forgot. One moment." She laid the bag over a chair to unzip it, then took out a long black velvet cloak and put it around my shoulders. "There! Now you are ready for your ball."

I leaned forward to kiss her. "It's gorgeous, Clara. Thank you." Quickly, I put the mask and my invitation to the ball in my evening bag and the evening bag itself into my large shoulder purse, which already held a flashlight and the tools given to me by Signora Renzini. Then, with a flourish, I wrapped the cloak around me and went out to meet Nick.

He was talking in the hallway below with Gianni. Both men looked up as we came downstairs—Clara made me pause before we reached the bottom to show off my costume—and Gianni cheered, so lavish, as always, with his praise that his stream of compliments almost covered up Nick's silence. I pretended not to notice the troubled glances Clara gave me when she registered that silence. But she said nothing, only squeezed my hand tightly before Nick and I went out the door. Through a curious kind of tact, none of us had said a word about what would happen when next we met.

Nick and I didn't speak to each other as we walked to the car; his impenetrable barrier was back in place, and I could feel my own defensiveness rise to meet it. Already the glitter that made the evening ahead with all its dangers tolerable was tarnished, and I resented Nick for spoiling what little fun I thought I deserved before I faced my unpleasant task. I knew I was being unreasonable; after all, he had a right to be angry, and I had made it perfectly plain that the risks I would take were more for Faltecchi's sake, and my own, than for any purpose of his. But still, I thought bad-temperedly, he might pretend not to mind—

and then perversely acknowledged to myself that undoubtedly I would feel even more resentful if he did.

Nick asked me in a toneless voice if I felt sure of all the plans we'd made with the Palmieris. Yes, I replied equally expressionless, I thought so, but perhaps we ought to go over them once more.

"All right." He shifted gears expertly but took the sharp turn just a little too fast. The tires squealed on the pavement. "You leave the ball as close to eleven-fifteen as you can. I'll wait for you on the Via dei Coronari, just before it opens into the Piazza Torreleone. We'll drive to Faltecchi and Stillitano together, but I'll let you out a block or so before it. That way you'll seem to be on your own if you run into anyone you know."

"Which is pretty unlikely at that hour."

"Granted. But it doesn't hurt to play safe."

"Oh, I agree. I do have a fairly well developed instinct for self-preservation."

Nick glanced across at me, one eyebrow raised. "So I've noticed. I'll park where—"

"What does *that* mean? What have you noticed?"

"Only that you seem to hedge your bets, Kate."

"You mean that I'm not totally convinced Alessandro is all you say he is."

"Damn Alessandro!" Savagely, he swung the Maserati at another corner, and the tires squealed again. Then, more calmly, he said, "Let's just stick to the matter at hand, shall we?"

How unfair, I thought resentfully, to serve me a foul and then change the rules to suit yourself. But I held my tongue. "All right. Go on."

He would park the car where he could watch the entrance to the building; if someone entered it while I was inside, he would sound two warning blasts of the horn. Gianni and Clara would be close by in their car, pretending to be lovers. All three would watch as I went in and would wait for my return. I was to leave both main doors unlocked, and if I ran into trouble, I would try to flick a light on and off twice in one of the rooms that faced the street. If that was impossible, I would simply scream as loudly as I could. The two men would come to my rescue while Clara called the *carabinieri*.

"Not the most inspired of plans," Nick said, "but—"

"The best we have," I finished for him. For the sake of the little resolution remaining to me, I found it better not to dwell on the many things that could go wrong. I reached into the large shoulder bag on my lap and took out my evening purse. "The picklocks and keys Signora Renzini gave me are in this." I showed Nick the shoulder bag and then put it in the backseat. "I'll leave them with you for now."

"Did you bring the flashlight?"

"Yes, it's there too."

"Fine." We were near the Palazzo Torreleone now, in the *centro storico,* the old part of the city where the streets twisted and narrowed, a warren of one-way alleys, many of which were closed to traffic. Without taking his eyes from the road, Nick opened the glove compartment and removed the gun Gianni had given him. He held it out to me. "Here, put this in your purse, too. Just in case."

Instinctively, if absurdly, I flinched back from the gun. "No! I don't want it." In a more reasonable tone, I added, "I don't even know how to use it."

"It's very simple. You let the catch off—like this. Then point it and press the trigger. It'll do the rest for you." He eased the catch back into place, much to my relief. The streetlights glinted off the dull black metal of the snub-nose little gun as it lay in his palm, looking disconcertingly like a child's toy. I wanted no part of it, that much I was sure of.

"Please, Nick. It would only make matters worse for me if I were caught with a gun, wouldn't it? Not having a license, trying to explain where I got it. I'd really rather not."

He didn't insist, and put the gun back into the glove compartment.

"Besides," I went on, more easily now that the gun was out of sight, "I'll feel better knowing you have it if you do need to come to my rescue."

We drove down the Via dei Coronari; Nick slowed and stopped the car within sight of the Piazza Torreleone. As we got out of the Maserati, I looked up at the sky. The moon was almost full, veiled from time to time by high, racing clouds; the oppression of the day had lifted somewhat, blown away by the wind, but there was still the threat of a storm in the air. I hoped it would hold off until the night was over.

Wordlessly, Nick and I stood facing each other. Finally, I said, "I'd better go now." I turned away, feeling oddly bereft, with the overwhelming sense of having spoiled something precious through my own carelessness or stubborn willfulness.

I had taken no more than a step or two when Nick said my name, and the way he said it—low, almost pleading—made me turn back to him so suddenly that Clara's cloak wrapped like a net around my legs and sent me stumbling into his arms.

He held me tightly, gazing down at me with those unreadable eyes, before he kissed me. "That's for luck," he whispered when his mouth moved away from mine and was soft against my hair. "I won't force it, Kate. You find your answers in your own way, then let me know. I'll wait."

I touched his cheek. "I wish I had the answers now. They seem so close, but . . . I'm sorry, Nick." Then I turned and went toward the palazzo.

Resolutely, I put all my confusion from me as I walked out into the Piazza Torreleone. Already it was so crammed with cars that I had to weave my way in and out of Fiats, Mercedes, Alfa Romeos, and, like some great sleek beast among the lesser breeds, an enormous Rolls-Royce, before I could reach the gates of the Palazzo Torreleone. The palazzo glowed with the light from the torches set into the walls by the gate, the yellow plaster made golden, shadowed in brown deepening to black where the light dimmed.

Signora Gambino stood by the gate, massive as a caryatid, her face solemn with the weight of the evening's responsibilities. Behind her, like an ominous shadow, was an armed security guard, the gun at his hip a grim reminder that in these times the parties of the rich were a temptation to more than the minor sins of *la dolce vita*. Once or twice I'd heard stories of nervous guards mistaking the curiosity or high spirits of guests for something more sinister, with unhappy results. I hoped this one was a cooler type. I smiled at him, but he didn't smile back.

Signora Gambino's face lost some of its unnatural seriousness when she caught sight of me; the white teeth flashed as she gave me a teasing welcome. "The lady of the pictures! You are wearing the costume that Count Massimo gave to you?" I opened the cloak to show her. "Ah, it is beautiful. Tonight you are a picture yourself."

"So are you, Signora Gambino. You look very elegant."

She ducked her head, pleased with the compliment. It wasn't flattery—she had arranged her thick hair in pretty coils on her head, and she wore the pleated black dress with its lace at the throat well. With her straight-backed, handsome bulk, she looked wonderfully like a statue of some formidable Roman matron of the Augustan age, large and secure in her authority.

"It is in honor of the occasion, this dress. I must look my best tonight. There is not only the ball, you see—later, when I finish here, I will go to a party at my son's house. Not so grand a *festa* as this, you understand, but the food will be as good. My daughter-in-law Anna is a cook like no other. I will bring you a piece of her *torta di mandorle* tomorrow, and you will see for yourself."

"I'll look forward to that." I gestured at the parked cars filling the square. "Has everyone arrived? Am I late?"

She laughed. "No, no. They will come until dawn. From party to party, you know. But many are here already, it is true, and you must go up and join them." She turned to open the gate for me, and I saw one of the palazzo's maids standing by the porter's lodge. "Gianetta will take your cloak. She will put it in my lodge."

"Do you know," I told her as I went past her through the gate, "I'm a little nervous."

"Yes?" She looked surprised. "But you have no need to be. Of course," she said, family pride strong in her voice, "the ball is for Signorina Daniella, and it is only right that she is the most beautiful. But you look lovely—the equal of any other lady here tonight."

Her warmth gave me courage. "If I do, it's thanks to this dress." Behind us, a car stopped in the piazza, more guests for the ball. I said good night to Signora Gambino, gave my cloak to Gianetta, and went along the arched passageway to the arcade.

A cobweb of tiny lights twinkled in the low boxwood hedges of the courtyard, diamonds spread out against the dark velvet of the grass. Branches of forsythia in enormous terra-cotta urns stood beneath the arches of the loggia; their blossoms shone like drops of gold in the light from the lanterns suspended above them. Torchlight gilded the water of the fountain and gleamed on the smooth flanks of the marble faun. Someone had placed a wreath of ivy at a rakish angle on his head, so that he looked more than ever like the spirit of revelry. I went over to him to offer a small tribute to the god of the place, and as I laid one of the camellias from my corsage on the fountain's rim I heard the clear, sweet notes of a flute. Startled, I looked about, then realized that the music was drifting out from the open windows of the long gallery above. I smiled at my own imaginings, and at the faun, and stood there listening.

But the moonlight dimmed beneath the clouds, and a cold wind came up, shivering the water of the fountain into a thousand gold pieces, dissolving the crystalline notes of the flute. I turned my back on the faun and crossed the courtyard to the great stone staircase that led up to the Salone d'Oro.

There was the sound of laughter behind me, and two women passed by in a mist of perfume. They paused to glance back at me, each with the identical stare of frank interest, gave me the same cool smile and brief inclination of the head, then swept up the stairs with a rustling of brightly colored skirts—and I in their wake, happy to think I could enter the ballroom under cover of their brilliance.

But I was not to escape so easily. At the doorway to the Salone d'Oro, splendid in a powdered wig and quantities of gold braid, a footman stood ready to announce the guests as they arrived. Resignedly, I waited until he had trumpeted the grander notes of *"principessa"* and *"marchesa"* and the two women in front of me sailed into the ballroom, then gave him my name.

"Signora Roy" simply doesn't have the same ring to it, I thought, as I entered the Salone d'Oro on the last note of my name. And then I forgot all my self-consciousness in the wonderful scene before me. The room that always seemed unsurpassed in loveliness was tonight even more beautiful, a Longhi painting come to life in a swirling mass of color and shimmering light reflected in mirrors, shining silver, and the prisms of crystal chandeliers. Laughter and music and tinkling glass combined to heady effect until I felt my heart beat fast with excitement. This was magic, and I would make the most of it until the hour struck.

My first instinct was to look along the walls for the Reni. But, as carefully as I scanned the paintings hanging there, I could not see the *Madonna and Child*. Perhaps Alessandro had managed his father, after all.

Then I heard my name again, spoken this time in a quiet voice with that trace of amusement so typically Alessandro's. When I turned, he was there beside me, dressed in the masculine version of my own costume, Harlequin's brightly checkered suit made from a fabric whose colors shifted in the light like the skin of some exotic chameleon. He wore a black half mask with slantng catlike eyes. The enigmatic, elusive Harlequin come to life.

"We're a pair this evening, you and I," he said with a teasing smile.

"Yes? I'm not so sure I can change my colors as easily as you." I pointed to a dark patch on his sleeve. "That, for instance—is it blue or green?"

"Does it matter? Tonight nothing is what it seems. It's Carnevale, after all."

I thanked him for the flowers. "It was kind of you to think of it," I added, somewhat lamely.

"Kindness had nothing to do with it." He took my arm. "Come, my father wants to welcome you."

We threaded our way through the laughing, dancing crowd, pausing frequently as Alessandro greeted friends or was caught and embraced. He always introduced me, no matter how brief the encounter—simply by name without explanation of who I was—and I sensed he enjoyed the curiosity in his friends' eyes, men and women both. I didn't flatter myself as to the reason for this curiosity; I suspected that any woman with Alessandro was bound to arouse interest.

Count Massimo and Daniella stood together greeting their guests in front of a large portrait of Baldassare Torreleone, the adaptable nobleman of the baroque who had built the palazzo. As Signora Gambino had said, Daniella was easily the most beautiful woman in the room. A provocative amalgam of innocence and voluptuousness, she was dressed as an *Inamorata,* one of the morally ambiguous lovers of the commedia dell'arte, in a full-skirted dress of rich gold taffeta cut very low in front, with a tall collar of stiff lace framing the sides and back of her head. Her hands, peeping out of the long, trailing sleeves, were folded demurely in front of her, and the eyes that gazed out from behind the white velvet *loup* sparkled with delight. Apart from the too knowing mouth with its hint of sensuality in the full lower lip, she seemed very much the picture of the young girl transformed for her first ball.

Count Massimo was in black with a white ruff around his neck that accentuated the pallor of his skin. His wire-rimmed glasses as usual were slipping down his nose, and he kept pushing them up again with an absentminded gesture. If anything, he looked more frail than he had when last I saw him at lunch on Saturday.

"Bellissima," he said when he caught sight of me, and I felt myself flush with pleasure. "I was certain that the dress would do justice to you, and I see that I was right. It was my wife's, you know." He took my hand and held it for a moment, then said in a soft voice, "I remember well when she wore it for her first Carnevale. She was very nervous until she put on that dress, and then, like magic, she felt the spirit of Carnevale."

"The magic is still there," I told him, and tried to thank him.

But he wouldn't let me, mildly protesting my gratitude as though it embarrassed him to be reminded of his generosity. "Your wearing the costume is thanks enough. It gives me pleasure to look at you. Now go and dance with Alessandro, and it will be as though my wife were here tonight."

Obligingly, Alessandro took my hand and led me out to the center of the room. At the far end, on a raised dais, musicians were playing a pretty waltz, the music as frothy and insubstantial as the dresses that many of the women around us were wearing. Alessandro held me closely, our bodies touching, and I felt his hand warm against my back through the thin fabric of the dress. He smiled down at me, and as we began to dance, he said, "You may remind my father of my mother, but I promise you my own feelings are far from filial. Although I have heard that a touch of incest adds a certain piquancy to a love affair."

"Then it's true what they say about Italian men—that their greatest love affair is with their mother?"

"Our enemies would say that the Italian male's greatest love affair is with himself. But yes, the cult of *La Mamma* flourishes. Perhaps if my own mother had been Italian I, too, would have been a victim, but she was Anglo-Irish—as you know. An uneasy mixture at best." As though this might sound disloyal, he added, "You mustn't misunderstand me—she was a wonderful mother in many ways. But very far from the traditional *Mamma*. She was always very cool, almost remote. I think the only intense expression of emotion that she permitted herself was in her religion. There she came close to being Italian."

"And are you an uneasy mixture, too?" I asked him. "Half your mother, half your father?"

He laughed, and the blue of his eyes seemed suddenly brighter. "Haven't you found out by now that in any mixture the Italian will prevail? The other never has a chance. But"—his mouth curved up in one corner—"it may explain why I'm always drawn to women with my mother's cool Anglo-Saxon temperament."

"My loss, then," I said dryly. "I don't think I ever told you that my mother was from Corsica. Her family came to Montreal when she was a girl, but they kept to Corsican ways. They wouldn't let my mother go out with my father before they were married without some member of the family along as chaperone. So my mother used to climb out her window to him. Finally, they eloped. My father, who is every inch a WASP—"

"And what is that?"

"WASP—White Anglo-Saxon Protestant. Anyway, he was so disgusted by her family's emotional, and sometimes violent, behavior that he refused to let her have anything to do with them after they married. She had to sneak off to visit them, still climbing out of windows when she was thirty."

"A romantic story. Did she ever change your father's mind?"

I shook my head. "After she died, when I was twelve, I didn't see my mother's family at all, and by the time I learned to stand up to my father, my grandparents were dead. But every time my hot blood gets the better of me, I think of them."

Alessandro held me infinitesimally tighter. "So you have hot blood, do you, Kate? And yet you seem so much the WASP yourself."

"A mask. Like your own. Perhaps we are a pair, after all." Before he could do more than raise one eyebrow at this, I changed the subject—it was becoming too dangerous. I asked him about the Reni. "How did you persuade your father not to hang it here tonight?"

He looked away from me, over my head, to acknowledge the greeting of some friends dancing by. "My father changed his mind. He has another idea for it now." But he didn't tell me what the idea was; instead, he whirled us around and in one gliding movement brought us to rest in front of his father as the music ended.

"I'll come back," he whispered. He turned and took Daniella by the waist, drawing her out with him onto the floor. They moved well together, the two cousins—one fair, one dark, each slim and beautiful.

I had my fair share of partners that night, but to my mind none danced as well as Alessandro, or perhaps it was simply that none charmed me as he did. I watched as other women fell under his spell, their inclination to surrender quite evident once they were in his arms, and I wondered if they in turn might have read me as easily.

Then Count Massimo asked me to dance. He moved slowly, but with Alessandro's grace—a stiffer, frailer version of his son—and held me so lightly that I barely felt the pressure of his fingers. His smile was as serene as ever, but the lines that cut into the pale skin of his face from nose to mouth were more deeply etched, and weariness was visible in the droop of his eyelids. I wasn't surprised when he told me that he would dance once more with Daniella and then leave the Salone d'Oro for his bed.

"I am at that time of life when doctor's orders take precedence over one's own wishes," he said. "But I must confess I am not sorry for the excuse. As we grow older, the pleasures of rest outweigh others. We grow dull, alas."

"Never that."

"*Grazie.*" He smiled. "To ourselves, then." He watched Daniella as she danced, laughing with her head thrown back, her whole being radiating delight in the ball, her partner, and—I thought uncharitably—herself. "There, my niece—*that* is youth. Tonight has been costly in many ways, but Alessandro is right. Some traditions are worth preserving. The young make their own lives, but we should not deny them something of the past, however little we may be able to give them."

My face must have shown my bewilderment—I felt sure he was speaking of more than the ball—because he went on, as though in explanation, "I have been selfish, Signora Roy, and it is time now that I made a sacrifice. I will sell the Reni. There is someone willing to pay what seems a remarkable sum for the painting."

I felt a chill premonition of disaster. "Does Alessandro know?" I asked, before I remembered Alessandro's words; this, then, was the other "idea" his father had for the painting.

"Yes, I told him this afternoon. Naturally, because he has always concerned himself with my feelings, he tried to persuade me otherwise. But it is too late. I am often slow to make up my mind, but when I do, I act quickly. I have given my word to a man who has long wished to buy the painting. I am sure Alessandro will be reconciled. It is, after all, what he has himself advised in the past."

So many thoughts were swirling in my head that I found it impossible to speak. If the Reni were sold, it would of course be exposed immediately as a forgery; any expert would see the charade for what it was. And then it would all come out. Alessandro could not afford to let that happen.

What, then, would he do? Once he found he couldn't change his father's mind, would he have the courage to tell him the truth at last? Surely Count Massimo would forgive his son yet again, the son whom he'd once forgiven so much. Or would he? How well, after all, did I really know the Torreleones? I saw only what went on between them when they were with others, the obvious affection, the respect. But I knew nothing of their private times together. Count Massimo was without doubt a kind and good man, but he also had a streak of pride and a firm sense of honor and right. What would he make of a son who not only flouted his principles but deceived him as well?

Even if Alessandro felt confident of his father's forgiveness, would he risk the blow to the old man's health the truth might give? There was also the whole other issue of his relationship with Stillitano. If Stillitano had some sort of hold over Alessandro, he might refuse to let him tell his father the truth, whatever that truth was.

But there was no time to think about any of these questions, because Count Massimo was asking me about my work for him—I managed somewhat incoherent replies. Then a servant approached us and spoke a few quiet words with the count. He nodded, holding out his arm to me. "In a moment supper will be announced. Let us see what there is before the locusts descend." His eyes twinkled, and for the first time I heard a touch of irony in his voice that sounded for an instant like his son's. "We Italians, I am afraid, lose our customary calm at the sight of good food. Unless you eat now, you may find it difficult later to reach the table unaided."

He led me through the double doors at the far end of the

Salone d'Oro and out into the gallery. Three musicians were seated together in a semicircle by the window, one of them the flute player whose music had sounded so magical in the courtyard. Beyond was an immensely long table sheathed in stiff white damask and covered with a Lucullan feast lit by tall candles in twisting silver candelabra.

The Torreleone crystal and silver alone were dazzling, but one hardly saw them for the delicious things they held. There were platters hedged with parsley and heaped high with curls of shrimp and glistening oysters on the half shell, plates of puff pastry pink with lobster, tiny mounds of foamy salmon mousse in cups of lettuce crowned with lemon, and mushrooms stuffed and oozing butter. Shining crystal bowls were filled with strawberries and dark red cherries, pyramids of gold-skinned apricots, and great bunches of green and purple grapes hazed in sugar. Little cakes, glazed pink and yellow, sat in geometric patterns on lovely gold-rimmed china plates, and at the far end of the table I saw wheels of cheese—straw-colored parmesan, ripe gorgonzola with its tracery of blue veins, and creamy smooth camembert. I had never seen so much good food; it was all I could do to subdue the locust instinct in myself.

"Champagne, Signora Roy?" Count Massimo handed me a narrow, long-stemmed glass filled with the bubbling golden drink. No, he shook his head at the waiter with the tray, he would not take anything himself.

I raised my glass to him. "Thank you, Count Massimo, for all you've done for me," I said, forgetting for once his dislike of the title.

But he didn't seem to mind and only smiled at me, inclining his body gracefully in a bow. "It is my pleasure. Now, I hope you will eat some of these wonderful things and enjoy yourself. I must wish you good night."

A stooping, gentle figure in black, he went through the double doors as though he were going back into a past more sympathetic to his own nature, and I was left alone with the music and the feast and my own none-too-pleasant thoughts.

But not for long. Almost at once the double doors opened

again, and a laughing, chattering throng came through them to supper. I looked at my watch and saw that it was already just after eleven; there was no time for that last dance with Alessandro. With a wistful glance at the feast, almost hidden now by the crowds around the table, I went down the gallery, past an oblivious couple kissing in the alcove of a window and a servant busy replacing guttering candles in their sconces, to the main staircase.

I paused at the porter's lodge to get Clara's cloak from Gianetta. The palazzo gate was open, Signora Gambino so busy with a fresh group of guests that she did not see me, and I left the light and laughter behind and went reluctantly out into the piazza to meet Nick.

He raised a quizzical eyebrow as I got into the Maserati. "Everything go all right?"

"Fine. For me, anyway. Alessandro may not have enjoyed the party as much as I did, though."

"Really? Why is that?"

I told him about Count Massimo's sudden decision to part with the Reni. "So this forces Alessandro to be honest with his father, or . . ." I left the alternative unspoken; I hadn't the slightest idea what it could be.

"Exactly," Nick said dryly. "Or . . ." He steered the car around some drunken revelers. "I'd give a lot to know just what he intends to do."

Soon, too soon for my taste, we had arrived. Nick stopped the car. The Via Livia lay ahead, shadowy in the streetlight, almost unfamiliar, and deserted apart from a lone car parked in a patch of darkness down the street from the entrance to Faltecchi and Stillitano. Clara and Gianni were in place.

I reached into the backseat for my shoulder bag, checked once and quite unnecessarily to make sure that Signora Renzini's tools were there and that the flashlight was working, then turned to Nick. "Is this really happening? It seems so unreal."

He took my hand. "It's not too late to back out."

With a show of cheerful resignation I straightened my shoulders and said, "I can't let our side down now." I reached for the handle of the door. "And the sooner I start, the sooner it'll be over."

Nick kept hold of my hand. "Remember, leave the main doors unlocked so that I can get in if I need to. Two blasts of the car's horn mean someone's coming. If you run into trouble—"

"I'll scream. Very loudly. You'll hear me, don't worry." I tugged the *loup* down over my eyes. "There, do I look the part?"

He pulled me to him and kissed me. "Be careful."

I got out then and walked quickly up the street, toward Faltecchi and Stillitano. In a moment, when I'd gone inside, Nick would pull forward and park where he, too, could watch the entrance. If anyone thought it strange that he should be there alone—well, perhaps they would think he was a jealous husband keeping an eye on Clara, the wayward wife, or a detective hired for the job.

Gratefully, I saw that there was no light shining from the window I knew to be Stillitano's. Even better, there were no lights on in the building at all. I unlocked the front door, and then, before I stepped inside, gave a quick glance toward the Palmieris' car. I could just make out two figures fused together into one, Clara and Gianni enthusiastically playing their roles as passionate lovers. But Gianni must have been watching all the same, because I saw his arm detach itself from the mass and make a brief but unmistakable thumbs up sign for luck.

Closing the door behind me was like shutting myself off from the world. I was on my own now. I remembered to leave the door unlocked, and then, by the light of my flashlight, made my way over to the elevator. Only after I was halfway up did it occur to me how stupid I'd been to take it rather than the stairs; I would never hear the car horn over its noisy clanking. Immediately, I punched the second floor button. The workrooms were on the third, but I wanted off right away.

Before I stepped out of the elevator, I saw the familiar little sign affixed to the wall beside the row of buttons requesting passengers to shut the outer door behind them as they left the elevator; with the door left open, the elevator was immobilized. In the past I'd cursed unknown culprits for their forgetfulness, but now it occurred to me that it would be a good idea if in fact the elevator were out of commission while I worked. That way anyone coming into the building would have to take the stairs, giving me a few extra seconds. Not many, because the elevator was almost as slow as walking, but enough, perhaps, to be crucial.

So I left the outer door gaping and slowly mounted the stairs to the third floor.

CHAPTER
17

I waited just inside the main door, listening. The workrooms seemed so quiet, unnaturally quiet. Somewhere there was the steady drip of a tap into a metal sink, but that was all. The corridor stretched dark and silent before me; no lights showed under the shut doors. I waited another long moment, then flicked on the hall light. Nothing stirred.

I went first to the storeroom for the supplies that were the excuse for my presence in the building. The soft clink of glass as I took the bottles of solvent from the shelves crashed against my ears; once a bottle almost slipped from my nervous grasp, and I had to lean against the countertop to calm my shaking. When I'd filled my containers with the solvents, I left them on the table in the middle of the storeroom and crept down the corridor to the door of Stillitano's office.

I paused, again listening to a silence that by now had taken on a life of its own. As I stood there, I was overwhelmed by a strange kind of lethargy, a sudden sleepiness, and the thought flickered far back in my mind that I would simply go home to bed and forget this madness. I shook myself then, hard, to slough off the inertia and set my mind to the job.

In the shoulder purse was the oblong plastic case Signora Renzini had given me, my burglar's bag of tricks. I fished it out, opened it, and took the key she and Paolo thought might be the one most likely to work on Stillitano's door, then fitted it to the lock.

The key stuck, but only for an instant before it turned roughly in the lock, clockwise, until I heard the click of the bolt giving way. With a faint creaking of hinges the door swung inward. I was past my first hurdle.

Then I gasped.

The light from the hallway shone on indescribable chaos. Stillitano's office, normally so neat as to seem bare, lay under a blizzard of manilla folders. Files drifted across the floor, chairs, and desktop as though blown there by some capricious wind, swirled up and out of the filing cabinet drawers, drawers that now gaped open and empty.

I moved slowly, unbelievingly, across the threshold of the doorway and into the room. It was airless and stank of tobacco smoke and cigarette ash; an ashtray on one corner of the desk was overflowing, with butts scattered around it on the carpet.

But when I looked more closely I noticed that although my first impression was of chaos, the folders themselves were shut and seemed less flung about by a careless hand than simply dropped down onto the first available surface in little piles of a dozen or so. I picked up one group; they were still in alphabetical order.

Suddenly I thought of the hall light. Anyone in the street below could see light shining from Stillitano's office window. Furious with myself, I turned and closed the door until only a crack remained. If someone did come into the workrooms unseen by Nick or Gianni, I wanted to hear them. When my eyes adjusted to the darkness, I picked my way carefully through the litter of files to the window. I looked down at the street below and saw, like watchdogs, the two parked cars. Then I closed the curtains and switched on the flashlight, keeping the beam pointed to the floor.

There was no time to think about what the mess around me might mean; I had to start to work right away on the desk. Taking a book from a shelf, I placed it on the carpet and propped the flashlight against it so that the light was trained on the drawer I hoped would contain Stillitano's notebook—right-hand side, second one down. I prayed Paolo's memory was accurate.

Abruptly, on the urging of unreasonable hope, I tried the drawer. But of course it was locked. What had I expected, a miracle?

I opened the oblong case and laid it flat on the floor beside the flashlight. I took out a key and began.

The first key I tried didn't work. Neither did the second. One by one, in the order suggested by Signora Renzini, I put the keys to the lock; one by one, I discarded them.

By now sweat was trickling down my face from under the velvet *loup*; I'd forgotten I was still wearing it. Impatiently, I pushed the mask up onto my forehead and wiped the back of one hand across my face. I was finding it hard to concentrate— half of my mind was focused on those warning blasts of the car horn that would tell me when someone entered the building. I strained to hear, but there was only silence.

None of the keys worked. I began on the picklocks. They were much more difficult to use, requiring a steadiness of hand I knew I couldn't manage for much longer. Each passing minute, ticked off to the beat of that wretched dripping tap as it echoed loudly in the silence of the corridor, undermined my courage a little more. I checked my wristwatch. It was close to midnight. Half an hour had gone by since I first entered the workrooms. I knew that the others waiting below would start to worry soon.

There were seven picks; I tried five of them without success. With a slight tremor in my hand, I discarded the fifth and took

231

up the sixth. To calm myself, I practiced a technique I'd learned from Faltecchi: closing my eyes, I took three deep breaths and in my head built an empty room, which I then blacked out with paint, wall by wall, until only a dark void remained in my mind. Finally, almost serene, I turned to the lock once more.

The sixth pick was longer and thinner, with a slight hook on its narrow end; it was also more flexible than the others had been. It did the trick. I felt it lodge firmly against the metal of the bolt, then, when I moved my wrist as Signora Renzini had taught me in an almost imperceptible increase of pressure on the pick, I felt the lock begin to give. A little more pressure and the lock snicked back.

I wrenched the drawer open. And struck gold. It lay there, a black leather-bound notebook on a pile of papers.

My hand was shaking hard, but this time with excitement, as I reached into the drawer for the notebook, then slipped it into my shoulder bag. About to close the drawer again, I hesitated. The papers were too tempting. I pulled them out and quickly riffled through them.

Then stopped. There, sandwiched in the middle, was a manilla folder with the name Brandini neatly penciled in tiny letters on the cover; it was the file Faltecchi wanted.

I looked at the other papers; at first glance they appeared to be contracts. There were a dozen or so, each one consisting of several pages stapled together, each signed on the last page with Stillitano's signature and the names of one or two others. One name jumped out at me: Alessandro Torreleone. I paused then to read the whole contract.

In brief, unmistakable terms it was an agreement on Stillitano's part to make a copy of the Reni and on Alessandro's to pay him a considerable fee. Oddly enough, the contract stated clearly that the Reni belonged to Massimo Torreleone. But the most damning aspect of the contract appeared in a short sentence near the end that stated that each party to the transaction agreed to its secrecy.

And there was something more. Above the signatures was a curious paragraph, in the flowery Italian equivalent of legal language, which promised "retribution in accordance with the rituals familiar to each party of this contract should either party fail in respect of any of the terms heretofore set out." Following this was a tiny drawing in red ink of a mason's trowel. Mestola Rossa.

Shaken, I glanced back over the other contracts. Each ended with the identical paragraph and the identical symbol.

I looked no further. Even if the notebook proved to be useless, the contracts were all we needed. I slipped the notebook, contracts, and manilla folder into my shoulder bag and shut the drawer. Stillitano would probably discover the theft in the morning, but what could he do about it? After all, he would hardly dare to call the police.

Carefully, I wiped the drawer clean of my fingerprints, picked up the flashlight, and replaced the book on the shelf. I closed the door on the scene and locked it, then went back to the storeroom for my vials of solvent. As I was leaving, I remembered the missing cap to the bottle of toluene and went back for an empty vial. Finally, I switched off the hall light and, with an immense sense of relief that verged on a triumph I didn't dare allow myself to feel yet, closed and locked the main door to the workrooms.

All I had to do now was go downstairs and join the others waiting for me in the street below and I could feel safe again.

I made my way cautiously down the stairs by the light from my flashlight. Near the bottom, clumsy with nerves and impatience, I stumbled over my own feet. I was desperate for fresh air and space, and most of all, light.

When I straightened, I heard it. Two short, sharp hoots of a car horn.

For one interminable, wasted moment I stood rooted to the bottom step, clutching the handrail as though glued to it by sweaty fear. While I hesitated I heard the all too familiar sound of a key in a lock and then, terrifyingly, Stillitano's voice. He was here, and he wasn't alone.

"Damn," I heard him say, "it will not open."

Only the fact that he'd inadvertently locked the already

unlocked door saved me. I knew I could never face him, could never pretend that my presence was innocent. I could only remember that he hated me and that he might be crazy. Like a fox at bay, I headed for cover, racing across the lobby to the broom closet where the porter stored his buckets and mops, to fling myself in just as the main door opened.

The metal edge of a pail dug painfully into my shin, but I didn't dare shift my position. The air was sharp with ammonia and soap, tickling my nose until I was afraid I would sneeze; to prevent it, I held my nose and put my hand over my mouth, taking short, shallow breaths.

A double set of footsteps crossed the marble floor of the lobby, then stopped. My heart stopped with them. There was a sudden line of light shining in under the broom-closet door. I heard Stillitano's voice again, crystal clear in the stillness. "Go straight there. Take only the painting, nothing else. For once show some sense. Signor Bassi was not pleased when I told him how you had bungled. If you fail us again—"

"*Porco Dio*! How in hell was I supposed to know that damned professor would come along?"

Marco! I felt sick at the thought of what might have happened had I stayed to bluff it out with Stillitano. My heart was beating again, slamming against my ribs with hard, painful strokes.

"Shut up." Stillitano's icy voice cut across Marco's self-justification. "I am not interested in your excuses. You have the opportunity tonight to redeem yourself, but it will be the last, I promise you. Listen now, it is important that you concentrate on what I say . . . I have an invitation to the ball upstairs in the office. You use that to get inside the palazzo."

"I thought you said Torreleone refused to invite you?"

"I reminded him of his obligations."

There was a snort of laughter from Marco at this. A match rasped, and I smelled cigarette smoke.

"*Merda!*" Stillitano said. "Where is that elevator? Some fool must have left the door open. Come, we will have to take the stairs. Now, I have sketched a plan of the part of the palazzo where you must go. We will go over it until no mistake is possible. There is an alarm connected to the painting . . ."

The sound of their footsteps on the stairs muffled the rest of his words; soon even the footsteps quieted, grew distant, and faded into silence. Somewhere overhead I thought I heard a door closing. I waited; for one eternal moment I waited. Then I opened the door to my stuffy hiding place, peering nervously around to reassure myself that they really were gone. My imagination was now at a pitch where nightmares start.

Easing off my shoes, I crept quietly across the lobby on stocking feet to the front door. Either Stillitano had forgotten, or else he had deliberately left it unlocked, for the door opened at the touch of my hand. I paused to replace my shoes and then, with an acute sense of release, slipped outside.

Before I could do more than step across the threshold, a hand shot out and grabbed my arm.

"Kate!" Nick's voice was a low and urgent whisper. At the sound of it I felt my fear drain away so suddenly it left me weak. If he hadn't got hold of my arm I would have fallen. "Steady," he murmured. "Are you all right?"

When I tried to answer him, my voice faded in my throat; I nodded instead. I tried again and in a hoarse voice managed to say, "Oh Nick, for one awful second I thought you were Marco."

His grip tightened on my arm. "Then that *was* him just now, with Stillitano?" I nodded again. "I saw them meet but wasn't sure it was Marco. He's in costume." He pointed to a black Alfa Romeo I recognized parked not far from the Palmieris' car. "That's Stillitano's. Marco's motorcycle is just down the street."

We were still standing in the shadows of the doorway, whispering like conspirators, the door open behind us. Nick reached past me to close it. "Where are they now?" he asked me.

"They went up to Stillitano's office."

"When the two of them headed for the building, I hit the horn. You heard it? God knows what they thought—I pretended to be waiting for someone to come out of the building across the way. Let's hope they were convinced. I'd just about decided to come in after you—" Abruptly, he stopped. "Kate, you're shaking. Are you really all right?"

"It's just nerves. I had to hide, but they never knew I was there, thank God. But Nick"—I clutched at his sleeve—"I did it! I got the notebook! And more besides, enough to— But let's get away from here. It makes me nervous. And we've got to find a telephone ... Stillitano's sending Marco to steal a painting from the palazzo tonight, during the ball. It must be the Reni they're after."

I tried to tell him what I'd overheard, but the fear came jolting back like an aftershock, all the terror resurrected now that I was safe and could afford to feel it. My whole body was trembling, and to my horror I heard my voice grow shrill, become someone else's voice.

Nick turned me to him, holding me tightly against his body, stroking my hair while he murmured, "It's okay, love. You've been so brave, but it's over now, it's over." And other words, tender words, repeated until the trembling stopped and I was calm again.

But the urgency remained. "We've got to hurry, Nick."

"Kate," he said quietly, "what does it matter? The painting's a fake. Let Marco take it. It's Torreleone's problem, after all."

"You don't understand. It's not the Reni I'm thinking of, it's Count Massimo. The Reni's in his study, and his bedroom is off that. What if he wakes up while Marco's there? What if Marco ... It doesn't bear thinking about. We've got to warn him."

He put his arms around my shoulders. "All right. But first let's go see Clara and Gianni. They'll be worried. Okay?"

"Yes, of course."

Clara and Gianni got out of their car as we came closer, broad smiles of relief on their faces. As Clara hugged me, Nick said, "I'm going to move my car into that side street down the way. I want it out of sight when Stillitano and Marco come out."

"I've never been so terrified, *cara*," Clara told me. "When I saw those two go in ... You must never do such a thing again!"

I gave a somewhat hollow laugh. "Don't worry. My career as a burglar is over. It was brief but glorious." I reached into my shoulder bag and pulled out the notebook and contracts. "The fruits of crime. Mine and Stillitano's," I said, handing them to Nick, when he came back to us. "I haven't had a chance to look at the notebook, but the contracts are interesting. But there's no time now," I said quickly as Nick gave the contracts to Gianni and began flipping through the notebook himself. "We've got to find a phone and call the palazzo. We've got to stop Marco—"

"The one in costume was Marco?" Gianni asked.

"Yes." I gave him and Clara a brief summary of all I'd overheard, adding desperately, "So you see, we've got to hurry. Marco has his motorcycle and—"

"Not anymore he doesn't," Gianni said dryly.

We all stared at him.

He held up a lethal-looking kitchen knife. "Clara brought this along. God knows what she thought I would need it for—"

"Why as protection, of course," Clara said indignantly.

He winked at Nick and me. "Clara's still a *Napolitana* at heart. You'd think she'd been a *scugnizza* on the streets to hear her talk sometimes. But the knife was useful. Doubtless Marco will blame it on Carnevale, the kind of honest fun he's familiar with himself. While I was at it, I gave Stillitano's tires the same treatment." He looked very pleased with himself.

"So that's what you were up to"—Clara laughed—"while I was saying Hail Marys in the car."

"With no disrespect to your Virgin, Clara," Gianni said, "God helps those—"

"Who help themselves," I finished for him. "The Italians say that, too?"

Nick grinned. "The Italians live that. So you can relax a little, Kate. Thanks to Gianni, Marco won't make it quite so quickly to the palazzo." His face grew hard. "Not that he's likely to make it anywhere. I have a score to settle with him."

I wasn't wholly persuaded. "I won't be able to relax until I've warned the Torreleones, Nick. I'm going to call them now. Has anyone got a *gettone* for the phone?"

"I think I do." Clara searched her purse. "And I'll come with you. Yes, here's one." She held out a token.

"Just a minute." Nick spoke so sharply that Clara's head jerked around, and she stared at him, surprised. "What do you intend to say, Kate?"

"Only what I overheard just now. Nothing more. I'll try to get hold of Alessandro. He can do what he likes with the information—call the police, whatever—but the main thing is to let him know what Marco intends. I won't involve you or Gianni or mention your investigation. If he asks, and I suppose he's bound to, I'll tell him what we agreed on—that I stopped by the workrooms and happened to overhear Stillitano and Marco."

There was a silence. Finally, Nick said, "Okay." But the consent was grudging. "Gianni and I will wait for you in my car. I want to photograph those," he pointed to the contracts in Gianni's hand, "and the Minox is there. We'll keep an eye out, too, in case they leave."

I turned and looked back up at Stillitano's window. The light was on. I wondered if even now he was discovering my theft, was pacing the floor, furious, as he tried to figure out who might have done it. Would he think of me? I shivered, then told myself he might easily have half a dozen enemies in the dirty game he played. Besides, it didn't matter what he guessed. I was safe; he couldn't hurt me now.

There was a bar in the next street that I knew stayed open late. I said I would telephone from there. Before Clara and I left, I remembered that Marco was in costume, and I asked Nick to describe it.

With obvious effort, he turned his attention away from the pages of the notebook. "What? Oh, something dark, I think. He's masked, a half mask, and wearing a cape that completely covers him. I couldn't see what was underneath. Sorry, that's not much to go on."

Gianni said, "You know, Marco has to get the painting out of the palazzo. That cape might be a way of smuggling it out. How big is the Reni, Kate?"

"Small enough so that it could be done that way, I suppose. Yes, you must be right, Gianni. How else would he manage it? There's a security guard at the gate, and he'll have to get the painting past him somehow. But if I hurry, it won't come to that. Come on, Clara."

As it was the only one open in the neighborhood, the little bar was crowded. A knot of men stood clustered in front of the barman, who was clattering a row of saucers down on the counter, followed by steaming cups of espresso. The coffee smelled delicious, and I longed for one myself.

When I asked to use the telephone, the barman shouted out across the room, "Hey, Flavio! Get off the phone! If you haven't persuaded her by now you never will. And the signorina here wants to use it."

The palazzo's number was busy; though I tried it over and over again, I could not get through. I didn't know Alessandro or Count Massimo's private numbers, and the operator was no help—the numbers, she told me, weren't listed.

As I put the receiver back in its cradle, Clara held out a cup of coffee. "No luck? Well, drink that. You can try again in a minute."

"Bless you. You read my mind." Black and smoky and barely cool enough to drink, the coffee went into my bloodstream like an injection of pure energy. Immediately I felt some of my flagging spirits revive. I tried the palazzo again.

But it was no use; the line was busy still. "Maybe I should call the *carabinieri* . . . ?"

Clara touched my arm. "Let Gianni do it. He'll know whom to contact."

Although I hated the idea of more delay, I knew it was good advice. The thought of trying to persuade some disbelieving desk sergeant that what I was telling him was more than some Carnival prank defeated me, and I disliked the idea of involving the police before I'd spoken to Nick. We went back to the two men; as I got into the backseat of the Maserati, I looked up at Stillitano's window. The light was still on.

Nick and Gianni were in front, partially turned to face each other, some of the contracts spread out over their laps. Anticipating my question, Nick said, "Don't worry, they're both up there. Did you get through to Torreleone?"

"No, the line was always busy." I put my hand on Gianni's shoulder. "Gianni, Clara says you'll know someone to call at the *carabinieri*, someone who might—"

"Danilo Cucchi," Gianni replied before I could finish. "The man who let us see his files on Studenti per l'Operaio. Marco's activities would certainly interest him." He looked across at Nick. "Shall I call him?"

Nick hesitated. "I wish we had more time to go through this stuff. It looks like dynamite. You're a terrific burglar, Kate." He grinned at me, and I felt an absurd pleasure at this questionable praise. "But we've got most of it on film now anyway, so yes, call him. Tell him to send a couple of men to the palazzo but to come here with reinforcements himself."

"*D'accordo.*" Gianni got out of the car.

When he'd gone, Nick told us what the two of them had learned from looking briefly through the notebook and the contracts. "They made it clear that Stillitano's up to his neck in Mestola Rossa—besides providing forgeries he may have acted as a go-between for stolen art works on behalf of lodge members, certainly on behalf of Bassi. Apart from the one contract for the Reni, though, it's unclear how deeply his involvement with Torreleone goes. As for his relationship with Marco, that comes through Bassi. Marco's just the sort of thug Bassi would use . . ."

"And is there enough there," I asked him, pointing to the papers on his lap, "to send Stillitano and Marco to jail? Because if not, I'm going back to Montreal. I'd rather risk freezing to death than face what might happen if either of them discovers what I've done tonight."

"We'll all emigrate together," Clara promised.

Nick laughed. "You don't need to pack yet. They'll go to jail. One of the last entries in Stillitano's notebook mentions paying Marco two million lire"—roughly a thousand dollars—"to do a job for him and Bassi on Saturday night. When Cucchi questions Marco about that, I don't imagine he'll have much trouble persuading him to explain it. Especially if Faltecchi can positively identify Marco as his attacker. Marco's not the type to sacrifice himself for anyone.

"But look," he went on, shuffling the papers together and putting them away in a leather briefcase, "I want a better vantage point than this. You two sit tight and wait for Gianni. I'm going closer to the entrance. Kate, may I have your keys? Just in case . . ."

I handed them to him through my open window. "Now it's my turn to say it—be careful, Nick." For an instant our fingers linked; then he was gone.

It seemed an age but must have been only a minute or two at the most before Gianni reappeared. "Where's Nick?" he asked as he slid into the front seat. We told him. "I see. I'm afraid I wasn't able to reach Cucchi. I tried his home; his wife said she expects him back soon. I didn't call the *carabinieri*. It would be better, Kate," he added when he saw my face, "to deal with Cucchi. Marco hasn't left yet, has he? Then we have a little time. I'm going to find Nick first. Then I'll try Cucchi again. Wait here." And he, too, disappeared around the corner of the alley.

Clara gave me a wry look, the parentheses around her mouth deepening, and shrugged philosophically. We settled back to wait.

The fear I'd felt earlier was gone now, as completely as if it had never been, like the memory of pain. I was only anxious, and angry. Angry at myself for good intentions gone wrong, for that well-meant secrecy that now seemed like deception. How would I explain to Count Massimo that I was, in one sense, responsible for what might happen tonight, that I could have prevented it if only I'd told him something of what I knew? How could I persuade him of my affection and concern? He would have every right to see my behavior merely as a patronizing assumption of his own weakness.

I was angrier still at Marco and Stillitano, although I think my fury with Stillitano was the greater because his guilt seemed so much worse. He had murdered friendship and the trust that is so crucial in our work. Marco was, as Giangiacomo had said, a hired gun; Stillitano was the real killer. Or so I thought, until I remembered Nick's sister.

I felt a cold determination rising in me now to ruin their plans and see them both in jail. How could we have let them get so far, suspecting all that we did? Little matter that only four days had passed from first suspicions to certainty, I was miserably conscious that I had failed to do the right thing—despite not knowing what that right thing really was. But now that I knew it, I would act.

These feelings may account for what I did next. I don't know how else to explain it.

The car windows were open. Clara and I heard the sound of footsteps coming fast along the Via Livia, surely Nick's or Gianni's. We leaned forward at the instant that a caped figure went past the end of the alley. He never looked our way, and in the blink of an eye he was gone.

"That was Marco!" gasped Clara. But I knew it already. We waited, but neither Nick nor Gianni was in pursuit.

I thought of Count Massimo, and I knew I couldn't sit and wait any longer. I had to warn him; I owed him that much. Instinctively, I reached into the front seat and opened the glove compartment. Nick's gun was still there. I took it out and put it in my shoulder bag.

Clara looked shocked. "Kate! What are you doing?"

"I've got to warn them. Tell Nick I won't do anything foolish, but I *must* try to warn them." I opened the car door.

"Cara, don't!" Clara grabbed my arm. "It's too dangerous. Wait for Nick or Gianni. I beg you! We'll go in the car . . ."

I pulled free of her grasp and slammed the door shut, then bent down to the open window. "Sorry, Clara. I can't wait." Before she could say another word, I turned and started running.

CHAPTER

18

Marco had vanished. But that didn't matter; I knew where he was going. He was moving swiftly when Clara and I saw him, but not so quickly that I couldn't reach the palazzo first if I ran as much of the way as breath would allow, or better yet, found a taxi. But even on the Corso empty taxis were hard to come by so late at night, and in the small streets of the *centro storico* they were virtually nonexistent. However, I told myself, if I couldn't find one then perhaps neither would Marco. Common sense added that he had no reason to risk a taxi. After all, he didn't know that he was being followed.

My greatest fear was that I would round some corner in my headlong course and run right into Marco or that he would look back, discover my pursuit, and lie in wait for me. Desperately I tried to visualize the route ahead. Would he take the same way as I? Did he know these streets as well as I did?

The cobblestones struck hard through the thin soles of my shoes, so rough and uneven that I stumbled once, clutching at the wall beside me, only to feel, to my horror, a greasy softness of cloth and underneath the bony shape of an arm. I screamed and jerked my hand away, then saw an old man's face, blurred eyes wide with fright, staring at me from a doorway, and smelled a sour reek of wine and garlic before he turned and scuttled back into the shadows, as terrified as I. After that I kept to the middle of the street.

All the while I was half-aware of a steady thumping sound, rhythmical and somehow ominous, like drums in the jungle, as though in counterpoint to the blood pounding in my head and the thudding of my heart. But I was too dazed to really take it in until I came around the corner to the piazza and up against a noise as fierce as a blow.

Ahead, where the street opened into the square, a maelstrom of bodies was moving in a black clotted mass. It was dark—I could barely make out the shapes as people—a strange darkness, because at night the streets and squares of Rome are always dimly lit by streetlights. Then, as my eyes adjusted to the unfamiliar darkness, there was a blinding flash of light, harsh and raw, as though some switch was tripped. When my sight cleared, the scene in front of me sprang into livid clarity.

In daylight this little piazza was a delight, scalloped on three sides by the rococo curve of peach-colored buildings and faced on the fourth by the massive gray bulk of a baroque church. But it was unrecognizable now.

I saw the scaffolding first, raised against the walls on the opposite side of the piazza, beyond the crowd ahead. On the scaffolding, like life-size gargoyles picked out by lurid red and yellow spotlights, were strange birdlike creatures crouched as though waiting for some command, at which they would swoop down on those below. An immensely fat woman in a tight black dress squatted in the center tier against the backdrop of huge shadows cast by those weird birds, laughing, her mouth a wide red gash in the chalk-white face. She was grotesque, like a leering mask of comedy.

The drums were louder now. There was a shout—it seemed to come from someone in the crowd ahead—and at once, as in a dream, the crowd parted, giving me a glimpse of something so bizarre that I could only stand and stare, doubting my own eyes.

Ringed by the crowd was a throng of masked and costumed creatures all moving, jumping, writhing, to that deadening thud of drums, as though taken by a mad tarantella. Like those condemned to dance until they forced the spider's poison from their bodies or dropped down dead, these dancers seemed stricken by some wild madness, capering and leaping without grace or pattern.

Almost against my will, I drew closer to the fantastic scene until I was at the front edge of the crowd. The dancers were costumed like the gargoyles on the scaffolding above, in birdlike masks with huge red-beaked noses and caped in black; with their arms stretched out behind them as they flapped and twitched, they looked like birds of prey quarreling over some victim. They rushed at the crowd, as though to peck at them, then turned on each other while the crowd jeered and laughed.

For one mad second I wondered if I'd wandered by mistake into another century, the wrong corner turned, the wrong road taken, and I was in an older age and part of a *danse macabre*. I stood there dazed until a man shouted and pulled me roughly back. The sight of his outraged face behind a pair of very modern aviator glasses brought me to my senses.

He cursed me extravagantly, and then, seeing my confusion, added more gently, "But you were in the way, signora. Soon you would have been in front of the cameras." He gestured to my left, past a bank of arc lights, and I saw the cameras and a group of men and women standing on the broad stone steps of the church. In their midst, perched on a camera crane while he shouted directions at the dancers, no longer creatures from a nightmare now that they had fallen still and silent but merely actors, was the director, streaky gray hair falling to his shoulders under the peaked cap.

"But how do I get around, over to the other side?" I asked the man in the aviator glasses. He was looking down at a sheaf of papers in one hand.

"I'm in a desperate hurry. Please, could you let me—"

"Impossible!" Dismissively, he flapped the papers at me.

Very well, I thought furiously, I've asked you politely, but since that doesn't work . . . You can edit me out later.

I plunged into the crowd of dancers while the man's back was turned, elbowing my way roughly through in absolute determination that no film crew, no matter how august the director, would prevent me from reaching the palazzo in time. There were grunts and some curses as I pushed and shoved my way across the square, but no one tried to stop me; perhaps because I was in costume myself, they thought I was part of the scene.

Stumbling, panting with weariness, I broke free of the crowd and darted under the barricade that blocked the other side of the piazza. Some men lounging by a parked car whistled and made feinting grabs at me, but only their laughter pursued me, and soon I was in deserted streets again, streets empty of people and traffic, everyone gone to see the film being made. There were no bars open here, no chance to telephone had I been willing to risk the delay of that busy signal. Marco would be far ahead by now, might even be in the palazzo, searching for the study. Fear gave me the energy I desperately needed; with a final surging effort, I raced down the endless streets and out into the Piazza Torreleone at last.

Rain spattered briefly on my face, then stopped. Like a threat, the storm hung over the city, ready to break. I could feel it gathering, pressing down on me. As I came up to the gate, I slowed to a walk, searching for Signora Gambino. But she was gone. Only her dark shadow, the armed guard, remained, watching me impassively as I approached.

I wasn't prepared for this. I'd thought I could simply tell Signora Gambino to warn the Torreleones of the risk of a robbery. But now, would the guard believe me at once, or would I risk precious minutes explaining, trying to convince him? What would he make of an unknown foreigner with a story of a robbery?

No, it would be faster to go straight to Alessandro. He could call down to the guard when I'd told him. Easier to give the guard my invitation and pretend I was a guest like any other.

I opened the shoulder bag and felt for the square of white cardboard, and felt again. All that met my hand was the touch of familiar objects and the cool metal of Nick's gun. The gun. Hurriedly, I shut the bag and looked no further. The guard's hand was too close to his own gun to leave me in any doubt of his reaction should he see mine.

But where was the invitation? Of course—in my evening purse, in the backseat of the Maserati.

Damping down my desperation, I went up to guard and, as calmly as I could despite my breathlessness, gave my name and said I was an invited guest who'd come earlier to the ball, left briefly, and was returning now but seemed to have misplaced my invitation. Signora Gambino, the *portiera*, knew me. Was she about? Or was there a guest list he could check for my name?

The guard heard me out, unblinking, his arms folded now across the row of brass buttons on his jacket. When I finished, he said, "I'm sorry, signora. The *portiera* has gone for the night. There is a guest list, but I have orders to admit no one without an invitation." His tone was polite; the look on his face, however, was not. He might as well have added what was clearly in his mind, ". . . and I have no intention of letting you in."

His eyes flicked coldly down the length of me, summing me up, and I was suddenly made horribly aware of how I must look: panting, disheveled—in short, a far from welcome guest.

For some ridiculous reason I had assumed until now that my urgency would carry everything before it, that my only real obstacle would be Marco, not some hired watchdog with disbelieving eyes. I could feel the accumulated frustration of the last few days rising up in me, twisting in me so painfully that it was all I could do to keep from screaming at that blank face barring my way.

"Please, please," I begged him, trying hard to keep the anger from my voice, "I've *got* to speak to Alessandro Torreleone or his father. It's terribly important. Couldn't I at least use the phone inside the porter's lodge? I know Signora Gambino wouldn't mind."

But at this he looked suspicious. He unfolded his arms and let them drop to his side, one hand resting on the holster. His gaze left me for a moment and carefully scanned the square.

I took a deep breath and was about to tell him I was no terrorist or lunatic and that he'd better reconsider or else take responsibility for the robbery doubtless under way while we argued when two things happened to distract the guard's attention from me, effectively destroying any chance of my telling him about Marco.

Several cars screeched into the piazza and stopped with a sharp squeal of brakes, horns blaring. Car doors slammed, and there was much shouting and laughter as a dozen or so costumed guests got out and started toward the palazzo. The guard stared at this noisy group, but before he could do more than take a step back in response to their onslaught the sky opened like a floodgate, and rain drove down on us.

The laughter changed to screams and curses from the men and women as they raced toward us at the gate, waving their arms frantically and shouting at the guard to let them in. For the first time, I saw him lose his calm as he stood caught between his orders and the converging mob of guests, whose shrieks were rising in direct proportion to the rate of the deluge. His obvious hesitation only added to their fury, and they bellowed at him to open the gate before they drowned.

They were too much for him. A spasm of panic crossed his face before his nerve broke and he turned to the gate. In a cursing, laughing, shoving throng they pushed through behind him.

And I with them, neatly sandwiched between two of the tallest, my mask pulled down over my face.

Inside, under the arched passage, there was massive confusion as the guests milled about while the guard shouted vain appeals for their invitations. The racket was deafening: men and women both wailed over their sodden costumes and ruined makeup. They ignored the guard's despairing cry that he must have their invitations before he could let them through to the ball, brushing him off with shakes of their heads while they tried to restore some of their by now soggy glamour.

As soon as I was inside, I stripped off the damp cloak; without it, and with the *loup* in place, I might escape the guard's recognition. But the problem of the invitation remained. The guard was obviously not going to let anyone through without one. Keeping to the far edge of the mob, I inched my way forward. My goal was the little stairway on the right, near the arcade, the stairway that led up to my studio and the southern wing of the palazzo. From that wing I could take a roundabout route along the gallery to the Salone d'Oro and Alessandro. It was slower than crossing the courtyard, but there was less chance the guard would see me.

The guests finally quieted sufficiently to hear the guard tell them that there were cloakrooms just off the courtyard where they could tidy up if only they would give him their invitations. With sudden comprehension and cries of eagerness, they produced those precious squares of cardboard and began to push forward again, all but overwhelming him.

In those few seconds of confusion I gained the stairs and raced up them two at a time, listening for the shouts of fury at my back. But I escaped unseen.

Near the top of the stairs the cloak tangled in my legs and almost sent me flying. It was heavy on my arm, a burden, and I looked for somewhere to leave it, then saw my studio door standing open. The paintings were gone, of course, and I supposed someone had forgotten or felt no need to lock up. Hardly breaking stride, I tossed the cloak through the doorway onto a chair and then, without pausing to think, put my body into overdrive and in one final burst of speed ran to the double doors that opened onto the southern wing.

I grabbed a handle and tried to wrench it open. Nothing happened. I tried again, with no better result. The doors were locked. Sobbing with weariness and frustration, I leaned my head against the wooden panels and banged with all my might on the doors. But I knew it was futile. How could anyone hear, so far away, with all the noise of the ball?

There was no choice. I had to go straight to Count Massimo, alone. Perhaps, with luck, I had won the race after all; perhaps Marco had been delayed. . . . I turned and ran back the way I'd come, past my studio and along the shadowy, silent gallery.

The eastern wing was deserted, closed off from the noise and life of the Salone d'Oro far away across the courtyard. My footsteps echoed in a dim, ghostly silence, an empty silence, for the gallery was stripped of all its furnishings, the tapestries and mirrors, chairs and tables, gone to decorate the western wing. Only a few portraits remained on the walls, too shabby or too ugly to be useful, staring indifferently down at me as I ran past. It was grim here, like the premonition of a future reality behind tonight's glittering facade.

When I reached Count Massimo's study, I stopped, one hand on the doorknob, brought up short at last by the hard fact of what might lie beyond. For the first time since I began my headlong rush to get to where I stood now, I thought about what it might mean to find Marco, to confront him alone, without help. Involuntarily, I took a step back, all my courage and unthinking determination seeping away. The weight of Nick's gun in my shoulder bag was no comfort. I would go back to the guard. I couldn't face Marco on my own.

A noise from inside the study, a muffled groan of pain, ended all my hesitation. I flung open the door.

Count Massimo lay faceup on the floor in the center of the room, moaning, arms and legs splayed out, his glasses in pieces by his head. I ran to him and knelt by his side, horrified to see blood pooling near his face. I was about to speak when another sound, a scraping sound to my right, followed by a sharp exclamation, made me rise and whirl about just as a man lunged out from behind the lacquer screen hiding the Reni. A man in a black cloak with a black half mask covering the top part of his face.

I only had a glimpse of him as he came at me with all the vicious force of a hawk falling on its prey, his mouth thinned with cruelty, his curving fingers reaching out for me. But that glimpse was enough. It was Marco.

Instinctively, I threw up my arm to ward him off as he struck at me. I caught him on the jaw with my elbow, my left elbow. The blow couldn't have hurt him much, but my scream of anguish, prompted by an agony so intense it left no room for thought of flight, a scream with all the pain and fear in me raw and pulsing, stopped Marco in his tracks for one long moment.

I doubled over, my arm pressed hard against my stomach while I cradled my throbbing elbow in my right hand and fought off the waves of nausea that washed over me. But I never took my eyes off Marco. Through a blur of pain and sickness I saw him stare speculatively at me, then down at Count Massimo on the floor beside me, and back at me again. Perhaps he thought we were both so wounded as to be negligible—a semiconscious old man and a terrified woman could be no threat. Whatever the reason, he suddenly turned away from us, knocked the lacquer screen aside, and grabbed the Reni from where it was lying on the prie-dieu. Either Count Massimo or I must have interrupted him as he was taking it from the wall. I wondered why the alarm hadn't sounded.

Stunned by pain into a blank passivity, I barely reacted to the sight of the switchblade that he drew from his pocket. He flicked it open with a sharp downward jerk of one arm and plunged it into the upper left corner of the canvas, cutting the painting away from its frame in one long ripping motion. When the canvas was free of the frame, he rolled it up and stuffed it under his cloak, then turned around to us once more. The knife was still open in his hand.

"If you're smart," he said with quiet menace, "you'll stay right where you are. But if you move or scream . . ." He made an evil little motion with the knife. "Understand?"

I nodded.

"Good." He walked quite casually to the door and drew the key from the lock. I supposed he was going to lock us in, and I wondered how he himself had got into the study so easily. But it was no more than a passing thought; my mind was flooded by relief. He was going, and we were still alive. I never once thought of using the gun in my purse to stop him; I only wanted him gone.

Then, with a fierce jab of panic, I saw his hand check on the knob of the door, saw him pause, jerk his head up as some thought registered, and swing around to us again. His eyes widened behind the mask.

"You!"

And I knew that until this moment he hadn't recognized me, had assumed we were strangers to each other and he could therefore afford to let me go. He must have realized that the blow to my arm hadn't been hard enough to explain that scream—and remembered.

There was a glint of something very like anticipation in his eyes, a look that promised he would take real pleasure in making me suffer, pleasure spiced by the knowledge of my fear. I think it must have been that look that saved me.

Like a white-hot flame the instinct for survival flared up in me again, burning away my paralysis until I felt my courage resurrected, phoenixlike, from the ashes of fear. The pain in my arm was fading, replaced by a dull ache that nagged at my flesh but left my mind clear. By my side Count Massimo lay with shut eyes and half-open mouth, his narrow chest rising and falling as he took in deep, frighteningly ragged breaths. But those breaths showed that he was still alive.

Slowly, deliberately, Marco closed the study door and turned the key in the lock, removing it again and putting it into his pocket. For the space of a few precious seconds his eyes left me, long enough for me to reach into the shoulder bag still hanging by my side, the right side, which was turned away from him, and quickly fish out the gun, hiding it up against me in the folds of my costume.

Like any sadist, Marco enjoyed lingering over his victim. The time he spent savoring my terror was all I needed. Gingerly,

I eased off the safety catch, then slowly straightened up to face him, the gun still hidden in my sleeve.

He smiled. "So, under that mask it's my friend the revolutionary. How did you come to be here so inconveniently for both of us?"

I said nothing. I was wondering about the range of the little gun.

"Never mind," he said shortly. "I've been told you have a bad habit of sticking your nose in where it doesn't belong."

"By Stillitano?" What did it matter now what I said to him? And anything that disconcerted or delayed him was to my advantage.

He looked startled. "You *do* know a lot." He shifted the knife from his left hand to his right, and I found myself staring at it, almost mesmerized by the long, gleaming blade. It looked terrifyingly efficient. Reflectively, Marco stropped the blade lightly with his thumb, as though he were testing its sharpness. "Perhaps I ought to find out just how much you know." He took a step toward me.

I raised the gun and pointed it straight at his chest, gripping it tightly in hands that were slippery with sweat; I was gratified by the look of shock that wiped the pleasure off his face.

"*Cagna! Puttana!*"

"Flattery won't work. Close the knife and drop it on the floor. . . . Now kick it toward me, but not too hard."

Marco obeyed my first command but then gave the knife such a vicious kick that it went clattering and sliding along the parquet floor to disappear somewhere behind me to the right. I didn't dare turn around to look for it.

At that moment, disturbed perhaps by the sound of the knife, Count Massimo stirred and cried out. Before I could stop myself, I glanced down at him. That gave Marco his chance.

He flung himself at me, grabbing for the gun. I fired, but it was too late. The bullet went wide, burying itself somewhere in the wall behind him. As he reached me, I flinched back, striking at him with the butt of the gun, which glanced off his temple before flying out of my sweaty grasp. It arced over his shoulder to fall on the floor somewhere in the shadows behind him.

Blood was streaming down his face from the cut on his forehead and there was a crazy light in his eye as he hit me. But the blood must have bleared his sight, because the blow landed on the side of my cheek, not in the middle of my face. It hurt, but not as much as he meant it to. Then he shoved me violently back and wheeled hard around to hunt for the gun.

Too hard. He stumbled over Count Massimo's outstretched arm and went crashing to the floor. Savagely, he lashed out with his foot as he fell. I heard a sickening sound of impact as the kick connected with that frail body. Count Massimo groaned once and lay still. He wasn't breathing anymore.

Dear God, I thought, he's killed him.

Marco was already scrambling to his feet, but the fall had cost him. It was clear that his leg was injured in some way, for he cursed, clutched at it, and almost fell again. I took a step forward. But he was between me and the gun. There was no point in trying for it; he would be there before me. And the study door was locked.

The secret passage was my only chance. I didn't wait to see what Marco would do next. In four steps I was at the panel, fumbling for the hidden spring.

CHAPTER
19

Frantically, I searched for the spring. Somewhere behind me Marco was cursing, his voice low and thick with anger. I risked a glance about. He was near the door, his back to me, stooping and looking about. Then he gave a yelp of triumph. When he straightened and turned, the gun was in his hand.

At the same moment my fingers found the spring. As I pressed down on the strip of wood, I put my shoulder to the panel below and felt it turn smoothly inward on its hinges. I took a fleeting satisfaction in Marco's shout of surprise, but I didn't linger to enjoy it, which was just as well, because as I dove through the opening, he fired. The bullet smacked into the paneling behind me with a crack of splintering wood.

I didn't look back to see if he was after me. He had to be. He couldn't afford now to let me go; I knew who he was, and I'd seen him kill. There was no time either to push the panel into place. If Marco got there first and if I had to struggle with him . . . The risk was too great. I fumbled in the shoulder bag for my flashlight. Let Marco find his own light, I thought as I plunged into the darkness.

There was light enough from the study for the few steps I took before I had the flashlight out and switched on. Its thin beam skimmed off the worst of the dark, lighting up the steps that curved down and away to the right. I ripped the mask from my face, then hurled myself down the circular stairwell, clutching at the clammy stones of the wall beside me for balance.

Down, down, down I spiraled in a nightmare come to life, winding down the ever-widening stairwell into a chilly gloom that smelled of must and damp and something undefinable yet familiar. The smell of stables, long gone but lingering in the wood.

Too quickly, Marco found the switch. I was only halfway down when there was a sudden flare of light. Naked bulbs strung on a wire looped along the stairwell's central pillar gave off a feeble glow, barely stronger than the flashlight. Footsteps sounded on the stone above, halting steps coming slowly because of the injured leg, but coming surely.

Some shred of sense persisted despite the panic clawing at my mind, or perhaps the memory of a movie I'd seen; I reached up and smashed the next bulb I came to with the handle of the flashlight—then the next, and the next. The pop of exploding bulbs and the tinkle of glass on the stone stairs were almost comforting. Now, I thought with grim pleasure, Marco might break his neck.

Savagely, I swung the flashlight up at a bulb that hung suspended from the ceiling on a line of flex. But suddenly the stairs grew shallow, fanning out like wedges of a pie around the central pillar, and my left hand slipped off the stone wall into air. Startled, I stumbled forward into the cellar and almost fell, saving myself only at the last second by grabbing blindly at a high wooden partition projecting from the wall.

But I dropped the flashlight. There was a loud and very final crack as it hit the stone floor; its light blinked once and failed.

Mercifully, a single bulb survived my destruction, the bulb I'd been aiming at when I stumbled. Struck a glancing blow by the flashlight, it swung wildly on its length of cord, sending my shadow skittering crazily across the wall. By its pale light I found the flashlight lying close to my feet, snatched it up, and snapped the switch off and on again. But it was hopeless; the bulb was broken.

Despairingly, I searched the shadows for a bolt hole. To my left a row of ceiling-high partitions retreated into darkness; to my right a rough stone wall continued for a dozen yards until the cellar opened up, stretching through a murky twilight into impenetrable night, cavernous and unfamiliar. I had a glimpse of labyrinthine passages; one of them must surely lead to an outer door. But which? No, I couldn't risk a possible dead end, a locked door or blank wall with nowhere to hide when Marco tracked me down.

Not long now, his footsteps seemed to say. They echoed in the well-like silence, slower than before because of the dark—as though he were feeling his way from step to step—but growing louder, growing closer. Panic raked me like a spur; a part of my mind stampeded me into reckless, frightened flight until the cooler half took over, curbed the fatal impulse, and forced me around the first partition.

It was a plain box stall: three wooden walls, a heap of dusty blankets, a bare-swept floor. No hiding place. I ran to the next. Apart from a broken trough in one corner, it was a duplicate of the first. With fading hope, I tried the third.

It was darker there; the light from the lone bulb barely reached it. But I could see that this stall was bigger than the others, with the rat-chewed remains of tack—bridles, harness, an ancient saddle—hanging on the far wall. Under these was a row of large, waist-high wooden boxes with hinged covers.

I ran from box to box, raising the lids, peering inside. Each was crammed full of odds and ends from the stables. Only the fourth was empty. Over the edge of the box I went, into that claustrophobic, dusty space to crouch on a bed of empty feed sacks. I lowered the top of the box down over me until only a hairline crack of light remained. If Marco came into the stall, I wanted to see him.

I knew my only chance was somehow to get around him and up those stairs again. Otherwise ... On the thought, the light went out. Through the darkness came Marco's familiar, vicious litany of oaths.

There were two possible explanations for the sudden dark: Either the bulb had burned out, or the light was on a timer. If it had indeed burned out, then the odds had shifted in my favor. The gun would be useless, and Marco would be handicapped by his damaged leg. But if it was on a timer, there would likely be another switch somewhere at the bottom of the stairs that might control a set of lights here in the cellar. And if I was thinking along these lines doubtless Marco was too, and was searching for the switch.

I crouched there, waiting.

At first I was conscious only of my own body, of my heart hammering hard at my ribs, the blood in my face, and of lungs desperate for air. Gradually, though, the memory of Count Massimo's murder, the smothering dark, and despair overwhelmed me. A long wave of terror, the backwash of all I'd been through, swept through my body like a tidal bore.

For a drifting moment I let it carry me with it until I knew I was going to scream. I fought it then, fought that lethal current with every bit of strength left in my mind, willing myself to relax until something like calm crept over me—perhaps simply the fatalistic calm that comes with the certainty of defeat. No matter; anything was better than that mindless fear.

As my terror subsided, the pain from my arm and cheek where Marco's blow had landed came back. I put my hand to my face and felt the stickiness of what could only be blood.

Then came a noise that froze my hand to my cheek—a faint scratching that rasped against the outside of the box, and at my quivering nerves. Had Marco found his way through the dark-ness to me already, precisely like the night predator he seemed? I clasped the flashlight tightly, the only weapon I had, ready to lash out at him the instant he pulled up the lid of the box.

Before I could move, I heard something else—a shrill squeaking and the patter of claws across stone. A rat, come to investigate the intruder in his cellar or to forage hopefully for the last grains of corn fallen between the flagstones. In any other circumstances those sounds would have horrified me, but now I was only relieved that the scratching had so innocent an explanation—as long as the rat, like Marco, stayed outside the box. But where was Marco? The cellar was silent once more.

Then he answered my question. The merest hint of light shone suddenly through the crack; my guess about the timer was right. Now surely it was only a matter of minutes before he discovered me.

I couldn't just sit there, crouched in the box like a rat in a trap of its own making, passively waiting for death. I had to know what he was doing. Cautiously, I raised the lid of the box a fraction more and peered out into the dim half-light, listening.

At first there was only silence. Even the rat had gone to earth. Then, as I strained to hear, came a whisper of movement, so eerily magnified and distorted by the cavernous space of the cellar that it was impossible to say what had caused it.

Suddenly, grotesque as a bat, Marco's shadow loomed on the far wall, huge and ominous in that twilight underground world. Like an unwilling spectator in a shadow puppet theater, I watched through the crack as the black image crept along the wall, paused, narrowed, and disappeared. He had gone into one of the stalls.

There was the noise of something thrown aside, something soft landing with a muffled thud on the stones—that pile of blankets, perhaps—before I saw the shadow reappear against the wall, grow larger, hesitate, and fade yet again. He entered the stall next to mine.

Once more I heard him moving about, heard now the sound of his breathing, and in frightened response tried to quiet my own; once more I saw the shadow towering before me, the gun in one hand distorted to terrifying proportions. Again he paused, again he moved forward.

And I saw Marco himself.

He stood there at the entrance to the box stall in which I was hiding, and I could have sworn he was staring straight at me, though some part of me knew that the light was so dim and the crack through which I was peering so narrow that it was impossible for him to see me. But it was all I could do to keep from crying out, to stop myself from giving up. After all, why prolong a hunt that could only have one, very final ending?

Only the sudden shift of his body as he turned to scan the stall saved me. No, he wasn't sure yet where I was. I clamped down on the cowardly urge to surrender.

His gaze swept over the stall, returned to the row of boxes, and stayed there. He took a cautious step forward, gun raised, into the stall—toward me. He moved to the left, to the far end of the row, out of my range of vision, so that I could only imagine his movements as I heard him slowly lift the lid of the first box. There was a protest of hinges, a sudden bang as he threw the lid back against the wall, and silence. Repetition. Then again, with the third box.

I was in the next, the fourth, along the row.

I saw Marco in front of me now, saw the black cloak block out the light, saw him lean forward to reach for the lid.

Before he could touch it, I surged up, flinging the lid back as hard as I could while I lashed out blindly with the hand that held the flashlight, my only weapon. His cloak cushioned the blow but shock caught him off balance and he went staggering back, grunting with surprise. I scrambled out of the box and raced for the stairs. As I reached the first step, I heard the gun and the simultaneous smack of a bullet into stone somewhere close by. I went up those stairs as though all the hounds of hell were baying at my heels.

As soon as I was on the spiral staircase, Marco couldn't get a clear shot at me; in any case, his injured leg would hamper him. The light faded as I ran upward until finally it disappeared altogether and I was running in darkness, oblivious to the danger of falling, only grateful for the shield it offered. Marco's limping footsteps sounded behind me like a distorted echo of my own.

The inky blackness lasted only a few seconds before I rounded the final twist in the stairway and saw the light from the study shining like a beacon through the open panel ahead. With the desperate hope that someone had heard the shots or my screams and would be there to save me, I forced myself, gasping, crying from terror and effort, up the last few steps, through the opening, and out into the study.

The room was silent in the golden lamplight, serene, almost reassuring with its book-lined walls and air of peaceful contemplation; it might have seemed a refuge but for that frail and broken body still lying on the floor.

Count Massimo was dead. No one had heard the screams or shots. No one had come to rescue me. The nightmare was real.

Marco burst through the opening behind me. Instinctively, I turned to face him. The gun in his hand came up, its wicked little snout pointed straight at me, but before he could fire I threw the flashlight at the gun, then hurled myself after it, grabbing for his arm. I felt the whisper of death as the bullet ripped into my jacket sleeve and harmlessly through again.

Possessed by a frenzied strength born of fear, I clung to Marco's arm while he struck at me with his free hand, hard chopping blows that fell on my right arm and side as I doubled over to save myself from being hit in the face or stomach. I kicked out wildly, connecting with his injured leg just as he brought his hand down hard on the back of my neck.

Locked together, the two of us crashed into a table and fell to the floor in a shower of papers and books, Marco on top of me. Smothered by the folds of his cloak and the rank smell of his sweat and crushed by the weight of his body, I lay stunned, pinned to the floor like a bird under a cat, barely breathing, defeated.

Marco rolled off and struggled to his feet. His eyes were unfocused, glazed with rage, and he had stopped swearing. He pointed the gun down into my face. I knew he was going to kill me now.

From a great distance I heard screams and only dimly knew

they were mine, saw Marco's face with a slow smile of sensual pleasure bent over me, felt . . . nothing at all.

What happened next is a blur of motion in my memory, a flash of color against black as Alessandro slammed into Marco from behind and knocked him sideways to the floor, scooping up the fallen gun in one fluid movement. Harlequin stood where Marco had been.

Behind him, I saw the old servant Mario kneeling by Count Massimo's body. He gave a sudden, anguished cry. *"È morto!"*

Alessandro never moved. Only the barest flicker of his eyes over Marco showed that he'd heard Mario at all. If he saw me, as he must have, he gave no sign of it. I tried to speak, to move, but I felt as though I were fighting my way through a fog of cotton wool; its dry thickness filled my head and mouth, stopping the words that struggled to get out. My head ached horribly. Only when I saw Marco stirring beside me on the floor did I manage to gather enough energy to drag myself, holding on to the table's edge, to my feet.

Apart from Mario, no one had said a word. As in a dream, everything seemed slower, each second dragged out; at the most, only fifteen of those seconds could have passed since Marco was standing over me with the gun, but it seemed an age, a lifetime. Unimportant details had a strange significance: A book with its back broken by the fall spilled its pages in a river of white across the edge of Marco's cloak; a small metal paperweight in the shape of a globe was still rolling across the wooden floor. It seemed to take forever to come to rest against a chair leg.

Then Marco groaned and rolled over, pushing himself into a sitting position. He rubbed his hands across his head as though it hurt him; he must have struck it as he hit the floor and been momentarily stunned. Finally, he opened his eyes.

When he saw Alessandro and the gun, his face grew tight and ugly with fear; all the menace and cruel pleasure in his own power vanished, replaced by a cringing terror. With fingers scrabbling at the floor, he tried to scramble backward, away from the gun, his eyes never once leaving Alessandro's face.

"No, Torreleone! Don't! You don't understand. . . . Stillitano sent me."

Alessandro did look at me then, briefly, consideringly, before his eyes flicked back to Marco.

"NO! PLEASE!"

Marco's last shrill scream of terror came simultaneously with the gun's report. Alessandro shot him full in the chest. Marco made a horrible sound in his throat, his eyes wide and pleading, before his body thrashed in a final spasm of life and lay still.

Alessandro bent over Marco, made certain that he was dead, and then put the gun down on the table and went over to his father.

At first I felt nothing more than an immense relief at my deliverance. I was safe; the nightmare was over at last. Grief, horror, anger were there too, but for the moment I knew only that I was somehow, miraculously, still alive.

But the fog was clearing, and as it lifted I began to see the glimmerings of other, more complicated emotions, among them a kind of shocked revulsion tinged with fear at the way Alessandro had killed Marco. He'd seemed cool to the point of cold-bloodedness, as though he were disposing of some loathsome insect rather than his father's murderer. And there had been just a trace of calculation in that glance at me before he pulled the trigger, so that I couldn't help but wonder if he shot him as much to shut his mouth as to avenge his father's death.

I told myself fiercely that no one would mourn Marco's passing, whatever the method. He had killed Count Massimo, he had killed Nick's sister, and he had tried to kill Faltecchi; he deserved his fate. And Alessandro had saved my life. I had no right to question the look on his face as he did it.

Nevertheless, those last words of Marco's echoed in my head. He'd spoken to Alessandro as though he knew him, as though he expected the mention of Stillitano's name to make a difference, to save him. Why? Because he knew the two men were in league together? Because Stillitano had some sort of hold over Alessandro? My aching head swam with unanswered questions.

But this wasn't the time to look for answers. Reluctantly, I crossed the room to the three figures grouped together like a tableau of grief: Alessandro kneeling by his father's body, one hand closed around Count Massimo's thin wrist, Mario hovering above them, moaning softly to himself. Alessandro's face had lost that icy blankness; now I saw only anxiety and a great tenderness. He bent his head to his father's chest and rested it there, and I thought he was mourning him until he raised his head and looked straight at me with joy in his blue eyes.

"He's alive! Mario, call Dr. Guareschi! Tell him to come at once, that my father may be dying. But"—and here he gestured at Marco's body—"not a word about this business. Do you understand?"

Mario showed no surprise, merely nodded, his face lit up with sudden hope. He went quickly to the telephone on the study desk but stopped in the action of raising the receiver to his ear. "Signore, look." He pointed down, behind the desk.

The desk had been moved away from the wall so that the wires of both the telephone and burglar alarm were visible. They had been cut. So Marco had known where to look for the alarm. Stillitano, of course.

Alessandro told Mario to use the telephone in the corridor outside Daniella's rooms; it was the closest on a different line. "Then wait for the doctor at the gate. We are not to be disturbed. No one is to come in here but the doctor. No one."

Mario went out, quietly closing the door behind him. Alessandro was stooping over his father when he thought of something, straightened, and crossed to the door himself. He gave an exclamation of annoyance. "Damn. The key's not here, and Mario has the other. But it was locked when we arrived. . . . Kate, do you know where the key is?"

I was about to say, "In Marco's pocket," when I thought better of it and shook my head instead. I did not relish the prospect of being locked in twice.

Alessandro gave a quick glance around at the floor, then gave up and came back to his father. He knelt, slipped his arms under Count Massimo's shoulders and knees, and slowly rose to his feet. His face was drawn and white, his mouth dragged down in one corner, as though he bore a weight far heavier than the body in his arms. He looked much older and very like his father. He said quietly, "Will you open the door to my father's bedroom, Kate."

I did as he asked, following them into the room. The bedroom was ascetic in its simplicity, the only furniture the narrow bed, a chest of drawers, and a massive walnut wardrobe in the corner by the curtained window. There were no paintings on the plain white walls, no decoration of any kind apart from the collection of photographs in silver frames that stood on the chest of drawers. A pair of worn slippers stood neatly by the bed, their leather cracked and peeling. As I looked at them, I felt tears sting my eyes.

Alessandro laid his father carefully down on the bed. He was reaching for the gray wool blanket that lay folded at the foot of the bed when he said abruptly, "The gun. We shouldn't leave it in there with the door unlocked. Please bring it to me, Kate."

Without thinking, I went obediently to get it. But as I reached down onto the table for it, an instinct stopped me, some memory from detective stories I'd read, or perhaps simply good sense. This was evidence, after all, and I knew I ought not to touch it. I left the gun where it was and went back into the bedroom. I'd been very careful to avoid looking at the body sprawled on the floor beneath the pall of the black cloak.

When I came into the bedroom, Alessandro was busy taking something from a small red case lying open on the bed and didn't turn around, saying merely, "Put it on the bureau for now."

Before I could reply, I saw him raise a needle inserted in an ampoule of clear liquid up to the light, pull the plunger slowly down, and withdraw the needle. Count Massimo's arm lay bare on the blanket.

"What are you doing?"

Alessandro calmly lifted his father's arm and pushed the needle into a vein. "This is for his heart. Don't worry, I've done it before. We can't afford to wait for the doctor."

When he finished and the needle was packed away in its case, he turned around to me. "Now, what happened here tonight? What—" He broke off; perhaps for the first time he really saw me, saw my bruised and bloody face, the torn costume, and realized how close to collapse I was. "*Dio*," he muttered. "Are you all right?"

I was leaning against the doorway; there was nowhere in the room to sit down, and even if there had been a chair, I'm not sure I would have taken it. It was almost as if I had to stay on my feet in order to think. Once I sat down, I might give way to the weariness that threatened to overwhelm me. Something told me I still needed to stay awake.

"Yes, I'm all right. Every bit of me aches, but it's no worse than that, though I suppose I must look awful. All I really feel is relief that your father's still alive. I was so sure Marco had killed him. Oh Alessandro, it was terrible . . ." I stopped, aware that I'd given myself away.

"You knew Marco?"

I looked straight at him. "Yes, I knew who he was. Though not as well as you and Daniella did."

If Alessandro was disconcerted, he didn't show it. "Then will you tell me what happened here?" he repeated.

"I'll try." As best I could, picking my way haltingly through the dangerous facts that mined my story, I told him the version of the story that we—Nick, Gianni, Clara, and I—had agreed on. The part about my stopping by the workrooms for supplies sounded so implausible that I hurried over it as quickly as I could, although Alessandro didn't question it and heard me through to the end without interruption.

"I realize now that I should have tried harder to tell the guard downstairs about the robbery, but it was so difficult. It seemed simpler to come straight to you. And when I found I couldn't because the door to the south wing was locked, I thought I should go to your father. I'm so sorry, Alessandro. Perhaps if I hadn't barged in like that, Marco would have gone away without hurting your father any more than he already had. I wish—"

Alessandro stopped me. "If my father had lain there all night he would surely have died. As it is, we can hope. . . . You showed great courage, Kate."

"You saved both our lives. How did you happen to come by at that moment?"

"A servant was passing and thought she heard someone cry out, but when she knocked there was no answer and the door was locked. She told Mario, who came to get me." He spoke slowly, looking over my shoulder, as though he were thinking about something else. Then he stared at the chest of drawers. "The gun? I don't see it."

"It's still on the table. I didn't think I should touch it, because the police might—" I stopped cold. Until that moment I hadn't given a thought to the police or to what I would tell them when they asked where the gun had come from and why I was carrying it. Reluctantly, I said, "What about the police, Alessandro? Shouldn't we call them?"

He smiled at me then, much as a grownup might smile at a child's naïveté. "This is Italy, dear Kate. Like the betrayed husband, the police are always the last to know. It's wise to learn all the facts before you involve them, especially the unpleasant facts. And one of the more unpleasant facts is our mutual friend Marco."

I ignored the last. "But isn't that *their* job, to find out the facts?"

"You're an innocent. And a foreigner. You may think you see the truth of what happened, but the police will doubtless see it very differently. We must answer our own questions before they ask theirs. I have many questions to ask you before we tell our story."

"Our *story*?"

But Alessandro chose to place the emphasis on my first word. "But of course 'ours.' After all, it wouldn't look well if we should disagree, would it? The police don't like confusion. They are, on the whole, rather stupid and, like most stupid people, are inclined to grow angry when they feel confused. It's in both our interests to make it simple for them."

"I see." And so I was to become Alessandro's fellow conspirator for the sake of simplicity; I might have laughed at the absurdity of it if I hadn't felt a prickle of fear along my spine. "In fact, it's far from simple, wouldn't you agree? This wasn't just a robbery."

"As you say." There was a silence as Alessandro put his fingers to his father's wrist again, feeling for the pulse. Satisfied, he touched the count gently on the shoulder, drew the blanket closer to his chin, then turned back to me. Reaching into the pocket of his Harlequin's costume, he took out a handkerchief. Before I could protest or move away, he had cupped my chin in one hand and was wiping the blood and dirt from my face. As I surrendered myself, half against my will, to his care, I wondered why the simple touch of his hand on my skin should confuse me so easily, why I was even in the room with him now that I knew he was guilty of much more than just collusion with Stillitano in the forgery of the Reni. Why did I give him such power over me? At that moment I had no answer.

We stood there, a tattered Columbine whose masquerade was ending and a Harlequin with a disguise like a second skin, so close together that I felt his breath warm against my skin. My eyes rose to meet his.

"Help me, Kate. I need you." The words were a whisper as his mouth came down on mine, offering the flattering illusion of confession from a man who seemed to need so little. I would like to forget that a part of me yearned to believe him, longed to lose myself and the memory of that terrible night under the touch of his skillful mouth.

Like a warning, Nick's voice sounded in my head, telling me to find my answers in my own way, and hard upon it came a curious flash of memory. I saw the image of Daniella's face as she had looked at Marco in the bar, that voluptuous submission of the will plain for anyone to see, and I thought, Now I know why she . . . A thought I wouldn't finish. It was enough to bring me sharp awake from the lotus dream. No, I was not Daniella.

The spell was broken. I accepted that from the beginning Alessandro's lovemaking had a single purpose: to bind me to him in a complicity of the body because he was afraid of what I knew. From the moment I saw the Reni, I was dangerous. The passionate urgency that pressed his body hard all along mine, that made him forget his father, came from the brain, not the heart. It was a passionate desire to save himself by using me.

I had my answers.

Those answers made me twist away from him and say, in a voice that held more anger than I meant to show, "It's no good, Alessandro . . ."

He let me go. "I was mistaken. *Mi dispiace.*"

The words were formal, a little cold, but I saw no trace of wounded ego, no anger visible at my refusal to play the game his way, just the shadow of Harlequin's mocking grin, suggesting that although the game might well be lost, it was worth a try. It struck me forcibly that Alessandro could hardly be touched by any rejection of mine, because he, like all the Torreleones, his father apart, was both egoist and pragmatist. Hadn't he told me so himself? The lovemaking had been one attempt at persuasion; that it hadn't worked didn't matter very much. He would simply try something else. And if nothing worked . . .

That cool self-possession was a part of what made him so attractive, of course, but also, now, very frightening. I suddenly saw him as a man capable of anything.

Perhaps he read something of what I was feeling in my face, because he looked amused and said, in a voice whose teasing tone didn't quite disguise a darker note, "Ah yes, I almost forgot. I must retrieve the gun." He went past me through the bedroom door.

No, I thought with weary desperation, the nightmare is far from over.

Before I could move, I heard the study door open and then Daniella's voice. "Sandro, what's happened? I heard Mario on the phone just now. What's wrong with Uncle Massimo?"

Then she screamed, and I'd swear there was more anger than grief in that scream.

CHAPTER

20

I spun around and took an involuntary step forward, then stopped. A warning signal from the brain held me back, rigid against the bedroom doorway, watching.

Daniella crouched over Marco, gold against black, her arms in their trailing sleeves flung across his body. The study's soft light touched the gold in her hair and glimmered in the folds of the taffeta dress, spreading out around her like a golden pool. I couldn't see her face, only the convulsive gesture of one hand as it closed on the black fabric of Marco's cloak. Alessandro stood motionless above her. Something in the awkward way he held his body, hands dangling by his sides, told me that for once he was at a loss.

It was a strangely beautiful scene—the golden girl prostrate on the body of her dead lover, Harlequin hovering above them like the unhappy spirit of a masquerade gone tragically wrong—but there was a frozen quality about it that made it seem curiously distant and unreal, as though I were watching from the "gods" while actors far below played out their final act, caught and held by the spotlight before curtain-fall. It was lovely, and it was certainly dramatic, but it was, after all, commedia dell'arte and had no business being tragic. In a moment the actors would leap to their feet, laughing, and take a bow. Then I could go home.

But real life made an entrance. Alessandro moved, laid the gun he was holding back down on the table, and reached out to touch Daniella—and the scene broke up, shattered by the violent jerk of her body away from him.

"*Assassino! Assassino!*"

He flinched back in time to save himself from her nails and caught her wrists, holding her away from him while she twisted and struggled in his grip like an angry cat, claws unsheathed, spitting with fury. A torrent of words poured out of her, obscene, violent, yet somehow closer to the rage of a thwarted child than a woman's grief, before trickling off into wordless sobbing. Finally, she quieted, grew slack in his grasp, and he let her go. She stood in front of him, hunched over and rubbing one wrist.

He began gently enough. "You knew him, Dani?"

"We were lovers." Her face was in profile to me, but the defiance there was clear, and even clearer in her voice.

He didn't speak; he simply went on looking at her. The silence thickened and settled down on the room like the deadly calm that comes with the eye of the storm. Daniella's nerve broke, and her voice took on a childishly plaintive note. "Why, Sandro? Why did you kill him?"

I moved farther back into the bedroom; Daniella hadn't seen me, and perhaps Alessandro had forgotten for the moment that I was there. Or perhaps he didn't care now what I heard. The implications of *that* terrified me.

Alessandro ignored Daniella's question, asking one of his own instead. "How did you meet him?"

271

"It was at a demonstration about a month ago. At the antifascist rally in the Piazza Venezia. He . . . he took my ideas seriously. You always laugh at them; you never take anything seriously." The defiance was back, and with it a petulance that sharpened her voice to a whine. The words tumbled out in a rush, an odd mixture of revolutionary rhetoric and the hurt feelings of a spoiled child. "You don't see the mess we're in, all of us. . . . There has to be a change, or we might as well be dead. You and my father, you think I'm still a little girl playing games. But I've grown up, I see what has to be done to change things. And I have friends who agree with me—"

"Those idiots in Studenti per l'Operaio, for example? Were you a member? Did *he* get you involved?" Alessandro nudged Marco's body with his foot. So he hadn't known until now that Daniella belonged to the group.

"Yes. So what? I was grateful to him for it." But her voice lacked conviction.

It wasn't likely, I thought, that Daniella and Marco had met by accident at the demonstration; far more probable that Marco had learned something of her revolutionary inclinations and capitalized on them, arranging the "accidental" encounter himself. Obviously he hadn't told Alessandro about his cousin's involvement in Studenti per l'Operaio; perhaps he hoped to use her in some way against Alessandro in the double game he liked to play. Whatever his reasons, Marco succeeded only too well with Daniella. For all her gloss of sophistication, she was no match for his way with a willing victim.

As the significance of Alessandro's words sank in, Daniella said uncertainly, "But you knew about Studenti per l'Operaio? And you knew Marco? How *could* you?"

"That doesn't matter now. Neither does he. All that matters is that we clear up this mess."

Again there was that deadly silence, again Daniella asked, "Why did you kill him, Sandro?" But this time she sounded hesitant, as though she'd had time to grow frightened of the answer. She was crying again, too, and I wondered unkindly how many of the tears were for herself.

"He attacked *Papa*."

"No! But why—"

"It seems he was after the Reni."

"The Reni? But he promised me . . ." The words trailed off as she realized what she'd said. No, I thought, she was no match for either Marco or Alessandro. Her hands twisted nervously in the long, shimmering sleeves of her dress. Abruptly, she took a step back and half turned. But it was too late; Alessandro had her.

"Don't, Sandro! Stop, you're hurting me—"

"You little bitch! Did you know about this?" He was gripping her by her upper arms, shaking her, and he looked furious. But for Daniella's sake, I thought, better that look of fury than the icy impassivity of his face at the moment he'd shot Marco.

"No, no," Daniella cried. "I never knew that he was planning such a thing, I swear it! Please, Sandro—you must believe me."

"What do you mean, then?"

"Nothing, nothing.'" But he shook her harder, and she went on. "Only that Marco was always after me about Uncle Massimo's paintings. He wanted me to steal one for the group, to prove my loyalty, he said. But I wouldn't, I wouldn't. I . . . I wanted to tell you, but he threatened terrible things if I ever mentioned it to anyone. He could be so frightening. He told me once that he killed a girl who was going to betray him. I knew it was just a lie to scare me, but still . . . She was in our group before I joined, so I never knew her, and she did die."

"Susanna," Alessandro said quietly.

"Yes, that was the name. How did you know?"

Once again Alessandro ignored her question. When he spoke, it was as if he were talking to himself. "So that's how she died. I always thought she killed herself. I even wondered if I might be to blame. But of course it was Gatti."

"What are you saying, Sandro? I don't understand."

"You understand very little it seems, dear Dani." Alessandro smiled coldly at her and dropped his hands from her arms. She made no effort to get away now. "Let me enlighten you, cousin.

Although none of it matters very much now." He turned and sat down in the armchair next to Marco's body, crossing his legs, his hands resting flat on the arms of the chair, as casually as if he had a pleasant story to tell and all the time in the world for it.

"Susanna and I had a love affair. It ended badly. She made no secret of her political allegiances, but she was very beautiful and I thought it might be amusing, and possibly illuminating, to learn why she believed what she did. You've accused me of right-wing sympathies, and I don't deny it. And in your own peculiarly contradictory fashion you've also accused me of political indifference. But there you're wrong. I have always believed that it's fatal to ignore the beliefs of one's enemies.

"Susanna introduced me to Gatti. I think she hoped to make us jealous of each other, but perhaps I do her an injustice. For a while I let them lecture me, but I quickly grew bored. Can you tell me why noble ideals so often degenerate into banality—and such intense and humorless banality? Of course, Gatti was hardly the pure revolutionary. Even Susanna began to realize it, and he'd managed to dupe her as thoroughly as he seems to have duped you.

"But he was a fool. As you have been, cousin." He smiled up at her. "You might easily have come to the same end as Susanna, you know. Gatti had no allegiances."

She gaped at him and moved uneasily away from Marco's body, as though he might rise up from the dead to attack her. She was, I reflected, recovering nicely from her grief. Perhaps she saw that Marco's death delivered her quite neatly from his terrifying, if exciting, attentions. Or perhaps it was simply that for the first time she saw his real nature.

"You're fortunate," Alessandro went on, still in the same relaxed manner, "that you are a Torreleone. Unlike that creature"—he looked down at Marco—"we know the meaning of loyalty. I can't solve the world's problems as you would like, but perhaps I can deal with this particular one. However, I haven't much time." He rose to his feet, and the tone of his voice changed, became harsh and urgent. "Go to your room now. And if you're asked about this affair, pretend ignorance. You enjoy deception; this is an opportunity to practice that talent. You know nothing. You were at the ball or in your rooms all night. Do you understand? Let's hope the police can't connect you with Gatti."

Mutely, Daniella nodded, undoubtedly grateful for the chance to shift her responsibilities to Alessandro's shoulders.

She was about to leave the room when it occurred to me that I very much did not want to be alone with Alessandro. I moved forward into the light. When Daniella saw me, she flinched as though I'd struck her. "You! What are you doing here?"

"Another friend of Marco's. Such a popular man," Alessandro said. "She, too, knew that Marco wanted the Reni and meant to steal it tonight. She followed him here, to stop him. She risked her life for *Papa*."

Daniella had the grace to look ashamed. Apart from her first moments in the room she had not asked after Count Massimo and now, belatedly, she said, "Is he all right?"

"We'll know when Dr. Guareschi arrives. His pulse and heart are weak, but steady. I gave him an injection. But . . ."

Daniella was silent for a moment, then quickly recovered; she traded that unfamiliar emotion, shame, for an easier one. And she had a target to hand for her anger. With a sneer, she rounded on me. "We used to laugh at you. We were never taken in by you, you know."

"I can return the compliment," I said evenly. "What's the term I heard someone use about Marco? Oh yes, a hired gun. An ambidextrous one, too. He liked to play both sides—even in the same family."

She looked startled. "What do you mean?"

"Ask your cousin. And now, if you'll excuse me, the party seems to be over." I started for the door, but I had to pass Alessandro to reach it, and I knew it was hopeless. He would never let me go.

He didn't. Without touching me, he stopped me by simply stepping into my path. "Leave us, Dani. Kate and I have a lot to talk about, and little time."

275

She crept past him without a backward look despite my desperate cry. "For God's sake, Daniella!" If anything, it only made her move faster. The door shut with a slam behind her.

Alessandro smiled pleasantly at me. "A brave girl, my cousin. Now, where shall we begin, Kate?"

My hands were trembling so violently that I hid them in the pockets of my dress; I wouldn't let him see how frightened I was. But I couldn't keep the trembling from my voice. "It's no use, Alessandro. Friends know I'm here; they'll be looking for me. And if you hurt me—"

"Hurt you!" He looked genuinely surprised. "Is *that* what you think? My dear Kate, for all that I shot Marco I'm not a killer. Do you doubt me? Here, here's the gun." He picked it up off the table and held it out to me. "Go on, take it. Then you'll feel safe."

I kept my hands in my pockets. Oddly enough, I believed him. And now that I'd seen what the gun could do, I wanted nothing more to do with it.

"No? A pity. It would make everything so much simpler for us, Kate." He looked amused at my incomprehension. "Why, yes. You see, if your fingerprints were on the gun you would have to do as I tell you. Otherwise I would tell the police that you shot Marco. In self-defense, of course. You would probably escape prosecution, and I would escape possibly embarrassing questions."

Of course Alessandro thought the gun belonged to Marco; he had no idea that my fingerprints were already all over it, precisely as he wanted. But as I had no intention of enlightening him on this point, silence seemed the safest response.

"However," he went on, "I must find another way of persuading you to cooperate. I could, of course, tell the police that you and your accomplice Gatti came here tonight to steal the Reni and that I managed to stop you. Although that seems rather ungrateful considering you risked your life for my father."

"Not to mention unconvincing since I knew the Reni was a fake. And your father knows the truth, after all."

"Does he? If my father lives he will not, I imagine, remember very much about tonight. It should be a relatively simple matter to fill the gaps in his memory with convincing details. He would be desolate, naturally, to learn that a young woman of whom he was fond schemed to steal from him, but ..." He spread his arms wide and shrugged.

"What about Mario? He knows that Marco wasn't any stranger to you. He heard him call out that Stillitano sent him. And he knows you didn't kill him in self-defense."

"Mario has been with the Torreleones all his life," Alessandro replied with chilling simplicity.

And I, I thought grimly, was a stranger. What happened to me was less than nothing compared to the well-being of the Torreleones. Mario would remember only what Alessandro wanted him to remember. I might have felt the desperation Alessandro so obviously meant me to feel had it not been for the certainty that my knowledge, combined with all that Nick and Gianni knew, made it impossible for Alessandro to succeed with any of his schemes. I still had a trump card to play, and now was the time to play it. The game had gone on long enough; it was frightening me.

As calmly as I could, I said, "You once complained about the movies' image of the decaying aristocracy going mad in their crumbling palaces. You've been watching too many of those movies, Alessandro." There was a gleam of admiration, even respect, in his eyes at that. Yes, I thought, he would like it this way. As long as I fought back, refused to be the doormat ego spread out for him to trample on, I would interest him; the instant I capitulated, boredom would set in. And I could not afford, now, to bore him. Very well, then, I would give him a taste of that independent spirit he claimed to admire in a woman and see if it really was to his liking.

"Nothing of what you've threatened would work anyway," I said. "I know too much."

"And what do you know?" He still looked amused.

"About the Reni, for a start. Then about your connection with Stillitano." I didn't know everything about that connection, of course—enough, however, to bluff with convincingly if

Alessandro probed. "And on top of that, I know about your work for Bassi. Friends of mine do, too; and two of them are journalists. So you see, I'm not your only problem. Setting me up wouldn't get you out of this."

The amusement was gone from Alessandro's face. Instead, for an instant, before he schooled his features to their customary calm, I saw dismay there. I pressed my advantage. "My friends have proof. Stillitano was indiscreet enough to keep a record of his transactions, and you and Bassi figure quite prominently in it. And when Stillitano finds out that it's gone, I wouldn't give a cent for his loyalty to the Torreleones, I really wouldn't."

I might have added that Bassi was about to be exposed, but that wasn't my information to give; Gianni had been told of the raid on Bassi's apartment in confidence, and perhaps, I thought, it would be wise not to reveal too much to Alessandro. I didn't want to make him so desperate that he decided he had nothing to lose by disposing of at least one of his problems. He would find out soon enough, anyway.

"How busy you've been, Kate. All this time I thought you had only paintings on your mind. You've been very clever at disguising what you know." He spoke with understandable bitterness.

But I could match him with a bitterness of my own. "A compliment from a master of disguise. I've learned a lot since I came to work for the Torreleones."

"So you have. How have you learned it all? I would be infinitely grateful if you would satisfy my curiosity."

Fine, I thought, I'll stand here all night talking if he likes. The doctor has to arrive soon, and when he does nothing will keep me from walking out that door. I had forgotten my aching face and the weariness of my body. They seemed quite separate from me, and I had the odd sensation of detachment from myself and everything around me, almost as though I were floating somewhere overhead, looking down on it all. It really doesn't matter what you tell Alessandro, I said reassuringly to myself; Nick will be here soon to take you home. You might as well kill time this way as any other.

"It started with the Reni," I told him. "Once I learned that Stillitano had worked on it and you admitted it was a forgery done to order, I began to wonder what he was up to. A friend who used to work for Faltecchi and Stillitano told me there'd been accusations of forgery against Stillitano. Stillitano was very eager to get rid of me, too. I knew I had to be dangerous to him somehow, and I could only be because of what I'd learned about the Reni. I figured I needed some sort of weapon to protect myself against him, so I took his notebook, thinking it might help. As well as those contracts for the forgeries, one of which is signed with your name."

Alessandro leaned back against the table, his arms folded across his chest. "I underestimated you."

I ignored this and went on, determined to spin my story out until help arrived. "Then there was Daniella. Quite by accident I overheard her quarreling with Marco—this was before I knew who she was. He was trying to persuade her to steal some paintings. I'm not crazy about your cousin, but she was telling the truth just now. She didn't want to do it.

"When I found out she was Count Massimo's niece, I wanted to tell him, or you, but I didn't quite know how to go about it. Or even if you'd believe me. I thought perhaps I ought to find out a little more before I gave her away to her family, so I managed to persuade her that I was sympathetic to her cause, and then she introduced me to Marco. That was my mistake," I added.

"Yes, Gatti was a mistake. For all of us."

And that, I thought with a flash of anger, is all he was to Alessandro. A mistake. A mistake that might have cost three people their lives, one of them his own father. Suddenly I was furious. "You use people as if they were puppets, and all you had to do was pull a certain string to get them to jump for you. A girl is dead, your father may be dying, and Faltecchi's in the hospital all because you chose the wrong puppet. And it was only a mistake. You're cold-blooded and heartless and I wonder if even your own father's death will move you. But what I really can't forgive is you and Stillitano sending your 'mistake' after an old man whose only fault is incorruptibility. If he dies—"

Alessandro straightened, surprised. "Surely you can't believe I'd send Marco to hurt my own father?"

"Not your father. Of course not. I meant Faltecchi. In the park when—" There was such obvious puzzlement on his face that I stopped, off balance.

Impatiently, Alessandro demanded, "What happened to Faltecchi?"

In a few words I told him what Marco had done, and why—or rather, my deductions as to the reasons why. I finished by saying that I assumed Stillitano and Alessandro were afraid Faltecchi would expose whatever racket they were involved in together.

Alessandro's surprise was replaced by a mixture of denial and affronted disgust. "Marco was an animal, granted, but I would never have turned him loose on anyone in such a way. Do you think I'm so vicious?" He seemed genuinely angry that I could have believed such a thing of him, and if the situation hadn't been so grim I might have laughed at his sudden self-righteousness.

However, I believed him. That I was still alive was some evidence that he preferred to use other means to achieve his ends.

He said, "I used Marco, that's true, but for information, not violence. It was useful for us, my friends and I, to know what insanity the far left was planning, and Marco could sometimes give us that information. For money naturally. But he was beginning to outlive his usefulness to us—I think his friends had begun to distrust him. God knows why it took them so long.

"But as for that other thing—no, never." He rubbed his face wearily. "And you know, I like Giorgio Faltecchi."

Then it was Stillitano, I thought. He had no such scruples.

"All right," I said. "You had nothing to do with the attack on Faltecchi. As for the rest, I don't know what dirty work you used Marco for, and frankly, right now I don't care. I'm not sorry he's dead. I'll go even further. I'm quite willing to say you killed him in self-defense or to protect your father or even me. Whatever you like. You don't need to threaten me. And I won't tell the police about Daniella's involvement with Marco, though I'll bet they already know. I think you probably underestimate them.

"But that's as far as I'll go for the pair of you. And I'm doing it for your father's sake, not yours. He's the only Torreleone who's genuinely noble."

Alessandro gave an ironic inclination of his head. "*Grazie.* On my cousin's behalf as well as my own. Although I don't imagine that Daniella has been guilty of anything worse than stupidity. If, as you say, the police did know of her relationship with Gatti, she'll have some uneasy moments, but perhaps she will learn a useful lesson."

I doubted that. There were some lessons I suspected Daniella would never learn. And Alessandro? What lesson had he learned?

To concede gracefully, perhaps, for he said, irony sharpening his words, "You're right, Kate. It wouldn't serve any purpose to prolong this charade. I'll ask Mario to call the police. We'll tell them what happened, you and I. But as to the rest"—he paused and gave a tired smile—"well, I warned you that we do things differently in Italy."

CHAPTER
21

As though on cue, Mario opened the study door. With him, the inevitable black bag in one hand, was a fat little man with shrewd eyes. The look of professionally calm appraisal he gave me as he came into the room didn't quite cover up his surprise, but before he could say a word Alessandro took his arm.

"Adriano! Thank God you're here." At once the two men started for Count Massimo's bedroom, Alessandro rapidly describing his father's condition as they went.

I was about to tell Mario to call the police when, in a voice so quietly urgent that it stopped Alessandro in mid-sentence, he said, "Signore, a word with you, please."

Alessandro looked back over his shoulder. "Is it important? Very well . . . Go ahead, Adriano. I'll join you in a moment."

The doctor complied but had taken no more than a step or

two before he was brought up short by the sight of Marco's body, hidden from him until now by the table and armchair.

"*Dio*, Sandro! Who is *this*?"

When he answered, Alessandro sounded surprised, as if he'd forgotten all about Marco, and impatient. "What? Oh, never mind him. You can't help him; he's dead."

Dr. Guareschi merely blinked. "Perhaps we ought to be certain of that." He set the bag down on the floor and, plucking at the pleats of his trousers to raise them slightly, knelt down by Marco's side, carefully avoiding the dark mass of blood by his chest. During the brief silence the room seemed filled by the doctor's heavy breathing. Finally, with a small groan of effort, he got to his feet again. "You are right. The police—?"

"—are coming," Alessandro coolly lied.

The doctor raised his eyebrows but continued without another word into the bedroom. Alessandro turned to Mario. "Now, what is it?"

Gravely, Mario said, "Two men from the *carabinieri* are already here, signore. With a Signor and Signora Palmieri. They are downstairs at the gate and insist on speaking with you. What shall I tell them?"

No mention of Nick's name. But surely he *had* to be with them.

"Damn!" It was spoken quietly enough, but Alessandro's self-control had been so remarkable that it made this small expression of anger more forceful than any amount of ranting and raving. I looked at him, wondering if the strain was at last beginning to tell on the smooth facade of his personality; a deep furrow scored the flesh between his eyebrows. He allowed himself one gesture of indecision, a glance at me while he rubbed his face, before he had himself in hand again. When he spoke, his habitual self-confidence and the swift flow of words disguised any fear or doubt. "Yes, all right. They may come up. But before you bring them, call *Questore* Barbato. Tell him what has happened, and ask him to come at once. Tell him that it is a matter of friendship. A matter of friendship," he repeated deliberately. "Use those exact words. And Mario—"

"Sì, signore?"

"I will tell the *carabinieri* what happened here tonight. That you and I rescued my father and Signora Roy from this thief, and"—there was a small pause, but Alessandro never looked away from Mario while he chose his words—"and that I shot him when he attacked me."

"Sì, signore." Mario did not show the slightest flicker of surprise. He went out, closing the door behind him, the good and faithful servant. I wondered idly whether his loyalty was to the father or to the son and whether Alessandro would be able to command the same unquestioning obedience when Count Massimo died.

"These Palmieris, are they by any chance the friends you spoke of?" Alessandro's voice was dry. I nodded. "Then I will leave you to greet them." After one short, unreadable look he turned his back on me and went into his father's bedroom.

Exhausted, I stumbled to the refuge of a big wing chair near the fireplace and sank down into it, desperate for the oblivion of sleep.

It came, but briefly. Minutes later the sound of voices startled me awake again, and I got wearily to my feet as Mario and the Palmieris entered the room behind two wary-looking men in plain clothes, obviously *carabinieri* despite the lack of uniform.

At the sight of me, Clara ran forward. "Kate! Thank God. But your poor face . . . What's happened?"

If only I never had to answer that, I thought as her soft arms went around me and I collapsed gratefully against her. The steel shaft in my spine that had held me upright and rigid all night long crumbled like chalk. I was safe; I didn't have to be strong any longer.

Gianni and the two *carabinieri* huddled around Marco's body while Mario stood nearby, I looked at the shrouded body on the floor. It no longer seemed the least bit frightening, or even human, spread out like a great dark stain, hideous, possibly infectious, but soon to be scrubbed away.

"Is that—?" Clara began.

"It *was* Marco," I corrected her. "He's quite dead. Even a

doctor's confirmation in case we were worried. Though personally I think a stake through the heart to make sure isn't a bad idea." I began to laugh as though I'd said something wonderfully witty and found I couldn't stop. The laughter gushed out of me like oil from a rich strike, black and uncontrollable. The men turned to stare while Clara held me at arm's length and shook me hard.

"*Basta*, Kate! Stop now."

As anxiously as a mother hen with a worrisome chick, Clara shepherded me over to the sofa and settled me down into the cushions, herself beside me, with one arm around my shoulders for reassurance and restraint. The cozy softness of her body was as comforting as a cup of warm milk.

"Clara," I whispered at last, "where's Nick?"

Instead of answering me, she called to Gianni. He crossed the room to us, fingering his unlit pipe with evident longing. He looked both tired and triumphant, his energetic walk subdued and slope shouldered but a small grin visible behind his beard.

"Damn it all, Kate," he began as he sat down on the other side of me, "you might have—"

Clara cut him off. "Don't, Gianni. You can see how it is with her."

I managed a smile. "I'm all right, Clara. And I deserve whatever scolding Gianni wants to give me. But before you scold me, Gianni, tell me where Nick is." My voice sounded thin in my ears.

"I wish we knew."

I must have moved or said something, because all at once Clara's arm was around me again. "Just tell her what happened, Gianni! Don't terrify her."

"*Va bene*." He leaned against the back of the sofa, holding the pipe between his hands; I could smell the fruity tobacco he liked to smoke. It was somehow reassuring, comfortably normal in the midst of so much that was not. "You must have wondered, Kate, why we let Marco go."

"Well, yes. I thought Nick at least would have followed him. Because of Susanna."

"I think he would have ordinarily. But perhaps he never got the chance to. When I left you and Clara to look for Nick, I couldn't find him. Then I heard a car coming up the street from the other direction. I was about to hide when someone grabbed me and pulled me into a doorway. It was Nick of course, but . . . To be honest, I'm not really cut out for this cloak-and-dagger business."

"I sympathize," I said dryly.

Gianni raised an eyebrow. "You do it very well all the same. Anyway, it was just as well that Nick and I hid, because the car stopped. There were two men in it; one got out and went into your building. It was Pietro Bassi."

"Bassi! But I thought—"

"That with every policeman in Italy out looking for him he'd be long gone? Exactly. Nick and I couldn't believe our eyes. He rang the bell, and Stillitano came down to let him in; he must have been expecting him. Then the other man drove off. Nick wanted to hear what was going on, and we agreed that while he tried to get close enough I would phone Cucchi again, and failing him, another contact I had. Not so good as Cucchi but better than nothing. Nick let himself into the building with your key, and I went off to the bar to telephone.

"But when I reached the bar it was shut, and when I got back the light in Stillitano's office was out. I could only assume that the three of them had left, with Nick following. I couldn't see him anywhere."

"Nick can look after himself, *cara*," Clara said, although I hadn't spoken.

"Yes, I know. Go on, Gianni." In spite of Clara's words, worry sat like an indigestible lump in the pit of my stomach. My taste for vengeance had died with Marco. All I wanted now was Nick.

"When I got back to the Maserati, Clara told me you'd gone after Marco. He must have got past Nick somehow, or else Nick decided Bassi mattered more. But of all the stupid things to do, Kate . . ."

"I know." I didn't look at him. I kept my eyes on my hands,

which were linked in my lap. I noticed with detached interest, almost as if they were someone else's hands, a swollen tenderness across the top of my right hand and two split knuckles. But the fingers moved easily when I flexed them.

Gianni went on. "We left a note in the Maserati for Nick in case he came back. Then we took our car. On the way to the palazzo we found a telephone and tried Cucchi again. This time, thank God, he was in. He's the one over there with the mustache." He pointed with the stem of his pipe to the bigger of the two *carabinieri*, who were now questioning Mario; Cucchi was a shambling, rumple-suited man whose drooping mustache badly needed a trim. A slow-moving, unintelligent type—Alessandro's "stupid" policeman.

Gianni disabused me. "Cucchi may not look like much," he said, reading my mind, "but there's a saying we have: '*Scarpe grosse, cervello fino.*'" Clumsy boots, clever brain. "People underestimate him at first. A mistake. Anyway, I told him about Bassi showing up and about Stillitano and Marco. I explained what had happened, and we agreed to meet here at the palazzo. However, Cucchi lives on the other side of Rome, and we knew it would take him a while to get here. But Clara and I counted on making it to the palazzo before you because we had the car." He grimaced. "We didn't know a film was being made."

I laughed. "Neither did I. Did you get stuck?"

He nodded. "So many idiots had come out to watch it, we couldn't get through them. Those *pazzi* seemed bent on suicide. They stood right in front of the damn car. I'd have been happy to oblige, but Clara wouldn't let me. That slowed us down. Then, when we finally got here, the guard at the gate made difficulties, and that superannuated Cerberus over there"—this time the pipe stem jabbed in Mario's direction—"kept us waiting till Cucchi arrived. Now, perhaps you'll tell us what you've been up to. None of it much good, to judge by that face of yours."

Clara touched my cheek with gentle fingers. "It will heal, Kate. I think you've been lucky . . . ?"

I nodded. "Do you know that old Chinese curse 'May you

live in exciting times'? Well, I understand it now. If you ever hear me complain of boredom, remind me, please, of tonight." As economically as I could, I described Marco's attack and Alessandro's rescue. Alessandro could tell his own story of Marco's death; I simply said that Marco had been about to kill me when Alessandro surprised him, managed to get the gun away from him, and shot him. To my relief, neither Gianni nor Clara pressed for details at this point.

"So you see," I added after I'd told my story, only too conscious that I was once more about to give Alessandro the benefit of the doubt, "he never knew what Marco had done to Faltecchi or that he had Daniella under his thumb. And I believe him. Marco actually boasted to Daniella that he killed Nick's sister—Alessandro had thought it was suicide. All that Alessandro seems to be guilty of as far as Susanna was concerned is callousness. He used her, as he used Marco, to get information on the far left for his friends in Mestola Rossa."

"He told you a lot," Clara said with surprise.

"Yes. I'm not sure why. Maybe because nothing he admitted to is actually illegal except for the forgery of the Reni, and he knows his father isn't likely to press charges. I'm afraid, though, that he didn't admit anything about any other relationship with Stillitano, or with Bassi."

"It doesn't matter," Gianni said cheerfully. "He will when we ask him certain questions about the information in Stillitano's notebook. His name turns up fairly often."

While we were talking, Cucchi had disappeared into Count Massimo's bedroom, leaving his partner to take down Mario's statement. The old servant was being frankly unhelpful, answering questions in one or two words, unwilling to give anything away, while the *carabiniere*, with a long-suffering look on his face, slowly drew out the few facts he would reveal. I wasn't sure which of them I felt sorrier for.

Cucchi came back out of the bedroom and over to us. I watched his approach with a certain amount of alarm. Gianni introduced him to me, and at once I saw what he meant; Cucchi's eyes focused on me like chips of ebony, hard and opaque. I was acutely conscious of my own far from legal behavior and guilty knowledge and, under that scrutiny, of a strong impulse to confess—perhaps simply to end the suspense, that same urge to give myself up that I'd felt in the cellars with Marco. Only the fact that others were implicated, especially Nick, whose gun still lay on the table nearby—the bullets safely removed by Cucchi's partner—kept me from saying more than a polite and far from truthful "*Piacere.*" But, for the moment at least, Cucchi wasn't interested in me. In a low, guttural voice he said to Gianni, "The doctor is finished now, and then I will question Torreleone. You may join us for part of it—as a material witness, so to speak. Strictly off the record, of course." A heavy lid closed over one of the ebony chips.

Gianni grinned. "Of course."

"Please remain here, Signora Roy," Cucchi continued. The words were simultaneously a polite request and an unmistakable command. "I would like to ask you some questions, as well."

On turning, the two men almost collided with Dr. Guareschi, who had come silently out of the bedroom. He told Cucchi he was going to look for the ambulance that should arrive at any moment.

Dr. Guareschi came back shortly in company with two orderlies and a wheeled stretcher. The two men paused when they saw Marco's body, but the doctor chivied them forward. "No, no, that is not the patient. This way."

When they returned, Count Massimo was lying on the stretcher, wrapped in blankets. The flesh of his face was sunken and hollow, the bones standing out sharply in relief; he looked carved from some gray stone. I felt as though I were already a mourner at his funeral.

As Dr. Guareschi passed by, I stood up, stretching out my hand to stop him. "Please . . . can you tell me if Count Massimo will be all right. I . . . I'm a friend of his."

Curiosity was on his face, and I wondered what, if anything, Alessandro had told him of the night's events, but if he had questions he kept them to himself, and when he spoke his voice was kind. "I cannot be sure, signora, until we take him to the hospital. He has internal injuries, serious ones. It is remarkable that he is still alive. But then he has always been strong, despite seeming otherwise. And now you must excuse me . . ." Before he left, he added gently, "You must get that cut on your face looked after. I am sorry that I have not time."

As he went out the door I saw him nod to someone in the corridor. There was the sound of voices, and then three men came into the room, two in the uniform of the *polizia*, the other so redolent of authority, large and smooth in a beautifully cut camel's hair overcoat and white silk scarf, that he needed no uniform to mark him out as someone used to giving orders. His graying hair waved sleekly back from a purely Roman profile of the early empire—plumply aggressive chins, thickish lips, large nose. Alessandro's friend *Questore* Barbato? Mario's welcome confirmed my guess; he was visibly relieved.

Cucchi's partner seemed less delighted with the *questore*'s arrival. Understandably so. To outward appearances colleagues, both police forces with overlapping responsibilities, the *polizia* and *carabinieri* were in fact rivals. It wasn't unusual for one force to keep vital information from the other when both were involved in the same case. I'd once read of a kidnapping case that had been badly bungled because of this rivalry, with one dead victim the net result. How could they? I'd raged to Clara, who heard me out and then admitted that to foreigners it must seem odd. But, she'd added, without that competition, with only one police force in the country, there was the risk of uncontrolled power and corruption. What would become of liberty? I'd muttered something about how typically Italian it was. I hadn't expected to see it at work.

Questore Barbato had clearly come to Alessandro's rescue, and he lost no time setting about it. After a heated discussion with Cucchi's partner, who vainly attempted to block Barbato and his sidekicks, and much gesticulation on the part of everyone except the *questore*, whose hands remained in the pockets of his overcoat, Barbato produced some trump card or other, at which Cucchi's partner threw up his arms in disgust, gave an ironical bow, and stood back to let them pass. One of the *polizia* remained in the study with us, as silently watchful as Mario, while Barbato and the other strode into the bedroom.

Gianni later told us that the *questore*, theoretically on shaky ground in his interference with a legal procedure already begun by the other force, had scooped Alessandro out of Cucchi's clutches with a few well-placed names and certain veiled threats, none of which appeared to worry Cucchi too much, as he knew that a magistrate would have to be called into the case immediately, anyway, and would make the final decision about jurisdiction. Besides, Gianni added, Alessandro had told Cucchi what he knew of the robbery attempt and Marco's shooting and was refusing to answer any more questions. The *polizia*, Cucchi said in his polite way, could have Signor Torreleone. For the time being.

I was standing by the window looking down at the street below when Alessandro came out of the bedroom with the others. I heard him behind me, but I didn't turn around. I had faced enough that night.

But he crossed the room to stand beside me. In a voice so low it was almost a whisper, he said, "Do you remember that once I told you I could love a woman who would not let herself be used by me?"

I simply nodded; I found I couldn't speak. I kept my eyes on the street, but I have no memory of what I saw there.

"A pity, isn't it, that some things happen too late. *Arrivederci*, Kate."

And he was gone.

A lot happened after that, but it passed me by in a blur of weariness. Reinforcements from the *carabinieri* arrived, as did another doctor to examine Marco's body officially, a photographer to take photographs, men to search for fingerprints and measure distances. The study suddenly seemed filled with people doing too many different things at once, all talking loudly and too much. It was stifling, unbearable.

When Cucchi questioned me, I found myself mesmerized by his shoes, Gianni's proverb running through my head. Clumsy boots, clever brain. The shoes *were* big and clumsy looking, the man equally so, but the black eyes above the ragged mustache convinced me of the clever brain. They looked as though they missed nothing.

After I'd gone through everything for him, shown him the secret passage, explained the forged Reni, which had been found tucked into a large pocket on the inside of Marco's cloak, and was clearly growing confused, stumbling in my answers to the simplest questions, Cucchi took pity on me.

"*Va bene, signora*. The rest can wait. Come to my office tomorrow—or rather, today. Shall we say four o'clock? I want to see Gianni and Clara, as well. They will show you the way." With a trace of sarcasm and a pointed look at Gianni, he added that the next time I felt inclined to play detective, I should come to him first. "It is better, Signora Roy, to leave such things to professionals."

"There will never be a next time," I promised him.

"Let us hope not. You may go now."

"But what about Nick?" I protested, turning to Gianni. "And Stillitano . . . We can't just go home as though everything's been taken care of. Don't you see"—this to Cucchi—"that Nick could be in danger?"

"I was about to say that we have men looking for both Bassi and Stillitano." Cucchi scratched his mustache. "They will find them. But until they do, it might be wise for you to stay with Clara and Gianni. If, as Gianni tells me, Stillitano sees you as a threat . . ." He left the rest of the sentence unfinished, but the implication was plain.

Clara put her hand on my arm. "We won't let her out of our sight."

"Good. Until this afternoon, then. *Ciao*."

"*Ciao*, Danilo," Gianni said. "And thanks."

"*Niente*."

We walked out into the corridor together and down the worn, echoing stone steps. The palazzo was silent, the ball over early. I neither knew nor cared what excuse had been made to get rid of the guests. My thoughts were a jumble of weariness and worry for Nick.

There was a new guard standing at the gate, one of the *carabinieri*, and he nodded to us as we walked through the archway and out into the piazza, now empty of cars, the guests at the ball gone in search of other amusements. Footsteps echoed under the archway behind us. Marco's body was carried past and loaded into the back of a police ambulance parked in the shadows by the palazzo wall. The ambulance door slammed shut, the motor started into life, and the ambulance drove off. Silence settled down again.

I shivered, and longed for Nick.

Clara saw the shiver. "*Cara*, you're cold! But where's the cloak?"

"Oh lord," I groaned. "I must have left it in the study. I'll have to go back for it. I won't be a minute."

Gianni said, "We had to park the car on the Via dei Coronari. We'll get it and meet you here."

The guard was on the telephone in the porter's lodge; I had to tap on the glass to get his attention. When he looked up I mimicked my errand for him, and he nodded permission for me to go back into the palazzo. Cucchi was surprised to see me again but stopped his work to help me look for the cloak. We'd just begun the search when I remembered that of course I had left it in my studio. I apologized for interrupting him and was about to leave when something held me back, made me turn and ask, "What do you think will happen to Alessandro Torreleone?"

He shrugged. "I don't know. First I must speak with Signor Stillitano and examine his notebook, which you so helpfully 'discovered.'" The inverted commas were so plainly around the word that I reminded myself to ask Gianni how he'd described my burglary to Cucchi. "But I am a realist," Cucchi continued. "As you saw tonight, Torreleone has powerful friends."

Then, perhaps because of something showing in my face, he added with sudden kindness, "I'm sorry, signora. Gianni told me that this has been difficult for you. You are a friend of the Torreleones?"

"No. Just an employee. But for Count Massimo's sake—"

"Ah, yes. He is an honorable man, I'm told. It's too bad the son isn't more like him."

"Yes. Good night."

"Good night, Signora Roy."

I found the cloak where I'd left it, flung over the chair in my studio. Quickly, I gathered it up, pulling it around my shoulders, and left the studio, eager to be quit of the Palazzo Torreleone with its haunted silences and sad dreams of the past. I wanted Nick, the unequivocal comfort of his body, the reassurance of his solidity. No more schoolgirl fantasies and fairy-tale illusion; I'd had enough of make-believe.

I was paying more attention to the drawstrings of the cloak than to where I was going when I collided with someone coming silently up the narrow stairs. "I'm sorry—" I began, then stopped and caught my breath. The man—it had to be a man he was so tall—stood on the steps below and still towered over me, looking weirdly like one of those bird dancers from the film, dressed all in scarlet, his face covered by a dead-white mask with a thick hooked nose and slanted eyeholes rimmed in red. It was a ghoulishly effective costume, like an evil being in a dream.

But it wasn't this, or the similarity to the dancers, that stopped me. It was the odd conviction that this strange figure, undoubtedly left over from the ball, was somehow known to me. If I'd been more awake, I might have wondered what he was doing in this part of the palazzo at such an hour. But I had only begun to take in that sense of familiarity when I felt his gloved hand on my arm, tightening, and then, before I could protest, the other grabbed my jaw, covering my mouth. He had a grip of iron.

The white mask came down until it was only inches from my face. I knew the eyes glittering behind the red rims of the mask.

"Always in a hurry, Signora Roy," Stillitano said. "*Pazienza.*

And do not struggle so. Otherwise I will break your neck. I have little to lose, and it would give me much pleasure." His whispered words came out in spasmodic, gasping spurts. He jerked violently at my arm and began half dragging, half pushing me up the stairs. As he propelled me along beside him, I hung as slackly in his grip as I dared, to slow us down. He was muttering to himself in a crazy, disjointed way that chilled me. "Somewhere to talk, somewhere . . . But there, yes, good . . ." We had reached the top of the stairs, and I saw the door to my studio still standing open. I'd been in such a hurry to leave that I had forgotten to close it. By the dim light of the corridor it was plain that the room was empty.

"Excellent." Stillitano shoved me ahead of him into the studio. He shut the door, dropping his hand from my arm to do so but keeping the other so tightly clamped over my mouth that I was held hard against his body. My lips were pushed back from my teeth, and I could taste the sour leather of the glove.

Moonlight spilled into the room through the tall, unshuttered windows, bathing everything in a queer grayish light. Stillitano was obviously looking about, because I sensed his head turning and his attention momentarily elsewhere.

"This is where you work, is it? No, do not trouble yourself to answer. I can see that it is. How appropriate for our conversation. Because paintings are precisely what I want to talk to you about. Or rather, one particular painting." He laughed on a high panting note that seemed about to skitter over into outright madness. "We are both such connoisseurs of paintings, are we not?"

While he talked, I searched the room with my eyes for some sort of weapon. But palette knives, scalpels, and razors were in a box under the table where I couldn't get at them. The easels, tightened into tripods, were large and unwieldy, not to mention unreachable. The worktable stood between me and them, with the solvents ranged in a row on top of it because I'd been in too much of a hurry to put them away.

The solvents.

My eyes swept over the row and found what they were

after: the small and deadly bottle of toluene with its cotton-wool stopper, lined up neatly with the others. If only I could reach it . . . But the few feet between me and it might have been miles so long as Stillitano had me in that unrelenting grip.

He was muttering to himself again. I had a hard time making sense of the disconnected, slurred Italian, but fear came through unmistakably in the tumble of words. By now I had a sixth sense for fear. He was terrified, but of what? Then a phrase jumped out; he repeated it once, twice—the one clear statement in a welter of words. "A matter of friendship . . . a matter of friendship . . ." The phrase Alessandro had used to Mario, that he had carefully repeated, when he asked Mario to summon *Questore* Barbato. But what did it mean?

Suddenly, Stillitano turned me around to face him, one hand still over my mouth, the other twisting my right arm up behind me, while he backed me up until the wooden edge of the worktable was pressing painfully into my spine. I stared up at his face, forcing myself to find the eyes that glittered behind the mask and hold them locked to mine. The solvent was my only chance, but to succeed I had to make him think that I was mesmerized, like a bird by a snake, unable to move.

He said, "I must have the Reni. Marco has failed. You will have to help me now." The words were distinct, sharply separated from each other, and his voice was as clear and coldly calm as it had ever been, as if he'd willed himself sane again, if only for the moment. "It was you, was it not, who took my notebook? No, it's no use shaking your head. You wear a distinctive perfume, very pleasant if somewhat too strong . . ."

I might as well have left my name on a visiting card in his drawer.

". . . and the contracts, as well. I wonder what you have done with them. . . . But I am sure you will tell me."

All the while I was inching my left hand free of the cloak and dragging it slowly, agonizingly slowly, up my side. I didn't dare hurry; he might sense the movement in spite of the muffling folds of the cloak. When I reached the top of the table, I bent my wrist back and felt the rough wooden surface harsh against my skin; a long splinter slid into my hand as I moved it backward over the table, but I couldn't risk raising it even fractionally higher.

In my mind I tried to visualize the row of solvents. Where exactly was the toluene? Groping blindly, my fingers touched glass and plastic, fumbling, feeling for the telltale cotton wool. No, not that one or that or that . . . At last, on the verge of despair, I had it. Carefully, ever so carefully, I eased the cotton wool from the bottle mouth. This was the hardest part; if I spilled any of it on my hand . . . But I mustn't think about that.

The cotton wool came free with a heart-stopping jerk that jiggled the bottle until my fingers were able to steady it. It took longer to steady my pulse. I dropped the cotton wool onto the table and closed my hand around the bottle again.

I was concentrating so fiercely on the toluene that I barely took in what Stillitano was saying, but now I heard him tell me that he wouldn't hurt me if only I would give him back his notebook and the contracts. "If I take my hand from your mouth, you must not scream, Signora Roy. Or I will kill you. You won't scream, will you?"

I shook my head. His hand moved an inch from my mouth, hovering just in front of it in case I disobeyed him. My lips felt bruised and dry; I ran my tongue across them.

"Now then—" he began.

I threw the toluene hard at his face.

But he must have felt the movement of my arm as it made its forward sweep, because he jerked back just in time and the bottle smashed instead against the wall behind him.

Even before I knew that I'd missed my mark, I was screaming and twisting free from the grip that had momentarily relaxed from surprise. Stillitano reached out to grab me back to him, but I bent and dove under his outstretched arms, pulling at the drawstrings of the cloak that hampered me like a shroud. By now the fumes from the poisonous little bottle were seeping into the air of the room. I was having difficulty breathing; behind me I could hear Stillitano choking.

I ran for the door. Reaching out his long arm, Stillitano

lunged after me and grabbed the cloak. For an agonizing instant the drawstrings tightened like a noose around my throat. I gagged, and tears stung my eyes. Then, like a last-minute reprieve, the drawstrings gave way. Still clutching my cloak, Stillitano stumbled back and crashed into a chair, but recovered almost at once. He sprang for the door, cutting off my escape. I turned and darted behind the long worktable.

Like children in a deadly game, Stillitano on one side of the table, I on the other, we edged back and forth, back and forth, until my nerves were shrieking, both of us gasping like fish in the poisoned air. I couldn't scream anymore; it was all I could do to breathe.

And then I heard Nick. Miraculously, he was shouting my name. "Kate! Kate! In God's name, where are you?" His voice came from the courtyard below.

"Here! In the studio!" I tried to shout, but the words came out in a whisper, like words choked off in a nightmare, my throat half paralyzed with the fumes. Desperately, I reached out for another bottle and hurled it straight at the windows overlooking the courtyard. This time my aim was true, and the bottle smashed through the glass.

"Hold on, we're coming!" Nick's answering shout faded as he ran for the stairs.

Stillitano was no longer watching me; his eyes were on the door. For a moment he hovered, indecisive, then started for it, but before he could reach it, there was shouting in the corridor and the door slammed open with a crash. Fresh air poured into the room. But the doorway was empty. Then Cucchi appeared, crouching low to one side, half-hidden by the edge of the frame, a gun in one hand. Behind him was Nick.

Stillitano froze. Cucchi shouted and at the same moment Stillitano turned and ran for the windows. I don't know what he intended—it was a suicidal drop to the stones of the courtyard, but maybe that's what he wanted. He never made it. Nick flung himself into the room and pulled Stillitano down with a flying tackle. The two men rolled over and over, a tangle of arms and legs in the moonlight. I heard a sickening crunch from under their thrashing bodies as they smashed over the broken glass on the floor. I couldn't see, couldn't make out whether Nick was in trouble or not; one moment he was on top, the next underneath as the bodies writhed in a frenzied confusion.

"The light," I shouted to Cucchi. "Put the light on! By the door . . ." But I was there before him, smashing my hand into the switch to force it up. I spun around again and saw a long arm flash up into the light from out of the tangled movement on the floor. At the end of it, shining like a knife blade, was a huge, jagged piece of glass. The two men were locked side by side.

"Nick! Watch out!" I screamed.

But before Stillitano could bring that lethal shard down into his neck, Nick twisted, pulled one hand free, and drove his fist into the side of Stillitano's head. Stillitano grunted once and flopped back onto the floor, unconscious. The glass dropped harmlessly from his hand to shatter on the tiles. Nick pushed Stillitano's body aside and got slowly to his feet, breathing hard.

Blindly, with tears pouring down my face, I stumbled into his arms. And then, from the fumes, the relief, and plain exhaustion, I went out like a snuffed candle.

CHAPTER

22

Five days later, on Sunday morning, I sat curled up in a wicker chair on the terrace of a house overlooking the Mediterranean. A breeze ruffled the water and rocked the small sailboat tied to the jetty; through the clear air I could hear the rhythmic ping of the halyard as it knocked against the aluminum mast. The breeze fluttered the edge of the tablecloth and tried, but failed, to reach me where I sat sheltered in the lee of the house, in an angle of plaster and stone that caught and held the sun, prompting the wisteria against the wall into an early, fragrant blossoming. On the table in front of me was a basket of rolls wrapped in a yellow napkin, a pot of apricot jam, and two cups of cappuccino sprinkled with cocoa. Beyond the table was the view. And beside me was Nick.

The house belonged to Clara's father, one of several that he owned on the Bay of Naples, that wide scallop of lovely, poisoned sea bordered by the sprawling city and hills checkered with orange groves and earthquake-shattered villages. Clara had commandeered the house for the weekend, and the four of us, she and Gianni, Nick and I, had escaped from Rome while the children stayed with their grandparents in Naples. The house had a name, La Rondinella, the swallow, and it clung to the cliff like the bird itself, swooping down the rock in a graceful series of roofs and terraces, a large, comfortable house of bright rooms and sudden stairways.

The view was Vesuvius. This morning the volcano floated in a pearly mist across the bay, little more than a gray outline, a sugar cone with melting flanks under the warm sun.

There is a certain combination of sunlight, luminous Italian air, and the sweet scent of wisteria that acts on the spirit as well as the senses. I was in that blissful state of grace where a pantheistic gratitude for the simple facts of nature—the twist of a brown vine against yellow-streaked rock, a flash of vivid green in the curve of a wave—goes hand in hand with complete sensual contentment. I yawned shamelessly and stretched, running my hand along Nick's arm. He folded the newspaper he was reading and dropped it onto the pile by his chair.

"Hungry?"

"Very." I uncurled myself, spread jam on a roll, and handed it to him. "There. Just to show you that I'm still capable of movement."

He gave me a pleasantly lecherous look. "Poor darling. Was I too rough last night?"

"Well, there *are* one or two bruises that look fresher than the ones Marco and Stillitano left behind. If you'd like to think that you're responsible . . . But actually, what I meant was that I've been spoiled to the point of complete idleness this weekend. I haven't lifted so much as a finger—"

"You weren't exactly passive between twelve and two last night. If that's any consolation." He leaned over and kissed me. Afterward, some time afterward, he settled back in his chair and looked at me thoughtfully. "I think we've struck the right balance between rest and, well, whatever you want to call it. . . . You're looking less like one of Lautrec's consumptive women and more like a Renoir this morning."

"Contentedly cowlike, you mean? Thanks very much." I pointed to the newspapers. "What was in those?"

"Some fact, more speculation. You've been lucky. The Mestola Rossa scandal has distracted them from Gatti's killing. Only one paper mentioned you by name. How did it go . . . ?" He looked up at the sky as he thought. "Oh yes, something about *la bella donna misteriosa*, etc., etc. They got quite excited by the fact that someone had seen you dancing with Alessandro Torreleone at the ball. You'll be sorry to know they spelled your name wrong." Grinning, he began to root through the heap of papers. "Would you like to read the article yourself?"

"Sadist." I pushed the proffered newspaper away with the point of the butter knife. "That's a lousy profession you've got yourself by the way."

"Isn't it?" he agreed cheerfully. "Still, you got off quite lightly, you know. Thanks to Cucchi."

"I suppose so." If I sounded less than wholehearted, perhaps it was because the memory of Cucchi's questioning was still too fresh. Like a skillful dentist working on a bad tooth, he had expertly extracted the information he wanted; the pain was minimal, but I still felt numb.

But yes, I had to admit that he'd been generous, willing to gloss over one or two awkward questions or even to answer them himself. Nick's gun, for instance. Marco took posthumous ownership of it. A *teppisto* like that would surely carry a gun, wouldn't he, Signora Roy? The way he said it made it more a statement than a question, and I didn't see any need to answer, but those ebony eyes stayed on my a face a fraction too long for comfort.

He allowed himself only the briefest look of disbelief when I told him why I'd gone to Faltecchi and Stillitano after the ball. If I hadn't been guiltily watching for it, I might never have caught it, it was on his face so fleetingly. "You went for supplies? At that hour?"

"Yes."

Then came the look. Gravely, he said, "You are to be complimented on your industry, signora." Still, because Nick and Gianni had turned over the notebook and contracts with the understanding that no questions would be asked about their source, he left it at that.

Step by halting step he had taken me back over the route I'd traveled that night, from the moment I overheard Stillitano order Marco to steal the Reni until Marco's body lay on the study floor. Gradually the facts spun out into a story that, while far from smooth and well tailored, wore well, according to Cucchi. Whether the investigating magistrate would agree was another matter, he observed dryly, and beyond his control.

However, he added that the investigating magistrate would have his hands full with Stillitano, who had collapsed into alternating fits of confession and self-justification tinged with hysteria, and Alessandro, who refused to admit to anything other than the shooting of a would-be murderer and thief in his house. It wasn't likely that he would go beyond Cucchi's report on my involvement. The interest would focus on Alessandro and on Stillitano and his connection with Bassi.

But Bassi still had not been caught and was unlikely to be, according to Gianni. Too many important people would suffer if he were.

Nick had done his best. Using my keys, he'd managed to get into Faltecchi and Stillitano after Gianni had gone off to call Cucchi. But while he was hiding, Marco had slipped out of the building unseen. Nick hadn't known Marco was gone until he got close enough to Stillitano's office to hear voices and realized Marco's voice was missing. Bassi and Stillitano were arguing heatedly, he told us later, with Bassi doing most of the talking. He hadn't been able to hear much of their argument, just enough to recognize that Bassi was putting some sort of pressure on Stillitano. At one point, Bassi made a phone call, but Nick couldn't hear what was said. Finally, after ten minutes or so, the two men left Stillitano's office, switching off the lights. Maybe it was at this point that Gianni returned, assumed everyone—including Nick—had gone, and took off with Clara in pursuit of me. Careful to stay hidden, Nick followed Bassi and Stillitano down to the lobby. Through a window, he watched as Bassi got into a black Mercedes. The Mercedes waited while Stillitano crossed the road to his car, stopped, gesticulated, pointed to his tires, and came back. The door of the Mercedes opened, and Stillitano climbed in beside Bassi.

Nick already had the front door of the building unlocked. As soon as the Mercedes' engine turned over, he opened it slightly to watch the car pull away and start down the street. Then he ran to the Maserati, nudged its nose out of the alley where it was parked, waited until the Mercedes turned out of the Via Livia, and shot off after it. Gianni's note was on the driver's seat; intent on the Mercedes, Nick hadn't seen it when he got into the car.

There was little traffic on the road; to avoid being spotted, Nick was forced to stay well back and once or twice almost lost the Mercedes. Then the storm broke. Under cover of the downpour he could pull closer, *had* to pull closer to keep them in sight. The Mercedes was heading east, going fast despite the rain. Eventually, it turned down the Via Appia Antica, the old road out of the city, bumping over the original Roman paving stones poking out through the worn skin of modern asphalt. Like sentinels in the rain, ancient tombs lined the roadside, huge humps of grass and stone, haunted now by dope dealers and prostitutes. Screened by trees and iron gates, down long, winding drives, lay the well-guarded estates of rich Romans who liked their country pleasures close to town. It was into one of these that the Mercedes eventually turned, closing Nick out. He parked on the verge, in the shelter of a clump of umbrella pines, and waited.

An hour passed. Nick was about to give up and go back to town to find us and to alert Cucchi to Bassi's whereabouts when the gates opened again and the Mercedes drove out. It sped back to Rome through the thinning rain. Nick kept on its tail as far as the *centro storico*, but there, caught by the double block of a red light and a delivery truck that chose to back out of an alley into his path, he lost it. While the truck maneuvered, Nick got out of the Maserati and ran up to the next intersection to search for the Mercedes' taillights. In vain. Cursing, he got back into his car—and saw Gianni's note, still lying on the seat.

As soon as he'd read it, he swore some more, squeezed the Maserati around the truck, which had finally, grudgingly, given way, and headed for the Palazzo Torreleone. He happened to come down the Via dei Coronari just as Gianni and Clara were getting into their car; at the sight of them he pulled to a stop. Explanations followed—Marco's attack, his death, Cucchi's arrival—and reassurances that I was fine and had only just gone back into the palazzo for my cloak. Cucchi was still there, they told him. Then they would collect me, Nick said, and go to Cucchi to tell him what he'd learned. There still might be time to pick up Bassi.

Together, the three of them went into the palazzo. They were crossing the courtyard when they heard my screams.

Nick shouted, waited, then shouted again. I heard only the second shout. When he realized where I was, he raced up the stairs, Gianni and Clara behind him. Cucchi, who'd also heard the screams, was a close second as they broke open the studio door.

Afterward, we realized that the Mercedes had dropped Stillitano close to the palazzo. He must have got past the guard at the gate while he was on the telephone, distracted. It was just my bad luck to meet him when I did.

His scheme was mad, of course. He hadn't a hope of getting the Reni. But then he must have been well on his way to a crazy despair at this point, doubtless helped along by whatever threats Bassi had made; his professional life was crashing around him, he faced exposure and jail if the police got hold of those contracts, and the one man who could help him was going underground. But if he could just get the forged Reni, he could eliminate at least one major piece of evidence against him. He must have felt that his luck was changing when he ran into me on the stairs. But then fortune abandoned him once and for all.

Others were luckier. Count Massimo survived Marco's attack. Recuperation would take a long time, but he would live. Signora Gambino came into my studio in the palazzo on Friday morning to tell me the news. I was there finishing up my work, for the simple reason that no one told me not to and because it was all I could do for Count Massimo. Signora Gambino accepted my presence as she accepted my part in what had happened, without questions. Though not, I suspected, without curiosity.

I'd written to Count Massimo expressing my sorrow and explaining as best I could my part in the whole affair, without any expectation that he would ever want to see me again. To my surprise and relief, Signora Gambino said that Count Massimo was pleased that I was continuing work on the paintings and counted on a visit from me when he was stronger.

She also told me that Daniella had left that morning for Washington, where her father was a diplomat. Home to Daddy and far away from the mess here. I wondered if Daniella would ever be forced to face the results of her actions. Not that I cared much, to be honest.

Signora Gambino did not volunteer Alessandro's whereabouts, and I did not ask.

So I worked and answered questions and fell into bed each night exhausted, and alone. Nick was caught up with Gianni in the Mestola Rossa story and working around the clock, rarely seen and barely there when we did manage a moment together. But it didn't matter. I knew what was coming, and I could afford to wait.

When the four of us met at the Palmieris' for dinner on Friday evening, Clara took a long and not very flattering look at my face, then another, equally sharp, at Nick's and Gianni's, and left the room without a word. After a few minutes she came back to say that it was all arranged. We would go south for the weekend. Unprotesting, we packed our bags and by late that night found ourselves at La Rondinella.

On Saturday morning Clara decreed that conversation was to be purely frivolous—not one word of paintings, plots, or murder. Again we obeyed her and gave ourselves up to the luxury of the house, the delicious food cooked and served by Carlotta and Pasquale, the husband and wife who ran the house for Clara's parents, and the sun that shone obligingly down on us with a heat rare for March.

Clara's edict held until mid-day Sunday. Gianni was the first to break. Unknown to Clara, he'd spent a part of Saturday on the telephone in pursuit of facts, in consultation with his newspaper, or simply to satisfy the need to know that made him such a good journalist. Nick told me this, adding that he himself was quite content to lie in the sun and think. Thinking was something he hadn't had much time for lately, he said. "Not that it stops me from writing, anyway." This with a wink.

Clara and I were lying on chaise longues in a sheltered patch of terrace, spreading sunscreen on vulnerable white flesh that hadn't seen the sun in months. Nick was offering to do the bits we couldn't reach when Gianni came out of the house to join us. With a slightly sheepish look at Clara, he said, "I've just been talking to Cucchi . . ."

Clara sighed. "I knew I ought to have had the phone disconnected."

"Stillitano finally confessed to using Marco to get at Faltecchi and the Reni." Gianni pulled up a chair and sat down beside Nick. "He says he only meant for Marco to frighten Faltecchi, but Marco went too far. He admits he wanted the Reni back because he was afraid Count Massimo would discover it was a fake. But he denies that it had anything to do with Bassi, and he refuses to admit that he was with Bassi on Carnevale. Says we must be mistaken. Cucchi thinks he's terrified—"

"He certainly *was* terrified when I saw him last," I said. "He kept saying something about 'a matter of friendship.' And you know, that's what Alessandro said when he asked Mario to get hold of Barbato for him. Mario was supposed to use that phrase when he told Barbato that Alessandro needed his help."

Nick took a cigarette from a pack on the table beside him. As he lit it, he said, "So Barbato is Mestola Rossa, too— Well, it was obvious enough anyway." In explanation to me, he added, "That's the code Mestola Rossa members use when they need something crucial from each other. 'A matter of friendship' —when you hear that, you're supposed to come through, or else . . . It's likely that Bassi told Stillitano to get the Reni back or suffer the consequences."

"But why is Stillitano still terrified?" I asked. "Didn't you say that the odds were that Bassi is in South America or somewhere equally remote by now. How could he be a threat to Stillitano?"

Gianni looked at me as though surprised by such innocence. "It wouldn't matter if Bassi were on the moon," he said simply. "He has friends."

"Oh."

"Remember that line at the end of all the contracts, the bit about 'retribution in accordance with familiar rituals'?" Nick asked me.

I nodded. "Voodoo."

"Exactly. Powerful voodoo intended to keep people quiet if things go wrong. Stillitano probably thinks that as long as he abides by his vows, he's safe. Bassi won't take revenge. Stillitano will go to prison, but at least he'll still be alive."

"So he *will* go to prison," Clara said.

"Sure. There's enough evidence to send him away for a long time," Gianni said happily. "If only for the attack on Kate."

"Thanks for the 'only,' " I told him. "But you know, I still don't understand why he was willing to risk his reputation and all those years of work?"

Nick tapped ash into a saucer. "Why does anybody get greedy? He stood to make a lot of money, the nontaxable kind, if he went along with Bassi. Maybe, too, he liked the idea of making fools of people, tricking them into thinking his copies were the real thing. Besides, from all accounts, Bassi is a spellbinder, with a genius for sensing weakness in people. He appealed to Stillitano's vanity, got him into Mestola Rossa, and once he was in, he couldn't get out."

"But why would Bassi want him in the first place?" Clara asked as she rolled over to sun her front.

I knew the answer to that one myself. "Because, apart from the Torreleone Reni—which was unfinished because Count Massimo asked to see it during his illness and it had to be rushed back to the palazzo—Stillitano is a first-rate forger, and Bassi collects paintings. I gather he isn't too scrupulous about their source or how he gets hold of them. The Reni is the obvious example. Perhaps Bassi bought up Alessandro's debts and then told him he would settle for the Reni. The painting wasn't Alessandro's to sell, but maybe Bassi suggested that he arrange for a copy to keep Count Massimo from learning the truth. When all this took place Count Massimo wasn't expected to live long anyway. After he was dead, the transaction could be announced officially, but in the meantime Alessandro had the money he needed and Bassi had the painting he wanted as well as a hold over Alessandro. What Stillitano was doing for Alessandro he was doing for others, too."

"But Stillitano made a fairly clumsy mistake, didn't he," Gianni asked me, "in using canvas rather than silk for the Reni? A strange mistake for someone with his knowledge."

"I know," I said. "That puzzled me at first, too. But Nick and I thought that perhaps it was important to leave one obvious clue in order to distinguish easily between the original and the copy—to avoid any possibility of confusion or dispute."

Nick leaned forward and ground out his half-smoked cigarette. "We know that in some cases the duplicated painting did actually belong to the seller, but there were good reasons to keep the sale to Bassi a secret. Money problems, for instance. If a businessman was known to be selling off his collection, people might rightly suspect he was in trouble. That wouldn't help business. Bassi provided a nice quiet market and a copy to hang on your wall as replacement to fool your friends. We suspect that Bassi's lust to own certain paintings was so great that he was willing to keep the fact of his ownership a secret, at least for a while. And when the owner didn't want to sell—well, the secrets that came his way from Mestola Rossa made for useful persuasion. As for Stillitano, he was in so deep he had to do as Bassi demanded. No matter how crazy it seemed. And trying to get the forged Reni back was pretty crazy."

"Why did they, then?" Clara asked.

"Because Kate knew it was a forgery. She could expose the transaction. All Stillitano probably wanted to do, possibly on Bassi's orders, was destroy the copy. Then the ball would be in Alessandro's court. He knew the dangers, but for some reason he'd been dragging his feet." Nick looked at me out of the corner of his eye, then went on. "Stillitano was frantic with fear, and Bassi wanted to force Alessandro's hand, so he told Stillitano to use Marco to get the Reni. Possibly he told Marco, behind Stillitano's back, to get rid of Count Massimo at the same time. That way Alessandro would be the legal owner. But I don't think we'll ever know that for sure.

"Torreleone must have been playing his own game all the while, and the Reni was the least of his worries. After all, his own father was hardly likely to take him to court over it, and he faced greater problems in his dealings with Bassi. He was busy covering his own tracks, because he could see that investigators were closing in on Bassi's trail. His major concern was with the financial arrangements he'd made on Bassi's behalf. That was what mattered. The Reni was hardly as urgent."

Gianni suddenly looked grim. "He's been damn clever. It's going to be hard to pin anything on him without Bassi." He glanced at Nick and added, "But at least Gatti's dead."

"Yes," Nick said quietly. "Torreleone's one good deed." After a pause, he went on. "I predict he'll stay quiet for a few years until the fallout from this scandal settles; then we'll hear from him again. Torreleone's a survivor—unfortunately." There was no anger or bitterness in the way he said this, only the faintest trace of a resigned cynicism.

"And a pragmatist, too," I said. "Like all the Torreleones, except his father. But I have to admit I won't be sorry if he escapes prison, Gianni. Count Massimo's suffered enough. And I can afford to be generous you see." Smiling, I took Nick's hand and got to my feet.

He smiled his slow smile back at me. "One quarry may have escaped, but the other won't."

"There's one last bit of news I haven't told you yet," I said. "But first let me get the champagne I brought." When I returned, bottle in hand, Gianni had glasses waiting.

"Clara was so strict about what was off limits that I thought I'd wait till just before we left today to tell you that Faltecchi's decided to go on with the business despite what's happened. And he's asked me to be a sort of junior partner."

When the general rejoicing died down, Gianni put his thumbs to the cork of the bottle and pushed. We watched the cork sail out over the Mediterranean, then raised our glasses. "To partnerships," I said.

"The permanent kind," Nick replied, putting his arm around me.

And we all drank together.